Heir of Corruption

A Dark Mafia Enemies To Lovers Romance

Sylvia Rae

Published by Lucky Clover Publications, LLC

For more information, contact Sylvia Rae

SylviaRae@Sylviaraebooks.com

Contents

MAILING LIST

Sign up for my mailing list, and claim your FREE steamy age-gap billionaire romance novella.

Click HERE to join.

Trigger Warning

Dear Reader,

This steamy romance explores the dark underworld of the mafia, so consider this your trigger warning! Things are about to get spicy up in here.

This book includes scenes featuring murder, violence, and more adult themes. So proceed with caution, especially if that's not your cup of dirty martini.

While I aim to provide thrills, chills, and heels-over-head passion, I know these subjects affect us all differently. Your mental health matters most! If you need something lighter, check out my other books for a less dangerous yet still steamy to sweep you off your feet.

But if you're craving a walk on the wild side complete with brushes with danger, alpha males and women who give as good as they get, buckle up! This book will take you for a ride.

Now grab your fan and cocktail of choice - your pleasure reading begins...

Prologue

Antonio

I have tasted her once.

The moment she felt my cock inside her, she realized her lifelong addiction to me.

Now, she thinks she can play games with me, and take control?

No, sweet angel, I am the one in control here.

She steps backward, her eyes locked on mine. A naughty smile touched her lips. She wants to play, but can she handle what she is starting?

I pull my shirt off and unbuckle my belt., letting it slip from each belt loop until it is free in my hands.

She looks at the thick stretch of leather in my hand, and her smile widens. She takes another step backwards. My mind has been hunting her for weeks, so this little taunt she is doing–she does not know how far I will take it.

My cock presses hard against my pants. I snap the belt in my hands and she grins, then turns to run towards the room.

Oh, I love a chase.

I walk through to the bedroom with a hunter's stealth, and find her sitting in the center of the bed, her legs crossed in front of her, her arms folder over her knees, looking coy and shy.

Her chance to play innocent with me is over.

I want to tear her to shreds with my cock.

“My little bird, I’ve been thinking about you all day, and the things I want to do to you.” I growl, stepping closer to the bed and flicking the belt in my hands.

She uncrosses her legs and moves them wider open, giving me the perfect view of her beautiful pink pussy.

I take a sharp breath in, pulling the button of my pants open. My cock is throbbing, desperate to be inside her.

I stand over the bed, naked, with my cock erect and ready. Her eyes are on it, she is biting her lower lip.

I lean forward and grab her ankle, and pull her lower down on the bed, flipping her over onto her stomach.

“Show your ass for me!” I command.

She does it with a soft giggle.

The belt sings as it cuts through the air and lands across her round ass cheeks.

She squeals in pain, but arches her pussy towards me again.

Little Seraphina, my angel, my innocent, untouched beauty. She is mine. And she will only ever be mine.

I angle the belt differently, so that when I slap her again with it, the thick leather stings against her pussy.

She cries out again, and her pussy turns bright pink, just like the streaks across her ass cheeks.

"You look perfect. Don't you dare move."

I toss the belt aside and cup my hand over her pussy, feeling how hot her skin is, wet and begging for my cock to thrust into her.

I dip one finger inside her tight little pussy.

"Do you think you can handle me?"

She nods, looking over her shoulder at me, her cheeks flushed.

I grin, walking around the side of the bed and pulling open the drawer of the nightstand. I reach in and grab the knife.

Turning back towards her as I run my finger over the sleek blade.

"Antonio?" She gasps, rolling onto her back and scooting up the bed away from me.

Then she sees the devilish grin on my face, and her eyes flare wide.

Not in fear, but in lust.

I kneel on the bed, inching closer to her. She squeals when I grab her throat in my hands and stare into her eyes.

"You are mine, Seraphina."

She nods, her eyes shining.

"Your pussy is mine. It will never belong to anyone else."

She nods again. "Yes."

"Yes, who?"

"Yes, sir." She whispers. My cock pulses.

I push my legs between hers and stare down at her body.

"The way your blood looked on my cock the first time we fucked-"

I close my eyes, remembering it. The feeling of penetrating her virgin body.

When I open my eyes, all I want is to see her blood on my skin again. To let her know, to remind her, that I am the only one who can ever fuck her.

I move the knife in front of her eyes and see the reflection of light the blade throws across her smooth skin.

"Lift your hands, hold on to the bedpost. If you let go, I will tie them there, and I promise you–you don't want that."

She does exactly as I have asked.

I press the blade between her breasts. She gasps as the sharp edge cuts lightly into her skin.

The thin line of bright red blood that springs from her skin causes a deep, urgent excitement to rush through me.

My lips pull into a sneer. I run my other hand up the inside of her thigh, slowly, until my fingers brush over her pussy. She is dripping. I slip my fingers inside her again.

"Good girl." I say, husky and low.

She arches her back and rubs her pussy against my hand. The movement causes the knife to press harder into her skin, more blood flows from her.

I pull the knife down across her stomach in a slow, deep movement. She cries out in pain and pleasure. I press my fingers deeper inside her pussy and feel her pulsing with need.

When I lift the blade and drop it onto the bed beside her, a fresh stream of blood pools in the curve of her stomach.

I press my hand into it, spreading it across her skin, letting it seep between my fingers.

Bright red, significant of my ownership of her.

With her blood painted on my hand, I grip my shaft and rub myself up and down in slow movements. Her blood spreads over my cock and electricity pulses through me. I am rock hard, so hard I know I am going to hurt her if I push into her now. But she is so wet, and my need is becoming far too intense.

As I withdraw my fingers from her, I dip them into my mouth, enjoying the taste of her.

As she moans at the emptiness I've left her with, I press my blood-soaked cock against her legs, allowing it to glide across her pussy.

With a look of desperation in her eyes, she rocks up against me, and so I thrust into her.

She cries out as I enter, forcing her wide open, plunging my cock into her pussy.

I grab her hips and thrust forward as the sensation of being buried inside her rushes through me.

As I thrust in and out of her tight little pussy, I run my hand over her stomach again, painting her blood up, over her breasts, up her neck, and then cupping my hand over her face.

The red handprint across her jaw excites me.

She rocks her hips upwards towards me as I thrust forward.

I grin.

Pushing harder, deeper, faster.

Her left hands drift from the bedpost, reaching down to wrap her fingers around my wrist.

I growl a warning and clamp my fingers around her throat.

"Do as I told you, my angel. Don't make me angry."

She gasps as I tighten my grip. She quickly reaches her hand up and holds onto the bedpost. I slam into her, jolting her body, again and again.

I lean down and kiss her, pushing my tongue into her mouth, letting it slip between her lips the same way my cock is sliding in and out of her pussy.

I feel her body trembling, a sign that she's almost there.

I press my face against her hair, letting the smell of her fill me up as I bury my cock inside her.

"You belong to me." I snarl.

She gasps, and her body arches beneath me, shivering and tense as her orgasm rushes through her.

I push my hips against her, thrusting into her, letting my pleasure explode from my cock deep inside her.

Seraphina will always belong to me.

From the moment my eyes fell upon her, until the day she takes her last breath, she will be mine and I will kill any man who tries to touch her.

Chapter 1

SERAPHINA

A loud snap echoes through the air in the tiny bedroom, and my ears are ringing. I feel dizzy and disoriented. I stare in horror at the dark figure standing over my mother's bed. In my fear, his form looks distorted and monstrous. He is standing dangerously still, staring right at me. He is so tall and so broad; I feel as though he could swallow me whole. Like a demon having crawled from the depths of hell.

All I see is red.

Only a moment ago, my mother sat up, ready to fight back, but she didn't even have time to scream, and now she slumps across the pillows, with dark, sticky matter splattering across the wall behind her. Thick, red liquid oozes down the headboard and across her blanket, dripping in syrupy trails onto the bedroom floor.

Even though It's dark, I can see the redness of it from where I'm standing in the doorway.

The walls are red, her pillow is red, his eyes are red.

Screams echo inside my skull as the demon moves and walks toward me, the pitch of it hurting my ears. I reach my hands up to clasp them over the sides of my head to block out the sounds, but then realize they are coming from me. My lungs are burning with pain, desperate for air. My mother is dead. She can never scream again. So, I'll scream for both of us.

I feel hands lift me off the ground and I think he has me. I think I'm about to die. I kick and fight and scream even louder. Snaps of gunfire fill the room again, and flashes of red lightning sting my eyes. My ears are ringing, and I don't even know if I'm screaming anymore. The demon turns to run; he leaps through the window, shattering glass in glittering splinters that land in the thick, red puddles of my mother's blood.

I bolt up in bed, choking on the scream that is sitting in the back of my throat. My heart is thundering behind my rib cage, threatening to shatter through the bones. I blink and blink again, fighting for vision in the darkness of midnight. It was a nightmare, Seraphina. It was another nightmare. Just breathe. Please, just breathe.

I gasp and fight against the horror of the visions still drifting in my mind.

Just breathe.

Slowly, I find my breath, and my heartbeat soothes down to a tempo that doesn't feel as though It's going to bruise my insides.

I take a deep, slow breath, and the familiarity of my bedroom in the beautiful city of Hong Kong takes shape. I reach out and flick my bedside light on.

I know I won't be able to fall back asleep tonight, and if I could, I would be sent back to that same room and that same horrific memory, which will keep replaying.

I was only four years old.

And even though it was over twenty years ago, the same nightmare continues to haunt me almost every night.

I throw the blankets off me; they are twisted and knotted around my legs because of how I have been kicking and fighting against them. Sitting on the edge of the bed, I rub my hands against my temples, trying to push away the remnants of those terrible memories.

Finally, I pull my long, curly, dark hair into a bun. Securing it with the ornate silver hairpin on my bedside table. I stand up on shaking legs and walk toward the kitchen.

I'll drink tea, sitting out on the balcony, watching the city lights and how the sky full of stars fades away as it changes from black to dark blue to orange, and eventually, the morning sun will pierce through my eyes and burn away the nightmares.

An gung still holds my mother very close to his heart. In his home, he has left her bedroom exactly as it was the day she left. I have spent many hours in there, learning about who she was. He even had her belongings sent back to Hong Kong after her murder.

My most treasured possession is her journal. From it, I could learn so much about my parents.

I was born in New York. My father met my mother on a trip to Hong Kong. She fell in love with him at first sight. His broad smile and dark skin were exotic to her. He always told her he was the yin to her yang. Her milky smooth, pale skin was such a contrast to his rich coffee-colored skin. She loved him deeply; I know that, and she was his entire world.

Even though they both grew up in the strict and overbearing world of the mafia - it was two very different worlds. He was from New York, and she was from Hong Kong. Their families held a rivalry, and their love faced forbidden boundaries. They moved around in secret at first, hiding from the world, lost in their own relationship. She fell pregnant, and they were so excited - but scared. He took her to New York, where he thought he could keep her safe, and he wanted to show her his world, his home, his life.

But not all stories are roses; some have more thorns than petals, and this story ends with my mother's death and my father being taken from me.

I was born in New York, and they were the happiest they had ever been in their lives. But there were problems. Even in New York, their love caused a stir. The war between the Hong Kong and New York families was at its worst.

I was young when ah gung finally gave in and answered the questions I had been begging him to tell me about.

I remember it like it was yesterday. He sat me down outside in the garden. It was a chilly day, and I wore a warm coat adorned with purple flowers and red mittens as he sat me down outside in the garden.

I had asked again, "ah gung, why did my parents die?"

He stood for a long time staring at me, with eyes full of quiet thoughts. Finally, he sat down next to me and started talking, although he did not once make eye contact.

"My child, your mom and dad, were not welcome in New York. When they arrived there, people threatened your father with exile."

"Why?" I asked. I wanted to know everything.

"See, kiddo, people just couldn't accept your dad and mom being together. They came from totally different backgrounds. He begged everyone to understand, to see the love he had for your mom. But, nope, they wouldn't have any of it. They decided they had to teach your dad a lesson, make sure he knew not to cross them. And to make sure everyone else got the message too, they took your mom away."

I sat watching An gung, the way his face strained as he spoke, the pain in his expression. Visions flashed through my mind of what I remembered of that night. The fear. The horror. Those memories have burned into the skin beneath my eyelids, and I can never unsee them.

An gung spoke openly that day, and it only added to the festering hatred and anger that was already growing inside me.

They used my mother as a lesson for my father, and they used my father as a lesson for anyone who wanted to disobey them.

As the men barged in and snatched me away, I caught sight of my dad just once more after that. They made it crystal clear, even to a kid like me, that New York was off-limits. "You're to be back with your own in Hong Kong," they said. That last time I saw Dad? We were in some dingy warehouse close to the airport. Suddenly, he burst into the room. His face was all beaten up, pain twisting his features. He yelled out for me, "Sweetheart!" Tears streamed down his face as they yanked him away, shoving him back into whatever hole they'd kept him in.

Then it was my turn to be hauled off. I was thrown into a car, dumped in the back seat, and then the door slammed shut, trapping me inside.

That was the last time, the very last. Deep down, I've always known they killed him, all because he dared to love the "wrong" person. And every day since that day, I have been planning my revenge.

Even as a child, a baby, really, I knew I would avenge my parents for what they did to them. I knew that one day, I would hunt them down and find out what happened. I have so much hatred festering inside me it hinders my ability to focus on much else.

My mother's father (ah gung in Cantonese) Muchen, took me back to Hong Kong and became my guardian. I became a ward of the mafia.

They kept me in secret at first, fearing that I would meet the same fate as my parents. I was not pure. I was tainted with my father's genes. I was half of my mother's world and half of my father's world, and my father's world was not welcome. Over time, things changed, and I was accepted into the family. I struggled with my identity and being different. My caramel skin is not as light as my family's, and my eyes are round and wide. My lips are plump, and the fullness of them contrasts against the beauty of my Asian cousins.

I used to wish I looked normal. I used to wish I looked like everyone else so that people would stop staring at me. As I got older, I became stronger. I realized that being normal was overrated. An gung would tell me there is great beauty in being different, and I believed it.

While I still don't think of myself as beautiful, I'm proud of my father's features. I don't wear them in fear anymore. I'm proud of the love they shared, and I have developed a deep, burning hatred and anger toward the people who took it from them.

The people who took them from me.

All I have left of my parents now is a photo. They took the photo a few days before leaving Hong Kong to celebrate their pregnancy with me. They looked happy and hopeful, never expect the ill future awaits them.

I keep that photo in my purse, and I stare at it often. I wonder what stories my mother would have told me as I grew older. What advice she would have shared with me - about boys, about love, about life and the lessons she had learned.

I wonder if my father would have taught me to drive. If he would have taught me how to defend myself and be strong. He was a boxer; he loved the sport. So, when I was old enough, I took up kickboxing. It was one way I honored him.

My mother was graceful. I struggle to honor her by being the same way as I think I'm clumsy. I try, though.

I wish I had known them. I wish that, even now, as an adult, I could sit outside in the garden with them and tell them about my day. They would ask me how I did with my studies at university, and they would know what my favorite food was. They would cook it for me on my birthday, and we would sit together on an enormous sofa in the evenings and watch movies until late into the night. My mother and I would plant flowers in her garden. She loved to grow things. An gung told me this as he has told me many things about her - but they are just stories from his perspective. I want to *know* her. I want to touch her warm skin and lean against her shoulder while she reads me bedtime stories.

Normal things.

Normal things that I never did with them and never will.

Someone made choices all those years ago that changed the course of my life so drastically that I'll never be that happy, carefree child ever again. I'll never grow up as I was meant to be. I'm me now, a very different version of who I was supposed to be.

The people who made those choices changed me, and in doing so, they cursed themselves.

I'll never stop hunting for them. I'll never stop until I make them feel the wrath of the pain they have caused me and I punish them for what they took from me.

Chapter 2

ANTONIO

I drop the dumbbell onto the gym floor with a thud and stare at my reflection in the mirror on the wall. Sweat is pouring down my body, my toned muscles are shining. I brush wet hair strands back away from my eyes.

I grab my towel and wipe across my brow. I have three more sets, and then I can start my cool down.

Tilting the water bottle over my mouth, I splash ice-cold liquid down my throat.

It is hot today, unusual for this time of year. Thank goodness the AC is on full blast in here.

I pull the headphones from my ears as Kalo walks into the gym on the second floor of my mansion. I have known Kalo since

I was very young. We grew up together, and I trust him with my life.

"What is it?" I ask, slightly out of breath.

"Are you almost done? They just called me to let me know that the shipment you were waiting for has arrived a day early. I know you wanted to be there when it came in. It should hit the docks in the next two hours."

"Yes, I'm almost done. Have Yuze put together something for breakfast. I'm starving."

"Alright, I'll have the chef whip up something, but hurry."

I raise my brow at him, and he throws me a half-smile. He knows I don't like to be told what to do.

I slide my headphones back in place and pick up the weights again, feeling my back muscles flex and tighten as I lift them.

***

At the breakfast table, I'm reading the news on my phone as Kalo slides in to the seat opposite me and dishes up his breakfast from the buffet spread out in front of us.

The server arrives with a fresh pot of coffee, and he pours the steaming, dark liquid into a white bone china mug to my left.

"After we stop to check in on the shipment, your mother has asked that we join her for a cup of tea," Kalo said.

My mother is dead. My *real* mother. She died many years ago, and I never had the chance to meet her or my father.

My father is an old man now, living in New York. I often read about him in the media. I follow the stories about him.

When I was much younger, I didn't know or understand why I looked so different from my peers. I asked my parents repeatedly, and they always told me the same thing; we love you just the way you are.

It didn't answer my questions, though, and I just knew there was something about me they weren't telling me.

One day, when we were having dinner, I snapped and demanded to know.

My dad looked over at my mom, and I saw her eyes fill with sadness.

Tears rolled down her cheeks when my dad told me I was adopted. They weren't my birth parents. I didn't take it well. I felt as though they had been lying to me for so long.

Later that night, my mother came into my room and gave me a wooden box with a dragon carved into its lid. She told me, "Antonio, this was your mother's. She left it for you so that one day you might know who you are and where you came from."

She walked out of my bedroom and left me alone with the beautiful wooden box. I remember how my hands were shaking when I opened it.

I took out each piece one by one, taking my time to examine it carefully, trying to understand.

Finally, at the bottom of the box, I found a letter from her. The paper shook in my trembling fingers as I read her words. That letter told me so much, yet also made me question everything. Everything about who I was as a young boy became a lie. My true identity hid in New York.

I was born in Japan after my mother fled New York city to escape from him. She feared for my safety and brought me here in secret. The day I was born, my mother handed me over to a family here, who were friends of her mother's, my grandmother. They raised me as their own and I have known no other family but them.

I think about my father often, and despite the horrific stories I have heard about the man, I still have a place in my heart for him. He never had the chance to know his son. He knew of me, but I was hidden from him. I wonder what that might be like for him.

He is a dangerous man, and many people risked their lives to keep me away from him and his world. The mafia boss of New York City. My Italian family in New York is of a mystery to me; although I read about them in the news often enough, I don't know even one of them personally. My father is an old man now, and soon I know he will die. I still hold on to a small hope that I'll meet him before that happens, despite knowing it is impossible.

My Asian mother met my father just as she was finishing college, and I was born as the result of an accidental encounter. One passionate night of forbidden love. He was much older than her, and they came from different worlds, yet they were drawn to each other. My mother fled the city when she found out she was pregnant and hid me in a small town in Japan. One day, when she thought it was safe, she returned to New York.

She and my father came in contact again, and while I don't know how everything happened, I know they fell in love and got married. But my mother never told him where I was or who I was. And they forbade me from ever contacting him. I have remained respectful of that to this day to keep my family here safe. And to stop my real father's enemies from finding me and using me against him.

So, the only family that I know is my adoptive parents here in Hong Kong, where I grew up. They treat me as they would their own son, and I love them both deeply. Except I have never felt like I truly belong. I have a space inside me that is waiting to learn everything about my Italian heritage.

My family here in Hong Kong doesn't treat me differently, but I know I look different. Made up of the genetics from two different worlds, with my father's features and my mother's charisma. My entire life, I have lived in a way that only expresses half of who I'm. It is a blessing and a curse. It has kept me safe and taught me to be independent and to rely on myself, yet it has a certain emptiness to it.

I have lived and learned many things about how this life works. And life has been good for me. I live in a mansion. I have more money than I could know what to do with and I spend my time, mostly alone, doing as I wish.

I prefer solitude over crowds. I'm well-liked by those I meet; I know I have a way with people, yet I hold them all at arm's length, never letting them get too close.

All except Kalo. I met him one day, a young child, while playing in the park. It was just an ordinary day and an ordinary park. I was playing games with a group of boys, and a fight broke out. They were calling me names, pointing out that I differed from them. That was the first time I got punched in the face. I was losing the fight until Kalo stepped in to fight by my side. From that young age, Kalo just decided that we would be friends and never gave me the chance to say no.

Kalo is my brother. Not by blood, but by honor. I might not have blood ties here in Hong Kong, but those whom I call family or friends are deeply important to me. I'll do anything to protect them, and I have.

I run my branch of the family business but keep it under the radar. Despite having power, I believe that strength is better showed through subtle maneuvers and strategic choices.

Much like a game of chess. You never want your enemy to know what your next move will be. As long as you know who is on the board and what your goal is, you can work out anything steps ahead of the average player. Those who need to know who I'm, do. And those that cross me find out quickly that I'm not a man to mess with. After all, I'm my father's son. His blood runs through me.

Kalo finishes eating and leans back in his chair. I stand up. "Alright, let's get going."

"I'll have the driver bring the car around."

I meet them out front and climb into the back of the car, drive toward the docks.

I step out onto the gravel and feel it crunch beneath my shoes as I walk toward the office. A man waves at me from the other side, closer to the containers, so I turn toward him. He is the one I want to speak with.

"Mr. Aoi, your shipment came in a day early. It was just unloaded now; we can head straight over there."

"Thank you, Yuki." I follow him through a maze of stacked containers until we stop at the large metal box with my company logo printed on the outside. Aoi Armor. I supply armored vehicles, clothing and equipment to military and defense forces. Of course, there are other aspects to my business that are not public record.

He takes a set of keys out of his pocket and slides them into the lock, pulling the chain free from between the handles.

They open a second lock with a PIN code, and finally, the doors swing open.

I step inside.

SUVs fill the container from wall to wall. They are all identical. Pitch black, tinted windows, four by four, bulletproof and menacing. The latest and best technology equips all the SUVs. Safety, luxury and beauty.

"How many?" I ask, eyeing the cars.

"Six."

"Excellent. Have them unloaded and delivered by tonight. You have the addresses?"

"Yes, sir."

I reach into the first car and remove the key from a pocket in the door. I turn and toss it to Kalo. “This one is yours.” He looks at the key in his hand with surprise.

“You bought me a car?”

“Not just any car.”

“Thanks man.” he grins.

“Thank you, Boss. Kalo.”

“Yes, Sir!”

I walk back toward where the driver is waiting. Kalo can drive himself home.

Chapter 3

SERAPHINA

I give ah gung a cup of tea and sit down on a pillow at the low table alongside him. "I'm so proud of you, Sera." His wrinkled face is shining with a smile spread across his lips.

I bow my head briefly and say, "Thank you. I'm looking forward to finishing everything."

It is my last few days of college, and graduation is just around the corner. I remained committed to getting top scores and giving my best throughout the journey.

"Now that you have finished your studies, will you spend more time with friends?"

I sigh, a little frustrated. He always worries about me. "I'm too busy for parties and things like that. I have to focus on my future."

It is true, and it is not true.

I could easily make time for friends and socializing, but I just don't have that sort of inclination. The one friend that I have, Maddy, is all I need. But even she complains often about how I need to get out more and enjoy life.

How can I, though?

I watch her, laughing and relaxing and surrounded by people who love her. Her family supports her in every way possible, and she has a mostly normal life. At graduation, her parents will be in the audience watching her. Ah gung will be there, but not my parents.

"Sera, I just want to know that you will be alright," he complains, sipping on his tea.

"I know, ah gung, I will."

"You spend too much time alone."

"I'm happy, though," I lie.

He eyes me carefully, knowing that I'm not.

I'm so consumed by the past that I have never allowed myself to focus on anything other than my goal of avenging my parents' deaths. While Maddy was dating boys and experiencing life, I was alone, painting to ease my pain, getting lost in textbooks, researching New York. I almost started dating a boy once, but as soon as he got too close, I pushed him away. I have never felt love and I have never been intimate with anyone. In college, Maddy tried to set me up on a few dates,it made me very uncomfortable. So, I'm still a virgin, and it doesn't bother me at all. It is not something I yearn for.

I'm consumed by sorrow and anger. I can't control it.

A year ago, Maddy and I had a fight, and she told me I was obsessed with what happened to my parents. We almost stopped being friends because of it. Despite how much it would have hurt me to lose the only friend I have, I would have let her walk away. I can't change who I am. If she can't accept me for me, then she should leave.

But she stayed, and she has been a good friend to me despite my seemingly singular focus.

She wants me to move in with her after college and find a job nearby; she doesn't want me to go to New York. I chose where I went to college based on the most favored schools in New York. I have geared every choice I have ever made in my life toward one goal.

I can't date. I can't party. I can't push the trauma of my past aside to enjoy my life until I have resolved what I need to resolve.

My need for revenge spills over into every choice I have ever made.

I know I'm damaged. I'm broken. I'm not the same as other people my age.

But I love deeply and take care of those people who are important in my life. If I see someone else in pain, I have an overwhelming urge to help them. I know what it feels like, and I don't wish it on anyone else.

I stare fondly at ah gung. His face is lined with age, and his skin is soft. He bruises easily, yet his strength is still obvious to anyone who looks at him.

He has been my rock, my home, and my mentor.

He knows me better than anyone else, as he has seen my pain when it was still raw before I learned to hide it so that I could blend in. He has loved me through my worst and continues to care for me to this day.

I realized when I was young that if I wanted to achieve anything in life; I had to put on a brave face. The people who meet me don'tknow the sorrow I carry beneath the surface. They see me smile; they see me laugh, and they think I'm just like them.

A few years ago, Maddy convinced me to go to therapy. It took a while and a lot of pleading on her part, and I knew it was coming from a place of love, so I agreed to try it. At first, I was excited about it. I held a small hope that therapy might ease the heaviness in my heart. But when the therapist asked questions, so many questions, I had to accept that it would never work.

I'm a ward of the mafia, and everything I know is confidential. Everything that I would need to speak about in order to overcome the trauma - I can't speak about. It is too risky.

Despite the therapist trying her best to convince me otherwise, I stopped going. I learned to bottle things inside of me, and I even tried to hide my true thoughts from Maddy. She knows me well enough, though. She sees through the veil into the festering wound that is inside my heart.

Apart from ah gung, my Hong Kong family knows very little about what I went through. They think I left all of that in my past, and the smile I plaster on my face when I'm around them is satisfactory to them.

Ah gung sometimes lets me speak about it. He tells me stories of the Italian mafia and the things they have done to other families, to parents, just like my own. My desire for revenge becomes even stronger.

I reach out and touch ah gung's hand. "I'm excited to be finishing college. I'll start applying for jobs soon, and my new life will begin."

"That is good to hear. Have you thought about where you will work?"

"You know, I have always wanted to see New York. I'll apply there. I have a list of the places I want to try for."

"Why does it have to be New York? Anywhere but there?"

"I want to see where my father is from. I want to learn about his life."

He looks down, his eyes tainted with sorrow. I want to change the subject. Speaking about New York with him is not the right thing for this moment.

"Will you be at my graduation?"

"Of course. I would not miss it."

I finish my tea and gently place the cup on the table. "I'm going to the market later this afternoon for some fresh vegetables. Did you want me to bring you anything while I'm out?"

"I can just have the housekeeper do it for me. You don't have to worry about this old man."

I lean over and hug him. "I'll always worry about you." I smile as he wraps his arm around my shoulder and kisses the top of my head. "And I'll always worry about you."

My apartment is near to ah gung's home. I moved out when I started college. He gifted me with this beautiful space to call my own. I visit him often during the week and we share a cup of tea and talk about what I have learned in college, and I make sure that he has everything he needs. His wife passed away before I got to know her, and he never remarried. He still runs much of the Hong Kong mafia; his status and power demand respect, and despite his age, he holds a position of power. Decades of knowledge give him an advantage over his rivals in his business.

I toss my backpack onto the sofa near the window and walk to the bathroom, turn on the shower. It is hot outside, unusually so, as we are nearing the start of winter. I wore a long jersey, thinking the wind would be cold, and now I feel uncomfortable. A quick shower will freshen me up before I go to the market.

My phone buzzes against the kitchen counter where I left it, and I run through to answer.

It is a message from Maddy.

Maddy: Sera, come over tonight and help me pick out what to wear for graduation.

Me: It hardly matters what you wear because your graduation gown will cover it.

Maddy: Don't be so boring. Of course, it matters. I'll order takeout for us.

Me: I'm heading to the market now, then I want to finish working on the painting I started last week. Can we do it another time?

Maddy: Fine, but you are not getting out of it next time. We are getting ready for the after-party at my house. No arguing about it. This is going to be such an amazing night.

Me: Are you more excited about graduating or the after-party?

Maddy: I think the answer should be obvious.

I smile. She is the life of every party. I know people are drawn to me. I could have so many more friends if I wanted that, but I don't know how to let people in. Perhaps that makes me so magnetic to them. Perhaps they see me as a challenge. I don't know.

I had a sheltered upbringing. Living under protecting the Hong Kong mafia is not something I would have chosen for myself, but it has taught me a lot about life and what is important. Family is important.

Feeling fresh and dressed in something more appropriate for the hot weather, I wander through the market carrying the fresh vegetables I have bought in a basket, swinging from my hand.

"Sera, I have your favorite. It was the last one, but I kept it aside for you," the man calls to me from behind the market stall.

He ruffles around beneath his table and pulls out a bright pink dragon fruit.

"Duka, you know me so well."

"Anything for my favorite girl."

I grin and reach into my purse.

"No, no, this one is not for payment. You can pay me next time."

I scowl at him. "You tell me that every time." I pull the money from my purse and try to hand it to him. "No, my favorite customer doesn't have to pay this time."

I shake my head and slip the money into the container on his tabletop while he tries to wave my hand away.

"You know I won't let you give away your things for free, Duka. You work too hard every day for that."

He bows his head slightly toward me and smiles. "Next week, I'll have something special, something you have not tried before."

"I look forward to it."

I continue to make my way through the marketplace until I reach the stall of an older woman. "Mrs. Yakati, I brought you that book I told you about last time."

"Oh, sweet girl, thank you for thinking of me ." I hand her the book from my bag.

"It is very exciting. You are going to love it. Then we can meet for tea when you finish reading, and you can tell me what you think of how it ends."

She is packing my usual order while we talk. Wild garlic and fresh turmeric, along with ginger and mung bean sprouts.

"Did you try that same recipe with the chili added in?" she asks.

"I did; it was so much better. I made some for ah gung, and he was very impressed."

"That is good to hear."

I finish at her stall and check inside my basket. I just need to stop and get coconut water, then I can head back home. I love walking around the market and often come here even when I need nothing. The people are friendly, and I spend some time chatting with them. They tell me about their families, their children and husbands and wives. Often, I'll bring gifts for their little ones, knowing how hard their parents work to take care of them. In a way, I enjoy this because it is my way of catching a glimpse into the simplicity of their family lives. The beauty of it.

After I have finished my shopping, I stop for an ice tea at the edge of the market and then make my way back home.

I unload my groceries onto the kitchen counter and then pack them away. The simple process makes me calm, and for a moment, I think of nothing else.

When I'm done, pain edges at my thoughts again, so I sit behind my easel and pick up my paintbrush. My mother was a painter. I have seen her work on the walls of ah gung's home, and knowing that I'm doing what she loved to do makes me feel closer to her. It turns out that I inherited the same talent that she had. The eye for color and detail in an abstract work of thick paint layered over stretched canvas.

I could have gone to visit Maddy tonight, but I feel better doing this in my space with my thoughts.

Chapter 4

Antonio

The boardroom is in a high rise in the center of the city. Glass walls along two sides of the room overlook Hong Kong. I sit at the table, drumming my fingers against the dark wooden surface.

"What is this meeting about?" I demand to know. It was not scheduled, and despite my asking more than once, I'm still in the dark regarding what I'm doing here.

"I'm so sorry, Mr. Aoi, he will be here in one minute."

I sigh and push away from the table, finding solace by walking over to the glass wall and looking out at the sight.

Finally, my uncle walks in. I resist the urge to call him out for making me wait. Diplomacy goes a long way.

"Antonio, sorry for being late."

I return to my chair and sit in silence, eyeing him, waiting to be told about whatever the hell is going on.

“We received news today and wanted to tell you in person before the media printed stories.”

“What is going on?”

My uncle leans back in his chair and pulls his mouth to the side, then leans forward again and sighs. “Your father, in New York, has passed away in the early hours of this morning.”

The words wash over me, but I don’t process them fully.

For a moment my mind is completely blank.

My father.

The understanding hits me like a ton of bricks.

He is gone.

I'll never have the chance to meet him. I'll never stand in front of him and introduce myself as his son. I'll never see him in flesh and bone and reality.

He is gone.

Any hope that I was holding onto of ever knowing who he really was has just been shattered.

I clear my throat, unsure about how I should react. My family has always made it clear they have a great distaste for him. They call him evil, brutal, cold, murderous - but he is my father. My loyalty is to the family who raised me. But he is my father. My blood.

“Antonio?”

“Thank you. I appreciate you telling me.”

“His funeral is going to be held tomorrow morning in New York.”

I nod. A funeral I can't go to. For a man I have never known.

My uncle is staring at me. Watching me closely. I lock my expression in place; he doesn't need to know the level of emotions sabotaging my insides.

I stand. “I have some work to attend to. Thank you again for taking the time to inform me in person.”

“It is no problem. Just be careful. The families in New York are undergoing intensive change now that he has passed away. We don’t know what to expect in the aftermath of this event.”

He speaks of it as though it is another business deal. The day-to-day ins and outs of things that we have to attend to. My jaw is tight, and I have to remind myself not to clench my hands into fists at my sides.

“I understand.”

I make my way out of the building, feeling dizzy and detached from reality.

I knew well that this day was coming, but somehow, I convinced myself that I would meet him before it happened. Even knowing that would never be the case. That hope still lived inside me. Now, it is gone forever.

I wanted to meet my father to discover that part of me I don’t know. I can feel him inside me. They tell me he is a monster, yet I'm half of him. I'm capable of everything that he is. I'm as ruthless as the stories they tell me about him. I have done things that match and even exceed his level of cruelty, yet they don't call me a monster.

My phone rings. It is my mother. For a moment I hesitate, not wanting to speak to her in this weird space my head is in.

But I sigh, sliding the green button across the screen to connect the line.

“Antonio, your uncle just called us and let us know the news.”

“Yes, he told me now as well.”

“I hope you don't feel bad for that man. I hope you don't let his death upset you.”

“Mama, I'm busy right now. Can I call you back another time?”

I don't want to talk about this with her.

"I know you are not busy, Antonio. I just want to make sure you are alright. That you don't let the death of that cruel man upset you. He doesn't deserve to have that effect on you."

"I'm fine, mama."

She sighs into the phone; she knows me well enough.

"When will you come for dinner?"

"Soon, mama. Thank you for calling."

We say goodbye, and I hang up quickly. My mouth clenched, my shoulders are tense, and my muscles throughout my body are tight. I think the best thing for me to do right now is to go for a session at my gym.

I don't know where else to put this heavy feeling that has settled on me.

My mother calls him a monster; she says he is cruel, but I'm him. I'm his son. His blood is my blood, so what does that make me in her eyes?

The more I think about it, the more I feel distanced from my Hong Kong family. It is a familiar separation that I have always felt; it just feels more intense right now.

I know they will never accept me for who I truly am.

Despite exerting more effort than usual at the gym that afternoon, I should be depleted of energy and emotion, but I'm not. I feel overwhelmed with questions that I'll never have answered.

Tomorrow afternoon is my father's funeral. I want to be there. Nobody would even know who I am. I don't even know if anyone on that side of the world knows that I exist.

I toss and turn in frustration until the small hours of the morning, when I finally drift off to sleep.

In the morning, I call my assistant and tell her to cancel everything scheduled for the day. I can't face meetings or clients. Not today.

I got out of a cold shower, just in time my housekeepers knocks on the door.

"Sir, your parents are here."

Fuck.

"Thank you. Please tell them I'll be out in a moment."

When I walk into the living room where my parents are waiting, my mother jumps up and rushes over to me. "Antonio, I brought you your favorite dim sum buns. I made them last night." She wraps her arms around me, and I hold her against me for a moment before stepping back. I'm not fond of intimacy, but I know she is just trying to show her love for me.

"Thank you, mama."

My father walks over to me and wraps his arm around my shoulder, giving me a brief half hug. "Dad, it is good to see you. Can I have the chef make some breakfast for you two?"

"No, no, that is unnecessary; we are just stopping by. We are on our way to the flower market. You know how your mama loves to spend time there."

"Some tea then?"

"We just wanted to come and check in to see that everything is going alright. What have you got planned for today?"

"I have taken the day off."

"Oh." I can see that this has upset my mother. "Is it because of what happened?"

"Yes, mama, I want to take the day to process it."

My mother twists her fingers together, fidgeting. "You don't need to live in fear anymore, Antonio."

I grind my teeth, taking a moment before I spit out the first words that come to mind. She is my mother. I have great love for her, but I didn't view him the same way they do.

"I never lived in fear of him, mama. Maybe he only hid me from his enemies."

She nods. I know she wants to disagree with me, but she presses her lips together. My dad is patting her back to comfort her.

"Your mama and I only want what is best for you."

"And you have always given me everything. I'll forever be grateful for the love you have shown me." I reply.

He smiles. "Well, I guess we had better get going. Call us if you need anything."

I walk them out to their car and hold the door open as they climb into the back. The driver pulls away. I breathe a sigh of relief.

I love them deeply, but I struggle to hear them speak badly of my father.

Glancing at my watch, I note the time and think about the funeral.

I spend most of the morning in the gym, trying to force the tension out of my body, but it doesn't work. Kalo calls and tries to convince me to join him for lunch, but I decline.

In the afternoon, I find myself in the atrium, sitting behind my grand piano with my fingers spread across the keys. I have not started playing yet; I'm struggling to press my fingers down to start. Things seem too far away from me, confusing and distant.

Finally, I press my fingers into the key and a melody drifts into the air, reaching into the high ceilings of the room. I feel it drift through me, and I close my eyes. My fingers know their way between the notes, and I continue to play, getting lost in the methodical journey of each chord.

By the time evening arrives, I feel even worse. The funeral starts in thirty minutes in New York, and I'm pacing the halls of my mansion.

Frustration increases and I call out to my housekeeper.

"Have Mr. Lee bring the car around. I'm going out."

"Yes, sir."

When Mr. Lee arrives, I open his door and tell him I'll drive myself.

I park out of sight, around the corner from a bar in the city.

Inside, the music is too loud and there are too many people. It is the perfect place for me to get lost, to distract myself from thinking about my father's funeral and how I can't be there.

I have only been here once, and I chose it specifically so that I would not bump into anyone I know. I order two shots of vodka and a drink at the bar. I down both shots right away, and before the bartender leaves, I tap the counter to order two more.

He pours them without question, which I like.

Within an hour of arriving, I'm more drunk than I have been in a very long time.

To my annoyance, it has not dampened the thoughts of New York and the funeral.

I sway slightly when I walk back from the bathroom and try to spot the bartender to order another drink. I have to kill this havoc inside my mind.

"What are you, half-breed?" A slurry voice reached me.

I look up at the man standing in front of me with a sneer on his lips.

He is obviously very drunk and doesn't know who I am, or he would not dare to even talk to me, never mind insulting my blood.

"Walk away," I demand.

"Why do half-breeds not have a spine?"

I take a breath; this is not worth it.

He grabs the collar of my shirt, trying to pull me toward him, but I don't even budge.

He reaches up with his fist, swinging it toward my face. I see it coming. I could block it easily, but suddenly, I wanted to feel the sting of his knuckles against my jaw.

His fist connects, and he shouts in pain as I hear his knuckles crack.

Fucking idiot.

Then I'm on top of him, smashing my fists into his face repeatedly. All I see is the rage that I feel from my father's death. The stranger's blood splatters across the floor and onto my shirt, and I don't stop. I hear screaming and feel the crowd pushing back around me, but I don't stop. Someone tries to pull me off, and I turn, and my fist connects with their face as well. His lip splits open, and blood pours down his face. He swings at me, and I don't dodge it. I stand and feel the blow.

Suddenly, a thick arm grabs me in a choke hold, and I'm elbowing it when Kalo's voice rings in my ears. "Ant. Stop. Stop, man. We have to get out of here."

Confusion floods me for a moment, then I let him drag me away from the chaos.

He shoves me into the open door of the car waiting outside, and I slump, drunk and angry, against the seat.

When he is inside the car, the driver takes off, driving toward my home.

"Stop the car," I demand. The driver pulls over to the side. Kalo protests.

"No, man, we need to get you home. The cops were called."

I should say thank you, but I say nothing at all. He pulled me out of there before shit hit the fan.

He leans back, letting go of a heavy breath. "It's going to be ok, man," he says. I glare in his direction, my focus pulling in and out. Then I climb out of the car and slam the door behind me.

Kalo climbs out and runs after me as I storm down the street. “Get back in the fucking car, Antonio.”

“Kalo, walk the fuck away from me. If you know what is good for you.”

He throws his hands in the air and accepts defeat, letting me go.

I make my way back to where I parked my car.

A young girl wearing a skintight red dress with revealing cutouts comes sauntering over to me. I eye her up and down.

“Honey, you look sad; let me put a smile back on your face.”

“Fuck off,” I sneer.

“Or you can fuck me. Wouldn’t that be more fun?” She giggles.

I keep walking, and she runs in her high heels, slipping her arm through mine. “Come on, it won’t even cost that much. I’ll give you a special price.”

Her red lipstick is messy and too bright for her pale complexion, but I can see she is pretty beneath all of that makeup.

She follows me all the way to my car. Continuing with her proposals for a fun time.

My nerves are grating more and more with each word she speaks. Her voice was a whining chorus in my mind.

I stop next to my car and she eyes it. “Driving this, I don’t even think you need a discount. Let me make you smile. You can do anything to me.”

I grab her around the throat and slam her against the side of my car. “Anything? Are you sure about that?” I whisper in a harsh tone against her ear. I release her from my grip, and she staggers away from me, gasping for air.

I open the back door. “Get in,” I bark.

“Actually, I think-“

I grab a handful of her hair and throw her onto the back seat.

She squeals and kicks at me, but I'm on top of her, slamming the door behind us before anyone hears her. I shove my hand over her mouth and start ripping her dress from her body.

Her eyes are wide with terror.

I grin. "If you behave, I promise you won't regret it."

She nods silently, a tear falling down her cheek. I release my hand from her mouth and pull a lever, dropping the back seat, giving myself more space to move. I grab her legs and pull them apart. She is not wearing underwear.

I tug my belt off, pulling my pants open to free my throbbing cock. Her eyes grow wide at the sight of me, and she tries to shift up the seat, away from my cock, so I grab her throat, leaning down hard, watching her eyes water. I press my cock against her pussy and thrust hard into her. Her body jolts, and a silent cry falls from her lips.

I run my hand over her naked breasts, ignoring the torn remains of her dress as I thrust into her. All of my anger and frustration and buried emotion all come pouring out of me. Every time, I thrust harder and harder. I feel her sobbing beneath me, and it only drives me deeper into her.

I release her throat to grab a handful of her hair, pulling her face away from me as I explode into her, my cock pulsing and my body shaking with adrenalin.

I lay on top of her, pinning her beneath me, while I catch my breath. Then I lift myself off her and sit on the seat next to her while she scrambles away from me. I pull my pants closed and toss a wad of cash at her.

"Get the fuck out."

She grabs the money and I can see she is about to scream at me until she looks down and realizes how much cash she is holding. Her lips smear into a dark grin.

"I said get the fuck out."

Clutching her arms across her chest, she tries to cover herself; her dress, now little more than tatters, offers no protection. And just like that, she vanishes from my life.

I wake up with a hangover and confusion. It is still dark; I'm still dressed. I pull myself off the bed to locate my phone. It is ringing and I don't know how long it has been ringing for.

I squint at the screen but don't recognize the number. All I know is that the area code is New York.

"Hello." My voice sounds rough. My throat is dry.

"Is this Antonio?" A woman's voice.

"Who is this?"

"My name is Rebecca."

"What do you want, Rebecca?"

"Antonio, I'm your father's sister. His younger sister."

My heart stops beating for a moment.

"Are you still there?" she asks.

"I'm here."

I stand up, walking through to the kitchen to pour myself a glass of water. I need to push away this foggy hangover. The shock of her introduction has woken me up fully, though.

"I know this must be a bit of a surprise to hear from me. I always knew about you. Your father didn't even know that I knew. I'm sure you have heard of his passing by now. The funeral was this morning."

"I'm aware." I don't know what to say; I have so many thoughts running through me.

"The thing is, I want to meet you, and I'm flying to Hong Kong in a couple of days. Are you able to meet with me?"

"Yes," I answer without hesitation.

"Lovely. I'm so looking forward to it. Family is important. I'm going to call you when I arrive."

"I'll wait to hear from you, then."

I end the call with a surge of excitement, tainted because this might be a trap.

It could be an attempt to murder my father's only son, to end his bloodline; it could be anything. I don't know. But I know it is worth the risk. I have questions, and I want answers.

Chapter 5

Seraphina

Maddy jogs next to me along the canal that runs through the city. It is beautiful and peaceful and our favorite place to run in the mornings. She keeps pace easily because I hold back a little when I run with her. When I run alone, I push harder, wanting to feel the pain in my muscles. Jogs with Maddy are more relaxed.

She laughs as we run past an owner being dragged along by the massive dog. He is stumbling and swearing under his breath, trying to keep the animal under control.

When we reach the water fountain, she stops to catch her breath.

"I'm so excited. It is going to be the best day ever." She jumps a little.

It is very early, and the sun is just beginning to rise. We have to be at the graduation ceremony in two hours, and she has been talking about it nonstop.

"You know these graduations are really long. It is going to be a lot more boring than you imagine."

"Nonsense. You are going to love it. Everyone is going to be there. It is going to be such an awesome vibe, and then tonight, we are going to the after-party. That is when the fun really starts."

I smile. I'm nowhere near as excited as she is. I'm happy to be graduating, but the process of the ceremony seems tedious and overdrawn. But I have to smile; I have to share Maddy's enthusiasm - for her sake.

"I really don't want to go to the party." I pull a face.

"Well, you are going."

"You have so many other friends there; if I didn't go, you would not even notice."

"Remember when you woke up late that one morning for Mr. Hanoi's class? Remember how I covered for you?"

"What has that got to do with anything?"

"You owe me, Sera. Besides, how would I survive without you? You are the best at keeping an eye on me and making sure I don't do stupid things."

I roll my eyes. Maddy often gets what she wants from me. She is my only friend, and I don't want to lose her. I put myself in awkward situations, like parties, in order to make her happy.

"You have been talking about what to wear to the party for weeks now. Have you decided yet?" I ask.

"No, you are going to have to help me pick something out. And I'll help you."

"I don't think my clothes really have that party vibe."

She laughs. “No, they don’t, but you can borrow something from me, obviously.”

She grabs my arm and pulls me back onto the running path. “Come on, I'll race you home.” She takes off at a sprint, and I catch up in a few strides.

I decide to push her a little and run just ahead of her until the end, when I pretend I have a stitch, and she shoots forward.

Outside her apartment, she leans against the railing, breathing heavily.

“I know you faked that,” she chuckles.

“I have no idea what you are talking about,” I grin at her.

“We all know you are a way better runner than me, but thanks for pushing me. Wow, that felt good. My legs are shaking.”

We make our way up the stairs to the fourth floor and into her apartment.

“You can shower first.” She throws me a towel.

We are standing in her bedroom, and I'm surrounded by dresses. She has made me try on at least eight of them and now she is getting frustrated with me.

She hands me the blue one that I said was too short.

“This one. This is the one. I don’t want to hear another word.”

I pull it onto my body. It hardly matters. The graduation gown will cover it, anyway.

“I can’t wait to start working,” Maddy says, pulling her own dress over her body. “It is going to be amazing to have that independence and not need to rely on my parents anymore. Aren’t you excited about that too? Have you decided yet? Are you going to move in with me?”

“I'm still looking at jobs in New York.”

She sighs.

“Does it have to be New York, Sera?”

“You know I want to go there,” I shrug.

“I also know why. I just want you to move on from all of that. You are so obsessed with revenge that you are missing out on your life. Do you know how many people absolutely adore you? You could have any guy you wanted. You could get married, have a baby, you could be happy.”

“I don’t know if I'll ever get married, Maddy.”

“Fine - then you could become the CEO of some major corporation and be a girl boss. What I'm saying is that there is so much more you could do than focus on revenge. Your life could be about so much more. I want more for you.”

“My life is not about revenge. Don’t be silly. "

Maddy falls silent and bites her lip. I can see she wants to argue with me. She knows it as well as I do - that my life is about revenge.

I made that choice so long ago, and I can't let go of it until that little girl inside of me, who witnessed the brutal murder of her mother, finds her strength again. In order to do that - I need to go to New York, and I need to do whatever it takes.

Maddy moves to stand in front of me, cupping my cheeks in her hands.

“Sera, you are so beautiful. You are strong and graceful and smart and funny and kind. In fact, I don’t think you know how strong you are. You are so much better than what those people did all those years ago. I wish you could see it. I wish you would let someone fall in love with you and treat you like you deserve to be treated.”

Her words touch my heart and I swallow hard to fight the emotions that form a lump at the back of my throat.

She drops her hands and smiles gently.

I want that. I want love. I want someone who values me, supports me, loves me with all their heart. I also want to share my love with someone. I'm human, and I know that I'm vulnerable. But my determination is stronger than any of those other needs.

My grandfather has arranged for a driver to take us to graduation and he is waiting downstairs when we step out onto the sidewalk. Maddy excitedly grabs my hand and pulls me toward the car.

The driver is holding the door open for us.

We slide into the back seat and find champagne waiting for us.

"This is so sweet of your grandfather." She pours us each a glass and says, "To our beautiful, happy futures."

Graduation is actually a lot more fun than I expected it to be.

As I step onto the stage, the announcer's voice fills the air, listing off my achievements. A surge of pride swells in my chest—I've poured my heart and soul into this. Knowing my grandfather is somewhere in the audience, watching, sends a wave of excitement through me.

"I wish I could be everything they hope for," I murmur to myself, managing a smile for the crowd. For a moment, I let myself bask in the feeling of normalcy, almost convinced I can leave the past behind and start fresh.

But then, my eyes sweep across the sea of faces, landing on the proud parents cheering for their kids. A familiar ache tightens in my chest, pulling me back to reality.

Later, on the university lawn, laughter and chatter fill the air as we snap photos and toss our caps skyward.

Ah gung pulls me into a warm embrace, his voice soft. "I'm so proud of you." Tears prick my eyes, a mix of gratitude and love washing over me. Sharing this moment with him means everything.

Maddy's parents envelop me in a hug just as heartfelt as if I were their own. Maddy and I laugh and celebrate together, wrapped in the joy and camaraderie of the day.

When the graduation is over, Maddy and I head back to her place to change into the dresses she has chosen for us to wear to tonight's party.

Chapter 6

Antonio

There is a sea of freshly graduated college students flooding the back garden of my mansion. Giant, transparent beach balls fill the pool, and gold and silver decor adorns the inside and outside of my home. Caterers run back and forth, and colorful drinks are carried out on large trays.

Music fills air, crowd dances in rhythm.

One of my cousins is amongst them. He graduated today, and he begged me to host the after-party here. Of course, I said yes. Despite not enjoying the massive crowds of people, I know what it means to him.

I'm standing on the deck overlooking the excitement.

My eyes have been fixed on a girl in the crowd all night.

Despite her youth, her graceful and controlled presence has captivated me. She is clearly mature for her age, not blending in with the crowd. Her extreme beauty makes it impossible for me to look away.

A boy walks past me, and I grab his arm. He looks at me with a shocked expression.

"The girl there, in the silver dress. Who is she?"

He squints into the crowd in the direction I have gestured.

"That is Seraphina."

"Seraphina," I repeat her name and taste how it feels on my lips. I release the boy's arm, and he moves away quickly.

Kalo chuckles. "What are you thinking, Antonio? Have you got your claws out?"

"Perhaps."

"I know what happens when you spot something you want."

"What is that?"

"You take it."

I chuckle.

"Who are you eyeing?"

I gesture with a nod in her direction. "The silver dress."

"Interesting. She looks slightly out of place, doesn't she?"

"That she does."

"She has no idea what is coming for her." He shakes his head. "I'll find a young student and see what she can teach me."

I hardly notice when he leaves. My sights locked on her.

When the waiter moves past me with champagne glasses glittering with gold liquid, I pick up two of them and make my way toward her.

When I'm standing close to her, I find her beauty is even more alluring. Her long, dark curls are falling loose over her shoulders and down her back. She is wearing a silver dress covered in sequins that shimmer when she moves. It traces the curve of her waist over her hip and sits short enough to tease any man who has his eyes on her.

Her skin is pale caramel and when she turns to look at me, feeling my presence behind her, her luscious lips curve in to a beautiful smile that lights her round brown eyes.

“Hello,” she says.

“Seraphina,” I say her name again, enjoying the sound of it.

“Do I know you?”

I hand her a glass of champagne. “My name is Antonio. This is my mansion. I wanted to say congratulations on your graduation.”

In a moment, her eyes narrow before she takes the glass. “Thank you,” she replies politely.

“You must be very proud of yourself?”

“I suppose that would be the normal process, yes.”

I chuckle. Her eyes move to my mouth, then back to meet my gaze.

“Would you like to join me on the deck? I have a bottle of champagne on ice.”

She glances around, not finding whoever it is she is looking for.

“My friend was here a moment ago. I should stay and wait for her.”

It’s uncommon for me to be rejected.

I reach out and gently wrap my fingers around her wrist, pulling her ever so slightly toward me.

“Your friend will find you, I'm sure.”

“Um, yes, ok,” she replies with hesitation.

I smile. Then place my hand on her lower back and guide her toward the deck.

I gesture at the seating. “Please, make yourself comfortable.”

“You don’t look-” she bites back her words.

"Neither do you," I chuckle.

"My mother was Chinese," she shrugs.

"My mother was Japanese, and my father was Italian. I never knew them, though. I was raised here."

She eyes me closely, her gaze drifting over my features.

"I heard a story about a boy who was half Italian, half Japanese -"

The corner of my lip turns upward. "I'm sure there are many stories; you can't always believe what you hear."

"I never really knew my parents, like you." Her voice drifts off, as does her gaze, leaving my face to look outwards over the crowds of people around us.

"So, you were raised by someone else?" Sadness shouldn't overshadow her beauty.

"My grandfather, Muchen Hanoi."

My body tenses up, the recognition immediate and chilling.

She's no stranger to me, not by any means. Rumors have swirled around her past, shrouded in a mystery that has never been officially unraveled. Whispers suggest the Italian Mafia's hand in the tragic fate of her parents. Her father, having whisked her mother away to New York, ignited the ire of the family back home. Their union, and the child it brought into the world—a little girl—was met with nothing but disdain. Her mother got killed, and she sent back across the ocean to Hong Kong to be raised under the watchful eye of her mafia family.

As far as I know, my father was responsible for her mother's death. He was the one calling the shots at the time of the murder, so he would have put that target on her head. I'm indirectly connected to her mother's death. I feel my jaw tighten. Her face turns back toward me. There is so much written in her eyes that it is hard to read her. She is a storybook that I want to know everything about, but now that I know I'm connected to her mother's death, I feel as though I should walk away from her.

She sips her champagne. "What was it like growing up half-Italian in this city?"

"I suppose you could say it was a challenge. Or it had its challenges. But, as you can see, everything turned out alright." I gesture around my mansion, and she smirks.

"Indeed, it turned out alright for you."

Seraphina places her empty glass on the table next to her. I lift the bottle I have chilling in ice out of the steel bucket.

"I don't think I should have another." She holds her hand up, declining me.

"Nonsense. You just graduated. Surely, the norm is to celebrate." I pour the champagne into her glass.

"I don't really follow the norm." Her smile is distant.

I stare at her. "Yes, I can see that. Nothing about you is average."

She brushes a curl away from her face, her elegant hands and perfectly painted fingernails moving gracefully.

"What do you do, Antonio?"

"I own a few businesses."

"Very vague," she smiles.

"What did you study?"

"Business strategy. It fascinates me."

"Strategy or business?"

"Strategy."

My gut is telling me that this girl is dangerous. I shouldn't talk to her. She's curious and knowledgeable, but I want this conversation to continue.

"Who are your parents, or - who raised you?"

"Mr. and Mrs. Aoi."

She nods as though she knows them. I assume she would, anyway. Her grandfather, being the person he is, would have knowledge of the world, its workings, and the players involved.

I feel so connected to her. Her story is so similar to mine. Without her parents and a different place to call home, she was raised in a whole new world. She doesn't know what the word family really means. Many find her presence unwelcome, as she is different and doesn't belong here. Her features are exotic and stand out. She is beautiful beyond words, and I know that has been a blessing and a curse to her.

I imagine she struggled with the same things I did. In school, children would have treated her differently, actually even as an adult now.

Some would bully, mock, or look at her with distaste. I imagine she doesn't see her uniqueness in the same way I do. As an artwork. An exquisite, priceless artwork.

A piece of art that I want to call my own. Something unique, only I can display and cherish daily. She is a one-of-a-kind piece, and I want her.

The more she dodges, the more intrigued I become. It's like she's crafted from a different mold. Most women? They swoon the second I flash a smile or hint at my status—dazzled by the money, power, the whole facade. But her? She scans my mansion with this nonchalant air, as if it's all just... ordinary.

It's not the usual awe I'm met with; it feels like a challenge. And damn, do I love a challenge! She's playing it cool, hard to get, and that just flips a switch in me. Now, it's like we're in this dance—she's the prey, I'm the predator. And I can't shake off this burning need to have her, to claim her as mine in every sense. This isn't just about wanting anymore; it's about winning, owning, consuming.

"Antonio, thank you so much for the drink and the conversation. I think I need to get going."

"Where is your friend?" I don't want her to leave.

"I see she has found her entertainment. Another boy to string along." She laughs and shakes her head.

"Why don't you have a boyfriend?"

"I guess I'm just not interested in things like that."

"What are you interested in, Seraphina?"

"I'm interested in things with more substance."

"That's very vague of you." I chuckle, using her own words against her.

The corner of her mouth curls upwards into a very alluring half grin.

"Stay for one more drink?"

"Thank you, but this really isn't my scene."

"The party? Or me?"

She looks me up and down with intensity in her gaze.

"The party."

"Can I give you a ride home?"

She laughs.

"I don't think that would be appropriate."

How is this girl turning me down so calmly, so smoothly?

"I see." Irritation prickles at me, yet I'm undeniably aroused. The sense of challenge intensifies. I have a history of getting what I desire, be it tonight or some other time. I will have what I want.

Seraphina stands. Her shapely legs catching my eye.

I stand as well, over a head taller than her. She looks fierce and composed despite her guarded nature and small build.

"It was a pleasure to meet you, Seraphina. I hope to spend time with you again soon?"

"It was a pleasure to meet you as well, Antonio."

I step aside so that she can walk past me, but only enough to allow a small space so she has to brush against my body. Her scent washes over me in exotic ways. She smells of rose and honey. Images of wild nature flash through my mind. Beautiful.

As she presses against me, her hand touches my waist. My blood pumps faster, and my skin heats under her touch. I resist the urge and press harder against her as my cock stirs.

Patience. This one requires patience.

She turns to look over her shoulder and smiles at me.

“Thanks again, Antonio.”

Then she walks into the crowd, her body disappearing from sight, and I'm left staring after her with my brows knotted in contemplation.

Chapter 7

Seraphina

My bedroom looks like a truckload of university supplies has crashed into it and overturned. I have boxes open, and I'm trying to sort through all of my textbooks, study notes and stationery. It's time to pack it all away. It feels strange to be closing this chapter of my life. I thought it would never end. It felt like it would never end, that's for sure. All those hours of studying. Late nights leaning over textbooks with the end of a pen dipped into my mouth, focused and taking notes. It's all over. I'll never have to do that again. The thought is difficult to comprehend, as it has been my only real responsibility for a few years now.

I have a sense of freedom, but the same sense of sadness and anger that I always feel weighs it down. The need for revenge.

Obsessing it. I know it isn't healthy. I know my life might be better if I could just forget everything. But I know I can't.

I slide one of the heavy textbooks into a box, letting my fingers drift over the spine for a moment. It's time for me to focus on the most important thing of all - finding out what happened to my parents. Learning who was responsible and plotting a way to take something from them to cause them as much pain as they caused me.

I think again about the man I met last night. I have heard about the boy who was raised in Hong Kong after his mother had to flee New York to escape his cruel, tyrant of a father. The mafia boss. My intuition tells me he is that boy from the stories. He avoided answering my questions, so many of them, but I'm almost certain.

I lay in bed last night, regretting not being more forward with him. Perhaps I could have learned more; perhaps he is the one who could have led me right to the people I'm looking for - in fact - he might be the person I'm looking for. If I'm right, his family killed my parents. But I didn't take full advantage of the situation last night, so I have lost that opportunity and now I must just focus on getting to New York.

I pick up another pile of textbooks and drop them into a box. Folding the lid closed, I place strong brown tape around the edges to secure it. I want to take the books to the local bookshop to see if I can sell them. I need to save for my trip to New York.

I don't want to ask for ah gung's help with this, as he doesn't even want me to go. I know it hurts him. I don't feel happy with my life. Not that I'm not happy with my life, though, it's just that I'm consumed by the horror of what I experienced.

One day, I'll have justice. After that day, things can change. Until then, I'm doing what I can.

Everyone heals in their own way, and I know what I need to do to heal.

I lift one box into my arms; It's heavy but manageable. The bookshop is near to here, anyway. I'll ask the doorman in my building to help me load them into the taxi.

It doesn't take long before I'm parked outside the bookshop. I called ahead and make sure that they were interested in purchasing textbooks before I wasted my time. The man sees me arriving outside, knowing I was on the way, and he comes out of the shop with his assistant to help me carry.

When everything is unloaded, he opens the boxes and unpacking the textbooks. He tells me it's going to be a little while, as he needs to check their condition and calculate an offer for me.

I smile; I love spending time in bookshops so he can take as long as he needs.

I browse up and down the aisles, taking in the smell of the pages and browsing through the books that catch my eye.

I'm lost in this world for a long time, reading, browsing, drifting. It's so peaceful and soothing.

A certain title jumps out at me from the rows of spines. *New York Mafia Mysteries. Tales of crime and horror.*

I slide the book out and open it. I read over a few paragraphs, opening it in different chapters. It's a book about the Italian family. Rumors, crimes, investigations.

I tuck the book under my arm. This one will come home with me.

“Miss?” the store owner calls to me. I make my way to the front of the shop.

“Your books are in beautiful condition. This is what I can offer you.” He slides a piece of paper across the counter, showing his calculations and how he came to the figure at the bottom of the page.

“That is great,” I say. “You can deduct the cost of this book from the total, please.”

He punches into his calculator, nods, opens the till and hands me the cash.

I slip it into my purse and slide the book into my handbag. I thank him and start walking out of the bookshop just as my phone rings.

“Hello?”

“Sera, it’s Kimmy. How are you?”

I don’t know Kimmy very well. He is one of the cool kids, coming from a very rich family. All the girls love him. I can’t imagine why he would call me.

“Hi, Kimmy.”

“Sorry to bother you, but I wanted to find out. You see, a friend of a friend says that there is a guy who is asking for your number. Apparently, you met him at the party last night.”

“Um, ok?”

“Well, I wanted to know if it's alright if I give him your number. I don’t want to just go giving your number out if you don’t want me to?”

Immediately, I think of Antonio. I don’t see who else it could be. Just this morning, I was regretting not having used that opportunity to my advantage and now I have another chance.

“Yes, that is fine. You can give him my number.”

“Great. Thanks. I guess you have an admirer, hey?”

“Maybe I just forgot something at the party, and he is trying to return it to me.”

He chuckles. “Yes, sure. Well, have a nice day, Seraphina.”

“You too, Kimmy.”

I slide my phone back into my handbag and grin. This is a touch of luck. Perhaps this is all the luck I need, and he can lead me to where I want to go.

I'm just going to play this. Men like him are dangerous. They are murderers. Killers. Sadistic and cruel.

Or - I could be wrong, and he is not who I think he is. That is a possibility as well, but there is only one way to find out. I wonder when he will call or if he will call at all.

Without the books weighing me down, I decide to walk home rather than catch another taxi. It's not far, and It's a beautiful day. When I get home, I want to search online for jobs in New York. I want to put applications together and applying. The sooner I get there, the better it will be.

I open my front door and walk inside my apartment; it was another hot day, and I need some iced tea. I toss my handbag onto the counter, and it thuds, and I remember I bought an interesting book today.

I pull it out of my bag, placing it on the counter as well.

Once I have poured some iced tea, I gather the book and my drink and head over to the sofa. The first few pages are an introduction and explanation of why the author chose a pseudonym and didn't use his real name. Blah blah. We know. It’s obvious.

I flip through the pages until I find the chapter one.

An hour goes by without me even realizing it. I only put the book down because I need to pee and can't hold it anymore.

When I return to the living room, I stand next to my coffee table, staring at the book, face down, pages open.

I wonder if there is anything online about Antonio and if I can find out if he was that boy that all the stories are about.

I rush to my room to grab my laptop, very interested in what I want to do.

I type in his name. Antonio Aoi.

It's like he doesn't exist. He is a ghost. There is nothing online about him. Not even about his role in whatever businesses he runs. Nothing. Literally nothing.

After an hour of scouring everything I can think of, I close my laptop and pull a face. It's frustrating, but also, somehow, it confirms my suspicions. If he was the boy who was hidden all those years, then, of course, there would be nothing online about him.

I grab my phone, checking to see if I have any new messages. Nothing.

Now, I'm even more eager to hear from him.

He is linked to the death of my parents, and I want to know how. I have to know how. This is the closest I have ever been to someone like him and gaining information about my parents' murder.

The rest of the afternoon seems to drag on and I keep checking my phone even though I pushed the message and ringing volume up to the fullest it can go. I'm so patient, playing the long game, but I feel this underlying excitement.

Perhaps I need to distract myself. This is ridiculous. I can't sound too eager on the phone if he calls.

I need to fill my time.

I grab my gear and head over to the gym. I can get a session of kickboxing in. If he calls or messages, I'll still hear it in the gym and if I don't, I can always call back. He is interested in me, so it's not like he is going to give up after one call.

The gym felt great. I worked out a lot of my energy, and I feel less agitated waiting now. I got home, had a long shower, and started cooking a simple vegetable stir-fry. I spread out the fresh greens I purchased from the market on the kitchen counter and I'm chopping and tossing them into the pan one at a time.

The methodical process is soothing.

I pad around the kitchen on bare feet, wearing oversized tracksuit pants I took from Maddy the last time I slept over there and a gym crop top. Her hips are fuller than mine, so I have to pull the drawstring tight around my waist, and they still slip down. But the fabric is so comfortable, and I love the dark green color; I just declared that they were mine, and when she laughed about it, I knew it was fine.

I toss the vegetables and lower the heat as they sizzle.

My phone rang so loud, I drop the bamboo spatula and laugh at myself.

I hold the phone in my hand, an unknown number on the screen, letting it ring two more times before I answer.

"Hello?"

"Seraphina, what a beautiful phone voice you have."

"Who is this?" I recognize his deep voice, but want to play it cool.

"We met the other night at my place. Or did you meet more than one alluring gentleman who has asked for your number?"

I giggle.

"Antonio, I thought it might be you."

"How are you? Did you enjoy your time at my home?"

"I'm good. I had a lovely time at the party. The host was quite charming."

"Is that so? I hear he is only charming to very specific people."

"I count myself lucky then." I giggle. It's fun talking to him, even if it's only to fulfill my mission.

"What did a beautiful girl like yourself do today? Now that you have finished college, I imagine you have a lot of free time on your hands?"

"Well, I spent some time in a bookshop this morning. Then this afternoon, I had a session at the gym, and now I'm making a stir fry."

"You are more and more interesting to me as the seconds go by. You cook, you love bookshops and - what do you do at the gym? Yoga?"

"Kickboxing."

He is silent for a moment, and then a deep, genuine laugh vibrates through the phone and sends shivers through my body. I smile at his charm.

"I think that shouldn't have surprised me, given that you seem to be in the habit of surprising me. Kickboxing. Remind me not to upset you."

I pull the pan off the flame of the stove and flick the stove off. I walk through the living room, still smiling, and slide onto the sofa, pulling my legs up beneath me.

"It's difficult to upset me, so you are in luck."

"Yes, I saw how calm and collected you were. A woman in control of herself is very attractive."

"How is your day so far, Antonio?"

"I had some business to attend to, boring things. I also had a session in the gym at home here. After that, I did a few laps in the pool, and my chef made lamb shanks for dinner."

"It sounds very luxurious, having someone cooking for you."

"Mm. It can be; I guess I'm used to it now. It's not always luxurious having so many people running around doing things for you. I do like my space and enjoy being alone."

"We are alike in that way, then."

"What else do you enjoy, Seraphina?"

I smile, thinking for a while. What kind of person do I want to portray? What kind of person do I think would lure him in and entice him? So far, just being myself has done the job perfectly fine. I decide to be honest.

"I love to paint. My mother painted. It somehow - connects me to her."

"Another thing we have in common. I don't paint, but I love art. What style do you paint?"

"Abstract. It's sort of emotional - provocative."

"Provocative." The word purrs from his mouth and I feel my body tingling.

Images of his strong jawline and dark eyes creep into my thoughts. His tall, muscular build and the way he stood so close to me the other night. He is gorgeous. I feel he knows it and has used it to lure many women into his bed.

The conversation is easygoing, and we talk for a long time. I smile often; his charm is obvious; I think to myself about how many women have fallen for it.

It's easy to flirt with him, to play the role of coy yet interested potential.

"Seraphina, I don't want to keep you up all night, at least - not unless you want to come over?" he chuckles, "No, I wanted to ask you if you would join me for dinner? I would love to spend more time with you in person and get to know you a little better?"

This is what I was hoping for. The chance to get closer to him.

"That sounds lovely. I would like that."

"Wonderful. Tomorrow night. I'll pick you up at seven. Will you send me a message with the address?"

"Perhaps I should meet you there, rather?"

"If you prefer that. I can send you the details of where I book for us. Are you sure you don't want me to pick you up?"

"Thank you, I'm sure."

"Independent and beautiful. You are quite something."

Almost reluctantly, we say goodbye. I feel as though we could have talked late into the night. Glancing at my phone, I saw that our conversation was already over an hour long. His flirting skills are off the charts. Years of experience, I presume.

I have what I want, though - a date. A chance to get closer to him. Perhaps I need to be more careful? What is he going to expect from me? I have not dated before, and I don't know what the *norm* is. I don't want to find myself when I feel awkward. He is also, if what I heard was true, a very dangerous man. I imagine he is used to getting what he wants. His confidence so far has been alluring, powerful and tasteful. How does he behave when things get more - intimate?

I'll just have to take things one step at a time. For now, I won't put myself in the back of a car with him. I won't be giving him my address. I'll be careful; I promise myself that.

Chapter 8

Antonio

The entire day, I have been watching the clock. I don't know what it's about Seraphina, but she has hooked me entirely. I can't get her out of my thoughts. I have to have her. However, my usual methods will not work. She is different, more challenging, more exotic, and not as easy as I have experienced it to be in the past.

Talking to her is quite fascinating. She has so many interests that are unusual. She is smart, mature and graceful. Topped off because she is stunning.

I have booked dinner for us at Santa Fey. A luxurious restaurant in the city, New York-style steaks and views that stretch around every wall of the high-rise building.

I'm very much looking forward to it.

But my plans are shattered when my phone rings, and I realize I'm talking to Rebecca. She has arrived in Hong Kong and wants to meet tonight. How can I say no? She is only available tonight as she is flying out again in a day or two, and the rest of her time here is booked.

Frustration tightens my lips. I can only hope that canceling on Seraphina won't make her upset with me.

“Can we meet tonight, then?” Rebecca asks again.

“Yes, tonight will be fine. Do you have a specific place you want to meet?”

“Somewhere safe? I don’t know if it's a good idea for us to be seen together. I know people here, and I don’t want to put either of us in a difficult situation.”

“I understand. I know a quiet place where we can talk without being interrupted. I'll send you the details, and we can meet at six?”

“Yes, that’s perfect. Thanks.”

I put down the phone and clamp and unclasp my jaw in frustration. This is a meeting I definitely have to go to. I can't miss out on this, but letting Seraphina down doesn't sit well with me.

I dial her number.

“Antonio? Did you miss me already?” She giggles, and I close my eyes, letting the sound of her laugh wash over me.

“I did, actually. I love to hear your voice. It brightens my day.”

“I'm looking forward to tonight.”

I sigh. “I was calling about that, Seraphina. I'm so sorry, but someone has flown in to see me, and this is the only night they have available to meet. I was not aware until only a moment ago. I really hope you don’t think I'm avoiding you. I very much want to take you out to dinner. Can we reschedule for tomorrow night? Same time? Same place?”

She is quiet for a moment, and I hold my breath.

"Of course we can." Relief washes through me. "Tomorrow night is great."

"I really appreciate this. Thank you for understanding."

"Honestly, there is no problem at all."

"Not busy enough to keep me away from you, beautiful girl."

She laughs again, and I hold the phone tighter against my ear.

"I'll see you tomorrow night, then."

"Until then."

At least she let me reschedule and seemed very easygoing about it.

It's already late in the afternoon, and I should get ready to meet my aunt.

I don't know what to expect. I could walk into a trap, but I have been in that type of situation before, and I know I can handle myself well.

Being ruthless is a part of who I'm, and it's the reason I'm rarely confronted. I had to make a name for myself and for my business.

I own the law. They are all on my payroll, which makes me untouchable.

I hold a certain power here in Hong Kong that is unquestioned, and that means I have very little to fear.

Ninety minutes later, I find myself at a table in a secluded corner of a quiet restaurant, far from the usual hustle and bustle. The moment Rebecca enters, there's no doubt in my mind—it's her.

Her foreign appearance makes her stand out here, but more than that, I recognize the resemblance. After hours spent poring over pictures of my father, the similarities in their features are unmistakable. She is his sister. However, she's much younger than he was, a gap of perhaps twenty or so years between them, placing her closer in age to my mother, maybe slightly older. It leads me to wonder, could they have been friends?

I stand up and raise my hand so that she can find me easily. She waves and rushes over. She doesn't hesitate - she wraps her arms around me and pulls me into a hug as though we have known each other for years.

“Antonio, oh my goodness, you are like the perfect mix of your mother and your father. I can see both of them in you.”

I return her hug, watching around me to see if anyone appears to have followed her.

I see nothing out of the ordinary.

After fifteen minutes of generic conversation, she says, “I can’t believe I'm meeting you. This means so much to me. I only wish your mother could have seen how beautiful you grew up to be. You look just like them.”

“Did you know my mother well?”

“We were so close, her and I. We were almost the same age. She was one of my most favorite people in the world.”

“Her and my father - what was their relationship like?”

“Your father was obsessed with her. His entire world revolved around her. I have always longed for a love like that, but we are not all so lucky. They meant to be together. I used to sit at the family dinners and events and just watch them together. They were always close, touching, holding each other. He would spoil her, and she would smother him with affection. They had these secret looks they gave each other as though they could speak without words. The love they shared was something unique, very special. I think it went far deeper than even I can imagine.”

I like my aunt. She is friendly, sweet and kind. She tells me stories about my parents make me smile. It deepens the longing in my heart to have been able to meet them. I wonder again how it would have felt to be their son, to be raised by them, to experience their love. I have never felt love like that. I don't feel as though I have ever experienced any kind of love.

My foster parents are absolutely amazing individuals, but their constant derogatory remarks about my father, my flesh and blood, have left me questioning if they could ever genuinely love me. Unconditional love. Perhaps it was just my own guarded nature, defending that part of myself that is my father's blood. Perhaps not. It's just how I feel.

The women who have come and gone from my life - there was no love there either. Sometimes it was about money; sometimes it was sex. Perhaps it was just me and my inability to let people get too close.

I wonder if I'll ever experience love. My parents' love is like no other, and even Rebecca acknowledges this. Most people never feel that in their lifetime. At this moment, I long to know what it's like.

"Your father spent many years looking for you, Antonio."

Her words jolt me into focus.

"He was looking for me?"

"Yes. He made a promise to your mother while she was alive that he would never ask about you or search for you. But after she passed away, I think he was so alone, so heartbroken. You were all he had. You were part of her, too, and he wanted to meet you. He hunted for years and could find nothing out. It tore me apart knowing he was looking, but I also made a promise to your mother, just before we lost her, never to tell him anything. It was too dangerous. He has so many enemies. I could not put you at risk like that."

Her confession makes me feel even more connected to my father. I thought he had just abandoned me, never wanting to meet me. Yet he wanted to meet me as much as I wanted to meet him. Regrets pulls at my heart.

"I'm sure you know that since his passing, seeing as you are his only son, you are the heir to his fortune - and his position in the family business."

"I thought there was a possibility that it might be the case." I ponder over what that might mean, not for the first time.

"I want you to come to New York. Not yet; It's still too dangerous, but soon before reading his last will and testament. I believe it's important for you to be there. I also think it's important for you to meet your family."

I nod. It's important to meet my family, and I want to do that. I worry, though, about the massive complications that can arise from me being the heir to my father's empire. A power struggle of unimaginable proportions. A position like that would attract many people, and I'm sure I'm not the only one.

I'll go to New York.

If I took over his role, I would be unstoppable. Untouchable.

When Rebecca leaves the restaurant, I wait a while longer, giving her a head start and just being cautious. I think about everything she has spoken to me about, about my parents. Going to New York will be the best way for me to learn more about them, understand their lives, and be close to them in the last way that is available to me. Talking to my aunt has made me even more determined to know my family in New York. I'm sure this hard process will have many challenges, but I have faced difficult situations before and I'm confident that I'll handle this one as efficiently as I have handled everything else that life has thrown at me.

If I'm the heir to my father's empire, I want to know. I want to face down anyone who disputes it. I have often thought about what it might be like to work alongside my father, to have learned from him and grown up under his protection instead of hiding from him.

Perhaps now I can find out.

I can find out who he was, not just the stories that were told about him, but who he was as a person.

Chapter 9

Seraphina

I place the phone down on the table in front of me and bite at my bottom lip. He has canceled. I feel upset as I have a plan, a mission, to find out everything he knows.

I sigh in frustration and pace around my apartment. The paint on my hands is still wet, so I go to the bathroom to wash it off.

I walk back into the living room and stare at the easel. I don't feel like painting anymore.

I may as well clean my brushes for now.

As I work over the kitchen sink, I run through my reaction on the phone. I think I sounded carefree and unbothered. I had to bite back my disappointment before I answered, as I don't want to come across as too eager, too demanding or suspicious.

I think it went well.

We have rescheduled for tomorrow night, but now, I can't get this single thought out of my mind.

What was so important to him he had to cancel his dinner plans with me?

Who has flown in to meet him? Where did they fly from?

I try to brush off the thought, but I can't. It might just be business, a client, something simple and obvious. But I can't let it go. I have to know.

I give in. As stupid and dangerous as it may sound, I decide I have to stalk him. What's wrong with a little secret mission, anyway? It might be fun.

I don't know where he is going or when, so I have to hurry.

Even though I prefer to take a taxi wherever I go tonight, I decide to use the car my grandfather bought me. At least very few people know that I have it, so it won't be recognized. I don't like to use it, because it is flashy and also, I find it inconvenient to find parking around the city. Never mind me not enjoying driving.

I slip into the driver's seat, wearing dark jeans and a long-sleeved dark t-shirt. I feel stealthy enough. My hair braided down my back, out of the way, and I have a peaked cap on. Perhaps I took it too far with the hat, but I don't want him to spot me.

I drive to the main road leading away from his mansion, knowing that he will have to pass me to leave his area. I park on the side, near someone else's home, as though I might be a visitor there.

I sit with my eye on the street for about forty minutes before I spot his ridiculous car. He is driving himself, which is odd. I know he has a personal driver, but he chose not to make use of him tonight.

I pull up behind him, keeping my distance.

While I follow him, I'm careful to keep a car or two between us and change pace now and then. He pulls into a parking bay at a restaurant I can't imagine him choosing.

I drive past, not wanting to be too obvious. Then I make a turn up the street and come around again, parking in the far corner of the parking lot. I climb out of the car and walk toward the restaurant. I can see him in the window. At least I know where he is sitting. He is alone. I find a spot at the bar, as far from him as I can be, with my body turned away from him. My heart is hammering in my chest.

If he notices me, there is no way that I'll explain my way out of this. I guess I can claim to be some jealous lunatic, unhappy about him canceling, but either way, my plans of using him as a pathway for my revenge will be destroyed.

When the Italian lady walks in, I know right away that she is here to meet him. Of course she is. When she hugs him, my thoughts are confirmed. They look as though they have known each other forever. That means that he is still very much in contact with his New York family, despite the rumors stating otherwise.

I can't make out what they are saying; I'm too far away, and I don't dare risk moving.

They are laughing and comfortable with each other.

Has he been planted as a spy here in Hong Kong since he was a baby? Was that the plan all along? I hold my breath with realizing what I have discovered. He is feeding information to his Italian family and has been for all of this time.

This information is massive. I have uncovered something so extreme tonight that I can contain myself. I think I should leave now. There is no point in taking any further risk of being spotted when I have the answers I came to find tonight.

I leave, staying close to the far wall, keeping my head low. When I glance back at the window, he is still deep discuss the woman. I wonder who she is. She is much older than him, perhaps just a contact, perhaps a family member. Either way, it doesn't matter. I know what I know now.

Anger settles in my stomach as I drive home.

He is a traitor.

He is a shallow excuse for a man, betraying the very people who took him in and cared for him. He deserves the worst kind of punishment.

I'm even more convinced now than I ever was before that he had some kind of involvement in my parents' murder. He knows something. He might know everything.

Just yesterday, I had this moment right after we got off the phone where I actually felt guilty about my plans. But now, I don't feel a thing. He's exactly the heartless mafia boss everyone says he is, a real-life monster. Thinking anyone could show him kindness seems ridiculous now. I mean, there he was, out in broad daylight, having a chat with someone from a rival family. His own family, no less. It's like he's living two lives. How does someone just go about their day keeping such a huge secret, betraying the people who are supposed to be closest to them?

I park my car in the underground parking garage and head upstairs, locking myself inside my apartment. I feel alive and high on adrenalin. There are so many thoughts rushing through my mind from every different angle. My plan is forming and becoming more concrete as each second passes.

Now I know no matter how many times he cancels on me or how long I have to play this game, and no matter what I have to do to trick him into believing I'm interested in him, I'll do it. I'll be patient, focused, and dedicated.

I'll have to be as ruthless as he is to play his own game against him.

This is what I have been waiting for my whole life, this chance. This opportunity is what I needed. I'm going to find out the truth, and I'm going to tear apart their lives from the inside out.

Chapter 10

ANTONIO

Ever since talking with Rebecca, my thoughts preoccupied with my parents, and when I think about family, Seraphina always comes to mind. She has not known family either, and she understands that pain better than anyone else I know.

It causes me grief, this intense guilt I have for the role I played in her losing both of her parents. My family name is associated with the murder, and now I'm asking her to spend time with me without even considering that my name, my blood, would likely cause her significant pain.

I can never let her find that out, though. If she doesn't know, then she can't hold it against me. I wince. I was never one to tell lies. I might hide information from someone out of necessity, but outright lying to them is not in my nature.

I don't want to lie to Seraphina. I'm going to have to take this one step at a time. Watch my words and where the conversation flows when I'maround her.

I don't even know who she is to me yet. All I know is that I want her.

Yet, if I pursue this, while I'malso the heir to my father's position and power, it could put both of us at increased risk. My family in New York would never approve of it, and I need to make a good impression when I get there. Do I care? I do. But not out of fear. No.

It is strategic. I must play each piece to my advantage, and Seraphina is not a piece that I can play in this scenario. She is a hindrance. I should just drop this entire pursuit and focus on the real goals.

I know I won't do that, though. She has caught my eye. I want her. She will be mine.

The danger of dating her and the challenges it represents are only making me want her even more.

In the conversations we have had over the phone, I'mso attracted to her. She is kind, gentle. She is so passive, yet I know there is a strength behind her eyes that is unmatched by anyone I have met. I want to know everything about her.

I have to. She has infected my mind with thoughts of her. She is so similar to me, yet so different.

We struggled with the same things, yet she became gentle, kind and empathetic, and I became cold, ruthless and determined to gain all the power I could. She is a different version of me. She possesses characteristics that I have not yet mastered and want to own. By owning her, I can own her gentle nature.

Things in my life are changing quickly. New opportunities come with my father's death. I have spent so long in hiding, my entire life having been lived beneath this veil of protection. I know it served its purpose, but that time is soon going to be over. I have so many things I need to focus on, and having met. Amid the midst of all of this, is not exactly convenient. I'm going to have to keep these things from her. I should just let her go, move on, forget her. But I know I'mnot going to do that. I know how to live in secret. I know how to hide parts of myself.

She may be a distraction, and her beauty might pull my attention away from where it is. I have lived my entire life beneath this veil of protection, always hiding, but I know who I'mand what I'mintended for. It will all be mine, including her.

All I have to do is keep the two worlds separate.

I message her to confirm our date for this evening.

Me: I’m looking forward to tonight. Are you sure I can't fetch you?

Seraphina: Me too. No, I'mhappy to find my way there.

Me: I'll see you at seven then.

I want to talk to her more, but I shouldn’t. That is why I opted to message rather than call. If I phoned her, I would have been so drawn to her voice that we would have spoken for an hour.

I have things to do before this evening.

At seven pm, I am waiting at the table that I have booked for us. It is right at the biggest window, with the best views of the city. The restaurant is playing soft music that romantically drifts through the candle-lit room, creating the exact atmosphere that I would want to spend time with Seraphina in.

I feel the hairs on the back of my neck rise, and I turn toward the door.

She is standing there; the waiter asking her who she was meeting.

They both turn toward my table and I stand.

She is wearing a short, silky, emerald dress that suits her caramel skin tone perfectly. Her hair is done in an elaborate style, with braids and curls falling around her face. She looks as though she was created as a mix of warrior and princess. Bold, yet gentle. Strong, yet obedient. She looks perfect. Absolutely stunning.

"Good evening, Seraphina."

I lean down and wrap my arm around her waist, kissing her cheek. Her scent breezes over me, and I close my eyes for a moment before pulling away from her. She blushes slightly, and it sends shivers through me. I have to have her.

She has this air of innocence that pulls me further into her.

"Antonio, this place is beautiful." But she is not looking around the restaurant; she is letting her eyes drift over my body. I smirk.

I stand behind her chair, and before holding it out for her to sit in, I move it closer to mine. She takes a seat, and I return to mine, our legs touching beneath the table and distracting me.

"I'm sure you know the meaning of your name, and tonight, it suits you perfectly. I have never seen someone looking so beautiful." I say.

"Thank you." She smiles and looks down at the table. She gives me the impression that she isn't used to receiving compliments.

"Have you had a good day? I'm so sorry about needing to cancel on you last night. Something came up, and I had no choice. It will not become a habit."

"It is honestly no problem at all. And yes, I have had a good day today. How was yours?"

"I spent most of my day distracted by this beautiful girl; she has been on my mind a lot. Luckily, I get to spend this evening with her."

"Are you always this charming?" She giggles.

“Most people would not describe me as being charming, but most people are not you.”

The waiter arrives, and I order a bottle of wine.

“Do you like steak, Seraphina? There are other things on the menu, but this restaurant is most well-known for its steaks. The chef is from New York.”

“I love steak. I don’t eat it very often, though. What do you recommend?”

“Let me order for us both. You will love it. I promise.”

She nods sweetly, and I place our order with the waiter.

Once the waiter has left us alone again, she grins. “You know you should never make promises you can’t keep.”

“And I never do. If I make you a promise, I assure you, I'll keep it.” I smile, whether I want to. I don't seem to have control over it when she is near me.

I’m fighting the urge to reach under the table and run my hand over the smooth skin of her thigh. I want to dig my fingers into her skin and leave bruises so that everyone knows she is mine.

The entire evening with Seraphina, I’m surprised to notice that I hardly think about anything other than her. She pulls me into the moment, makes me present, to enjoy what is happening right in front of me. Nothing else matters. I don’t worry about New York or my family or business I need to attend to. I’m entirely, completely focused on her.

I’m laughing more than I have laughed in years, perhaps ever. Her gorgeous lips curl so easily into a smile, and I can't look away from her.

Every movement she makes turns me on. Every word she says captivates me.

She is far smarter than I thought. She is amazing in every single way.

I want to invite her to come home with me, but I know intuitively that she won't allow herself to be treated that way. Played like that. She requires respect; she demands it, in fact.

I'll have to be patient, even though it might drive me absolutely crazy.

I believe it will be worth every moment I have to wait, every thought I have to hold back, every time I have to stop myself from touching her. When I claim her, it will be completely. It will be the most perfect experience.

The waiter clears out dessert plates away and Seraphina declines a cup of tea or coffee. Our first date has ended, and honestly, I'mreluctant to say goodbye. We are standing in the restaurant's foyer; soft, warm lighting is falling over her and complimenting every inch of her.

"Are you sure I can't drive you home? It will be no problem at all."

"No, I'm going to catch a cab." She looks up at me and her brown eyes flaked with gold.

Her long lashes flutter when she grins.

I have held myself back all night. I have completely drained my ability to control myself. I step closer to her and brush my thumb over her luscious lips.

"Has anyone ever told you that you are the most beautiful creature in the world?"

My voice is low and edged with need.

She shakes her head.

I lean into her and press my lips against hers. She doesn't move away, so I wrap my hand around the back of her head and press harder into her mouth. A soft sigh escapes her lips, and my cock stirs. My other hand slips around her waist and pulls her body against mine.

I slip my tongue into her mouth and hold back the growl that wants to escape me.

I struggle to stop, but I have to. I stare into her eyes for a moment, watching as her pupils dilate. I smirk. She wants me.

Don't worry, princess, you will feel me soon.

With my hand still around her waist, I walk out onto the street with her and wave down a taxi. I open the door, and before she climbs inside, I kiss her one more time. Fuck, I want her so badly.

When I release her, she climbs into the seat with a wide smile spread across her lips.

“I'll call you tomorrow,” I tell her.

“I'll be waiting.”

I close the car door and watch the taxi drive away. I have a massive smile painted on my face and I just know; I know, without a doubt, that she is mine. She belongs to me, and I'll make sure she knows it when the time is right.

Chapter 11

SERAPHINA

When I step into my apartment and flick the light switch on, it is almost midnight.

My date with Antonio this evening went really well. Much better than I could have hoped for. We spoke about so many things, and to be honest, I find him to be quite charming.

Never mind how gorgeous he is.

I won't be falling for any of that.

I roam into the kitchen, kicking my high heels off on the way, and flick on the kettle. I need a cup of tea. My mind is feeling agitated with excitement. So many things in my life are aligning perfectly, and finally, after these years, I feel as though I might be on the path that leads me to the thing I want most.

Revenge.

I know that if the people who killed my parents are still alive; they have no right to be. I want them dead. But before I kill them, I want them to know what it is like to lose someone they love. This dark, hidden side of who I'm is not something I'm proud of. But it is what they have created inside of me. Those murderers made me this way. They created that darkness. It has had years to fester in my heart and one day, they will come face to face with their own creation, and they will regret it. I want to *see* that regret in their eyes. I want to see their pain.

I lean against the kitchen counter, lost in thought. Antonio was telling me very little about New York or his family there. He pretends he doesn't know much about them, wasn't expecting I saw his secret meeting with the Italian lady. A smile drifts across my face.

The kettle clicks just as the water boils furiously.

I pull my favorite mug from the shelf and select a vanilla and rose tea bag from my bamboo box. I pour the steaming water into my mug while thoughts of Antonio and his family run through my mind. He seems to be quite taken with me. That is fantastic. It is going to help me carry out my plan. As long as I can keep up this ridiculous act and make him believe I'm actually interested in him as well, I'll find out what I want to know.

I drop the tea bag into the hot water and watch the color bleed from the thin papery walls into the surrounding liquid. Streams of bright gold that swirl and twist like blood flowing into water. My eyes locked onto the beautiful flow while thoughts of revenge drift in the same manner through my body. Antonio is the key to everything.

I'm more determined than ever to go through with my plan now.

I grasp the mug, making my way to the bedroom, mindful of the tasks that await me tomorrow. Settling my thoughts for a night of rest is paramount, yet I'm aware it won't come easily tonight. The thrill of a new opportunity surges through me, both exciting and energizing, but it's crucial not to let this distract me from my other plans. Diversifying my focus is essential—I can't afford to pour all my energy into a single aspect.

In the morning, I'm woken up by the sound of my phone vibrating against my bedside table.

I reach out and grab it, wanting it to shut up so that I can get at least another thirty minutes of sleep. But then I think to myself that it might be Antonio, and I prop myself up on my elbows to stare at the phone.

It is ah gung. Considering that a phone call from him is rare, I slide the green button across the screen to answer it.

"Seraphina, I hope I didn't wake you?"

"Good morning, ah gung, no, I was just getting up now. How are you feeling today?"

"I thought that today would be a lovely day for breakfast in the garden. I was hoping you would join me?"

I push myself out of bed; my bare feet are cold against the floor. I actually wanted to speak to ah gung today in person, so this is the perfect chance to do that.

"Of course, I would love to. I can be there in forty-five minutes."

"Wonderful. See you soon."

I won't have tea here then, even though it is how I prefer to start my morning; I'm just going to hop into a shower and then go straight there.

While the water runs over me, I think about everything that I want to say to ah gung. I need to ask for his help, but I know it is something he has been reluctant to speak about ever since I first brought it up. I have to get to New York. It is an expensive trip, and while I have been saving for a while now, I know I don't have enough yet.

But how can I ask ah gung to help me when he knows the truth about why I really want to go there?

I scrub shampoo into my hair, enjoying the scent as it steams around me.

When I'm out of the shower, I spend a little tiny massaging Argan oil down the long strands of my hair. I blow-dry it halfway dry and then curl it up into a neat bun, securing it with my silver hairpin.

Ah gung stays close by. I'll enjoy a morning walk and sort through my thoughts on the way there.

Ah gung's housekeeper opens the doors and welcomes me in.

He bows his head and smiles, wishing me a good morning.

"Your ah gung is by the koi pond. "

"Thank you, Hikara." I nod my head, smiling.

"Seraphina, how have you been enjoying your time now that you no longer have to study?"

Ah gung has his back to me, leaning over the koi pond, sprinkling flakes of fish food onto the surface of the water. He doesn't turn around when I step onto the stone pathway that leads toward him. "How did you know it was me, ah gung?"

"Ah gung knows these things."

I stand next to him and slip my arm around his waist, looking down at the golden, yellow and white fish hungrily grabbing the food into their mouths. "Good morning."

He wraps his arm around my shoulder.

"It seems we have lost one; it must be the neighbor's cat again," he mumbles, looking for his black and white koi.

"Ah gung, you can't blame the cat; he has not been back here since you threw him into the pond," I chuckle, remembering the look of disgust on the cat's face as he clawed his way out of the pond. "It might be a bird."

"I'll have Hikara look through the security footage. We can sort this out."

Ah gung is not fond of cats.

I smile and shake my head. He finally turns to me and takes my shoulders in his hands. He looks me up and down, holding me at arm's length.

"Well, despite being all grown up and ready to face the world, you look just the same. Beautiful as always."

"Come on, I'm dying for a cup of tea."

I slip my arm through his, and we walk toward the large outdoor decking where the chef is setting up our breakfast.

"Seraphina, of course, I want to see you, but I invite you here for another reason this morning. There is something I wanted to talk to you about."

Do I tell him I also want to talk to him? Perhaps I should wait and find out what it is he wants to say first.

Ah gung takes his seat and I push his chair in behind him, then sit next to him, picking up the pot of fresh tea and pouring us each a cup.

I remain silent. It is the polite thing to do. He will say what he wants to say in his own time.

"You are finished at college now, and it is time for you to start your life," he says, watching my face. "I'm an old man, and soon I want to stop working, but I want to hand over my business to someone I can trust. Someone strong and determined."

My heart tightens in my chest.

"Seraphina, I want you to come and work with me. I want to teach you everything so that you can take over, and I can step back and relax in my later years."

I don't want to take over his business. I have other plans.

“Ah gung, you are still such a long way from retiring. Perhaps one day I'll come and work alongside you, but for now, I have plans of my own.”

“You have plans?” he mutters, trying to hide the disappointment on his face.

“Yes, ah gung, I want to go to New York.”

His expression sinks. It breaks my heart a little to see the regret in his eyes. “There is so much more to live for than that.”

“I want to find a job there. Start a life. Learn about my father.”

“I know what you want to do, Seraphina. This is not about your career or your need to travel. I had just hoped that maybe you would let it all go.”

As we continued our breakfast, ah gung, and I exchanged pleasantries, carefully steering the conversation clear of anything related to New York. In a gesture that was both generous and unexpected, he presented me with a stunning pair of diamond earrings and a Hong Bao, filled with twenty thousand dollars, as a graduation gift. "Book a trip, enjoy yourself, and take a friend along," he suggested warmly. It was a thoughtful offer, especially considering I had been diligently saving money for years, building a substantial safety net on my own, without ever seeking financial help.

I hugged ah gung goodbye, then, walking home, I pull out my phone and message Antonio.

Me: Good morning, thank you for a lovely night last night.

Antonio: It was my pleasure. How are you today? Do you have plans?

Me: I have a few things to do today, but it won't take up all day. What are you up to today?

Antonio: I'm just having a meeting in town at a little restaurant that I think you would like, actually. It's called Kimara Ruka. Have you heard of it?

Me: I have, but I haven't been there yet.

Antonio: I will have to bring you some time. Do you have plans for this evening?

Me: Not yet.Antonio: Good. Be ready at five. Send me your address. My driver will be there to pick you up. Wear something warm.

I bite my lip. I guess I can't avoid giving him my address forever. Besides, soon I'll be in New York and it won't matter. I send him my address and tell him I'll see him at five.

I waved down a taxi. "Kimara Ruka, please." I don't know what I'll find out, but at least try, the cat and mouse excite me.

I sit at the cafe across the street and watch Antonio talking to a group of men. They are all locals, wearing business suits. A pretty boring meeting, from what I can see.

Antonio stands out; his crisp, custom suit is tailored to fit his perfect build. He has a quiet strength about him that demands the respect of the other men around him. I can tell that they have respect, or fear, for him by the way they move - their stance and their mannerisms. The meeting drags. I had a couple of cups refills, finally I gave up. Nothing interesting about Antonio today.

I have a few hours before he comes. Better hurry back home to make a change. Tonight is going to be interesting.

Chapter 12

Antonio

Seraphina smiles when we arrived.

The driver stops outside the boatyard, and I climb out to open the door for her.

"Are we going on the water?" she asks, a bright light shining in her eyes.

"Yes, I thought we might have dinner on my yacht." I hold my hand out. She slips her fingers between mine. Her innocence pulling me deeper into her.

She looks out toward the row of yachts. "Which one is yours?"

I stand behind her, leaning around her, pointing: "That one over there. The black and white one."

“It’s beautiful,” she whispers, glancing sideways at me instead of toward the yacht. Her hair brushing across my cheek, and the scent of her skin teasing my senses.

I slip my hand into hers again and lead her toward the boat.

The captain welcomes us aboard.

Tonight is ideal for being in the water. The ocean is calm and clear; the wind is warm and the white clouds that are scattered across the sky promise a beautiful sunset.

Seraphina and I sit on the front deck of the yacht with cocktails on the table in front of us.

She is sitting too far away from me, though, so I slip my arm around her waist and pull her closer, sliding her along the wide seat that surrounds the deck. She giggles and leans against me when I wrap my arm around her.

“I'm so happy you could join me tonight,” I say, running my fingers through her dark curls.

She smiles, and I see her cheeks flush pink.

“I can’t stop thinking about you, Seraphina. I smile when I picture your face.” She turns that beautiful face toward me, and I brush my hand across her cheek.

My heart races in my chest.

Her bright eyes lock with mine, and when she doesn’t look away, I lean down, pressing my lips softly against hers. I don’t know what it is about her, but I'm steadily becoming obsessed with her. Obsessed to own her, making her mine. Possessing her in every way possible.

She breaks away from the kiss, smiling, looking out over the calm water.

“I think about you, too,” she says, and I grin. I run my hand over her side, feeling the curve of her waist down to her hips. Her response neither encourages nor rejects my advances. I must proceed cautiously rather than risk pushing her away.

"The chef has prepared a seafood dish for us tonight. I thought it was fitting, given the view."

"This view is breathtaking. How amazing it must be to come out here whenever you want."

"I guess I don't enjoy it as much as I should, to be honest. Work consumes a significant amount of my time. It's been a while since I last took the yacht out. "

She reaches out and places her hand on my thigh. Heat spreads through my leg into my groin. The slightest movement of her fingers increases the growing tension in my body. If I were here with any other woman, I would have already been pulling her clothing off and bending her over the railing. With Seraphina, though, I can tell that it would not have the desired effect.

No, she is different. A slow hunt. More of a challenge.

The corner of my mouth curves into a smile, and I lift her chin toward my face.

I rarely pay much attention to how it feels to kiss a woman, but her full lips keep drawing me in. I press my mouth into hers again, and she sighs softly against my lips.

My cock stirs. I need to stop before I'm unable to.

"Come." I stand, pulling her to her feet and leading her to the dinner table.

Seraphina and I sit in the late afternoon light, watching as the sun sinks lower, almost ready to dip into the ocean, while being lost in conversation.

"Why New York?" I ask, dipping calamari into the dark chili sauce.

"I have always wanted to go there. I guess it is because I was born there. It is my father's home, after all."

"I also want to go to New York soon."

"How many times have you been there? What is it like?"

“I have not been there yet.” I shrug my shoulders.

“You haven’t been?” she asks, surprised.

“Not yet.” Her eyes are gripping me with their intensity. I chuckle. “Why is that so surprising to you?”

She shakes her head and sips her drink. “I don’t know; I guess I just assumed that you have been everywhere. Especially New York. Don’t you stay in touch with your family there?”

Guilt ripples through me. Should I be speaking to her about my family in New York? Probably not. It’s frustrating to hide parts of myself, but it’s my norm.

I decide to steer the conversation in a different direction rather than focus on her.

“Any plans for New York?”

“I have been applying for jobs there. I don’t know yet. I just want to explore.”

“Perhaps one day I shall take you there then,” I comment, knowing that it could never happen. It’s risky for both of us. I don’t know what awaits me in New York if I go.

Seraphina tells me about all the things she wants to see there, and her eyes light up while she speaks. The sky is glowing orange, and it is reflecting against her skin, making her hair glow and her lips seem more appealing than ever before.

I realize that, after a long time, I'm finally having fun. Rarely can I simply appreciate living in the present moment. Seraphina’s magical presence helps me let go of constant thoughts and just relax.

I really love being around her.

“Dance with me.”

She laughs. “I don’t think so.”

“It was not a request.” My voice deepens as I guide her to the deck and pull her against my chest. She hesitates, then grins and wraps her arms around my neck. The sun is now dark red behind her, colorful streaks catching the lining of the clouds as it sinks close to the water. Dipping its fiery body into the ocean. She looks up at me, and the sky reflects in her eyes, and it is as though I can see the fierce storm of her soul. I wrap my fingers around the back of her neck as I press my mouth against hers. The sweetness of her drink touches my tongue, and my body pulses with need.

She slips her tongue across my lips, and I moan deeply.

With my hand on her lower back, I press her hips against mine so that she can feel my body's response. She stiffens slightly, but her lips remain against mine.

Slower, Antonio. Careful. Have patience.

She is driving me crazy, though. Why doesn't she seem to want this, or is it just how she is? Does she know how her body is taunting me? She must be aware of it. She gives me just enough to lock me into her, but doesn't fulfill my desires. She is a curiosity, a wild bird that I must tame slowly.

We dance slowly, moving against each other under the now dark sky, with the stars glittering above us. My plan was originally to have her stay on the yacht with me tonight, but I know I won't be able to control myself. I must take her home soon. I must play her carefully if I want to have my way.

When I walk her to the entrance of her apartment building, I take my time kissing her again. If she were to invite me in now, I would do such wonderful things to her body. But she steps away, her lips plump with desire, and says goodnight. *Alright, little bird, I will wait.*

*****

Kalo slides the glass across the bar toward me. I wrap my fingers around the cool surface and draw it up to my lips. Yamazaki. They keep this brand specifically for me. A rare yet perfectly crafted whiskey.

“Where were you last night?” Kalo slides into the set next to mine.

“I took Seraphina on the yacht.”

“You are spending a lot of time with her lately.” He mutters.

“She is quite captivating. And beautiful. I enjoy spending time with her.” I turn my body toward his, noticing how tight he is pulling his mouth.

“Do you notice that since you met her at that party, you speak about her every time we are together?”

“Is that a problem?” I shrug, unsure what he is getting at.

“What is it about her? You rarely give this much attention to women. They keep you entertained for a moment or so, and then you move right along.”

“She is different. I don’t know what it is about her yet, though.”

“What? Is she good in bed? She looks a little innocent, to be honest, but I guess you never can tell.”

“I wouldn’t know.” I grin, thinking about her innocence and how I want to find out what she is hiding behind it.

“You don’t know? You haven’t fucked her? What the hell?”

I lift the Yamazaki up to the light, swirling the golden liquid in small circles.

“Some things take time and patience. Like this, the longer it takes, the more exquisite the flavor.”

“Just fuck her and get over her.”

I glare at him. It bothers me he is speaking about her like that. Just one of those girls who I will brush aside once she has served her purpose.

I know it is usually that way with women. I use them for a good time, then push them aside until I feel the need to entertain myself again. I don’t focus my energy on chasing or courting anyone. Even I'm surprised to myself by doing that with Seraphina.

Regardless of the circumstances. I will be the one to decide. Not him.

“What is your problem, Kalo?”

“That girl is up to something. I don’t like her.”

“Don’t be ridiculous. What the hell could she be up to?” I shake my head. Perhaps he is jealous that he didn't catch her attention before I did.

“I know her family. Just watch your back,” he grumbles, looking bitter.

“Watch my back? Since when do I have to worry about things like that? Her grandfather doesn't scare me.”

“Antonio, I have been your friend forever. Can’t you just take my advice sometimes with no need to overrule it? Stop being arrogant. You have been different since you met her.”

“And people can’t change?”

His eyes drift across my face, trying to read my expression. He is pushing my buttons, but he is still my friend. He has a certain leniency with his words, but he knows I have my limits, even for him.

He shakes his head, and I can see him refocusing his thoughts. “I'm glad you got home ok the other night, the night of your father’s funeral.”

“Yeah, thanks for pulling me out of that dingy bar. I was just letting off steam.”

“No problem, man. Any news about New York? "

“Not yet. I may go there soon. Just to see.”

“Watch your back there. It’s not a safe place.”

Chapter 13

SERAPHINA

I stare excitedly at the email open on my laptop. The buzz of the coffee shop fades away as I read it again, lost in the wave of ideas that are flooding my mind. I received a job offer as an intern from a company in the city. The pay is horrible, and New York is expensive, but they offered to pay for my flights to get there. The rest I will sort out on my own. I grin. Things are coming together so nicely for me.

The waitress stands alongside my table and stares down at me with a smile on her face. I look up at her and realize she must ask me something while I was readying the email.

"Sorry?"I say.

"Need anything else? refills? "

"Oh, no, thank you so much. Just the check, please."

I can't be wasting my money on restaurant lunches anymore. I need to save it for New York. I will make something to eat at home.

I close my laptop and start packing.While I'm waiting for my bill, my phone rings. It's ah gung.

"Hello," I say happily into the phone.

"Seraphina, you sound full of life this afternoon. How are things going?"

"I applied for a job in New York. They replied today with an offer."

There is a silent pause on the other end of the line. "A job."

"Yes, it's the starting point."

"New York is expensive, Seraphina. You can't just go there and expect to manage on very little pay. Are you sure you don't wanna work with me?"

"Ah gung! Please be happy for me. You know how much I want New York."

He sighs a long breath. "I will help you with whatever you need. Your rent and your flights."

As much as his help would be welcome and would take the pressure off me, I can't accept it. I realized in the days since I applied for the job that whoever else I involve in this plan - I'mputting them at risk. If I get to New York and everything goes according to plan, and I'mable to get revenge - if they find out that ah gung funded my trip, they will assume that he was in on it as well.

I can't put his life at risk. Not without knowing all the players and all the pieces.

"That is very generous of you, but I think it's time for me to figure out in life. I can do this on my own. It won't be easy, but you raised me to be strong."

"You never were very good at accepting help, even as a little girl. Well, I'mhere. If you get stuck, you must call me. If you get there and you change your mind, you will be on a flight home that very same day." I can hear in his voice he doesn't want me to go, but I'm happy he seems to accept it.

"Thank you, ah gung. I really appreciate that."

After the call ended, I messaged Maddy.

Me: Guess what? I got a job in New York!

Maddy: Are you serious? So quickly? No, you aren't allowed to go. What am I going to do without you?

Me: I'm not gone forever. Besides, you are gonna be so busy with your life you won't have time for me anymore.

Maddy: You are the one who has been busy. What is this I hear about you going on a date with the guy who hosted the party?

Me: I will have to tell you about it over a drink.

Maddy: Better make it soon. I don't like that other people know what is going on in your life before me. That is not how it works, being friends.

I smile at the messages. Then another notification pops up on the top of my screen.

Antonio: Fancy meeting you here.

I narrow my eyes at the message. I don't understand it.

Antonio: Blue really suits you.

I glance down at my blue sweater. What the hack! I look around, confused and slightly stressed.

Through the window of the coffee shop, I see Antonio. He is smiling at me through the glass. I grin and shake my head. My eyes follow him as he makes his way inside and takes a seat at my table.

"Are you stalking me, Antonio?"

"Of course I am. What else should I be doing with my day?"

He waves the waitress back to my table, then turns to me. "What are you having?"

"I was just finishing up."

"No, you weren't. You were just waiting for me, and now you'll have lunch with me."

I am rolling my eyes at how controlling he is being. He seems to enjoy it, so I decide to let him have his way and play along with his games.

"I was waiting for you, but you were late." I grin cheekily.

"I'm so sorry about that, my love. My meeting ran longer than expected, but of course, as a professional stalker, I get to you in time." He raises one eyebrow, smirking at me.

The waitress looks between us, smiling at the playful conversation we are having.

"I'd like the steak, and she will have,.." he waits for me to decide.

"I will have the Thai green curry."

The waitress nods and heads off to arrange our food.

"Bumping into you like this has made my day." He reaches across the table and rests his hand on mine.

“Are you sure you weren’t stalking me? I might like the idea." My eyes sparks of mischief. When he replies, his voice is low and dark.

“Seraphina, if you want to be hunted, I will most happily oblige. But I can't be held responsible for what happens when I sink my claws into you.”

My heartbeat rapidly, sending hot currents through my body. I bite my lip and try to hide the genuine rush of lust that surges in my blood.

He grins. Saw through me.

“I'm glad I bumped into you, though, sincerely,” he says, leaning back in his chair, his long legs brushing against mine underneath the table. “I got some news.”

“So do I, but you go first.”

“I will travel to New York soon; My father’s lawyer has contacted me. I need to be present for the reading of his will.”

“I thought you lost contact with your father.”

“I didn’t. But he left instructions with the law firm. I have to be there.”

“When are you leaving?” I sound disappointed at the idea of him going. I think it is the fact he can just hop on a place and fly there at a whim while I have to take a job, doing something I'm not even interested in, to scrape my way there.

“In about two weeks. Will you miss me when I’m gone?” His eyes are narrow and focused on my mouth.

“I will, but not for too long.” I grin.

“Mm. Is that so? You said you had news as well. What is it?”

“I got an offer today from one company I applied. I'm heading to New York in four weeks, then work.”

He watches my face,

“Come with me?”

“What?”

"Come with me to New York. You will get there earlier than needed, but you can fly with me."

"I can't, Antonio. The company is paying for my flights and besides, I don't have anywhere to stay until I start working." I shrug; as much as I want to go with him, I'mnot paying for my own flights and probably can't negotiate much with them when they book.

"I'm taking my private jet. You can fly with me. You don't have to worry about accommodation either. Just come with me. We can spend some time together. I have been really enjoying getting to know you now."

My thoughts churn with all the possibilities. I will get to New York two weeks earlier, so I will have enough time to get an apartment before work starts. I can even save a little money. If I find my way there, perhaps the company credit airfare toward my accommodation. It will give me a little more leeway while I settle in there.

Besides, if I go there with Antonio, maybe I will meet his family and get into the right crowd.

"Actually, I might just take you up on that offer."

His face brightens with a massive smile.

"That is what I wanted to hear. I will be busy when I'm there. But I will make time to spend with you. We will have an amazing trip together."

Him being busy works out great for me. It means I can do my thing without him breathing down my neck all the time. He's just a piece of a puzzle in my plan for revenge.

Every time the image of my mom, abandoned and lifeless, flashes through my mind, a surge of hatred wells up within me. He might not be responsible for her death, but there's no doubt in my mind—his family played a part.

He makes my skin burn when he touches me or if his lips fill me with desire when they brush across mine. It's overshadowed by a relentless, blinding rage. I may misdirect my sorrow and my need for vengeance may blind me, but one thing is crystal clear: someone must pay!

“That's settled, then. I will make all the arrangements and send you a message with the details once it's booked. You will fly with me to New York.”

His leg moves against mine, pushing his knee between my thighs. I know what he wants from me. It's pretty clear what he's after. I'm trying to keep things slow for now, but if push comes to shove, if I really have to go there to keep his interest—well, I'll cross that bridge when I get to it.

The waitress drops off our lunch, and Antonio scoots back a bit, pulling his leg away from mine. Suddenly, there's this chilly gap where we were just touching, and I catch myself missing how his skin feels like against mine.

Chapter 14

Antonio

I stand at the desk in my office at home; the phone pressed against my ear and my laptop was open in front of me.

"Yes, you can make those arrangements. No, I don't know how long I will go for. Inform the pilot and book the hotel. Penthouse. Yes." I nod as my assistant takes notes. "I have one guest joining me on the flight. No, you do not need to book an additional hotel room. Good. Confirm once it is done."

I place the phone down on my desk and stare at the email. They have confirmed the date to read the will. I'm expected to go there and claim my position as the heir to my father's estate, his company, his position. I know I'm not the only one who has received this news, and it is most certainly causing a stir in New

York. The idea of my taking over will provoke the anger of a multitude of individuals. It is going to be a dangerous trip.

I close my laptop. Stupidly, I have invited Seraphina to join me.

I'm putting her at risk by taking her with me. Just being close to me during this time can cause so many issues.

I'm going to keep her under the radar while I'm there. I don't want them seeing her and thinking they can leverage her against me. I've also got to be slick about keeping my real identity from her. Given her mom's death linked to my family, she'd probably hate me if she found out what I'm hiding. I'm just getting to know her and don't want to scare her off. Can't let that happen.

She has this pureness about her, angelic and sweet, and I don't think she will accept me if she knows everything there is to know about me. I can't taint her perspective of me with that truth. My darkness. I will keep it hidden from her.

I sigh. *I will make it work.*

I want to travel with her. Having her spend that much time with me, I will win her over.

I need to clear my head.

I walk out of my office toward the atrium. My grand piano is in the center of the room. I slide onto the seat, running my hands across the ivory keys. I close my eyes and play. The melody slips between my thoughts and eases my mind. My face relaxes. I feel the tension ease from my shoulders. My fingers move expertly across the keys as though I were caressing a lover's body. I imagine my hands running over Seraphina's stomach, trailing over her hips.

When we are in New York, I will have her all to myself. She can't withhold what I so desperately want from her.

I feared her reaction upon learning about my oversight.

I tell myself this is the reason we will share a room, but I know better.

I skip a key, and the tune falters. I slam my fingers against the piano, and an ugly rush of sounds erupts from it.

Fuck.

I should never have invited her.

I'm being selfish. I don't want to feel that way. I have put her in a horrible position by asking her to come with me.

I push myself away from the piano. Playing is not helping me now, as it did.

I walk back to my office to attend to the admin I need to finish, feeling frustrated and annoyed because I want what I want but don't have it yet.

In the evening, after I finish my work for the day, I sit out on the balcony of my mansion. The air is crisp and bites at my skin, but I like it. Anything to distract me from feeling guilt for inviting Seraphina.

I have to let this go. She is coming. I want her there.

The next morning, when I wake up still feeling the knot of worry in my stomach, I live at the fact that I'm going to revoke the invite. It is too risky. If I knew what I was walking into in New York, it might have been a different story, but it is not.

I run my hands across my face, rubbing my eyes in frustration.

I better tell her today. Just get it over with before I change my mind and let this risky plan go forward.

I reach out and grab my phone, lifting it off the charging station.

"Open curtains," I say to the room, and light fills the space as they draw upwards, disappearing into the ceiling,

I pull myself up against the headboard, resting my back against the pillows, opening the chat window to Seraphina.

Me: Good morning, gorgeous girl. I hope you slept well - and dreamed of me. I know I dreamed of you. Are you busy today? I would like you to join me for a walk in the botanical park. Perhaps breakfast or lunch in the gardens?

Seraphina: Good morning. I had amazing dreams last night. What I dreamt of - well, that is for me to know. I have to do a brief run around preparing for New York this morning, but I can meet you for lunch. What time? Shall I meet you there, seeing as I will be close to the area, anyway?

Me: Fantastic. I will find you at the garden entrance, on the South side. Where that orange blossom tree hangs over the walkway. One o'clock?

Seraphina: Perfect.

She adds a little heart icon, and I smile at it. But then I'm filled with guilt again. I have to uninvited her. It is the last thing I want to do, but I know I have to.

At one o'clock, leaning with my back against the tall stone wall that runs around the gardens, with my arms folded across my chest, I wait for Seraphina.

She doesn't keep me waiting long, though. I spot her walking toward me, wearing a long, flowing skirt that dances around her as she walks. Her hair falls around her shoulders and flicks to the side as she turns her head. Her smile instantly captivates me, and my lips spread into a grin.

I push myself away from the wall, and when she is close, I pull her against me.

I press my lips into hers and stand on her tiptoes to return the kiss.

"You look incredible," I say, wrapping my arm around her waist and walking with her into the gardens.

She eyes me up and down with eyes that tell me she is hungry to feel me. "You always look incredible."

We stop near the entrance, at a little coffee stand. I order us each a cappuccino. Then, we make our way along the pathway through the lush greenery, breathing in the freshness of it all.

"I'm so excited that everything is coming together." She chatters.

"With?"

"My job in New York. I'm a little nervous, though. I'm not sure how the first few months will be. I think it will be a challenge, um. But I know I can make it work."

I bite at the inside of my cheek. I need to tell her she can no longer come with me. I can't even tell her why, though. I have to come up with something that sounds plausible.

She continues to chat about what part of the city her offices are in and how she is looking for somewhere close by or somewhere that is close to a train station.

I listen, and my thoughts wander.

The longer I roam through the gardens with her, chatting about the future, the more resistance I build against un-inviting her. I want to go *with* her. I want to have that time with her. After this trip to New York, I don't even know when I will see her again. If I return to Hong Kong and she stays in New York? What will happen?

Perhaps by then, I will have tasted her properly, and this obsession and need I have to possess her will have subsided.

She is going to New York, with or without me.

What harm will it do if she just goes earlier - with me? I would help her. I'm not the one putting her at risk. I will just be helping her.

“You say that. It will be a challenge. Is your Gung Gung not assisting with this trip?”

“He offered, but I think this is something I need to do without him. I somehow feel the need to prove myself to him. I don’t know. I'm being silly, not accepting his help, but I know he doesn’t want me to go.”

“Why doesn’t he want you to go?”

“He wants me to take over his company here in Hong Kong.”

I wonder why she wouldn’t want to do that. He is the one who runs a massive corporation. I guess I understand, though. She was born in New York. She has the same pull I have - to find out what it is like there. Perhaps she always wants to answer questions she has had since she was little.

“I will pay for your accommodation. I mean, after you work, I will find you an apartment and cover the cost of it.”

“Not a chance. I can't accept that from you. Why would you do that?”

“You can and you will. I will do that because I want to see you smile.” I say the words and feel the truth in them. I want to make her happy. I want her to need me. Reply to me.

“Antonio," She shakes her head.

“We don’t need to talk about it anymore. We can find you a place to stay while we are there. I will send you the details of our flights and the hotel where we will stay later this afternoon. My assistant has made all the arrangements for that.”

She seems to accept my offer as a soft smile plays across her face.

“Thank you. You are very sweet to me.”

And that is how it comes about that I'm still going to New York with her, despite the risk. I will just move carefully and tactfully. I will play my pieces across the chessboard with an eye on every corner. I will keep her safe from finding out who I really am as much as I will keep her safe from my enemies being able to get to her.

“Are you nervous?”

Her question puzzles me. “Nervous about what?”

“To attend reading your father’s will?”

“No, I'm not worried about it. Nothing leads me to believe there will be any issues.”

“What if he leaves you everything?”

“I don’t understand the question.”

“His home, his company. Would you move to New York?”

“I can't decide to like that until I know all the facts.”

She nods, her hand finding mine, our fingers intertwining effortlessly. A smile crosses my face. Filled with the certainty in New York, she'll open up to me. I'll see to it.

Chapter 15

Seraphina

Maddy pulls at the reins of the mare she is riding. Steering her toward the clearing. I have not been horse riding in so long, but I love it, so when Maddy invited me I was quick to say yes.

"So, this is where you will do your internship?" I trot my horse alongside hers.

"Yes, the ranch owner is a friend of my father, so I kind of had a first choice here. The vet who works here is brilliant, though. To work as his assistant will kick start to my career."

Maddy study to be a vet, and I know she'll be an incredible addition to any team that takes her on.

"I'm still mad at you for going to New York," she says, pulling at the reins to slow her horse down to a walk. We guide them onto the path leading to the outside. I feel that the horses have walked it so many times in their lives that we need to tell them when to go.

I relax in the saddle, taking in the beautiful scenery.

Maddy shoots me an angry glare, although there is a smile on her lips.

"So, were you ever planning on telling me about this date you went on? Why am I the last to know?" she huffs.

I grin. "We have been on more than one date, actually."

"How dare you," she laughs.

"I think I might like him." I fall a little silent as my thoughts turn inward, and a pang of guilt spikes through my heart. I have been spending more time with Antonio; the more time I can spend with him, the more I can find out about this and his family - but in that time, I kind of have to admit that I have grown fond of him.

"Earth to Sera," Maddy shouts.

"Sorry, what?"

"Jeez, where were you drifting off to now? Dreaming of this new boy?"

"More of a man, actually."

"You said you like him? But I have never heard you say that about anyone before. Why has he suddenly got your attention?"

"He is mature. I guess. I don't know. He has this way about him that makes me feel really special."

"Girl, you don't need a man to make you feel special, but - I'mkind of happy to hear you talking like this. It is about time you focused on normal things, like guys, dating, maybe falling in love?" she laughs.

"Let's not get ahead of ourselves."

"What happens when you go to New York? Won't you miss him?"

"Mm. He is coming with me for a bit."

"You are going to New York with some guy I haven't even met? Who are you, and where is my best friend?" she shouts, and the horses spook a bit. She leans down and pats the mare on her neck. "Sorry, baby, I didn't mean to be so loud. It just seems that someone has been keeping a lot of secrets from me." She turns her eyes on me, throwing me a look that could kill.

"I'm sorry." I laugh. "It all happened quickly."

"What else happened? Did *that* happen?" she looks shocked.

I shake my head. "No. Not that. No."

"Mm. Ok. I would definitely expect you to tell me if *that* happened."

I grin, thinking how I'd probably be too shy to share if something like that ever happened. Honestly, I'm not even sure how I'd react if he made a move. Sure, he's shown interest, but he's been nothing but respectful, never pressuring me. Yet, the thought of spending so much time with him in New York makes me nervous. But I'll handle it—got enough on my plate as it is.

The ride continues quietly, the morning peaceful, and I mull over how Antonio treats me. I confessed to Maddy that I like him, and it's true. The more time I spend with him, the more my feelings grow. It's easy with him; smiles and conversation flow naturally, no need to pretend. Sometimes, I catch myself getting lost in his gaze, curious about his kisses. But I can't let that distract me. I'm on a mission—a mission to avenge my parents. No guy, no matter how appealing, can divert me from that path.

"You are crazy, though. You are making this big move, and you don't even know what New York is like. What if you hate it?"

"That is not the point."

"It is, though. You don't even have a friend there. What about me?"

"You can come and visit me. I can visit you. You are overthinking this whole thing. It's not like we won't be friends anymore just because I'min New York. "

Maddy rolls her eyes. "Do you have any idea how impossible you are? I can't even get you to go out with me here. It's like drawing water from a stone. How will I get you to stay in touch when you are on the other side of the world?"

"I promise I will."

"Fine." I could see the sadness in her eyes. I know it is not only about going to New York; she is sad about why I'm going to New York. It makes me sad, but I have to do this.

After our morning horse ride, we have a packed picnic on the front lawn of the ranch, overlooking the stables. It is such a beautiful place, and I'mexcited about Maddy. She is going to be fine. When she works here next month, she won't even be thinking about me. I push aside my guilt about being a rotten friend. Maybe one day when this is all over.

I have never thought about what happens afterward.

I don't even know if I'll be the same person anymore.

I have only ever known Hong Kong.

I have only even known this embedded anger.

I have only ever focused my goals on seeking revenge.

I don't know what is going to happen next. I only know I'mon the right path now.

After lunch, I say goodbye to Maddy and make my way back home.

Inside my apartment, I'm stripping off my clothes, rich with smelling horses and dust. I dump them into the washing machine and then walk into the shower.

Often, I leave only the cold water running, even in winter. It aches against my body, tensing my muscles, which I have to focus on relaxing. I feel in control under the icy water.

I stand under the flow until I shiver. Then, I switch to a warmer temperature and wash myself.

Focused and refreshed. I slip into a comfortable pair of track-suit pants and a warm top, then wrap the towel around my hair and carry my laptop and my phone through to the living room.

I want to spend some time researching New York; perhaps I can find an article about Antonio's father and his death and any rumors around it.

I get comfortable on the sofa.

Before I open my laptop, I check my phone.

I have messages from a number that I don't recognize.

I slid open the notification.

Unknown: I have my eyes on you. I'm watching you. I know you are spending a lot of time with Antonio.

Me: Who is this?

Unknown: All you need to know is that if you cross him, you cross me.

Me: Big words coming from someone who is too scared to tell me their identity.

Unknown: We haven't met. My name is Kalo. Ask around. You will find out I'mnot one to be messed with. I want you to stay away from Antonio.

Me: Why? Is he not allowed to date anyone without your approval?

Kalo: Watch yourself, Seraphina. I know more about you than you know about me.

Me: I'msure Antonio is capable of making choices about who he wants to hang out with. Perhaps you are receiving less of his attention since he met me? Talk to your friend about that. Your threats mean nothing here.

Kalo: I know him better than you ever will. I know what is good for him. And you are not it.

I press the button to turn off my phone. This is ridiculous. I don't need high school style threats from some jealous friend who is upset over nothing.

He sounds jealous. I bite at my bottom lip. Is there more to this? Does he know something about me? How would he, though? If anything, he might know of my ah gung. Perhaps there is a history there that I'munaware of. I consider asking ah gung - but then I'll need to tell him why I'm asking. I don't want to open a can of worms.

I can't ask my Gung Gung without explaining who Kalo is and how I know or am linked to him. Then I might have to tell him I have been seeing Antonio.

I didn't even want Maddy to know I was seeing Antonio. Ah gung will know who he is. He'll realize my underlying reasons for pursuing this.

I push the phone away from me, trying to dismiss the worry in my thoughts.

I'll keep Kalo in the back of my mind. I'll watch my back and monitor him, but for now I don't want to be distracted by his, most likely, empty threats.

I type in Antonio's father's name. Massimo Rossi. A name I have typed in many times before.

I browse through the articles about his death. Old age. Nothing suspicious about it. This man didn't deserve to live in old age, not in the comfort that he was living.

Chapter 16

Antonio

We are flying to New York in a couple of days.

I could have waited until then to see Seraphina, but I don't want to. I can't get her out of my thoughts, even when I should have all of my attention focused on what is going to happen in New York. I invited her for dinner at my place. I need to spend time with her. If I don't, I'm going to drive myself crazy thinking about her.

I stand in front of the long bathroom mirror and splash cologne on my skin.

I pull the collar of my black shirt straight. Leaving the top few buttons undone. I can see the curve of ink running up my neck, the start of a tattoo that travels from my hip, over my shoulder, all the way down my back. A dragon design similar to the one I saw on my father in a photograph many years ago.

I pull the cuff of my sleeve out and roll each sleeve up over my forearms.

With one last glance in the mirror, I turn to leave the bathroom.

Seraphina will arrive at any moment now.

I wait in the atrium until security informs me that my guest has arrived. I tell them to welcome her in and walk through to the entrance hall to greet her.

Seraphina is stepping inside the doorway when I walk into the room. The breath is knocked from my lungs.

Her choice of a short black dress, body-hugging and leaving very little to the imagination, openly invites me to take her passionately. All the boys she has experienced in the past will be nothing in comparison. I'll leave her wanting nothing but me for the rest of her life.

“Seraphina, welcome back to my home. You appear attractive tonight.”

She smiles and leans forward to kiss me. “Thank you for the invite.”

“My chef, Yuze, has prepared one of my favorite dishes. I hope you like blue cheese. I have a specific brand important, as I can't seem to get enough of it.” My eyes drift over her ass, how the dress sits just low enough to taunt me.

She places her hand over her stomach, a subconscious gesture that doesn't suit the dress she has chosen.

I grin.

Slipping my arm around her waist, I lead her to the dining room, wondering if I can make it all the way through dinner or if I'll spread her out on the table and tasting her pussy within the next hour.

She sits down, and I slide into the seat next to her. I sit close so that she can feel me against her. She wants this as much as I do, obviously.

She reaches out and brushes her hand across my forearm. Her fingers trailing the muscles below the fold of my sleeve. "You look gorgeous, Antonio." She doesn't look up. I can't read her eyes.

My chef arrives.

"Good evening, Ms. Seraphina. May I get you something to drink?"

"She will have the champagne," I answer for her.

"Yes, sir."

"If you keep brushing your fingers over my skin like that, I may have to skip dinner altogether and find other forms of entertainment for the night," I growl.

Her eyes widen, and she pulls her hand back, grinning.

"Perhaps I should behave myself then." She giggles.

"I doubt you intended on behaving yourself when you chose that dress for our dinner."

"I, um, borrowed it from my friend."

"Your friend has good taste. She may as well just let you keep it, seeing as it looks better on you than it could on anyone else."

"It's one of her favorite dresses."

"So, she will not be pleased to find out I have ripped it off your body?"

Her lips part in shock.

A reaction that turns me on even more.

Yuze returns with champagne and pours us each a glass. "May I begin with the first course, sir?"

"You can go ahead, yes."

Throughout dinner, Seraphina is flirtatious. She is laughing often and as the evening progresses, I can focus on anything but how her body looks beneath that tight black dress.

I run my hand along her thigh, pulling her legs open beneath the table. She bites her lips as I glide my hand up the inside of her leg.

Then she moves and crosses one leg over the other, and I smirk. The little temptress seems to enjoy taunting me.

Once our dinner plates are cleared away, I ask Yuze to wait for a little while before bringing out the dessert. I know I can't wait any longer.

"Join me out on the deck. I thought we might get some fresh air. I'll pour us another glass of champagne." She giggles, already tipsy from the bottle we have finished.

I take her hand and lead her outside toward the daybed overlooking the swimming pool.

I sit down and pull her with me.

I can't contain this need for a moment longer. The bulge of my penis is already pressing against the fabric of my trousers.

I wrap my fingers around the back of her neck and press my lips against hers. She moans into my mouth. My cock throbs, desperate to feel her sliding onto me. I grab her thighs and pull her onto my lap, her dress riding up her legs, sitting high on her hips. The black lace of her underwear is beauty.

I grab her hips and press my cock against her pussy as I kiss her with more urgency.

She seems to hesitate, and a shy laugh rustles through her. I rock her back on forth over my cock, and she moans again.

I can't wait a second longer. The need to possess her has become painful.

I pull my belt off and unbutton my pants. My cock jumps free. Her eyes fall upon it with a wild expression. I grab her hips again, lifting her dress higher.

I slip my fingers under the lace of her underwear and dip them into her. She is drenched. I pull my fingers out and slide them into my mouth.

"You taste like heaven, Seraphina."

"Wait," she murmurs.

"I think I have waited long enough," I whisper against her ear, pulling her underwear aside.

She moves away from me.

I narrow my eyes. Why is she playing hard to get?

I lift her in my arms and lay her on the daybed, on her back, pulling her legs apart so that I can push my hips between hers.

Her breathing is heavy with need, and her eyes look desperate.

"You have been such a good girl. You deserve to feel this pleasure," I say, hovering above her, gripping my shaft in my hand, sliding it over her pussy.

I lean forward, ready to thrust into her, ready to be consumed by the pleasure of my cock being buried inside her pussy.

"Wait!" she cries out.

I freeze, confusion stalling my movement.

She scrambled backward, away from me. Her cheeks are flushed luminous red. Her eyes are glittering, as though she might fight tears.

I stand up. I can't imagine what has upset her so much.

She pulls her dress over her body and climbs off the daybed.

I cock my head to the side. "What is going on? What happened?"

"I have to go," she stammers, grabbing her shoes from the floor.

“Seraphina,”

But she has already turned away and is running back into the house.

I pull my pants up, struggling to zip them up over my cock.

“Seraphina, wait!” I shout.

When I run into the house, she is nowhere to be seen.

I dash to the front door and rush out onto the steps, just in time to see her car driving down the driveway, moving away from the house.

What the fuck just happened?

Should I go after her?

This is a situation I have never been in. My entire life. No one has stopped me. Ever.

I storm back into the house. A mix of worry and anger filtering at intervals through me.

I grab my phone and dial her number.

It rings for ages.

I hang up and try again. She cuts off my call.

I have to fix this. I have to fix whatever happened. She has to come back. She can't leave me like this.

I type out a message.

> *Me: Seraphina, I don’t understand what happened. Did I upset you? Please, come back. We need to talk about this. Why did you leave?*

I stare at the phone. She doesn't come online.

I type again.

> *Me: whatever happened - I'm sorry. If it was something I did to offend you. Just answer me.*

Nothing.

What the fuck is going on?

Is this part of some fucked up game she is playing? Was I not forceful enough? Who the hell does she think she is - leaving me in this state? How dare she taunt me and tease me all night, begging me to fuck her on the dinner table and then deny me the satisfaction?

I storm through the house and bump into Yuze.

“Are you ready for dessert yet, sir?”

“No, I don’t fucking want dessert, for fuck's sake.”

I push past him toward the drinks cabinet, pulling out the vodka and pouring a double shot. I down it, needing to feel anything but the unquenched thirst for her body.

I pour another double and wait for it to burn all the way to my stomach.

“Fucking bitch.” I mutter the words and regret them.

I can't speak about her like that. Anger courses through me, despite my mind being at odds with the situation.

The vodka warms my blood. It eases the tension in my body. Just enough for me to think a little clearer.

I pick up my phone again. She has read my messages but has not replied.

Me: Seraphina, talk to me. We can forget about everything. Unless you want to talk about it. Either way, just reply. Better yet - come back?

She reads the message again and then goes offline.

She is fucking with me. She is playing hard to get. She wants me to chase. She has just changed the rules of this game, but she doesn't know how hard I like to play.

Fine. I'll play her games. Next time I see her, I'll not be so gentle. If she wants to provoke me, to entice me, to bring out the devil inside me, then that is what she will get.

I know women love that. I had intended on being more gentle with her, but that is not what she wants. And I want her. So, I'll make sure that I get it.

I smirk. This is going to be fun.

But at the back of my mind, I'm still haunted by concern.

Chapter 17

Seraphina

Antonio pushes me onto the daybed overlooking the pool. I'm so torn at this moment.

I knew it was coming, eventually, but now that he has pulled his pants open and I'm staring at his cock, I'm panicking.

All night I thought I could go through with this.

He drives me wild. He makes me feel things that nobody has ever made me feel. I *want* to sleep with him. Or I thought I did.

My body was buzzing in ways I never imagined possible when he pulled me onto his lap.

I almost passed out from the pleasure of feeling his fingers dip inside me. He knows what he is doing and the way he moved. Fuck, I wanted to spread my legs wider, feel him press his fingers deeper.

But I panicked.

He stood up, lifting me in his arms, and I tried so hard to push that panic aside. When he leaned over me, though, and I saw how large he was, and my emotions became too raw, I knew I could not go through with it.

Intense fear and guilt flooded me and caused me to lock up inside.

I had to run.

Never mind the fact that he can tell I was a virgin. That alone would have been so embarrassing. But also the fact the first time I ever have sex with someone, it would have been my enemy. Someone I'm supposed to hate. Someone linked to my parents' murder.

Tears rush down my cheeks as I drive toward my home.

I feel so ashamed of myself. I thought I was stronger than this.

It's only sex, isn't it? So why do I feel so emotional about it?

I'm willing to do anything to get revenge for my parent's murders, so why couldn't I do this?

My phone rings with his name across my screen. I ignore it.

It rings again, and I reach out to press the red button to decline the call.

I can't even think straight, never mind speak to him on the phone right now.

What would I say?

What would he think of me?

I hear messages coming through, but I force myself to focus on the road ahead of me. The painted markings of the lanes, the streetlights, the night sky.

Anything but him.

By the time I arrive home, I feel more in control of myself, but fearful that I have ruined an opportunity. Will he be angry? Will he speak to me again?

The first thing I do when I get into my apartment is climb out of this ridiculously short dress. I pull on some comfortable pants, feeling more secure in them.

I slump down onto the couch and open his messages.

Antonio: Seraphina, I don't understand what happened. Did I upset you? Please, come back. We need to talk about this. Why did you leave?

Antonio: whatever happened - I'msorry. If it was something I did to offend you. Just answer me.

His messages don't seem angry. He seems upset, yet but not angry.

Should I reply? What should I say?

I drop my phone onto my lap and press my fingers against my eyes, trying to stop the tears that are stinging me. It doesn't help. I switch my phone screen off. I can't reply now. I don't know how to deal with this.

I can't even imagine how to go about telling someone that I'ma virgin. Especially someone like Antonio, who, without a doubt, has had many women.

It might reverse him away from me. He'll know that I'minexperienced and won't know how to pleasure him in how he is used to.

The thought of him being with other women sets a knot in the pit of my stomach.

Why am I jealous? I don't even care about him. I'm just using him.

I sit on the couch for ages, feeling the weight of what has happened, sitting on my shoulders. My phone chimes again, and I open the message.

> *Antonio: Seraphina, talk to me. We can forget about everything. Unless you want to talk about it. Either way, just reply. Better yet - come back?*

I'm going to have to tell him. I don't have a choice.

But not tonight. I'm too overwhelmed right now. I have to calm myself down first. Perhaps I can try to tell him that doesn't push him away.

I push myself off the sofa and slink toward my bedroom, falling onto the bed.

I close my eyes, wanting to fall asleep and forget today ever happened.

Images of him rush through my mind.

The way he pulled me onto his lap and kissed me as he rocked my hips against his cock.

I feel myself tingling. I try to push the thoughts away.

But his hands are between my legs, his fingers sliding in and out of me.

I roll onto my back and sigh in frustration. How does he make me feel this way?

He pulls my legs apart, gripping his cock in his hand; he lowers himself over me, pushing my legs even wider with his hips. I gasp as his body pins me to the bed.

My hand drifts down my body beneath the fabric of my pants. Touch the lace panties that his fingers brushed across not that long ago.

I pull them aside and dip my finger inside myself.

I can't believe how wet I am.

I groan and rock my hips against my hand, picture him above me on the bed.

He pins my arms above my head and traces kisses along my neck. "You are so wet, Seraphina. You drive me wild," he says against my ear. His voice vibrating through me. I tilt my head and feel his lips against mine. His tongue slides into my mouth, and I feel him pressing his cock against my pussy.

He slides his cock into me, pushing into me. I feel my pussy opening as he fills me up. The pressure is indescribable. I shudder as it slips deeper.

Pain mixes with pleasure, and he rocks his hips back and forth.

"You are such a good girl," he breathes.

He releases his grip on my wrists, and I wrap my hands around his neck, arching my back as I try to feel him deeper inside me. "Mm. That's a good girl. I know you can handle this."

I gasp at the pleasure of it. I did not know it would be this amazing.

He thrusts faster. I wrap my legs around his waist, and he slips his arm under my back, pulling me up toward him. He pushes into me, and my body shakes.

"Antonio," I whisper.

Then, an orgasm engulfs every fiber of my body. The intensity sends currents of lightning through me.

I lay on my bed, panting. Blinking against the darkness. My hand still resting against my pussy. I can't believe how amazing that felt.

With the heated need satisfied, I go to the bathroom to wash my hand and splash cold water on my face. I stare into the mirror.

Tell him tomorrow, Seraphina.

I roll my eyes at my reflection. What is going on with you? Why are you thinking about him like this? He is your enemy, not your lover.

I climb back into bed and toss and turn for hours before drifting off to sleep.

I didn't have the same nightmare I had every night. I don't dream at all for the first time in as long as I can remember.

I wake up feeling rested and fresh, but I'm hit with anxiety.

I reach out and pick up my phone.

Antonio has sent another message.

Antonio: If you don't call me, I'm going to come to your place.

No, I can't handle that. I can't face him in person. I can't even bring myself to dial his number.

I type, and my anxiety grows worse.

Me: Antonio, I'm really sorry about last night.

Antonio: what happened? Are you ok?

Me: Yes, no, maybe.

Antonio: Just talk to me. You can tell me - whatever it's. If I did something, tell me.

Me: It's not you. It's me. I guess there was no way for me to keep it from you, anyway.

Antonio: Don't make me beg to understand what is going on.

Me: Antonio, I have never had sex before. I'm a virgin.

I hold my breath. I can see he is typing a reply. Then he stops and goes offline. I stare at the screen. He comes back online. He is typing again. I can't handle this.

Time seems to move at such a slow pace as I wait for his message to come through.

I don't know how he is going to handle this.

my heart shudders with nerves as a message splashes across my screen.

Antonio:, I had no idea that you were going to say that. I would have guessed so many things before I assumed that.

I bite my lip, seeing that he is writing more.

Antonio: Thank you so much for being honest with me. I want you to know that if I had known before last night, I would never have behaved in that way. You are such a beautiful girl. Everything about you. Of course you drive me wild and turn me on in ridiculous ways, but I promise you I'll not push for anything from you. If you are ready, you can let me know. There was no reason to run out like that. I think you are special. Rare. Even more rare than I could have dreamed. I appreciate you being so honest with me. Don't let last night change your mind about me. I still want to see you. I want to spend time with you.

I read his response three times. It's so accepting and caring that I'm taken aback. I never would have expected this type of response.

He doesn't feel repulsed or put off by discovering this about me. He still wants to see me.

All this time, I imagined he was just pretending to be this charming, romantic man, just toward one goal, sleeping with me. I thought he hid that villain beneath the surface of the mask he wore around me, yet now, I'm questioning myself.

Perhaps the mask is the one the media gave him. Built by rumors and stories. Perhaps I have been seeing the real him all of this time.

Antonio: Will you still come to New York with me?

New York. In all of this chaos, I had not even thought about New York.

Can I still go to New York with him?

What if he *isn't* the monster I think he is?

I guess, either way, I need to go to New York to find out the truth. The truth about who killed my parents, and the truth about who Antonio is.

Me: I'll still go to New York with you. I'm sorry I didn't tell you before. Thank you for understanding.

Antonio: My angel, you have nothing to be sorry for. We are going to have an amazing time together in New York.

I smile and close my phone.

Throwing the blankets off me, I climb out of bed to start my day. I have to pack for New York today. I'm going to fulfill my lifelong obsession to avenge my parents. I'm going to hunt down the murderer and pay them back.

Chapter 18

Antonio

I wake up much earlier than I do, still tight with anger and confusion about why Seraphina left last night.

Even a cold shower has not eased the lust I'm struggling with.

I snatch my phone in anger from my bedside table. I type out a message that I have every intention of following through with. I'll sort this out. I'll not have any woman play with me like this.

Me: call me ASAP, or I'll come over.

I fling the phone onto the table, skeptical she's awake this early. However, once she's up, she'll have to answer me. I'll wait until lunch. No response by then? I will knock on her door.

I toss the blankets aside, huffing in annoyance, and pad barefoot to the kitchen.

The house is quiet, even my staff are still asleep.

I make a cup of coffee and carry it outside so that I can watch the sunrise.

Something has been bothering me.

What if Seraphina stopped me last night because she knows I'm the heir to my father's business? Perhaps she knows my family had something to do with her parents' death. It can't be the case, though. I have been so selective about what I share with you.

She was asking the other day, though, if I would stay in New York. Was my answer too suggestive? If she had any concerns, she would have surely declined the invitations I sent her to see me after that. No, it can't be that.

It has to be something else.

As the sun's rays pierce through the mist and clear the sky, I sit and think about New York. Claiming my rightful place as heir of the New York mafia, the power the position offers me is something very alluring to me.

If I had someone like Kalo by my side, I would have someone I can trust. Would he move to New York if I accept the position? I believe he would. He has never said no to me before.

Rebecca's texts popped up on my phone again. Each message prodded for the same details: my accommodations and flight schedule. I hesitated, thumb hovering over the keyboard. Despite the unexpected warmth I'd felt towards her, trust was currency I wasn't ready to spend—not yet.

"I'm not laying all my cards out, Rebecca," I finally typed, the decision settling in with every tap. "I'll let you know when I've landed."

I could almost hear her calculating response, a mix of frustration and understanding. "Alright, I get the game. Just... be safe, okay?" she replied.

If she truly knew the stakes of the world we were navigating, she'd know better than to press further. Setting down my phone, I couldn't shake the unease of unseen eyes and ears that might await. Trust had to be earned, especially when every shadow could conceal a spy or every room with a hidden camera.

She offered for me to stay at her home, but that is never something I would do. Even if I trusted her. I'm too private. I like my space. And Seraphina is coming with me.

Is she still going to join me on our trip to New York?

My stomach tightens. What if she has changed her mind?

I sit still as the sun reaches higher, beginning to warm my skin.

I'm about to get up and go inside when my phone chimes. Seraphina.

Seraphina: Antonio, I'm sorry about last night.

Relief floods through me.

Me: what happened? Are you ok?

Seraphina: Yes, no, maybe.

She is responding but not telling me what is going on. She needs to explain herself. If she does not tell me, how will we work past this?

Me: Just talk to me. You can tell me - whatever it is. If I did something, tell me.

Seraphina: It's not you. It's me. I guess there was no way for me to keep it from you, anyway.

I can't handle this suspense. She needs to just say it. Whatever It's. I want to reach through the phone and shake her. My fists clench with frustrating it all.

Me: Don't make me beg to understand what is going on.

Seraphina: Antonio, I have never had sex before. I'm a virgin.

My jaw drops open.

A virgin?

No man has ever been with her. Her exotic beauty remains untouched and untainted. Now I'm more determined than ever to be the first and only one to have her. She'll belong to me in ways that very few people can ever understand. She'll be mine. My cock throbs at the thought of her untouched body. I'm in absolute shock. I was so worried it had something to do with me, something I had done, something that she had maybe found out. But this - this information has my heart racing.

Me:, I didn't know you were going to say that. I would have guessed so many things before I assumed that.

I'm relieved that I didn't sleep with her before I knew this. When I penetrate her for the first time, I want to be thinking about this. I want to know this.

Me: Thank you for being so open with me. Had I known what you shared before last night, I would've acted differently. You're incredibly beautiful in every way, and yes, you have an undeniable effect on me. But I promise, I won't pressure you for anything. When you're ready, just tell me. There was no need for you to leave like that. You're special, truly one of a kind, more than I ever imagined. I'm grateful for your honesty. Please, don't let last night change how you see me. I still want to be with you, to spend my time getting to know you better.

She is quiet for a long time. I stare at the phone, a smirk across my lips.

I am picturing how I'll claim her in ways she has never experienced before. Once I have thrust myself inside her, I'll never let another man touch her. I'll own her.

Even now, I'll kill anyone who so much thinks of her in those ways. If I see a man's eyes trace her body, that body which belongs to me, I'll rip them from his skull and feed them to the wild birds. She hasn't replied for a long time, and I wonder if her telling me she was a virgin was also her way of trying to tell me she could not see me again.

I'll not allow that.

Me: Will you still come to New York with me? Seraphina: I'll still go to New York with you. I'm sorry I didn't tell you before. Thank you for understanding. Me: My angel, you have nothing to be sorry for. We are going to have an amazing time together in New York.

She does not know the things that I'm going to do to her. But not yet; the anticipation can continue to grow. Now I know what she was hiding from me. All this time, I saw an innocence in her, yet I could never have imagined it would be such an intoxicating reality.

I breathe out a heavy breath and shake my head.

My beautiful Seraphina.

I check my watch and note that my meeting for today is starting in the next hour.

Yuke has prepared my breakfast by the time I step back inside. After breakfast, I have a quick shower and then climb into the car, ready to complete all the things I need to tie up before I make my trip to New York.

I don't know when I'll come back, so I need things to be in order.

Is it even worth risking my safety to come back to Hong Kong if I take the position in New York and assert my rights to the place my father left for me?

The tension between our families is still thick and violent.

I have the first meeting of the day in the boardroom.

I suffer through the boredom of it. Finances and reports. Afterward I go to my office and call for my assistant.

"Coffee," I said when she arrives at my door.

"Yes, sir. Kalo has just arrived as well. He asked for you while you were still in the meeting. Can I tell him you are out?"

"Yes, I need to speak with him."

She hurries away from me, and not long after, Kalo steps into my office.

"When is your flight booked for?"

"Day after tomorrow."

"Listen, I've got most of the shipments covered. I can handle that, but there are some new clients I need to run past you before you leave." He shifts his feet. "Also, I wanted to ask, are you planning on coming back?"

"I can't answer that yet. But if I decide not to come back, will you move to New York?"

The questions stun him for a moment.

He stands up and pacing, tapping his hand against his chin.

"Move there? To do what?"

"Run things with me."

I lean back in my office chair and fold my arms across my chest, eyeing him.

“I won’t be welcome. It'll be dangerous.”

“It might be, but when I'm in charge, I'll change a few things.”

"You can't expect to just arrive and start changing everything on a whim. Being there, and potentially being offered a position, will anger many influential figures."

I huff. “They will learn their place. Besides, this is just a projection. I want to know if you would consider it.”

Kalo stops pacing and stares at me. “What about your businesses here? I could stay and run these.”

“These business run themselves. I'll leave Aloma in charge. He has been with us since we started. I can also fly between New York and Hong Kong if needed.”

Kalo shrugs. “Yeah. I mean. I like my life here, but yes, I would move if you need me to.”

“That is all I wanted to know for now. We can just see how things play out and decide as we go along. While I'm away now, though, you are in charge here.”

“Noted. Can we run through those new clients?”

“Yes, sure, pull up a chair.”

Kalo sits down, tossing a file onto the desk. “Are you still seeing that girl?”

“I'm still seeing Seraphina. Why?”

“She hasn’t - uh - said anything?”

I lock my eyes on his. “About?”

“Nothing in particular. I mean, maybe about New York? Anything.”

I know him too well. I know he is keeping something from me. “Kalo, what are you not telling me?” My voice is low with a threat. He knows I hate secrets. Knowledge is power.

“Look, man, I’m sorry. I messaged her.”

“What the fuck did you message her for?” I slam my fist onto the desk.

“Jeez, I just wanted her to know not to mess with you. I don’t like her. I don’t trust her. She needed to know someone was watching your back and someone has their eye on her.” He stumbles over his words.

“Did you threaten Seraphina?” I'm furious.

“Not. Sort of. Come on, man. Honestly, she handled herself well. I didn’t want to tell you. I knew you would react like this.”

“Of course, I would fucking react like this. She is with me, which means she is under my protection. You will treat her with respect.”

He nods, tight-lipped.

“Now, tell me about these clients.”

I shove the anger away. Kalo has good intentions, even if his actions sometimes suggest otherwise.

Chapter 19

SERAPHINA

I grin as Antonio pushes me up against the wall of the balcony in his home. He grabs my hips and spins me around, pushing me forward so that I'm bending over the edge.

He runs his hand down my back, over the arch above my ass, then cups my ass cheeks, pulling them apart. I rock back against him, feeling his rock-hard cock pressing between my ass cheeks.

He moans a deep sound and whispers my name.

I feel him moving, then his cock slides all the way down my ass, between the cheeks, and over my pussy. I push against him again, desperate to feel what it's like to have him inside me.

"Are you sure you are ready, my angel?"

"I'm ready, please, Antonio," I beg.

He chuckles. His massive hand comes over my hip and guides his cock into my pussy. I cry out.

I wake up with the sound of that cry still on my lips and grin, turning to bury my face against my pillow. I can't stop having these dreams about him.

They are erotic. Sometimes, I wake up in a sweat, with my hands on my body.

As the dream fades, my eyes shoot wide open. Today is the day.

We are flying to New York.

Excitement clouds my vision, blocking my sight from my true reason for going there.

I should stop this nonsense and refocus, but I decide that just for now, I'll let myself be excited. When do I ever felt excited?

Besides, part of the reason I'm excited is that I'm so close to finding out the truth.

I rush around my apartment, making sure I have everything I need. I won't be back here for a very long time. Months, possibly a year. The job I have taken is a six-month contract with the option to renew after six months if both parties are happy.

This is it. There is no more time. Antonio's driver will be here any moment to fetch me. I haul my suitcase to the front door and push it out into the hallway.

After I have locked up, I push the case into the elevator.

I can't believe I'm leaving.

The elevator doors slide open, and I look up to find Antonio standing in the foyer.

"My angel, let me get that for you." He takes my case from my grip and wraps his arm around me, pulling me close against him and kissing my lips.

I grin.

"I can't believe I'm going on a plane." I blurt out.

"This is your first time flying?" His brows shoot up.

"Yes." I nod, and he shakes his head. "I guess there are a lot of things in this life that I take for granted and a lot of things in this life that I can show you." The side of his mouth curves up in a mischievous grin, and electricity rushes through my body.

I have been having way too many dreams about this man.

"Come on." We step outside and his driver takes the case from his hand, carrying it to the back of the car as Antonio holds the door open for me.

The entire ride to the airport, I'm grinning. The closer we get, the more often I see planes flying overhead.

we pull through a private gate and onto the tarmac of the runway.

Not only am I going on a plane for the first time, but it will be a private jet.

I climb out of the car and stare at the massive machine. I feel Antonio pressing against my back. He leans over and says, "It looks even better inside." He steps around me, taking my hand in his, and leads me to the stairway to climb into the jet.

I'm doing my best not to look out of place, but I don't think I'm doing an excellent job. Antonio looks cool and collected. I'm grinning nonstop, and my face aches.

"Are you going to be smiling like that all the way to New York?" he chuckles as he gets comfortable.

I bite my lip. I'm not doing a good job of hiding this excitement. "That depends. How long is the flight?"

"Around fifteen hours."

"I might take a break about halfway there."

He packs up laughing and pulls me closer to him so that my face is against his chest. He kisses the top of my head. "I'll make sure they bring out the snacks at the same time so it aligns with your break, ok?"

"Perfect," I say, breathing in the warmth of his scent.

Our flight is long, but comfortable. I stop smiling, at least some of the way, and even fall asleep with my head resting on the curve of his body with his arm wrapped around me. I woke up confused about where I was, but then full of excitement again.

"There it is." Antonio gestures toward the window. "New York City."

I lean close to the window and feel him behind me. It's late in the evening, and the city lights are sparkling like scattered stars across the landscape beneath us. Colorful lights in no specific arrangement blend across each other, creating a picture I'll never forget.

The plane touches down, and we disembark, climbing straight into the car, waiting for us.

The driver knows where we need to go. Antonio doesn't say a word to him.

I turn my face toward the window for the entire drive as I take in the city. Buildings that look like nothing I have ever seen before, a city so unlike Hong Kong. The lights are different; the signs are different, and the roads look different.

I feel far from home, yet I have this sense that I'm where I need to be.

Is this how my mother felt we she arrived in New York? Was she as enamored with the differences, the brightness, the energy and the smells?

Antonio rests his hand on my thigh, and it's just about the only thing that I can focus on apart from the views.

The car pulls over outside a massive hotel.

Three men walk toward us, dressed in red jackets with gold trim.

They open the car door. "Welcome, Mr. and Ms. Aoi."

"Oh, um,"

"Thank you," Antonio responds, didn't bother to correct them.

"You may go right up to your rooms. We will bring your luggage."

Antonio's hand drifts to my lower back as he pushes me toward the towering hotel doors.

Chandeliers hang from the ceiling in the foyer, and mirrored tiles shine as we walk past.

A man hands Antonio a key card, informing him that should he need anything at all, he must just ask.

Antonio walks through the hotel like he owns it, even though I know, or he tells me, he has never been to New York before.

Perhaps he was lying, or perhaps it was just his confidence.

I shrug off the thought. I don't want to focus on those things right now.

Inside the elevator, Antonio swipes the keycard through the slot above the button panel, and the elevator carries us upwards.

"Um - will I also be getting a key card for my room?" I ask.

"You and I are sharing the penthouse," he replies.

I bite my lip. I'm sure the penthouse is massive. I'm sure there will be plenty of space for both of us.

The elevator doors slide open on the 68th floor, and we stand in front of two massive wooden doors.

Antonio takes my hand again and moves toward them, swiping the key card against the lock.

I hear a soft click, and the doors pull open. Antonio ushers me inside.

I stroll into the magnificent space. It's beyond luxurious. Opulent.

I stand against the wide glass windows that surround two sides of the penthouse. My stomach knots and my head spins as I look at the view. I have never been this high in my life.

"Are you satisfied?" he slips his hand around my waist, and I feel his body press against my back.

"Do you mean - do I like it?"

"Yes."

"It's incredible."

"Come, see the rest."

He tours me through the living spaces, the kitchen, which looks big enough to cater for a restaurant, a bathroom straight out of a designer magazine - and the only bedroom - with one gigantic bed.

I turn to shoot a glare at him. "There is only one bedroom?"

"I told you we are sharing the penthouse," he says, as though this is not a problem at all.

"But,"

"I made a promise, Seraphina. I won't do anything you are not comfortable with. Not until you are ready."

His promise doesn't reassure me because all I can think about is ripping his clothes off and feeling him inside me. What if I have a dream about him while I'm in the same bed as him, and I wake up touching myself? I'll die of embarrassment.

It's too late now, though.

"Let's have a shower, get some rest, and tomorrow morning, we can go out for breakfast."

"That sounds perfect."

When I climb out of the shower and wrap the soft hotel gown around my body, my heart beats faster. I'm so nervous about climbing into bed next to him. I open the door, step out of the bathroom, and walk into him. He reaches out to stop me from tripping, and the gown falls open; his hand slides beneath it, across my naked waist.

He freezes, his hand on my skin, his eyes on mine. I can't even move to pull the robe closed.

Every cell in my body is alive with need.

He takes a deep breath. I see the immense control in his gaze as he doesn't once break contact, even for a moment, to run his eyes over my skin.

He drags his hand, letting his fingers trail over my stomach. Gripping the edges of the gown in his hands, he pulls it closed, tying the cord around my waist.

I take a slow breath, almost regretting his control. For a moment, I thought I'll let him push me against the wall and spread me wide open.

I blink away the thought.

"I won't be long. Make yourself comfortable. Our luggage is in the bedroom."

I smile and make my way to the room.

I want to get dressed so that he doesn't see me.

I pull out my pajamas and cringe. I only packed one. A soft, white silk pajama that are almost transparent. I did not know I would share a room with him. I get dressed and hurry to climb under the blankets. Sitting, waiting for him to walk in.

When he does, he grins, a towel draped around his waist, staying up. The v-shaped muscular groove of his Adonis belt taunting my eyes, leading them to the area the towel can barely cover. I pull my eyes upwards, but it doesn't help because now they are tracing over the defined six-pack of his abdomen.

My cheeks burn.

"You can look all you want, my angel." He leans over my side of the bed, his face inches from mine. "And when you are ready," he cups my chin in his hand, the muscles of his thick arm flexing as he moves. He presses his lips against mine and kisses me. I feel the area between my legs ignite.

When he pulls away to look at me, he is chuckling again.

He turns his back to me and drops the towel. I bite my lips and knot my brows as my eyes glaze over his perfect ass. He is doing this on purpose. He steps into a pair of gray sweatpants, and I roll my eyes at the audacity of this man. Has he no shame?

He slips into bed next to me and wraps his arm around my waist beneath the covers. He pulls me up against him, and I let out a small whelp.

"I promised. Remember."

I nod. There is no way I'll get any sleep tonight. "

Chapter 20

Antonio

Even though it's my first time in New York, from the moment we land, I feel as though I belong here. Absolutely everything about this place feels like home. As though I have known nothing else my entire life. It's obvious in my blood.

Our first night in the hotel is possibly the most teasing experience of my life.

I'm lying in bed with Seraphina's magnificent body pressed against mine, and it's taking everything in me not to take her right now.

We are alone, in the dark, with no one here to stop us. The things we could be doing. The things that I could do to her.

I push the thought out of my mind. I want her to feel comfortable with me. She will come around sooner than I think. I saw the way she looked at me. Her eyes were falling from her skull with the way her gaze dragged across my body.

As morning light filters in, I awaken with a smile, comforted because despite some shifting in the night, Seraphina has remained close, pressed against me. I find myself on my back with her head resting on my chest, her breaths gentle and rhythmic. Her hand lies across my chest, and I gently entwine my fingers with hers, drawing her even closer.

I'll show her all the respect that she deserves. I'll be patient with her, even though it's a challenge. When she is ready, I'll be as gentle as I can.

"Good morning," her sleepy voice mumble across my chest.

"Good morning, my angel. Did you sleep well?"

She rolls off my chest onto her back, rubbing her eyes. "I did. I didn't dream."

"Is that good or bad?" I ask.

"Oh - it's good." She sits up, and I notice how transparent her silk top is. I grit my teeth together. I can do this.

My eyes trace over the outline of her nipples as her full breasts press against the delicate fabric.

I feel my cock stir.

"I'll make us coffee." I push the blankets off and move away from her.

"Or do you want to just go straight out?"

"Let's go get bagels," she says.

"Bagels." I chuckle. Of course.

I leave the room, trying to give her some space so that she can get dressed without my eyes locked on her. I had enough strength not to look last night when the robe fell open, but I can't trust myself to do that again.

She walks out wearing these super tight jeans that look amazing on her. She's got a simple white sweater and some white sneakers on. Grabbing her phone, she stuffs it into her little black backpack and says she's all set to go check things out.

"I'd better get ready then," I say, heading into the bedroom.

A short time later, we step out onto the streets of New York. I'm hit by an array of sounds, colors, and smells that fill me with energy. Next to me, wrapped in my arm, Seraphina is a ball of excitement. I watch as her gaze darts from the cars to the buildings, scanning every coffee shop and staring at the fashion people have worn.

"Where do you want to go?" I ask.

She shrugs, pouting her bottom lip.

"Alright, then I shall take you somewhere." I trail my hand down her back, letting it rest on the arch above her ass. I love the way it feels beneath my touch.

We walk along the main street outside of the hotel, and I select the most New York-style cafe I can find. Leading her inside with me.

I order us each a bagel and a coffee. And then sit with her by the window, looking out onto the street.

"I can't believe how differently they dress to us. And the food in the restaurant windows doesn't even look like home. Everything is so strange."

I chuckle. "Good strange, I hope?"

"Yep!" she exclaims with enthusiasm.

"How are you feeling?" I wonder as I stare down at her.

"I'm thrilled to finally be here. It's a bit surreal, though; I've imagined this moment for most of my life." She gives me a once-over. "It's not quite how I envisioned it, but I've always pictured coming to New York. And now that I'm here, it's like no time has passed from when I first decided to come to this moment right now."

Strangely, I know exactly what she means. I have also wanted to come here my whole life. And as a young boy, I knew I would. The space between that young boy making that choice and me here today - seems minuscule.

“I guess that is why they tell us to enjoy the journey as much as the destination.”

We enjoy our breakfast by the window, watching the people come and go.

When we stand up to leave, Seraphina slips her arm through mine and leans close to me. She seems to love being here, but she clearly feeling a little overwhelmed with all of it. So, she is giving me the control to take the lead and make all the choices, while she trusts me and just follows. I quite like this. Her handing her choices over to me. I feel as though this is how it should be.

In the late afternoon, after a few hours of exploring New York, I receive a call from Rebecca. They need me to come into a meeting before reading the will. They want to establish who I'm. I guess all I'm required to do is to show up, show face, and stand my ground.

Rebecca warned me it might get a little challenging, as some of the family members are very against me being here.

Seraphina and I head back to the hotel and I let her know I won’t be gone for too long. I would prefer if she did not go out without me, but I know I can’t ask that of her. She is going to be starting a life here soon, and as much as I want to control her, it's not realistic.

She pulls out some books that she purchased at a corner bookshop we found when we were exploring and settles down on the sofa to read for a while. I stare at her for a moment. What is it about her that has me so captivated?

"I'll let you know when I'm on my way back." I lean down and kiss her.

She reaches up and pulls me closer, kissing me more intimately, and now I don't want to leave anymore. I low growl leaves my lips when she pulls away. "I hope everything goes well with your meeting." She smiles.

"You are a temptress, my angel." I brush my hand across her cheek.

"I'll be back soon."

Sitting at the boardroom table at a New York office building high rise, I'm biting my tongue.

We have been here for two hours. People are standing, yelling, throwing accusations, and all-round being disrespectful.

I'm still watching the mayhem. Learning who each person is. Mentally taking notes on who I need to watch out for. Unfortunately, it seems that I need to watch out for every single one of them except for Rebecca, who keeps glancing in my direction, looking stressed and embarrassed.

the lawyer, Blake Maritzio, stands up as well and shouts to be heard over everyone else.

"Can we *please* all just calm down?"

I feel like he needs a whistle and a handful of red cards to toss at people when they step out of line.

The room falls silent for a moment as everyone stares at him.

"Please, if everyone would take their seats, we can address the concerns one at a time in a *civilized* manner."

He has been working with the family for many years; otherwise, I doubt someone would let him get away with speaking.

Lucas, stands up, a gruff-looking man with gray hair, a cropped beard and dark, menacing eyes.

"How do we know he is who he says he is?"

"Antonio provided full identification when he entered the building, Lucas."

"Oh, please, we know how easily that can be faked."

A younger man stands up, one of my cousins.

"Why should he even be included in the will?" Lucas's son Arton snaps. "He knows nothing about this family. He deserves nothing."

The attorney raises both hands. "It's not our place to dictate Massimo's wishes. We don't even know what the will says yet, but whatever it says is what we will follow."

"We want to dispute the will." A woman who has otherwise been quiet smirks a comment toward me.

"How can you dispute what has not even been announced yet?" the attorney sighs.

"He would not have been called here if the will did not involve him. We know Massimo was obsessed with his son, his only heir. It's too a far stretch to assume he has left everything to this - *outsider*," Lucas snarls.

The room erupts again as everyone speaks at once.

The attorney looks at me with an apologetic silence in his expression.

I stand.

"Thank you all for your time. I don't feel that this meeting is progressing or serving any purpose."

"Nobody gives a fuck what you think."

I nod toward my uncle. "Lucass, I'll see you at reading the will. I hope you all have a wonderful evening. Blake, thank you for your time."

I turn to leave as the noise explodes behind me. How dare I walk out? How dare I speak to them this way? Who do I think I'm? I ignore all of it and push the glass door open. When it swings closed behind me, I take a deep breath and walk away. That was a disaster.

I have no one on my side. Rebecca seems quiet and withdrawn, not saying much to defend me. The rest of them are gunning for my throat, wanting blood.

I'm questioning my choice about coming here. Is this what I want?

On my way back to the hotel, I called Kalo.

"Antonio, how is New York?"

"I'm booking you a flight. I need you here. Just for now. I need someone I can trust."

"That bad?"

"Yes, that bad."

"Alright. Have you been in and out of meetings with the family the entire time?"

"No, Seraphina and I have been enjoying the city as well. That part of it has been amazing."

"Hmph." Kalo huffs in annoyance.

"Kalo?"

"Nothing. I asked about the family, not that girl."

"That girl? I believe you mean - *my* girl."

"Sure, man, *your* girl." I can hear the bitterness in his voice. "Anyway, I can arrange the flight from my side. I'll be there as soon as I can. I just have a few things to sort out here in Hong Kong."

"Good. Let me know."

I hang up and sigh. All I want to do is get back to the hotel and wrap my arms around Seraphina. Well, I want to do a lot more than wrap my arms around her, but yes, I need to be near her. Touching her. I just want to forget about the absolute mayhem of that meeting.

Chapter 21

Seraphina

"His name was Marcus Moretti" I repeat the tenth time, confused why it's not coming up on her system.

I tap my fingers against the counter. Trying to track down where my dad's buried. It's been a wild goose chase through government buildings and nobody can tell me anything—it's like he never existed. At the courthouse, they wanted proof we were related, but of course, I had nothing on me. Then, at the huge New York Library, I spent hours digging through old newspapers and obituaries until my eyes hurt. The government records were a total dead end. After waiting forever to talk to someone, they just told me they couldn't help and suggested I check out local graveyards myself.

I'm pretty sure they never gave my mom a proper gravesite, but my dad was different. He was born here in New York, a citizen. But the thought of sifting through hundreds of graves looking for him.. it just feels so bleak.

As for my mom, I connect with her spirit in nature—hiking up mountains or sitting by a serene lake. I feel her presence in the breeze, the water, even the soil. Everything's more vibrant with her spirit around—trees greener, flowers more colorful. She's out there, free, touching every beautiful corner of the earth.

"Can you spell that for me one more time, my dear?"

"M-o-r-e-t-t-i."

She types each letter into the keyboard and then squints at the screen. "No, there is nothing coming up for him. We don't have a record of the burial location for him. I'm so sorry."

"Is there anything on the system for him?" I'm feeling desperate.

"We have a place of work, but no - it's from over twenty years ago. I doubt it will be of any use to you?"

"Give it to me, anyway. I have to start somewhere." I sigh.

"It might not even be open anymore." She slides a piece of paper across the counter toward me with an address and company name written on it. *Allure Custom Furniture.*

Standing outside on the pavement, I type the address into my phone. It's a few miles from where I'mnow, so I decide I'll walk there. It will give me a chance to see New York on foot.

The streets are filled with people hustling back and forth, dressed in fashion I don't recognize. I love it. I love the energy and the strange shops I walk past. I stop outside, many of them to peer through the windows. People are of assorted natures here. Some greet me with wide smiles, and others stare, looking me up and down as though I fell off the back of a truck. I smile at them anyway. Kill them with kindness.

Glancing at my phone to make sure I'mheaded in the right direction, I find the street that the furniture shop is supposed to be on. It's quieter than the main street. I make my way to where the pin is on the map.

When I reach the correct point, my heart sinks. There is an old building there, faded with paint peeling off the walls. Across the top of a door, I see some broken lettering. Once the name of the furniture shop, now a scramble of nothingness.

I sigh and rub my hands across my face. What am I going to do? How will I find out where he is buried?

Next door to the old building, I see a small general store cafe. I need something cold to drink so I head inside, and behind the counter is an old lady who looks so frail I'msurprised she can hold herself upright.

“Hello dear. What can I get for you today?” Her smile is sweet and kind.

“Can I please have a bottle of water?”

She gets up, shuffles over to the fridge behind her, and pulls out a bottle of still water. She places it on the counter, confirming the amount I owe her.

“How long has this shop been open?” I ask, wondering if my dad ever purchased a cool drink here before?

“Oh, my goodness, almost seventy years now, I think. My memory is getting a bit faded, though.”

“And have you worked here the entire time?”

“Yes, ever since I turned eighteen, my father used to run the store alone before I started helping,” she says, and I feel a tug of pity pulling at my heart for this old woman who has lived her entire life in the four grubby walls of this cafe.

“Did you ever meet a man called Marcus Moretti? I understand he worked at the furniture shop next door.” I know it's a long shot, but I have to try.

“Marcus, of course I did. He was in here every day when that furniture store was still open.”

“Do you maybe know where they buried him?”

“Buried? Is he dead? Oh no, he was such a good man, always had good manners. I mean, I saw him just the other day, and he looked fine. When was it now? Spring? No, Autumn. What happened to him?”

“Oh, no, I think we are thinking of different people. Marcus died many years ago.”

“Did he? That’s terrible. You know he used to live in town here.” She smiles at me.

“Do you know where?” I'mnot even sure if we are talking about the same person anymore.

“Oh yes, let me write it down for you.” I wait while she scribbles down an address. I don’t have too much hope attached to it. She hands me the piece of paper.

“Can I get you anything else, dear?”

I put my money on the counter and pick up the water. “Just this. Thank you so much. Keep the change.”

I step out of the little cafe and back into the city sunshine. Unscrewing the cap, I take a sip of cold water and smile. That poor old woman knows what day it's. I wonder if she ever met my dad. I walk over to the now abandoned building that used to be where he worked. I glance up and down the street, picturing him arriving here every day, going into the office, and talking to the surrounding people.

What I would give to go back in time and see him walking past me now.

I type in the hotel's address on my phone's map. It's too far to walk. I caught a taxi this morning to get to this side of town; I guess I'll have to call one to get back to the hotel.

I think about Antonio. I wonder what he is doing today. I smile, looking forward to seeing him later this afternoon. I have to be careful around him now that I'mfinally in New York.

Today was unsuccessful, but I felt like I'mslowly adjusting to being in New York. The first few days were crazy. I guess I never understood the term culture shock until now. Thank goodness Antonio seems so confident around here. Almost as though he has been here before. I still think about that. Wondering about whether he perhaps has - perhaps he has been meeting with his family here. I don't know, but soon I'll find out.

When I arrive back at the hotel, I'msurprised to find Antonio already back.

"Seraphina?" I hear his voice calling me from inside the room when I open the door.

"It's me. I didn't expect you to be here?"

He comes out of the room, a sly smile across his lips. "And are you disappointed or pleased to find that I am?"

My eyes graze over his naked chest and hover over his hips, above the line of his pants.

"Well, seeing as you are topless, I might say that I'mpleased."

He chuckles and pulls me into an embrace. He kisses the top of my head. "Did you find your father's grave?" he asks, holding me against him.

I sigh in frustration. "No. Can you believe the system has no record of him to show where he was buried or if he was cremated? It's driving me crazy."

"That is odd, isn't it?"

"Maybe not, though? Maybe he didn't get a grave? I mean, people die all the time and just end up nowhere."

"Well, he can't be *anywhere.* That is impossible. There has to be something that tells us something."

"That is what I thought until today. I don't know where to look next. I met this ancient old lady at a cafe near to where he once worked. She swore she knew him, but I don't think she would know her own kids' names if I had asked her. She gave me an address, though, where he used to live."

I shrug, pulling the paper from my pocket and staring down at it.

"I'll hire you a private detective. You can sit with him, tell him everything you know, and he can find out whatever you need. I doubt it would even take long."

My eyes stare into his for a long time. It's a sweet gesture, but it's too risky for me to accept. If he hired a private detective - what else would they stumble upon about me - what information would they feed back to Antonio? I can't take that chance.

"That is kind of you, Antonio, but I think I'm going to keep trying on my own for a while."

"If you change your mind, just say the words, and I'll make it happen, little bird."

"Little bird?" I giggle.

"Yes, you are my little bird." A mischievous grin spreads across his face.

"And what do you do to little birds?" I wiggle my eyebrows.

"One day, you might find out." He traces his fingers down my arm, and my skin warms beneath his touch. My eyes trace over his torso again, each muscular curve and river that forms his beautiful body.

He cups his hand under my chin and pulls my face toward his. I feel his lips against mine, hot and inviting. I press my body against his chest and let my hands slide down his back. He feels amazing beneath my fingertips. I want more of him. I want all of him.

Chapter 22

Antonio

Early in the morning, I receive a message from Kalo to let me know he has landed in New York and was in a taxi on the way to the hotel.

I booked him a room in the same hotel that I'm in, figuring it was easier that way. He should be here within the next hour.

Me: Take some time to settle in, then we can chat at lunchtime. I'm sure you are tired from the flight.

Kalo:, I slept most of the way here. But I could do with a shower and some good food. I'll give you a shout later.

Me: Perfect. I want you to get started this evening already on some investigations. But we can chat in person.

Kalo sent me the thumbs-up.

I place the phone back on the bedside table and roll back toward Seraphina. She is still sleeping. I wrap my arm around her waist and pull her against me, feeling her stir and hearing her mumble something in her sleep I can't make out.

Who are you, beautiful girl? I lay my head back on the pillow and close my eyes. This feeling of being so close to her, yet not having her as my own yet, is driving me crazy. Sleeping in the same bed as her has made everything so much worse, yet I would not change it.

I feel her shift closer to me, pressing her ass cheeks against my pelvis. Mm. The things I want to do to her.

"Are you awake, little bird?"

"Not yet." She whispers.

I chuckle. "Do you want some coffee?"

"Mm." She sounds so cute when she is half asleep.

I lean over to kiss her neck, and a small smile traces her lips.

Then, I climb out of bed to head toward the kitchen.

I like this coffee machine. I think I should get one for home. Wherever home is going to be after this New York trip is over.

The first meeting with the family went badly. At least now Kalo is here. I can have him gather some more information on my behalf. I want to know if anyone is on my side. At least those who aren't are very vocal about it so far. I need to build up a team of people I can trust. Perhaps people who were close to my father. I don't even know yet who he got on with? Did he get on with my uncle? My cousins? They seem like such bitter, power-hungry people.

I pick up the two coffee cups filled with steaming, frothy cappuccinos and turn to find Seraphina standing in the kitchen doorway, rubbing her eyes.

I put the coffee cups down and lift her into my arms, muzzling against her neck.

She giggles and wraps her arms around my neck.

"Did you sleep well?"

"I did. Did you?"

"Yes, I have a meeting this afternoon, around lunchtime. Then, after that, I'm free. Do you want to go for dinner with me tonight?"

She reaches behind me for her coffee and sips it, closing her eyes for a moment.

"I wanted to ask you a favor. The address that the old lady from the shop gave me, I thought that if he lived there, perhaps one neighbor remembers him? I'm nervous about going there alone because when I looked online, it didn't look like the best of neighborhoods. I don't just want to go knocking on doors without some kind of muscular looking back up. Will you go with me?" She grins.

"If you need muscle for backup, I'm the right man for the job. Can you wait until after lunch, though?"

"Sure, of course. Tomorrow is fine too."

"No, today is good. I'll keep you updated about what time the meeting ends."

She nods and carries her coffee out onto the balcony. We sit together, watching the morning light grow brighter and stretch across the city.

At lunchtime, I go down to Kalo's room. She doesn't need to know that I'm having my meeting in the hotel or that it's with Kalo.

I know she and Kalo don't see eye to eye, to say the least. Kalo is set against her, but I hope to change that.

"Ant, how are you, man? Come in."

I step inside his more modest, yet still very luxury room.

He pours us each a drink and sits down in the living room with me.

"So, what is it you want me to get to work on?"

Straight to business, I like this about him. He knows when to fuck around and when to focus.

"I'll give you the names of everyone I know of here in New York. I want to know how they connect to each other and who gets on with whom. If you can find out whether my father liked them, then that would be a tremendous bonus."

"Consider it done. When is reading the will?"

"Soon. So, I need the info ASAP."

"Do you want to grab something to eat?"

"No, I have plans with Seraphina this afternoon. I don't want to keep her waiting longer than I have to."

He rolls his eyes. I throw him a warning look.

"Come on, man. You know how I feel about her. I won't hide that from you. I'd rather be honest with you."

"But what is your actual problem with her? What did she do to you?"

"Nothing, yet, but that is my problem. I don't trust her not to. I just have a feeling she is up to something. I'll figure it out."

"Kalo, leave her alone."

He stands up, placing his already empty glass on the center table. "You can't grab a quick bite to eat? It feels like forever since I last saw you. Ever since you got this new girl, you don't even hang out with the guys anymore."

"Fine, we can go to the restaurant here in the hotel." I take out my phone to let Seraphina know I'll be an hour or two, max.

Kalo grins, looking triumphant.

After lunch, I head back upstairs, texting Seraphina that I'm done.

I walk into the hotel room to find her dressed and waiting for me.

"I chatted to someone I know here in New York, and they let me know that this neighborhood is, as you suspected, dodgy. I thought perhaps before we go knocking on doors, we first scope out his old house for a bit. See if we are lucky to get someone talking."

"You mean like a little detective work? I like the sound of that."

"Good, I have already ordered us a delivery from the local store. Snacks and drinks are the most important requirement for a good stakeout."

A broad smile stretches across her face.

"Thank you for going with me. I appreciate it."

We are parked on the street near her father's old house. The rental car has dark-tinted windows, so we can see out, but it will be difficult for someone to see into the car.

We have been here for a few hours, watching the people come and go, and what we have been doing is laughing.

The sun has already set, but no one has come or gone from the old house, although we had made notes on the neighbors living on either side of it.

Seraphina leans close to me, her eyes glittering in the dim lighting of an old streetlamp a little way away from the car.

"Alright, it's my turn to ask a question."

"Yes, it is. Shoot."

"How many stakeouts have you been on?"

"I have never been on a stakeout that I enjoyed as much as this one, and I have never been on a stakeout with such a beautiful girl."

"Mm. I think that is cheating. You didn't answer the question."

"Does that mean I have to take a penalty?"

"It does." She grins.

"What price should I pay?"

"Kiss me."

I'm surprised. Of course, I have wanted to kiss her the entire time I have been sitting here with her. I just wasn't sure if she was thinking the same things as me.

I don't hesitate or wait for her to ask me again. I lean over, grab a handful of her long, dark curls, and press my mouth over hers. She gasps as the force behind my kiss, not expecting it.

Once I kiss her, though, I find it hard to stop.

I run my hand down her chest, cupping her breast. She gasps. Her hand runs down my chest and, to my surprise, settles with her fingers over my cock.

I'm rock hard. She is playing a dangerous game with me. My self-control has been hanging by its last thread with her so close to me these last few days and now she is being very direct regarding her invitation.

I grab her hips and lift her out of the passenger seat and onto my lap, pushing the car seat further back to give us room. My kiss gets deeper, and I press hard against her mouth.

I slip my tongue inside her lips and taste her.

My cock throbs.

I grab her waist and press her down into me, feeling her grind against me.

Fuck.

My fingers wrap around her throat, and I tilt her body backward, arching her back over the steering wheel as I thrust my hips against her.

She wraps her hands around my wrist, feeling the slight restriction of air. I grin; she is mine to take; she wants this.

When I release her throat, she gasps for a breath of air, then leans forward to tug at my shirt.

My heart thunders as I slide my hands between her legs, pressing my fingers against her pussy.

But when her fingers grip my belt, I stop her.

“Wait, little bird.”

“What is it?” she asks.

“This is not how your first time is going to happen. Not in a car. Not like this.”

“But I-”

“But I won’t do this to you here. I want to linger over your body, exploring every inch of you. I want to hear you moan.”

She grins at me. I lift her off me and place her back in the passenger seat, feeling the painful need of my cock throbbing against my pants.

When I glance over at her, I'm smiling as well. Because now I know she is ready. I know she wants me. I won’t have to wait much longer before I make her mine.

“Look.” she says, pointing at her father’s old house.

An old man has just stepped out of the front door carrying a garbage bag.

We watch him as he walks toward the end of his driveway, close to where we are parked.

Seraphina is breathing hard, staring at him with her mouth dropped open.

She reaches out and grips my thigh. Her fingers digging into my flesh. It turns me on even more.

“What is it, little bird?”

“That's my father.” She whispers, enough for me to hear.

I stare at the man. Dark skin, short hair, walks with a slight limp.

"You sure?"

She nods without taking her eyes off the man. He glances up and down the street, dusting his hands across his pants. Then turns back toward the house.

Seraphina looks as though she might puke.

“Are you ok?” I ask, leaning close and brushing my hand across her face.

“That is my father,” she says again.

Chapter 23

Seraphina

"Are you sure?" he asks, but I hear it. My body is begging to shake.

"I'm fucking sure." I snap, swallowing hard to ease the lump forming in my throat. The shaking intensifies as my stomach knots tighter and tighter. No matter how hard I breathe, no air seems to reach my lungs.

"Antonio, I want to leave. Get me out of here. Now. Please," I beg as tears stream down my face in salty rivers.

He starts the engine. "It might not be him, little bird."

I lean forward, digging around in my handbag, finding what I'm looking for. I pull out the photograph and hand it to Antonio.

He is about to turn the wheel of the car and pull into the street, but he stops to stare down the picture of a black man with short-cropped hair. The edges are the photograph are torn, and the picture is cracked, faded over time, but it's him.

He is older now, he looks more worn down, as though life has been hard on him. But there is no mistaking the fact that the man we just saw is my father.

For the entire drive back to the hotel, I'm contemplating everything that this could mean. It's beyond what I can comprehend in this moment of absolute shock.

I just go numb, unable to deal with the horror of what I have just learned.

I follow Antonio up to the penthouse, not registering my surroundings or anything he says to me.

He guides me toward the sofa in the living room, saying something about tea. I sit still, staring at the wall, trying to get my thoughts to either process or quiet down. Neither seems to work. I feel nothing at all.

"Seraphina?"

I glance up, staring at him. "Your tea is cold. Do you want me to make you another one?"

I look down at the teacup sitting on the coffee table in front of me. I do not know when he put it there or how long I have been sitting here. "Little bird?"

His voice is soothing, but I can't seem to reply.

Antonio leans over me, wrapping his arms beneath me. He lifts me up, cradling me against his broad chest, and carries me to the bedroom.

He places me on the bed, then kneels down beside the bed to remove my shoes. I watch him without a thought.

He unbuttons my jeans. I don't say a word.

Then pulls the covers back and places me beneath them, pulling them up over me. He climbs into bed next to me and, wrapping his arms around my waist, he snuggles me against his chest, holding me close, his presence a comfort I wish I could feel.

I don't know if I slept or not. I seemed to just lay in bed, drifting on nothingness.

In the morning, I don't remember waking up. I'm just lying here, staring at the same spot in the ceiling's corner, wondering if what I saw was real.

Antonio is already up; I can hear him in the kitchen. I roll over, forcing myself to look at something else. I close my eyes as tears sting against them.

I have one thought, one prominent fear, that has crept into my mind over the hours since I found out my father was alive. I came to this, considered, but.

My father has been alive all this time, yet he has never once tried to reach out to me. He must have known where I was. And if he didn't, then it would not have been hard for him to find me. I kept his surname. I'm on social media. I have not hidden or lived in secret.

My father did not want to find me. He was not interested in knowing me, or speaking to me, or explaining anything. The only reason I can imagine for doing such a thing is - he killed my mother.

All I saw that night was a man standing over her. A man leaped from the window, shattering glass across the room. A man who could have been anyone. Who could have been my father? Where was he otherwise? He wasn't in bed next to her. He didn't run in when my mother was shot. Where was he?

"Little bird, I made you some coffee." Antonio places a cup of coffee on the bedside table, and I watch the steam drift off it, disappearing in long tendrils into the air.

Antonio leans over and strokes my hair, his fingers brushing across my cheek.

“I'm going out for a few hours. I don’t want to, but I have to. I will be back as soon as I can. If you ask me to stay, though - I will?” he looks at me with what appears to be hope in his eyes.

I roll over to face the other direction again.

I hear him sigh softly and then walk out of the room.

My father is alive.

My father is alive.

All this time. All these years. He never cared enough about me to message me. Not once.

I feel that he has been hiding. Perhaps in shame or perhaps in guilt. Maybe both.

Have I been angry at the wrong people for my entire life? I think I have. I think I have projected so much hate onto Antonio’s family, his father, just assuming they were responsible, I didn’t take the time to consider anything else.

The more I think, the angrier I become. Not only for what my father has done, murdering my mother, but for never reaching out to me as well. For being alive. For letting me fester in my thoughts of hate, revenge and misery all these years - alone.

I pull the duvet over my head. I don’t know how to deal with any of this. I wish I could just disappear, vanish into nothingness. I wish I could not exist for a moment just to feel relief from this emotional torment.

When I pull the blanket off my head and glance at my phone, I'm shocked to see almost the entire day has drifted past. It's around two o'clock, and I have not bothered to get out of bed.

For a moment, I get angry at myself. Get up, Seraphina, get up and do something about this.

But I can’t. I just don’t have the will or motivation to do anything at all.

I hear the hotel door opening and footsteps as Antonio walks into the living room, past the kitchen, and then toward the bedroom.

"You are still in bed, little bird? Are you ok?"

He sits on the edge of the bed and pulls the duvet away from my face to look at me, but I can't look at him. I'm so broken. I feel shattered and torn. I don't want him to see me like this.

I grab the edge of the blanket and pull it back up over my face.

"You didn't have any of your coffee? Have you eaten? Little bird, you can't do this to yourself. I'll make some food."

He disappears again and I feel tears roll down my cheeks. When he is near me, I feel weaker. When I'm alone, I have to hold it together for myself, but when he is here, and he acts like he cares, I feel myself needing him.

I can't need him. It isn't right. It's not how it's supposed to be.

I seethe with anger towards him, too. Why does he have to make me feel this way?

I never asked for this. I wanted no of this. *He needs to leave me alone.*

I sit up in bed, fueled by an anger that increases as each second ticks by.

I know somewhere in the subconscious reaches of my mind I'm being irrational in having this much anger toward Antonio. This anger is not for him - it's for my father. But when he walks into the room carrying a plate of food, I feel I lose control of myself.

He places the plate of crackers, cheese, and cold cuts on the bedside table.

In a rage, I swipe my hand across the small table, sending the food flying and the plate crashing against the wall. Antonio blinks in astonishment, then sits down on the bed near my feet. He places his hand on my leg.

"Little bird, I know you are upset, but you can't do this to yourself."

"Do what? I think I can do what I want. Who are you to tell me anything?"

"Excuse me?"

"Who the hell are you to me?"

"I'm someone who cares about you. But I'm warning you - watch your tone when you are speaking to me."

"Watch my tone?" I laugh, a bitter, dry sound that is foreign to my own ears.

"Little bird." His voice is thick with warning. "All I want is for you to be alright. If you tell me how I can help you, I will be here for you."

"I'd prefer it if you left me the hell alone."

He shakes his head as the muscles along his jaw clench and unclench. I stare at him with fire in my eyes.

"I will not leave you in this state."

I push the blankets off myself and stand up, storming out of the bedroom. He follows me to the living room.

"Don't you get it, Antonio? You are *nothing* to me."

"I know that isn't true."

"All I ever wanted was revenge for my parent's murders. All I ever wanted was to hurt the people responsible. *Your family.*" I shout. As soon as I say it, I know that I'm digging myself into a very dark hole.

"Revenge?" his voice is low, and his eyes are growing darker by the second.

"Why do you think I have been getting close to you?"

My heart stops as I hear my words. Now that they are out of my mouth, they hang in the air between Antonio and me. He is frozen in place, as am I. The air feels ice cold and full of static.

He steps closer to me.

“You got close to me in order to get revenge?”

I bite my lip, forcing myself to shut the hell up. I can’t believe I just said that.

His stare becomes so intense that words fall out of my mouth again.

“That *was* my plan, *originally*. That is all I ever wanted. I knew who you were. I thought - I thought your family killed my parents. It was how it all started when I first met you.”

It isn't how it's now, though. That’s not how I feel now. I realize with shock. My heart sinks. Confessing my reason for getting close to him has made me realize that it's no longer what I want from him.

I have fallen for him.

“Is that so?” Antonio says.

“Wait,” I say as he picks up his phone and his wallet from the counter.

He walks straight past me without another word, out of the hotel, closing the door behind himself.

What have I done?

I love him.

The truth shocks me to my core. I'm in love with Antonio.

I run to the door and open it, but he is gone. The elevator doors have already closed, and the number above the doors tells me he is close to the ground floor.

I need to let him go.

I don’t think he will ever forgive me for what he just found out.

I close the door and return to the bedroom, climb back into bed, pull the covers over my head and disappear from the world again.

Chapter 24

ANTONIO

I stand inside the elevator, feeling claustrophobic. The rage inside me is spinning so that I swing left and punch the elevator wall, smashing the mirror panel. Glass shards glitter to the floor, and I stare at them, feeling betrayed.

The doors slide open, and the lady behind the reception desk stares in horror at the mess I'm walking away from.

"Add it to my bill," I snap, leaving the foyer and walking out onto the busy New York street.

She has been playing with me this entire time. Her words twist and churn in my mind.

She was using me in some revenge plot.

What does this mean?

It means that she has been keeping secrets from me.

I walk with my hands shoved into my pockets, then take them out because I don't know what to do with myself. I just don't want to be lashing out like I did in the elevator.

I keep my head down, as I'm not in the mood to greet anyone. I walk past, and I know my face is dark with anger. I'm hurt. It's difficult to admit that, but I'm hurt.

Did she feel anything for me? At any point in our being together?

It all felt so real to me. I was so sure that she had fallen for me. I was so sure that there was something going on between us. Am I that blind?

I walk past shops, people and restaurants. I do not know where I'm going. Turn down a pathway leading into a garden of some sort, a city park. I walk along the edge of a tree line. I just keep going, heading nowhere. Trying to push this anger out of my body, but feeling every moment.

I want to kick her out. I never want to see her again. The thought stabs a knife into my chest. No, I can't do that. She is mine. She belongs to me. I want her close to me. How did I fall for someone who never even felt anything for me? Someone who was using me?

I have fallen for her. I know this because even in this fury, I still want her around. It's the most ridiculous thought. It makes me even angrier to realize that she has some kind of power over me.

Kalo was right all along.

I can't believe this is happening. What happens from now? Do I kick her out of my hotel room?

Will I ever speak to her again? I know I can't trust her. She has been hiding things, keeping things to herself, tricking me.

The same thing you have been doing to her.

I shake my head. No, It'sn't the same.

Isn't it? I knew, or thought, that my family had a connection to her parent's murders - and I hid that from her. How is it different from what she kept from me?

I reach the edge of a large pond. Ducks are gliding across the surface. I stare at them, not knowing what to do.

I fucking love her.

She lied to me.

You lied to her.

I run my fingers through my hair and brush my hand across my chin.

I lied to her. I kept things from her. I did that - and I still developed genuine feelings for her.

I want her. I don't want to lose her. Is it possible that she feels the same? When I think about her words to me earlier, she told me *that was my plan*. Was. Not is. Perhaps along the way, things changed. All the time we have spent together meant something.

I turn back toward the hotel. I need to speak with her. We are both in the wrong. I'm angry, but that doesn't make what I did right.

I walk back, no longer filled with that dark rage. I'm still upset; I'm hurting, but I know how I feel about her.

By the time I have reached the hotel, I'm calmer and a lot more in control.

The receptionist avoids making eye contact when I walk in. The glass in the elevator got cleaned up, and now there is only a blank metal wall where the mirror panel used to be. I stare at it all the way to the penthouse.

Outside the penthouse door, I take a deep breath. I'm going to get some answers; I just don't know how to go about doing that.

I don't even know how to start this conversation.

I push the door open and walk inside.

I find Seraphina in the bedroom. Her eyes are red, as though she has been crying. I walk to the edge of the bed and stand over her. What do I say?

She sits up, then raises herself on her knees. She reaches out and touches my chest. Her eyes are soft, almost pleading.

When she wraps her fingers around the front of my shirt and pulls me closer, I don't stop her. She presses her lips against mine, kissing me.

The intensity of this kiss seems to spear something deep inside me. Anger, hurt, betrayal, love, passion. I pull open my belt buckle, yanking the belt free from my waist. I push Seraphina hard, and she falls back onto the bed, looking up at me in shock, but not moving away from me.

I kneel over her, grabbing her wrists and wrapping the surrounding belt. Then I loop the belt through the bedpost. She opens her mouth to say something.

"Not a fucking a word, little bird."

She closes her mouth again; her eyes are wide and glowing.

I grab the edges of her t-shirt and tear the fabric from her body. She gasps in fright; the nervousness that runs through her is visible.

Then I pull her pants off, and she lays naked on the bed with her arms tied above her head.

She shifts, rubbing her wrists together, trying to free them.

I pull my shirt off and step out of my pants. My eyes are on her the entire time.

My hungry gaze hunts over her body, her beautiful curves, her smooth skin.

My cock is rock hard and throbbing.

She thinks she can get away from me. Betray me? Lie to me?

I will show her who she belongs to.

I grab her legs and pull them apart with force, then lay over her, my hips forcing her to open her legs around me.

She cries out with fear and tries to wiggle her body away from me, so I grab her hip, wrapping my hand around her and push her into the bed.

"You move when I say you can move," I growl.

"Anton-"

I press my hard cock against her pussy, and my name freezes on her lips.

I rub my cock up and down, and a sly smirk teases across my lips when I feel she is dripping wet.

"You can tell me no, but your body is betraying you. I know you want this."

I say, pushing my cock into her pussy. Inch by inch, forcing her pussy wide open. She cries out in a moment of pain, and I pause, letting her adjust to the size of me.

Her breathing is heavy and fast. Her breasts are rising and falling with each breath.

I lean over her, my mouth against her ear, and as I push my cock deeper into her, all the way to the base of my shaft, I whisper, "You belong to me now. You will always be mine."

She shudders. Perhaps pain, perhaps pleasure.

I lift my chest to look down at her as I thrust in and out of her.

Her lips are open. Her eyes are still wide.

I glance down at my cock, watching it slide into her pussy.

When I pull out and see blood coating my shaft, a deep moan of excitement rumbles through my chest.

I pull out of her, loving the sight of the red wetness on my skin. I wrap my hand around my cock and slide it up and down, coating my hand in the blood. I dip my fingers into her pussy and bring it out.

I dip my fingers into my mouth, then trace my hand over her breasts, leaving red handprints staining her skin. My cock throbs, almost painfully, at the pleasure I get taking in the sight of the fresh blood over everything.

I lean forward and press my blood-stained lips against hers as I slide my cock back inside her pussy. My pussy. It belongs to me now.

The taste of iron against my tongue and the sight of her covered in blood, smeared across her lips, across her breasts, down her stomach, fuels me.

I thrust harder, and she screams. This is not about her pleasure, though; this is about me claiming her body as my own.

I fuck her. Slamming into her, she fights against her restraints.

I clamp my hand over her neck, and she tilts her head backward as if inviting me to do so.

My cock thrusts into her, again and again, and soon she is arching her back and lifting her hips toward me.

"That's right, little bird, let me take you, enjoy it, feel it."

She shakes; first, her legs wrapped around my back; I feel them quiver against me. Then, her entire body is shuddering. Her pussy pulses over my cock. She closes her eyes. "Open your eyes. Don't you dare close them?"

Her eyes lock with mine as her orgasm rushes through her. Her pupils dilate, and she moans. I shove myself deep inside her as I felt my release pulsing. The most intense orgasm I have ever had shoots through me, erupting inside her.

I collapse onto her, panting, her body pinned beneath me. I take my time to catch my breath, and when I press myself up to look into her face, I see the strains of tears that have run across her painted cheeks.

It gives me a fright.

I pull the belt loose from the bedpost and lean back, pulling her into my arms and holding her close against my chest.

She leans into me, her hands still knotted in my belt. I stroke my hands down her back, through her hair; she is so beautiful. So soft. So delicate. And she is mine.

She is all mine. She will only ever be mine.

I won't allow another man to touch her, ever, no matter what happens from now onwards.

She belongs to me.

Chapter 25

Seraphina

I am leaning against him, my heart thundering in my chest, my hands still twisted together with his belt, locking my wrists against each other. His muscles are flexed and glistening with sweat. He smells of blood and salt and something else. Is that what sex smells like?

I breathe him in. Feeling intoxicated by everything.

He wraps his arms around me, and I feel incredible.

I could never in my life have imagined that sex would be this amazing. My skin is burning, alive, and tingling. My legs are still throbbing as the muscles ease after such an intense orgasm. My lips feel swollen and tender from his kisses.

I am no longer a virgin. There was such an intense physical and emotional release in all of this.

It hurt quite a bit, but not for long. I think the pain of it, the intensity of everything, is what gave me the space to *feel* the emotions that were infecting me. The space that I needed to just let go. The complete release of pain, fear, pleasure, and confusion pulled me back toward myself. It was *absolutely incredible*.

He was so rough and forceful. I don't think that it's how your first time is supposed to be, but I wouldn't change it for the world. It was what I wanted without knowing that it was an option.

I didn't think that my first time would be so heavy, yet somehow, it was the sexiest thing I have ever experienced in my life. I have never been more turned on by someone or something they did - ever.

I lick my lips and taste my blood on them. It should disgust me, but it doesn't. After seeing how much it turned him on, I was also turned on by it.

"Little bird, I am so sorry."

I tilt my head up toward him, confused by his words. I am the one who should apologize to him for lying to him the entire time we have spent together.

"What do you mean?" I ask. "What are you sorry for?"

"For being so rough with you - I didn't mean to. I honestly never wanted to hurt you."

"You didn't hurt me, Antonio. It was incredible."

He wraps his hands around my waist and leans my body away from his so that he can look at my face. He frowns, a look of concern traced over his expression.

"But you were crying?" he says, brushing his thumb across my cheek.

"Oh, um, yes, afterward, I cried a little. I just felt some very intense emotions."

"Emotions? Not physical pain?"

"I felt pain. I mean, it hurt, but that isn't why I was crying. I just got overwhelmed."

"It wasn't too much for you, Seraphina? Honestly, I know I got carried away - for your first time. I had intended to be so gentle with you."

I smile at him. I reach up and brush my fingers over his blood-stained lips. "Well, um, you changed your mind at some point?"

He chuckles. Relaxing at the sight of my smile.

"I guess I did. Fuck, honestly, that was the most intensely satisfying experience I have ever had."

I shift my body back a bit, wiggle my butt across the bed, and hold my hands up toward him.

"What?" he grins. "Do you want me to untie you?"

I nod. "I need to talk to you," I say, knowing that it will not be a straightforward conversation.

He pulls the belt loose, weaving it off my wrists, and tosses it onto the floor next to the bed.

"Let's hop in the shower; let me wash you, then we can talk over a cup of tea. I bet you still have eaten nothing."

"I haven't."

I don't feel hungry at all, though.

He climbs off the bed and takes my hand in his, leading me toward the bathroom. When the shower water is flowing, he steps in with me. And he rubs soap all over my body. The water runs off my skin, bubbly and pink, stained with my blood, then it runs clear.

He washes himself, so I take the soap from him, and he leans his hands against the shower wall above my head while I wash his body.

We are both quiet. Perhaps he is as lost in thought as I am.

I am thinking about so many things. I am trying to figure out what I want to say to him and how best to say it. I am also thinking about my father and how much hate I have for him.

Antonio leans past me to switch off the water.

He reaches out of the shower to grab a towel, which he wraps around me.

He rubs his hands over the towel. Over my body. Then holds me close against his naked chest. I feel him tracing kisses across my shoulder, into the curve of my neck, and it sends shivers through me.

"Come on, get dressed, dry your hair, do whatever you need to in order to feel fresh and get your mind out of where it has been all day. We can talk after that, ok?"

I nod. Grateful that he isn't rushing me or putting pressure on me to explain myself. He is giving me all the space I need to figure it out.

When I walk out of the bedroom, my hair blow-dried and pulled into a messy bun, a pretty lace blue top on, and my favorite dark blue denim jeans, Antonio has made me a cup of tea, and he is sitting out on the balcony with his own coffee.

I pick up my tea and walk out into the fresh late afternoon air.

I sit next to him at the small breakfast table.

"Antonio, what I told you this morning isn't everything that I should have said."

"Alright," he says patiently.

"It's true. I started interacting with you, thinking that you were linked to my parents' deaths and planning to take my revenge out on you - or to use you to get close to your family. But then, we spent so much time together, and the more I was with you, the more my feelings and goals changed without me even realizing it."

He nods, waiting for me to continue.

"I fell in love with you." I struggle to lift my eyes to meet his. Terrified of what his response will be. I am terrified that I will see instant rejection in his expression.

But I see nothing even close to rejection.

I see tenderness. My heart beats faster, almost excited, because now I do want to hear what he has to say. I feel hope perhaps I am not the only one who is feeling this connection between us.

I feel his hands run up my thighs, sending electricity through my body.

He leans toward me.

"I am in love with you, little bird."

His words rush over me like a cool rain in the middle of summer. It's soothing, relieving, and exciting. It's exactly what I wanted to hear.

An excited laugh bubbles from my lips and I jump up, wrapping my arms around his neck, kissing, trying not to smile while I do.

I giggle, feeling happy, and I hear his low chuckle.

I lean back.

"I thought you were going to ask me to leave. After what I did. I am so sorry, Antonio."

"You can't leave, little bird. I want to be with you, always."

He pulls me onto his lap, and we sit watching the view for a while, enjoying the closeness and this newfound truth.

After a while, my stomach grumbles, protesting the fact that I was on an angry hunger strike for the entire day.

"I think we had better get some food inside you."

"Mm. Maybe."

"I am going to take you out somewhere special. We have something to celebrate."

"What?"

"Us." He smiles, kissing me.

Then he lifts me to my feet and goes through to the room to fetch his jacket.

"I don't think I am dressed properly," I say, looking down at my jeans.

"DO you want to put on a dress?"

"I have one here that I borrowed from my friend."

"You don't own dresses?" he asks, surprised.

I shrug. "Not really."

"That will not do. Tomorrow we are going shopping for you. We will find you the most beautiful dresses."

I shake my head, grinning, as I walk through to the bedroom to change. I slip Maddy's short black dress over my body. Looking in the mirror, I feel pretty. I slide the high heels onto my feet and grab a small clutch, all belonging to Maddy, all on a long-term loan for my New York adventure. She insisted I take it with me, and I am glad that she did.

When I step out of the room, Antonio's eyes light with a hungry fire. "Fuck, you look so sexy. Maybe we don't need to eat. Maybe we should just stay home so that I can eat you."

I smile. "I might be a little tender right now."

He chuckles. "Yes, I would imagine so."

The restaurant is breathtaking. The views across the city at night are magical and the romantic atmosphere is making me lean closer and closer to Antonio.

Soft candlelight flickers across our table, playing in his eyes, making them bright and dangerous. He sips the wine he has ordered for us, tasting it. Then he nods to the waiter, confirming that he can pour a glass for each of us.

I glance over the menu, unsure what I feel like eating, lost in my thoughts again.

I am so happy that Antonio and I feel the same way about each other, and I am excited to be here with him, but honestly, my heart is so heavy with shock after seeing my father yesterday.

Everything in my world has been spun around and flipped upside down.

I bite at my lip as anxiety increases.

"What do you feel like eating, little bird?"

"Um, I don't know."

He reaches out and places his hand over mine. "Do you want me to order for you?"

"Yes, please," I say, relieved.

Antonio orders us a seafood platter, and it sounds perfect.

I sit staring out of the window, watching the lights of the buildings around us and below us as they glitter against the dark backdrop of the night sky.

"Seraphina, where are your thoughts right now? You seem very far away from me."

"I'm sorry. I know I am being distant. It's just everything, you know."

"With us?"

"No, that is the one thing that is bringing me peace. No, it's everything with my father. I can't believe he is alive."

Antonio nods, his fingers massaging my thigh.

I clamp my teeth. Should I dare to tell him what I am thinking about?

Now that I have found love for the first time in my life, do I tell him who I am? Do I risk having him pull away from me because of my honesty?

I don't want to hide things from Antonio. It never served me well, keeping secrets in my friendship with Maddy, my relationship with my grandfather - and my relationship with Antonio.

Secrets have built walls around me my entire life, and I have never felt comfortable enough to let someone get too close to me for fear that they would see who I am.

The dark, angry energy that I carry around everywhere with me.

I never wanted people to see how damaged I actually was because of my parent's murders.

"Little bird, you have gone quiet again."

I sigh softly. "I am sorry."

"Talk to me. Whatever you are thinking, I am here to listen. I am here to help you."

I stare into his eyes, and I believe him. I believe he means that.

I open my mouth to speak, and the waiter arrives with our dinner.

I lean back and say a polite thank you.

When we are alone again, Antonio picks up the white cotton napkin and drapes it over my lap, letting his hand drift against my leg.

My stomach is in such a knot I know I can't eat until I tell him.

"Antonio."

"Yes?"

"I want to kill my father."

Chapter 26

ANTONIO

It has been two days since Seraphina told me she wants to kill her father.

At the restaurant, when she first said the words, I took her hand in mine and reassured her it was natural for her to want that. I told her to think about her choice for a few days, and if she still felt this way, then we should talk again about it.

Killing her father is not in my favor at all. Quite the opposite, in fact.

He has Italian mafia ties, ties to my family. Ties to the mafia that I'mabout to inherit.

It would look bad if people discovered I was involved in this man's death.

No, it's not a personal thing. I don't give a shit about him. If Seraphina wants him dead, then I would want that for her, but it's inconvenient. Especially right now, just before reading the will.

I want to give her the world. I want to give her everything her heart desires. But this is going to cause problems.

Kalo paces up and down his hotel room. I stretch my arm across the back of the sofa behind me.

"I don't know, Antonio. This girl is not worth it. She is not worth the drama."

""I've warned you, Kalo, not to speak ill of her," I snap, irked by his comment. Should I even be discussing this with him? He's my right-hand man, my closest friend—the one who's always got my back.

"Does Seraphina even know why you are actually in New York?"

"She knows my father passed away."

"Does she know you are here to accept your position as heir to the New York throne?"

"No, I have not told her yet."

"It's because you don't trust her," Kalo snaps.

"No, it's because the time has not been right. I want to tell her, especially after she told me everything. It's only fair that I tell her. But I need to wait."

"For what?"

"After the reading of the will. There is no point in telling her I'm going to be heir to the family but then declining the offer if things don't look good. I will wait, go to the reading, learn who is who - and then tell her once I have decided for myself."

"But you are going to take the position, aren't you?"

I shrug. "I'm almost certain, yes, but I like to be one hundred percent sure. I like to have all the pieces on the board so that I know what game I'mplaying."

Kalo sits down opposite me.

"Kalo, there was something else. I know you have pieced together a very good layout of who is who and who I can most likely put my trust in, but there is another thing I need you to look into."

"What is it? Anything."

"The last two days, when I was out and about, I noticed a woman following me. She isn't trying to hide the fact that she is following me, either. I was going to corner her in an alley, but decide perhaps I should find out who she is first. She is -"

"A Japanese woman?" Kalo smirks.

I stare at him, looking unimpressed.

"What is going on, Kalo?"

"Alexia is a friend of mine. She is a hired gun. She also does some private work in the security sector. I actually told her to stay out of sight, but I guess she had her own ideas."

"You hired this woman?"

"She has been staying close to you since you got here. I was just unhappy with the idea that I couldn't be around if something happened and you needed backup. I trust her with my life, man. You can, too."

"You should have told me."

"I didn't want to bother you with it. Plus, knowing you, you would have told me not to arrange it."

"That is what I would have done. But, in hindsight, I'mgrateful for it. I did not know my family was going to be against me being here. Any support I have is valuable. Thank you."

"Don't even mention it."

"I want you there at the reading."

Kalo pulls a sour face. "I know why you want me there, but it's going to upset many people. I'm from Hong Kong; I will not be welcome."

"I realize that, but I want you there. I doubt they will do anything but share their annoyances at the reading."

"I don't like to assume anything, but alright. I will be there."

"It's in two days. You can ride there with me. For now, I'm going to head back to my hotel and talk to Seraphina about her father. I need to make her think she doesn't want to kill him, at least not yet."

"Good luck. You brought that drama upon yourself." He snorts an indignant laugh.

"Little bird?" I call out as I walk into the penthouse.

"I'm in here." Her voice drifts from the bedroom, then she walks out of it toward me. My lips curl into a smile. She looks incredible. Her hair is pulled up into a messy bun; the way her jeans hug her hips and cling to her legs is seductive. She is wearing an oversized pink hoodie that says *New York* across the front.

"You look like you belong in New York," I chuckle.

She laughs. "I thought it was cute," she says, pulling at the front of the hoodie.

"Mm. Cute. Yes."

She stands on her tiptoes to kiss me. I wrap my arms around her narrow waist and lift her against me.

"Do you feel like doing a bit of shopping? I have a few places I want to take you."

"I feel like doing anything with you." She nuzzles into my neck.

"Get your shoes on. Let's go exploring."

We step out onto the main street outside of the hotel. I slip my fingers into her hand, pulling her up against me. "I'm loving this place. The energy here is amazing," she says, taking quick steps to keep up with me. I notice and slow down a little, so that she can walk comfortably.

"Would you like to live here? I mean, I now know the real reason you came here was not because you wanted to move to New York, just because of those - other reasons."

She smiles and looks away from me. "I thought I was just coming here for that and that I would go home to Hong Kong afterward, but I have been wondering what it would be like to live here."

"Me too. It's very different from home."

"Are you thinking about living here?"

"I don't know yet. The thought has crossed my mind. I want you near me, though."

She smiles a wide, beautiful smile that spreads across her face.

I don't need to tell her yet about me taking the position as heir to my father's estate. I don't know how she will feel about it all. She might hate the idea of being that involved with the mafia. For now, I'll wait and see what reading the will show me. I might decide that this place has nothing to offer but drama. I might just head right back home to Hong Kong. Either way, I want to keep Seraphina with me.

"When does your new job start?"

She glances at me with a sour look. I laugh. "You never wanted that job, did you?"

"It's a horrible job. I just needed to get here. I start in two weeks."

"Don't do it," I say, as though it was an obvious option.

"I have to, though. I need money to stay here. I need to pay for my apartment, food and whatever else happens in New York."

I nod, but I know I will take care of her. I don’t need to talk to her about it yet, but whether it's in Hong Kong or New York, my little bird will never have to work a day in a job she doesn't enjoy.

We spend a few hours roaming the high fashion stores along Fifth Avenue. Everything that Seraphina likes, I buy her, despite her protests, and her continuously telling me she is just browsing. I want her to feel incredible. I want to spoil her.

I tell the stores to deliver the bags directly to the hotel for us so that we don’t have to carry them around all day. Then we head over to a cafe for some food.

I choose a table out of the way from the crowds because what I want to talk to Seraphina about is not a normal conversation to be overheard by nearby people.

I hold her chair out for her and then slide it in behind her when she sits down.

Our legs touch beneath the table, and I wonder if perhaps we should just go home so that I can explore her body instead.

“Little bird, I was thinking about what you told me the other night.”

She nods. She knows what I’m talking about.

“Is it possible that death is too kind?”

Her eyes meet mine with a questioning look.

“What do you mean?”

“I mean, there is so much suffering that can be gifted to someone in life. And is that perhaps not a better form of punishment? Death is final. Once off. Then they rest afterward.”

She bites at her bottom lip, pondering what I have just said.

She looks up at me with a dark sparkle in her eyes. “I think you are right.”

I breathe a sigh of relief. That is one thing that I do not have to deal with right now.

I run my hand along her thigh. She grins, not a friendly or happy grin, but a grin filled with a wicked undercurrent. I find myself especially turned on by this. She is darker than I could have imagined she would be.

She is perfect for me.

"I'm going to give it some thought. But you are right. All these years of my life, they have been a sort of torture to me. Maybe I need to give him the same gift he gave me, somehow. Years of mental torment."

The waiter arrives to take our order, and we spoke no more about her father or what plans she might create in her mind. That is a conversation for a private place. I have planted the seed and she can move in whichever direction she wishes with it.

When the waiter is gone and we are alone again, I cup her face in my hand and pull her close to me so that I can whisper against her ear. I feel her hands running along my thighs as she leans toward me.

"Are you feeling strong enough again? To handle me? Has your body recovered after our first time together?"

My heart pace speeds up at the thought of being inside her again.

She smiles and looks down, her dark lashes filtering her eyes from my gaze. The innocent yet flirtatious smile that drifts across her face is killing me. "Perhaps a few more days," she whispers.

"It will be worth the wait. Just know that I think about you every moment of every day. I can't get you out of my mind. You drive me crazy."

She lifts her eyes and presses her lips against mine. I slide my fingers along her neck and feel the electricity beneath my touch upon her skin.

Chapter 27

SERAPHINA

I am alone, out in the City of New York, sitting at a coffee shop. My table is near the window, and I love the views of people rushing past, going about their lives.

I think about my father's life. His miserable house in that beaten-down part of town. The unpainted walls and empty gardens. The gray bricks and that sad expression on his face when he came outside.

I think about how he walked. Hunched over as though he were uncomfortable.

I slide my fingers over the photograph of him in my hand. In this picture, he looks vibrant and happy, full of life and with endless possibilities for his future.

My mother took this photograph. I found it tucked into the pages of her journal. She loved it, caressed it. It must have brought feel fondness to her heart when she gazed at it. It used to fill me with sadness and love. Love that I thought was lost in death. But then I found out that he is still alive and now the photograph has a very different meaning for me.

It is an insult of sorts. All of those hours that I have spent looking at it and wishing for this man, the thought was taken from me. All of those hours were a mockery of my heart. He was alive this entire time. My whole life, I have been living without that truth.

Antonio is right. Death is too easy for him. Even though I can see that his life is miserable, maybe lonely, I want to make it worse. He doesn't even deserve the comfort of that falling apart home of his. He doesn't deserve the comfort of a warm meal in his stomach.

He should shiver, shaking and cold, hungry and in pain on a cold cement floor. That is what he deserves.

“Would you like another coffee?” the cheerful voice of the waiter pulls me from the darkness I was drifting in. I smile up at her, confused for a second.

“Oh, yes, thank you.” She smiles.

“Who is that in the photograph? You have been holding it for ages. It must be someone special to you?”

“It is someone important to me, yes. My father.”

“I lost my father when I was very young, too. He had cancer. It is never easy losing one of your parents.” She shares a sad smile, one that says to me *you and I are the same. We have had the same hurt in our lives.* I smile back. She is wrong, though. We are nothing the same, her and I. She can't faith the hurt I have had, because of this man.

"I'll get you that coffee," she says and picks up my empty mug, carrying it away.

"Sorry," I call her back. "Can you please make it a takeaway?"

"Of course."

It is still early. I am going to catch a taxi on his street. I think I want to watch him, see what his life is like. Follow him around, or maybe I can get a closer look at his home. I need information. I need to know if there is *anything* that he loves. Anything close to his heart. Anything that I can take away from him.

Perhaps I need to do this in slow increments of frustration. Mess with his head upset his days, little by little, driving him to wonder if his sanity was slipping.

Of maybe I will just do it all in one go. A devastating blow that rips his life from beneath his feet. Tears his world apart and leaves him gasping and pleading for death - which will not arrive.

I walk out of the cafe holding my takeaway coffee cup. I am filled with a strange sense of energy. A new focus, a new purpose. It is the most directed purpose that I have had since the beginning of all of this. Before, I did not know who to focus on, where to look, who was responsible. I only had ideas. Hints, suggestions and things that I needed to find more about. But now I have a singular hyper focus. And nothing is going to distract me from this.

I wave down one of the iconic yellow cabs and climb into the backseat, giving him the street name. I spent so much time wasted on hating the wrong people.

Perhaps they were involved? I don't know, but he is the one who dealt that devastating shot. It was his hand. His choice. His actions. And then afterward, he chose never to reach out to me. He didn't even try.

The driver stops a few houses from my father's and asks me if this is alright. I thank him and climb out of the car. I look around me. Before, I did not want to come here alone. I didn't want to risk the danger of this neighborhood. But now, I feel so driven toward my goals that none of that seems to matter.

I stroll up the street. Walking as though I belong here. There is a worn, splintered wooden bench under some trees on the pathway, so I sit down in it, crossing my legs, leaning back and watching his house.

His windows are open, and now and then, I see him moving past them. Working in what I imagine is the kitchen, then walking through to another room. After around two hours, he comes out of the house, dressed in shabby clothing that suggests he has lived in them for many years. He walks in the opposite direction from where I arrived. My eyes are locked on his.

A young kid comes riding past me on his bicycle, then skids to a stop and backs up.

"Hello," he says happily.

"Hello."

"Are you new here? I live just over there. My name is Tommy."

"Hi, Tommy. I am new around here. I live just around the corner on the next street. But I just moved in."

"Oh, my friend lives around the corner, and my other friend lives over there and then we also play in the park over there, and then sometimes we just ride our bikes all over the place."

"That sounds fun. Have you lived here long?"

He puffs out his chest, proudly answering. "I have. Everyone knows me."

"And do you know everyone?"

"I do. You ask me anything, and I know," he grins.

"What about the old man who lives in that house over there?" I point toward my father's house.

"Mr. Moretti?"

"Yes."

"Well, he is alright. For an old person. Do you know him?"

"I used to, long, long ago, before I can even remember."

"He's nice to us. Sometimes, he makes us sandwiches if our moms and dads are working late."

"That sounds nice. Does he live with anyone?"

"No, he lives alone. And I never see him have visitors, either. He seems boring."

"What does he do all day?"

"Nothing. Sometimes, he just sits in front of his house on a chair."

I nod. "It was nice to meet you, Tommy. Maybe I will see you again."

"Well, if you are going to live around here, you are going to see a lot more of me. I ride around here all the time," he laughs, then rides off, waving as though we were best friends.

My phone rings, Antonio's name bright across the screen. I forgot he asked me to let him know what I would do today. I haven't spoken to him since we left the hotel early this morning, and it's already early evening. I glance up and down the street, then slide the green button to answer the call.

"Hello, little bird. Why am I sitting alone at the hotel when I could have you by my side?"

"Are you back already? Did you have a good day?"

"It was good. I got things done. Where are you?"

"I am just about to head back now."

"Must I come and fetch you?"

"I don't want to bother you with that. I will find a taxi."

I haven't seen a single taxi driving past here since I arrived, and it is getting closer to sunset.

"No, I am coming to fetch you. Just send me your location."

I bite my bottom lip. At first, I am reluctant to tell him where I am, but then I realize he knows what I want to do. He knows my plans; it should be no surprise to him I am here.

And I don't want to hide any part of myself from him, anyway. If our relationship is real, then he should know all of me.

"Alright, I will send you the location now."

"I am already in the elevator."

I smile.

After we hang up, I message him the pin to my location. He sends me a thumbs up, nothing else. That is good. I slide my phone back into my small backpack and feel grateful that he phoned. I would never have asked him for a lift, and I think I might have been stuck in this neighborhood after dark, not knowing how to get a taxi from here. I guess I could have phoned for a cab. But this is easier.

Antonio's car pulls up alongside the bench where I am sitting. It is far too flashy for a street like this. I see one or two people eyeing it as I stand up and climb inside. Then they turn away, minding their own business. I imagine in this neighborhood, many people turn away from things they witness and mind their own business.

Back at the hotel, I was still thinking about my father and what Tommy had told me about him. His life sounds bland and lonely. Antonio places the takeaway bags on the countertop.

"You are silent tonight?" he comments, pulling me close to hug me.

"Sorry, I am just thinking a lot."

"Well, let's get some plates. Do you want to eat on the balcony or at the table inside?"

"Outside. I like the views."

I go to the bedroom to kick off my shoes. When I come back out, he has already carried everything outside and set up our dinner. I slide into the chair next to him, and he grabs the leg of the chair to drag me closer to him.

I grin.

We eat in comfortable silence, looking out over the edge of the balcony.

After the food is finished, Antonio wraps his arm around me, and I lean against him as we watch the now dark sky.

"Where are you, little bird?"

"I'm here with you."

"But where are your thoughts?"

I shrug, snuggling my face against his chest.

He runs his fingers down my cheek, along my neck, and across my collarbone.

"You can talk about anything, you know. You don't have to keep it all inside."

"I know."

But I don't feel like talking right now. I don't even know what I would say. I am so focused on this one thing that I don't even feel like asking Antonio what he did today or where he went. I do care, but I also don't. I have my own things I need to do.

He gently kisses my forehead.

"Well, I am here. Alright? For anything you need."

That is something I deeply appreciate about him. He seems to sense whether to push me, to get me to talk, and when I just don't need to. He seems at peace with not knowing sometimes and letting me just be near him without taking my energy or demanding my attention.

He is perfect for me. And perfect for me.

Chapter 28

ANTONIO

I spend the evening with Seraphina, lying against my chest on the enormous sofa out on the balcony. We are both quiet, lost in our own thoughts. I like that about her. I don't always have to speak. I can think and be myself. Especially now, with reading the will come up tomorrow. I have so much to consider, so much to take in. Everything that is about to happen and my lack of knowledge about my father's last will and testament are occupying my mind. His last wishes.

We go to bed, wrapped up in each other, but quiet and distant.

In the morning, my stomach is tense. Knotted with the unknown.

I am pacing up and down Kalo's hotel room, waiting for him to finish getting ready. I arrived here earlier than I was supposed to, so he was not late. I just couldn't sleep anymore, and I couldn't wait in the penthouse. I didn't want Seraphina to notice how agitated I am.

"If we leave now, we are going to be much too early," Kalo calls from inside the room somewhere.

"I know. We can wait here longer or go get a coffee on the way."

"How are you feeling?" he asks, walking into the living room area.

"I don't know if I can answer that. I just want to be prepared for anything. I guess I just want to get this over with."

"I understand that. You will know where you stand once this is over. Then you can decide how to move forward."

He picks up his phone, sliding it into his pocket, then nods to let me know he is ready.

I glance around the hotel room. "Let's go get that coffee. I need some air."

We drive to the area close to where the lawyer's offices are and find a coffee shop there. On the outside, to anyone observing me, I appear together. Calm, alert, and ready for anything. On the inside, I feel an undercurrent of chaos. Knowledge is power, and I won't be able to make the right choices until I conclude this meeting.

"It's time," Kalo says, glancing at his wristwatch.

He gets up to settle the bill, and I wait on the street outside. Taking a few slow, intentional breaths. We walk toward the tall building together, and inside, they point us to the correct floor.

We ride the elevator in silence. In the lawyer's reception area, they point us toward the glass boardroom. Inside, I see my family.

They glare at me as I push the door open.

“Who the fuck is this?” my uncle snaps, glaring at Kalo.

“This is a close friend and business partner,” I say.

“He can’t be in here. None of us brought someone to hold our hand. Get him out.”

I glance back at Kalo with no expression on my face. He nods and steps back out of the room. He takes a seat in the waiting area, with his eyes on the boardroom. On me.

I take the seat that has been reserved for me near to where the lawyer is going to sit.

The room is full of hushed whispers. There are nine people seated and waiting. Thanks to Kalo, I now know not only their names but their relationships with each other and with my father. Who does business with whom, who interacts and who avoids each other?

I nod toward my cousin, who, despite our previous interactions, which were not pleasant, to say the least, I am now aware, hates his father. He was closer to my father and fed him information under the table about my uncle. My cousin Philip nods back at me.

Blake Maritzio enters the boardroom with high energy and a broad, professional smile.

“Welcome, everyone. I am glad we could all be here. I won’t take up a lot of your time; we can get straight into it unless anyone has something they want to say first?”

“Just get on with it,” Lucas snaps. My uncle is a man of many manners.

Blake sits down, opening a leather folder in front of him. He turns his attention to me.

“Antonio, the covering letter is addressed to you, but I am going to read it out loud for everyone to hear.”

To my only son,

I wish I could have known you.

In my death, I hope you can learn about who I am by living in my life in a small way.

I trust you will find my last wishes for your satisfaction.

Your father, Massimo.

Blake slides a sealed envelope across the table toward me. "This one, he requested you read in private, in your own time."

I pick up the envelope and slip it into the inside pocket of my suit jacket.

A murmur of comments runs around the table.

My uncle's eyes are boring into me, so are my other cousins and family members. Lucas is sitting. When his father does glance at him, he sneers as though to support his father's sour expression.

"Alright, the will is now going to be read. If everyone can, please remain silent until the end. All and any comments are welcome at the end, but please understand that they will be final and can't be contended."

We sit in tense silence as Blake flips through the pages and then reads.

First, he lists assets. Vehicles, houses, holiday houses, art, jewelry, furniture, bank accounts, investment accounts — the list goes on and on. My father did very well for himself in his life.

Then he moves on to list business assets, cars, and everything linked to businesses in my father's name.

Around the table, eyes are growing wider and wider. Perhaps they did not know the extent of his wealth. Perhaps he was a secretive man.

The tension increases when Blake turns to the last page and reads the line that everyone has been waiting for.

"I leave all the above to my son, my one and only son."

I don't move a muscle.

Lucas leaps from his chair and slams his fists onto the table. I hear shouting, and chaos erupts in the boardroom. I close my eyes for a moment to block it all out. When I open them, my eyes meet Kalo's. Blake is standing, begging for everyone to take their seats again.

"How the fuck do we even know he is who he says he is? He crawled out of the dirt, arrived in New York, and wants to believe he was the son of the great Massimo Rossi? His name is not even on the will. It just says *my son.*"

"Lucas, please, take your seat. We can address your concerns in a civilized manner."

"I won't sit. Fuck civilized. I want blood tests. I want proof. I need evidence," he fumes, sitting down anyway.

"Yes, we want blood tests." A few of the people around the table shout. "We do not know who this person is."

I can see the level of patience and control the lawyer is displaying. I suppose he deals with this sort of thing all the time. His eyes are on me. "Antonio, we were prepared to face this exact request because you have been out of the picture for so long. We have your father's DNA records, and if you would allow us to take blood, we can do it right now. We have a nurse available."

I don't know if I am supposed to be offended by my uncle's request for proof, but I'm not. I can't be bothered less. I know who I am. I have nothing to hide. If this shuts him the hell up, then so be it.

"I have no problem with that."

Lucas stands again. "I want to witness the blood being taken. No fucking around here."

Blake looks at me, and I nod.

He sighs, standing up and waving his hand toward the receptionist through the glass walls of the boardroom. She nods, stands up and comes to the door.

"Please have the nurse come in here," Blake says, and she nods once to confirm, then disappears.

I sit in my seat with my shirt rolled up over my biceps. The nurse dabs alcohol over my arm, then presses a needle into my vein. She takes a full vial of blood, smiling at me. Her eyes darting over my body before her cheeks flush pink.

I think of Seraphina and how her lips swell when I kiss her.

"Once the blood results are in, the requests in the will be completed, and no additional proof of evidence will be required," Blake says from where he is seated. "How long will the results take?"

"I can have them before the close of business today, sir," the nurse confirms, packing her things.

"Good. Did everyone hear that?"

Comments shift back and forth across the table, agitated chatted. They are not happy with the will. Perhaps they thought they would get something. A small piece of something. Perhaps my uncle thought he would get it all.

"Does anyone else have anything else they would like to say while we are all here?"

Blake glances around the table. "Nothing? Alright. I will be in touch with each of you once the test results come in. Thank you for your time."

My uncle is the first to storm out of the office, grabbing his son's arm and pushing him through the door. Philip walks along with him, nodding as his father spews out his distaste for what he has just heard.

I wait for everyone to filter away, ignoring the glances filled with hate and anger.

When I step out into the waiting area, Kalo stands. He stays silent until we are inside the elevator, alone.

"From the outside, that looked rather exciting. Did they take your blood?"

"Yes, proof that I am who I say I am."

"So, I assume you got a sizable piece of whatever your father left behind?"

"I got everything. Everything."

That evening, Seraphina and I are relaxing at the hotel when I get the call to confirm that I am who I say I am. My blood tests confirm I am my father's son, and everyone who attended the meeting is being notified.

Not even fifteen minutes later, the first threat arrives from a hidden number.

Then another, and another.

They want me to return to Hong Kong along with Kalo. He will die. He will be skinned alive. The threats are all pretty standard, and all want the same outcome. For me to turn down everything that my father has given me and go back to where I came from. Except, they have forgotten one thing. I am *from* New York. This is where I was created and where I belong.

I grind my jaw, annoyed at their assumption that I will just let this bullshit slide. Do they think I am so weak-minded that these words, these threats, will drive me off?

I think it is time for me to make an example of someone. It is time for me to show them just how much like my father I am.

I have decided that I will take my father's position.

I will take what is mine.

I glance at Seraphina, sitting on her phone. She needs to know who I am. I don't need to tell her about being heir to the mafia family, not until that is concluded within my family. But she needs to know about me, the truth, to prepare for when I tell her that. No more hiding and holding back. I want her in my life.

"Little bird, I think it is time I told you some things about me."

Chapter 29

Seraphina

Antonio is out with Kalo, and I am alone at the hotel. Last night, he told me why he was in New York. He told me that his father left him a lot. That is why he came to New York to claim his inheritance. Why would that be such a secret?

It was a lot to take in, but none of it bothered me. He told me he was scared it would push me away from him or overwhelm me. He reassured me he wants to be with me, that his feelings for me are real.

I listened to him and felt a little detached from it all. I am happy that he felt he could share it with me. I also wondered why he did not tell me sooner. He was keeping his own secrets while I was keeping mine. When I opened up about my secrets, he continued to keep his.

I wonder if he told me everything.

Is he perhaps hiding more?

He told me that his father left him a lot. That is why he came to New York to claim his inheritance. Why would that be such a secret? He mentioned some issues with his family that he was sorting out, but again, nothing so dramatic that it needed to be a secret.

The thing is, it might have upset me to know he felt he couldn't tell me in the beginning, but I am so lost in my own worries and my own tasks I can't process everything all at once.

I guess I took what he told me and stored it away in the back of my mind to look at later. The only thing that was important in all of it was that he wants to be with me still.

I want to be with him, too, but I can't focus on that either right now.

I am struggling more and more than the days go by, knowing that my father was alive all this time.

I have given in and phoned my grandfather and ask him if he knew.

Was he also kept in the dark? I imagine he would have been to keep it from everyone makes sense.

"Seraphina, my angel. How are you doing in New York?" My Gung Gung's voice is instantly reassuring to me. It feels like a safe space and reminds me of home.

"Ah gung, are you keeping well? Are you looking after yourself? I worry about you."

"Oh, stop that. I am perfectly capable of looking after myself. I got this far in life, didn't I?" he chuckles. "Tell me about New York."

"Ah gung, I found out something." I hesitate. "I saw my father. He is alive. I saw him with my own eyes."

There is heavy silence on the other end of the line. I hear my Gung Gung take a deep breath. What is he thinking about? Is this a shock to him? Is it as much of a shock as it was to me?

"Ah gung? Are you there?"

"I am here, Seraphina."

"My father is alive," I say again, then wait for his response.

"Are you alright?" he asks, and it tells me nothing.

"Did you know?" I hold my breath.

After a moment passes, he says, "I knew."

My heart is gripped by cold talons. They pierce into it, and the pain sears through me like acid.

"You knew?" my voice is shaking. Tears are running down my face.

"I knew. I couldn't tell you."

"Why not?" I am filled with anger and confusion. "Why did you keep this from me? Do you know what this has done to me? That is a secret you had no right to hide from me."

"I am so sorry, angel. I just could not tell you."

"But why? I need to know why. What else do you know about him you can tell me? I need to know everything. I have to. Please."

"I am sorry. I can't speak about this."

"Gung Gung," I shout into the phone, knowing the disrespect of losing my temper but unable to hold back.

"Please know that I am sorry."

I hang up the phone. I am in complete shock; my entire world falling apart more and more. Everything that I knew, everyone that I know, is in question.

My phone rings again. It is him. I don't want to speak to him. I decline the call.

He phones again, and I decline again.

Ah gung, of all people, knew the truth about the anguish I experienced every single day of my life caused by the loss of my parents. He knew I was focusing my hatred and need for revenge on the wrong people; he knew everything yet kept it from me. Why? Why would he do that to me?

What else don't I know?

My phone rings. He is not giving up.

I have nothing to say to him. He told me he could not answer my questions.

I have so many questions now. More questions than answers. I feel betrayed to my core, and, I don't feel like he is home to me anymore. I don't feel as though I belong with a family who keeps secrets like that from me.

Where do I belong, then? Nowhere? Anywhere?

The hotel room feels small and suffocating. I need to get out of here.

I stare at my phone, watching it flash as it rings again.

I slide it away from me so that I can't see his name on my screen.

I need to get out of here, and I need to leave the damned phone behind. I need to leave my Gung Gung behind and think to figure out what all of this means.

I scratch around in the drawers and find a piece of paper and a pen. I scribble across it.

I have gone for a walk. I won't be long.

See you a bit later.

XOXO

I leave it on the kitchen counter for Antonio to find later when he gets home.

Antonio also kept secrets from me.

My father, Ah gung, Antonio. Am I not worth the truth?

I push open the hotel door and make my way down to the street below. I walk, going nowhere. I just need to go somewhere. Anywhere.

I wish my mother was here right now. I wish she could wrap her arms around me and tell me that everything is going to be alright.

How can I be so alone in all of this?

I wonder if my Gung Gung always knew or if it was something that he found out later on. If he always knew, then why would he need to hide that from me? Does anyone else know? Am I the only one who was kept in the dark? Was he involved in the decision not to tell me? I can’t handle these questions rushing through me. I can't handle the chaos of it. The unknown aspects of my *life.*

I feel as though I might never go home now. What is there for me? Nothing, no one who cares enough about me, to be honest. I think about all the times I confided in him when I was feeling scared, hurt, or broken. He listened and gave advice. He tries to guide me, all the while knowing something so massive that it could have changed the entire course of my life.

I wave down a yellow cab. I know where I want to go. I want to speak to the one person who I can trust. My mother. I need to get to the water.

The beach is near to me, and it is the only place where I will clear my mind and speak to my mother.

The taxi driver drops me off on a sandy shoreline. I climb out of the car and pull my shoes off right away. Stepping onto the sand, it soothes the soles of my feet.

I walk along the edge of the water, contemplating everything that has happened in my life. The waves reach out to me, splashing against my feet, cool on my skin.

When I find the right spot, I drop my shoes into the sand and sit beside them, staring out across the massive stretch of blue water, churning and moving with the tides and the wind.

I squint against the sun reflecting off the surface.

"Mom?"

"I need you."

Tears fall on my cheeks again. Tears of anger and hurt. *Please, mom, I need you.*

I push my thoughts out into the water. I release them from my mind toward her so that she can send something back to me. Reassurance? Comfort? Anything to let me know I am not alone.

Hours go by, and the sun sinks low against the edge of the ocean. Still, I don't get up. The sky grows darker and darker, and behind me, the lights of buildings shine. In front of me, the stars are flickering in the sky. Still, I do not move.

I am waiting for her reply.

When it comes, I will know what to do?

A drunk couple sways passed me, giggling and laughing, pushing each other and being playful. I watch them for a moment, then turn my eyes back to the midnight black water.

My mother has nothing to say to me today. Maybe her silence is her answer.

Is she telling me I am strong enough?

Am I strong enough to do this on my own?

I don't want to. I want her to be here with me.

I stand up, dusting the sand off my legs. I am strong enough. I have always been strong enough and I have always done everything on my own, anyway.

It is time for me to take action, and to find my own resolutions to whatever is going on.

I walk off the beach and wave down another yellow cab. I should get back to the hotel. Antonio will probably worry about where I am.

Chapter 30

Antonio

I walk into the hotel after a long morning of going through my father's assets with Kalo. I must decide which assets I want to keep and which ones will be auctioned off. The family will be allowed first viewing of the auction items, to give them a chance to make their own offer on any pieces they want.

There are some pieces that I know are investments and some that, in my father's personal letter to me, he insisted I don't sell. I guess I'll find out why when I have time to go to his mansion and look at everything for myself.

"Little bird?" I call into the space, feeling that she is not here. It's too quiet.

I check the rooms anyway, just to make sure, then come across her note on the kitchen counter, next to her phone.

Why in the world would she leave her phone behind? I press the button on the side, but it's locked. Glancing at my watch, I see it's still early; she might have just left.

With all the threats I have been getting, I don't like the idea of her being out there alone with no way of me being able to contact her. She has not been in a good place, and last night; I told her almost everything about me. Everything except for me being heir to the mafia legacy. I'm supposed to take my position as the mafia boss of New York. That was the only thing I left out. I want to tell her, but only once it's official.

She hardly spoke. I have no idea how she feels about everything I said.

What if she left because of that?

I try to push the worry from my mind, telling myself she just needed some time alone.

I make a coffee and sip it, wondering where she could have gone.

Finally, I can't take it anymore, and I have to look for her.

With everything going on, there are too many factors at risk here. I spoke to Kalo about the threats I had received; he told me his Japanese friend is going to be staying closer to me now, and of course, he is here as well.

I should call him and ask him to look for Seraphina as well.

I dial his number on the way down to the hotel lobby, but he doesn't answer. I dial again, no answer. Perhaps he is in the shower.

I message him.

Me: Seraphina is not at the hotel; she left her phone behind, and I'ma bit concerned, considering everything going on. I'm going out to look for her. Please do the same. Let me know when you get this message.

I slip my phone into my back pocket, stepping into the underground parking area where my rented car is parked.

I don't even know where to start. Did she leave on foot or in a taxi? Where would she have gone? Surely not to her father's place. She would not do something risky without first letting me know, would she?

I drive up and down the streets, staring into coffee shops, going around in circles, trying to imagine where she might be. I drive for two hours, feeling useless and frustrated.

Then I park the car and climb out to walk the main street on foot. I'm getting more and more worried as time goes by. I keep phoning Kalo, and he is not answering. He has not even read my text.

What the fuck is going on? Where are they?

My stomach aches, twisting with nerves, and I realize I have not eaten all day. Perhaps that's why I'mso jittery and uncomfortable. I need to take a moment and recoup my thoughts.

I step into the first cafe I find, not caring much about what type of food they have.

I order a bagel and a drink, then watch, hoping to see Seraphina walking on the streets outside.

I feel alone right now, staring down at my food. One plate. One seat at the table. I glance around me, half expecting to see her smile or hear her laugh.

I have spent much of my life alone, but since I met Seraphina, I don't want to be alone anymore. I was fine with it then. But not now.

Wherever she is, she should be here with me. Where she belongs, by my side.

The longer I sit here alone, the more intensely I feel about this. The love that I have for her is very real, and I'll do anything to keep it.

I'll kill anyone who tries to take her away from me. Without hesitation.

I push the plate of half-eaten food away. I can't just sit here and not know where she is.

I try calling Kalo again, and this time it goes straight to voicemail. It's getting late in the afternoon, and none of this is making me feel at ease. I have to get back out of there.

The one place that keeps bothering me is her father's house. I hope she has not gone there alone again, especially so late now. It's not a safe area.

I head back out onto the street. I make a trip down to his street. Even though I don't want her to be there, I do hope I find her sitting on that bench. At least then, I'll know where she is and what she has been doing.

It takes me an hour in the evening traffic, which for some reason is much thicker than usual, testing the limits of my patience. But Seraphina is not there. I wait in the street for a little while, watching her father through the window of his home, He appears to me completely alone and at ease.

She is not here.

Frustrated and getting angry, I turn my car around to head back to the hotel. By this time, it's dark, and the thought of her being anywhere alone is getting troublesome.

What if my New York family saw me with her and took her?

Would they be so stupid? Could they possibly be so stupid that they would take action against me that will ensure their death?

I'll tear them apart from the inside out. Every single one of them will experience pain beyond what they can comprehend.

I grip the steering wheel so that my knuckles turn white.

I keep checking my phone, expecting Seraphina or Kalo to call me. If she was back at the hotel, back with her phone, I imagine that the first thing she would do was message me or phone me to find out where I am.

My phone is quiet this evening.

I park the car back in the underground parking, my stomach knotted worse than before. I jog up the short flight of stairs to the elevator, climb inside, and wait impatiently for it to climb to the top floor.

I push open the door with a loud thump and rush inside.

Seraphina jumps in fright, spinning around to face me.

"Little bird." I rush over to her, pulling her into my arms and holding her so tightly that I hear her breath catch.

"Antonio." She pushes against me. "I can't breathe."

"Where were you? What happened?"

She pushes against my chest again, and I lower her to the ground, releasing her from my arms.

"Nothing happened. I just needed space, that's all."

She wanders toward the kitchen, where she is making tea. I follow her, unsure about what is going on and why she pushed me away.

I feel as though she is moving away from me, not wanting me near her. Perhaps she has decided that she doesn't want to be with me anymore.

I stand quietly, giving her the space to speak to me while she makes her tea. But she says nothing.

She finishes and carries the cup past me to the bedroom.

"I'm going to bed," she says when she sees me following her.

"Little bird, what is going on? Is it something I have done or said?"

"You? Um, no, Antonio, it's not you."

"Is it us? Do you still want this? Please, talk to me. I was so worried today."

I don't want to lose her. I love her.

She places her tea on the bedside table and sits down on the bed.

Her eyes look tired. The dark rings beneath them tell me she has not had a good day at all.

I sit down next to her, wanting to wrap my arms around her and comfort her, but unsure about whether she wants that from me.

“Seraphina, what is bothering you? I know sometimes you need your space to think, but I can’t handle this. I need to know what is going on.”

Am I losing you?

“it isn’t you, Antonio. it isn't us. I still want to be with you. My feelings for you are still the same. I'm just overwhelmed. I still can’t believe my father is alive. I don’t understand it. I'm trying to process how everything I have ever known is not real. I lived my whole life knowing things, only to find out it's not how it's.”

She sighs heavily, pressing her fingers against her eyes to try to ease them.

“I imagine that must be very difficult for you,” I say, wrapping my arm around her, relieved that she still wants this. She still wants us. “Is there anything I can do?”

She leans into me, shrugging slightly, as though she doesn’t know if there is anything anyone can do at this point.

“I'm really struggling with the pain of knowing that he was alive all of this time, and he never once tried to find me or contact me. Does he hate me that much?”

She cries, and I press her head against my chest, letting my shirt soak up her tears.

“Ah gung knew. He knew my father was alive. He never told me. Why do people hide things like this from me? Don't I deserve the truth?”

My heart pangs with guilt. I need to tell her I'mthe heir. Now is not the time, but I don't want her to have the same thoughts about me. I thought she did not deserve to know the truth. I want to tell her. I have to.

I stroke her hair and kiss the top of her head.

"I'm here for you, beautiful girl. I'll always be here for you."

We lay down on the bed together, my arms wrapped safely around her.

After a while, her breathing becomes even and slow. I know she has fallen asleep.

I carefully slip my arm out from beneath her and lift myself off the bed without disturbing her. I want to go down to Kalo's hotel room. I have still not heard from him, and it's becoming a problem.

I'm silent when I leave the room and even quieter when I close the penthouse suite door behind me. She needs to rest. I'm only going to be a moment. I just need to see that he is ok.

The elevator beeps when it arrives on his floor, and the doors slide open. I walk down the wide passage until I see his room number, then knock lightly on the door.

I knock again.

And again.

I'm feeling sick to the stomach by the second.

I twist the door handle and push against the door, and it springs open.

Stepping inside, I half expect to see the place ransacked, but it isn't.

Nothing is out of place. Everything is neat, and there is no sign of foul play.

I look around to see if I can find his cell phone, but I can't.

His wallet is not here either. What is going on?

Did that idiot go out drinking and forget to charge his phone? It's entirely possible.

I gave him the afternoon off. I told him I didn't need him for anything.

I guess I'm going to wait until tomorrow when hopefully, he will come home, charge his phone and fucking respond to me.

I leave the door unlocked when I close it, just in case he has forgotten his keys inside.

"For fuck's sake, Kalo. You can be an idiot sometimes."

I make my way back upstairs into the penthouse, quietly sneaking back to the bedroom. Seraphina is still asleep. I strip out of my clothing and climb beneath the blankets with her.

I struggle to fall asleep, worried about where Kalo is. But I'm deeply grateful to have Seraphina in my arms. The woman I love.

Chapter 31

SERAPHINA

The sunshine of a new day bleeds through the open hotel curtains and onto my pillow. My eyes flutter open in lazy, slow motion, and a soft smile spreads across my lips when I feel Antonio has his arms wrapped around me. This is how I want to wake up every morning, wrapped up in his body, laying close against his chest, feeling his warmth and care.

I snuggle closer to him and close my eyes again, wanting to savor this moment.

I need to show him what he means to me. I am incredibly skilled at isolating myself and keeping others at arm's length, but with him, he deserves more of my attention and affection. I should open up and let him in. I should do something special for him.

Today, he said he met somewhere. Maybe I should follow him, and afterward, when the meeting is done, I can take him for lunch or somewhere nice. He would be surprised to leave the meeting and find me waiting for him. I think that would be nice.

He moans softly and pulls me closer, and my smile grows bigger.

"Good morning, my angel."

"Good morning, sexy." I roll over to face him and trail kisses over his warm skin, along his neck, and down across his collarbone. He grins, and the curve of his lips makes my heart flutter. He is so gorgeous. I could look at him all day and never tire of his face.

"What are you doing today, my love?" he asks without opening his eyes.

"I think I'll go for a walk, maybe find a cute little coffee shop somewhere. I just want to sort out, take a quiet day, and enjoy some peace."

"It sounds great. I have that meeting this morning, around ten. Then I'll be back."

He opens his eyes and looks at me, and my heart sings. His gaze is deep and intimate.

He leans down to kiss me and my body sparks to life at the touch of his lips.

"I had better go shower." He grumbles.

"I'll make coffee." I sit up, stretching, slow and lazy.

"You look so cute when you wake up and your hair is all wild like that."

"I know other ways to make my hair look all wild like this." I giggle.

"Mm. Don't tempt me. If I didn't have this meeting, I would lie in bed all day with you."

I toss the blankets off and slide my legs off the side of the bed, stretching again. I feel superb this morning. A little lighter, a little more like things will be ok. Antonio, taking the time to talk to me last night, helped me understand he wants to be here for me - and that I'm the one pushing him away and trying to struggle through everything alone. It isn't necessary. I have someone who wants to support me and help me. I have to appreciate that; I just didn't know how because I have never had someone this close to me in my life. But it was my choice, and I want to make different choices now.

I pad, barefoot, through to the kitchen. Antonio follows me and slips his arms around my waist, kissing the back of my neck.

"I'll be in the shower."

"Your coffee will be ready when you get out."

He disappears, and I miss his warmth already. I smile while I'm making the coffee. My heart bursting with happiness.

After coffee and a quick shower for myself, we are both dressed and ready to leave the hotel.

I slip my phone into my handbag. Antonio wraps his fingers around mine, and we catch the elevator down to the ground floor. On the street outside, he turns toward the left. The meeting spot is close to the hotel, so he is going to walk, and I pretend to turn toward the right, saying goodbye and telling him to have a good morning.

He kisses me, grins and tells me he will see me later.

I watch his perfect form walking away from me, then when I'm sure he is far enough along the road to not notice, I hurry after him, ducking low if he turns around, smiling like a naughty child, enjoying the fact that I'm going to surprise him.

I watch him going into a nearby restaurant, and sit down at a table with a group of men. They all look Italian. Some of them greet him in a friendly manner, and some look pissed. Maybe they are just not morning people. Maybe they are just asshole businessmen, who knows?

I sit in the coffee shop across the street and watch and wait, looking forward to when his meeting is over, and we can do something fun.

His meeting lasts an hour and I have a cup of coffee and a breakfast muffin while I wait.

When I see them standing up and ending the meeting, I get up too so that I can go out onto the street and wait for him.

I walk across the road toward him and stand just outside the coffee shop where they had their meeting, far enough away to not interfere with the end of his meeting and close enough for him to notice me if he looks around. I'm grinning, feeling silly and fun because of the surprise.

The men step outside onto the walkway; two of them march off in a huff, and another two stay behind to share a few more words with Antonio.

"Antonio, it will not be easy getting them to accept that you are the new heir to the mafia family here in New York. It's a big thing you are taking on. Are you sure you are ready for this?"

"I have been ready for this since the day I arrived in New York, Arton, and you would do well to not question me."

"I know, man, I'm just saying. Look, my father is very bitter about it all. He has always been a bitter man; ever since his brother was in charge, it got worse. Massimo was a good leader for our family. My father would never have been able to do what he did. I'm sure you are going to prove yourself well enough."

"Thanks. I appreciate that." Antonio holds out his hand, and a man around the same age as him shakes it.

My heart is hammering in my chest. The heir?

Is he the new mafia boss of New York City?

He has been hiding this from me the entire time. He told that man that he was ready for this from the moment he landed in New York. This is something he knew about; he came here for this. This was not just about reading his father's will - this was about inheriting a heritage, and becoming the new Mafia Boss.

My stomach knots. I feel the blood drain from my face.

Was he ever going to tell me?

Does that mean he is moving here? Was he intending to keep me around or toss me aside when he took up this new position as the heir?

The other man walks away from Antonio, leaving just one more person to say goodbye to. Antonio glances around himself, spotting me. He grins, but then his face falls dark.

My eyes narrow, and my brows knot together.

My father lied to me, my grandfather kept secrets from me, and now the man I love has done the same thing. Antonio has kept massive secrets, even after I have been so honest and open with him.

"Seraphina," he says, his voice strained. He knows I have heard everything.

"The new boss of New York?" I whisper.

He doesn't know what to say; he knows he has hurt me. It would be impossible not to see the pain etched across my face.

I glance down, trying to calm my thoughts. I look up again, and he is still staring at me.

The last man from the meeting is trying to say goodbye to him, but he is staring at me.

I can't be here anymore. I spin on my heels and bolt.

I run, at full speed, through the streets of New York. I duck around people, bump into them, and don't even bother to say I'm sorry. I run and run, not even knowing where I'm going. I just know that I have to be far away from all of this.

I don't look back, not even once. I don't want him to follow me. I need to be alone.

How can I trust him? How can I open up my heart to someone who has not done the same in return?

My body gave up on me, leaving me gasping for breath and completely worn out after my marathon-like run.

I walk around the streets of New York for another hour, but I know he'll look for me, and I don't want to be found. So when I spot a dodgy-looking motel with filthy walls and peeling paint and a broken sign that is only half lit up, I walk straight into it.

"I need a room, please."

"Hour rate or night rate."

Gross. "Night rate, please."

The clerk looks up at me, confused. "You want to stay over?"

"Yes, can you please hurry?"

"Sure, yes. Here is your room key. I'd be extra careful to make sure the door was locked at night. We don't have room service or anything, but I guess if you need something, just come down and talk to me or the other guy who will be on duty."

"Thanks."

After checking in, where they don't even ask my name or for any of my information, which is perfectly fine with me, I climb the stairs to my room.

It's dark and smells damp. I pull open the curtains and push the windows wide open. Daylight streams in, and the cool breeze carries away the stuffy smell.

At least the bedding smells clean, and the little bathroom off the side of the room smells like bleach. I sigh and slump down onto the bed.

I pull my phone out of my back and check it. There are seven missed calls, and as I switch it on, it rings again.

Antonio.

I press decline.

He phones again right away.

I press decline.

What would I say to him, anyway?

He just keeps phoning, though, and no matter how many times I decline, he calls right away again.

Finally, I give in and answer the call.

"Seraphina, please don't hang up, just listen, alright. Give me a chance to speak."

He sounds flustered and desperate.

"Speak, Antonio."

"I was going to tell you. Of course, I was going to tell you. I was just waiting for all the pieces to come together after the meetings and the legal stuff so that I knew what was what. I had to figure it all out, and then I was going to tell you. I swear. I was waiting for the right time. Please believe me. Seraphina, it was a lot for me to process, you know. I didn't even know what it all meant. I just had to sort it all out in my head, and then I was going to sit down with you and talk."

I don't know what to say. I hear his words, but words are words, and his actions really let me know who he is.

"Seraphina?"

"I'm so sorry, my angel. I'm really sorry I kept it from you."

Tears spring to my eyes at the softness of his voice. I can't process any of this.

I drop the phone from my ear, letting my hand rest in my lap. I can hear his voice still coming through. I slide my finger across the screen, dragging the red button to hang up.

Chapter 32

Antonio

Seraphina has been gone for two days. I have been looking for her, but not with my full effort, as I also feel as though she doesn't want to be found and I need to respect that.

I send her a message in the morning and a messaging in the evening to let her know I'm thinking about her and to tell her I'm sorry.

I think she just needs time. And I have to give it to her. If I push her, I might push her away, and I can't handle the thought of that happening.

The attorney met with me yesterday to hand me the keys to my father's mansion, along with a thick folder containing some documents, as well as letters from my father, addressed to me.

The housekeepers are still living there and taking care of the place, but everyone, well, those who are on my side, is telling me it's time to move in.

I think my moving into the mansion will solidify everything for the family. Things are up in the air for them as much as it's for me with this massive changeover.

Lucas has been sending messages here and there to let me know he is still not happy. He has been making it clear, even when he is trying to be subtle, that I'm not fit for the position.

Arton and two others are to support me.

So, I received the keys yesterday, and today, I want to head over and take a proper look around. I mentioned to Arton that I want my father's belongings moved to storage before I move in. However, he insisted I take the time to look through them first, in case there's anything that should remain in the house. I feel petty, but I believe a fresh start would be a good idea.

Even I like my father's taste in furniture and art, I need to establish my dominance in this family. And that mansion is a meeting ground, a backbone of family events, and a symbol of the person running everything. It needs to reflect on me.

Then, something else that is eating at me is that Kalo is still missing.

I have hired a private detective here in New York to look into it, but so far, the detective has found nothing. I need to act as though nothing is bothering me, but, It's eating me alive.

I pick up the keys to the mansion from the hotel kitchen counter. I slip my phone into my pocket and grab the keys to the car I have rented.

It's time to go to my father's home. My stomach flutters at the thought of it. I'm about to walk into his space. A space filled with his life, every corner representing who he was as a man.

The hallways he walked down with my mother. Their home.

If I hadn't been sent away, I would have grown up in that home.

My jaw muscles flex, and I take a deep breath. It's time to go.

Driving down the streets of New York, I spot a dark gray car tailing me. They are not even trying to be subtle about it. I turn random corners, and they follow. I pull my Glock out, placing it on my lap, ready for whatever is about to happen.

It could be anyone—my family, harboring bitterness and plotting to get rid of me; or, hell, it could even involve Seraphina.

The bottom line is that the best way to deal with whoever it's, and whatever they want, so to ask them.

So I pull the car into an alley, big enough to maneuver in and with an open end on the other side in case I need to make a getaway.

The gray car follows me in and parks a little behind me.

I pause a moment and then climb out of my car. I stand leaning against it, waiting. Inside, I'm alert, tense, and ready - but on the outside, I appear casual and calm.

A figure steps out, hooded, keeping their face low.

I notice they are petite, narrow-shouldered, and very feminine in the way they move.

My eyes narrow.

Then she looks up at me, pulling the hood off her head. She turns to look behind her for a moment, checking to see if anyone else is cornering her in. She braids her long dark hair in a silky plat down her back. Beneath her black coat, I see the outline of a small sword sitting along her spine.

She looks at me.

"Antonio."

Her features tell me who she is.

"You must be Kalo's friend," I say with a sigh of relief.

"Rei."

"Nice to meet you, Rei."

"Where is Kalo?" she asks, walking toward me.

"Actually, I was hoping you could tell me."

"You don't know?"

She pulls her mouth to the side in annoyance and thought.

"I have been looking for him for a few days. He is not answering his phone and has not been back to his room."

"Shit," she mutters.

"When last did you see him?"

"He hired me to tail you, not himself. I was not keeping much of an eye on him, but we were in touch over the phone."

"I see."

"Look, just take my number and give me yours. If you hear anything, please tell me."

We exchange numbers, and she turns to walk back to her car. "Wait, the girl I was with. Have you seen her?"

"Seraphina? No. Is she also missing?"

"Not missing in the same way Kalo is, but she seems to have taken some time to herself."

"Well, I think it's best to give her time to herself, if that is what she wants?"

I nod, and Rea walks away from me. Her poise and elegance tell me she is far more dangerous than she looks.

"Rei." She turns back again. "Would you be interested in working for me?"

"We can talk when you sort out all of your shit," she grins darkly. "In the meantime, I'm close by, even when you don't see me."

I chuckle and nod again. I never see her. That is why I want to hire her. She is excellent at what she does.

“See you around.”

“See you around.”

I climb back into my car and continue my journey toward my father’s mansion.

The place is massive. My father loved extravagance, and he was loud about his wealth and status.

I have been here for most of the day now, going through the rooms and learning about who my father was as a person. From what I can tell, he was a complicated man. However, something that stands out to me is his love for my mother.

There are pictures of them in almost every room. The look on his face in every single one of those pictures is one of love, obsession even, the way his eyes are always on her, and the smile on his face. He loved her. It must have been a terrible thing he went through when he lost her.

In his office, the top drawer, the one he must have used the most - are folders filled with documents, all detailing the private investigators he hired and his search for me.

He has been searching for over ten years. Holding the folder in my hand, I sit down in his office chair. A lump forms at the back of my throat. My father was determined to find me. The folder contained the last email, which I printed out and added, and it was dated only a few weeks before he passed away. Even nearing death, he never gave up.

My mother gave nothing away regarding where I was; she never betrayed my safety, and my father never gave up looking for me.

Both of them loved me.

I wish I had followed my gut instinct and come out here to meet him before he passed away. Just once. I wish I had sat with him, had a whiskey, a chat, a laugh.

It's too late for such wishes now.

I slide the folder back into his top drawer.

"Antonio?" Lucas calls from somewhere in the house.

Fuck. I'm not in the mood for him today.

"Lucas, in here," I call back, standing up and heading out of the office. I don't want him to snoop around my father's house, although I'm sure he has already searched through these rooms many times behind my back, looking for things that might not be noticed.

I step out into the hallway and spot Lucas. He walks toward me into the more private section of the house, but I walk toward the living room, getting him to follow me in that direction.

"Antonio, I wanted to see if you needed any help. Moving things or sorting things?"

"That is kind of you, but no. I don't need any help for the time being. When I'm ready, I'll let you know."

"I can also give you the rundown on how things work around here. I know how your father liked things to operate."

"Thank you, Lucas, but while I respect my father's methods, I have my own. I'll work with the family, but they are going to get used to my way of doing things."

"Your way? Do you think you can just walk in here and change age-old methods?" he snaps.

"Everything changes. Change is not a bad thing. Bringing modern aspects of processes will only boost business for the family."

"You fucking idiot. What do you know about the family or about our business?" His mask slipped this time. I stare at him, my face blank.

"Lucas, get the fuck out of my house!"

"Your house? You child. This house was mine long before it was yours. You are too weak to handle the responsibility that someone has thrown at you. You don't know what you are in for.

You are going to learn quickly who is really in charge here, just like your father had to learn." he spits the words in my face and my temper flares.

He sees my clenched fists and throws the first punch. It hits my eye, but I don't even flinch. He is an old man, and his strength is leaving him.

My fist swings too, for him to even realize what is happening.

A loud snap cracks through the air as it smashes against his nose, breaking it and sending blood flooding over his chin and down the front of his shirt.

He collapses to the floor in shock, and I stand over him, glaring down at him.

"You ever dare speak to me like or about my father like that again, and I'll break more than your nose."

It's time this arrogant man learned about his place. I don't take insults.

My uncle staggers to his feet, spitting blood onto the carpet. He sneers at me with blood-stained teeth. "You little shit." He grins, looking wild and manic. "I suggest you look in the wine cellar. Someone left a little welcome home gift for you there. And believe me, there is more where that came from. I suggest you leave, sooner rather than later, if you don't want to see how far this can go."

He spins on his heels and storms out of the house.

I wait until he is gone, then tell the security that I never want him in here again without my consent. If he ever visits, he is to wait outside until I let him in.

The security nods, confirming my instructions.

I turn to hurry toward the wine cellar to deal with whatever is down there.

My heart feels constricted.

I rush down the marble stairway into the temperature-controlled room.

It's dimly lit with rows of wine bottles along each wall. In the center, on a large oak table, is a small black box.

I reach out to pull it toward me, biting down as I lift the lid.

My insides churn with rage, shut my eyes and force myself to freeze.

When I open them again, I look into the box.

It's Kalo's finger. His ring was still around the severed edge. The silver dragon with emerald eyes was custom made for him, so there was no mistaking this.

I slam the lid back down, pushing the box away from me.

Then, after a few moments, with the world spinning and my head churning in murderous thoughts, I pull the box back toward me.

I open it and lift the severed finger out.

I slip the ring off, sliding it onto my finger.

Kalo will want this back, and I'm going to make sure he gets it back.

This is a warning. He is still alive; I know he is otherwise, it would have been his head I found inside a box.

Lucas is the one spearheading this attack. He has mistaken my quiet nature for weakness, and now he is going to learn just how wrong he has been about me.

Chapter 33

Seraphina

On the morning of the third day, I wake up in the same stuffy, horrible motel room and roll over in the otherwise empty bed. I'm overwhelmed with a heavy, desperate need to be wrapped in Antonio's arms.

I have been doing nothing but lay in bed for the past two days, staring out of the tiny dusty window and thinking about all the things Antonio has said to me, trying to piece together why he would lie to me and why he would keep things from me.

The thing that I can't deny or push aside is that I know he loves me. I don't have any doubt about that. Even though, at first, I wanted to accuse him of using me, disregarding me and having no respect for me, I just can't keep those thoughts solid. I know it's not true. He loves me.

So, whatever his reason for not telling me he was going to the new Mafia Boss of New York City, - It's not because he doesn't care for me.

The conclusion that I have come to this morning especially, is that I need him. I love him, and I want him in my life. And I want to be in his life, regardless of who he is and what his future holds.

I have never felt this close to someone before.

I have never had the chance to be connected with another person.

I roll over in bed and rub my eyes. I think it's time for me to check out. I can't let this fear and trauma hold me back anymore. I need to dive in - and take a chance, accept the risk - and with that risk, find amazing rewards waiting for my heart.

It's time for me to go back.

I sit up, stretching my legs out in front of me, my muscles aching from this horrible bed with a sunken mattress. I don’t know how I stayed here for so long. I guess I was not even aware of my own surroundings, so lost in my thoughts.

I toss the blanket aside and get up. Pulling my clothing on, piece by piece, collecting all of my things that are scattered across the small dressing table, and tossing them into my handbag - I'm packed and ready to leave.

Leaving the motel, the guy behind the front desk waves in a friendly manner. I don’t think he often has guests stay this long. I thank him for looking out for me while I was here; he was friendly enough and checked in on me once or twice.

Then I step out into the bright morning light and take a breath of fresh air. It's so good to be out of that stuffy room.

I walk down the main street toward what I think is the right direction, then stop, realizing that I have no idea where I'm.

I don’t even know how I ran when I left.

I pull out my phone and punch in the hotel's name on my map and it tells me I'm around fifteen minutes away if I catch a taxi.

I hurry toward the busy street I see in front of me and wave down a yellow cab. My stomach is filled with butterflies at the thought of seeing Antonio again. I want to stop running away from things, and although It's how I process them, I think I need to learn a different way of dealing with challenges, Especially if I have someone who is patient and willing to help me through all the doubt.

The cab seems to take the longest way around, and I get impatient. All I want to do is get there. I can't even know if he will be there, but I need to be there. Now.

I stare out the window at the traffic along the street. Sighing, I notice that this is not a fifteen-minute ride in morning peak hour traffic.

"I'm going to get out here, actually. Thank you."

"Wait, mam, you can't just -"

I pass money through to the front and ignore whatever protests he has. I can walk there faster, and this agitation that is building up over my impatience is making me anxious.

At least if I'm walking, I'm moving and getting rid of this nervous energy.

It's a beautiful day anyway, and the taxi took me over halfway, so it's not far.

I glance into the coffee shops and clothing stores as I walk past. If Antonio is going to be living here, would this be a place I'm happy to live as well?

It would. I like it in New York. I'll just need to figure out what to do for work, something more permanent than that horrible job I applied for before and something that I'll enjoy.

I follow the directions on my phone, and in no time at all, I'm on a street I recognize as being the one the hotel is on.

I slide my phone into my handbag and walk a little faster.

My heart skips a beat as I step into the hotel foyer.

"Good morning, Miss. Aoi," the receptionist greets me.

I grin. "Good morning. Is Mr. Aoi in at the moment?"

"Yes, mam, he is."

"Thank you." My heart flutters. He is here.

I hold myself back from running to the elevator. Once inside, I do a little happy wiggle, feeling so much excitement run through my body that I can't stand still.

I push open the penthouse room doors and step inside the hotel room, and Antonio rushes over to me with a massive smile on his face.

I'm grinning from ear to ear.

He lifts me into his arms and holds me against his broad chest. I wrap my arms around his neck and snuggle my face into him. He smells like home.

"You came back, my angel; you have no idea how much I have missed you."

"I missed you too, Antonio. I'm sorry, I just needed a little time."

He lowers me to my feet and looks into my eyes. I notice the bruise across his eyes. I reach out and touch it, and he pulls his face away. "What happened?" I ask, worried.

"It's nothing, Just a petty argument with an irate old man who doesn't seem to accept the new regime," he chuckles, seeming to be unbothered by it.

"Your family?"

"Yes, my family. They aren't all like that, though. I'm figuring out who is who and who is on my side."

"It looks pretty bad," I say, reaching up again and tracing my fingers over his eye.

“It’s just silly family drama, my angel. But that is how the world works. You can't choose your family, but you can choose who you fall in love with.”

He presses his lips into mine, and all of my worries fall quiet. My mind is silent, peaceful, and beautiful. He makes me feel this way. He makes me feel better just by being near me. I forgot about this calming sense of safety I have when I'm around him, and now that I'm wrapped in his arms again, it's all coming back to me.

“Antonio, you mean everything to me,” I whisper against his chest. Resting my head on his toned, muscular body.

“My love, you are my entire world. I love you more than you understand. I'm sorry that I kept those things from you. I'm so happy to have you back with me. I honestly love you. Please, next time you need space, let’s talk first. Let’s try to work it out."

“I understand, and yes, I agree. I thought about all of that. I want to change how I react to things. I know you give me the space to be myself, and I know you will listen to me if I have something I need to say.”

“Always,” he agrees, kissing me again.

I giggle as he lifts me into his arms.

I push away from him. Trying to wiggle free. “Wait, I need to take a shower. The place I was staying was not that great.”

“Where did you stay?”

“A motel on the other side of town.”

“Seraphina, never do that again. If you need space, I’ll book you into a hotel. A proper one. Not some motel. At least let me do that for you.”

“I won’t need space again.” I smile up at him.

I won’t. I want to be with him.

Chapter 34

Antonio

When Seraphina walked into the hotel room, my heart leaped into my throat, and I ran over to her, desperate to have her in my arms.

She was smiling and welcoming and did not seem to be angry with me anymore, but she also looked exhausted. When I looked into her eyes, I could see that she drained; there was pain in her eyes, but she was back.

I watch her walk away toward the bathroom and head into the kitchen to order her some food.

She takes a long time to shower, and the room services arrive before she finishes.

When she steps out, wrapped in a soft silk robe, her hair damp over her shoulders, I can't help but go straight to her again.

"You were gone too long, my love."

"I know. I missed you the entire time."

"I ordered some food for you. I didn't know what you want, so I ordered a bit of a selection."

She grins up at me, pulling the cord of her robe, letting the knot slip loose.

"it isn't food I want."

My heart thunders, my skin catches fire, and my cock stirs.

She tilts her shoulders back and lets the robe fall to the floor around her feet.

I take a deep breath and step back to admire her beautiful naked body.

She steps backward, her eyes locked on mine. A naughty smile touched her lips.

I pull my shirt off and unbuckle my belt. She steps back again. My cock presses hard against my pants. I snap the belt in my hands and she grins, then turns to run into the room.

Oh, I love a little chase.

I walk through to the bedroom with a hunter's stealth and find her sitting in the center of the bed, her legs crossed in front of her, her arms folded over her knees, looking coy and shy.

"My angel, the entire time you were gone, I was thinking about you."

She uncrosses her legs and moves them wider open, giving me the perfect view of her beautiful pink pussy.

I growl, pulling the button of my pants open. My cock is throbbing, desperate to be inside her.

I stand over the bed, naked, with my cock erect and ready. Her eyes are on it; she is biting her lower lip.

I lean forward, grab her ankle, and pull her lower down on the bed. She lands on her back, and I force her legs wide open.

Then she spots the knife in my hand. She did not notice me picking it up off the nightstand, but now her eyes are locked onto it. I have a devilish grin on my face. Her eyes flare wide.

Not in fear, but in lust.

I kneel on the bed, stalking closer to her. I grab her throat in my hands and stare into her eyes.

“You are mine, Seraphina.”

She nods, her eyes shining.

“Your pussy is mine. It will be no one else’s.”

She nods again. “Yes.”

“Yes, who?”

“Yes, sir.” She whispers. My cock pulses.

I push my legs between her and stare down at her body.

“The way your blood looked on my cock,”

I close my eyes, remembering it. The feeling of penetrating her virgin body. When I open my eyes, all I want is to see her blood on my skin again. To let her know, to remind her I am the only one who will ever fuck her.

I move the knife in front of her eyes and see the reflection of the light the blade throws across her smooth skin.

“Lift your hands, hold on to the headboard. If you let go, I will tie them there.”

She does as I have asked.

I press the blade between her breasts, and she gasps as the sharp edges cut her lightly.

The thin line of bright red blood that springs from her skin causes a deep, urgent excitement to rush through me.

My lips pull into a sneer. I run my other hand up the inside of her thigh until my fingers brush over her pussy. She is dripping. I slip my fingers inside her.

“That’s my good girl,” I say, husky and low.

She arches her back and rubs her pussy against my hand. The movement causes the knife to press harder into her skin, and more blood flows from her.

I pull it down across her stomach in a slow, deep movement. She cries out in pain and pleasure. I press my fingers deeper inside her.

When I lift the blade and drop it onto the bed beside her, the curve of her stomach is pooled with a fresh stream of blood.

I press my hand into it, spreading it across her skin, letting it seep between my fingers.

Bright red, significant of my ownership of her.

With my blood-covered hand, I grip my shaft and rub my hand up and down my cock. The blood spreads over me, and electricity pulses through me. I am rock hard, so hard I know I am going to hurt her if I push into her now. But she is so wet, and my need is becoming far too intense.

I pull my fingers out of her, dipping them into my mouth, savoring her taste.

She moans at feeling being empty, no longer feeling me inside her, so I press my blood-soaked cock against her, letting it slip over her pussy. She rocks up against me, so I push into her.

She cries out as I enter her, forcing her wide open, plunging my cock into her.

I grab her hips and thrust forward as the sensation rushes through me.

As I thrust in and out of her tight little pussy, I run my hand over her stomach again, painting her blood up, over her breasts, up her neck, and then cupping my hand over her face.

The red handprint across her jaw excites me.

She rocks her hips upward toward me as I thrust forward.

I grin.

Pushing harder, deeper, faster.

She lets go of one hand from the bedpost, reaching down to wrap her fingers around my wrist.

I growl a warning and clamp my fingers around her throat.

"Do as I told you, my angel."

She gasps as I tighten my grip. She reaches her hand up and holds onto the bedpost. I slam into her, jolting her body again and again.

I lean down and kiss her, pushing my tongue into her mouth, letting it slip between her lips the same way my cock is sliding in and out of her pussy.

Her body shakes, and I know she is close to coming.

I press my face against her hair, letting the smell of her fill me up as I bury my cock inside her.

"You belong to me," I snarl.

She gasps, and her body arches beneath me, shivering and tense as her orgasm rushes through her.

I push my hips against her, thrusting into her, letting my pleasure explode from my cock deep inside her.

We lay in bed for hours, talking, connecting, and sharing stories about ourselves. I love this girl. I can't picture my life without her. She has become my entire world. Everything about her is perfect for me.

"Seraphina, I got the keys to my father's mansion - well, my mansion now."

"Did you go there?"

"I did. It is a beautiful place. My uncle was furious about me inheriting it. Honestly, he is furious about the entire situation. He is the one who has been the biggest pain in my ass. But I will sort that out; no matter what I need to do to show him I am the one in charge, he will learn."

"Isn't it scary, inheriting all of this - being the heir - it is so much responsibility?"

I chuckle. "I have had none issues with taking on responsibility, my love. What I have to watch out for is those who don't want me around. It is not the safest situation at the moment, but I will establish myself, and then things will normalize."

"How? When?"

"Soon enough. I am going to move into the mansion in the next few weeks. I am just having some things changed in there. But what I wanted to ask you is - will you move in with me?"

"I want to be with you, but what about your family?"

"They will come around. I know they will not be happy with it, to begin with, but things need to change around here. Seraphina, if they don't accept you, and they are going to make our lives miserable, then I will leave all of this behind me, and we can go back to Hong Kong together. I want nothing in my life except for you. Anything else that exists for me is a bonus, an extra, an addition that falls beneath the single, most important thing for me - *you*."

"Antonio, you should not disregard your family . You should appreciate them. At least you still have a family. Do not run away from them."

"I will, for you, my love. I will do anything for you."

She grins and pulls herself closer to me. "I won't let you. I will help you rather, however I can, to make things work here. Yes, I want to move in with you, and yes, I want to be with you."

"That is all I need to know. The rest we will figure out as we go along. I will always take care of you, my angel."

I press my lips against her head, closing my eyes and letting this moment imprint in my memory.

I will always take care of her. Those words will never fade away.

Our conversation flows to different things. Things about life, the future we see for ourselves, places we want to travel to, and amusing arguments about what color we would paint our bedroom.

"You still haven't eaten," I say, pushing myself away from her.

"No, don't go." She complains, with her hand against the sheets where I was lying.

I glance over at the blood stains on the bed. "I am going to warm up that food I ordered ages ago. Go hop in the shower, and I will straighten out the room."

She sighs, rolling off the bed and heading toward the bathroom.

I neaten the room and throw fresh blankets over the bed. I imagine that housekeeping is going to be in for a bit of a surprise. I chuckle at the thought.

When she gets out of the shower, I climb in and tell her to get cozy in bed again.

After my own shower, I carry a tray of assorted sushi through to the bedroom, and we have an evening snack, lying naked on the bed, continuing our conversations until late into the night when neither of us can keep our eyes open anymore, and she falls asleep against my chest.

I wake up with my phone vibrating against the bedside table.

I pick it up and slide out of bed, and going into the living room, I answer the call.

"Yes?" I say, not sure who the unknown caller might be in the middle of the night.

"Ant, it's me," Kalo's voice comes through the line.

"Kalo? What the fuck. I have been looking for you. Where are you?"

"Ant, listen, it's bad." This is when I notice how weak he sounds, strained, scratchy, exhausted.

"Kalo, tell me where you are," I demand. Filled with rage.

"Ant, "There is a sudden sharp sound, and then another voice filters through the line. Clearer. Stronger. "If you don't leave, your friend dies. I want you out of New York within forty-eight hours, Antonio."

"Who the fuck is this?" I say with deadly calm.

"You heard me loud and clear, right? I won't say it again."

"You don't know it yet, but you are already dead."

"You have forty-eight hours."

The line goes dead.

I try to return the call, but the number beeps, telling me it can't connect.

I have so much anger pushing through my body at this moment at the thought of where Kalo is and what they have been doing to him. I grit my teeth until my jaw screams in pain.

Then, when I brought my temper down to a functional level, I message Rei.

> *Me: They have Kalo. I just got the call. Threatening his life if I don't leave. I don't know where he is, but I am going to find out.*

> *Rei: Send me the number they called from. I will see what I can do as well.*

> *Me: Focus on my uncle, Lucas. He is behind this. He doesn't seem like being the one who is the force of the operation. He wouldn't stand a chance against Kalo in that sense, but he was orchestrating it somehow.*

I message her the details. Then go back to the bedroom. My head is a war zone of thoughts, considering every angle and every option.

I need to figure out how to find my friend, and who is here in New York can help me.

Chapter 35

SERAPHINA

This morning, Antonio told me about the phone call he got last night about his friend Kalo.

I never got on with the guy, but that sounds terrible. He is distant and lost in thought. I have heard him on the phone, trying to figure things out, trying to find out where his friend is, and I am doing my best to be supportive but also to give him the space he needs to do whatever he needs to do.

It also shows me a glimpse of what his family is capable of. We both assume that it is his uncle behind it all. He told me that Lucas has been pretty blatant about letting him know he was involved,

While he is busy with that, I have been in my own thoughts.

I am sitting out on the hotel balcony, staring over the city views. Watching as far below, people move back and forth like ants. Insignificant, tiny, and even though their lives matter to themselves, from up here, I think about how if one of them was to disappear, the rest would just keep moving.

The thing is that Antonio's family issues have me thinking about my father.

I can't help but get lost in the idea of revenge again. I keep trying to push it away, wondering if it is worth it at all. My father's life looks miserable. He looks miserable. He seems to be so alone, and I know what torture that is.

Also, I have found love worth living for. That is where my focus should be.

But I have so many questions. There are so many things I need to know still, and I don't think I can have closure without the answers.

Even if I don't chase revenge, perhaps I can just ask him. A conversation, a rather intense one, but one that gives me the answers I need. In the biggest scheme of things, my father is nothing in my life. He is one of those ants hurrying around far below the balcony. His existence doesn't affect my life and the choices I can make from here on. But, knowing - knowing that I do not know. It is driving me crazy.

Antonio steps out onto the balcony.

He presses his hands over my shoulders and massages the tense muscles.

"My angel, you have been out here for hours."

"Did you find out anything about your friend?"

He sits down next to me. "I am working on it, but nothing concrete yet. Why are you sitting out here? What is on your mind? Something is bothering you; I can sense it."

I nod, letting a heavy sigh fall from my lungs.

"You are right. But I don't want to bother you with things right now. We can talk another time."

"No, my love, remember what I told you? Talk to me. I am here for you. It doesn't matter what else is going on in my life. You are the most important thing to me."

I stare at him, studying his expression. So sincere, so caring.

"Seraphina, if you don't talk to me, it will worry me. If you tell me, I might help - or at least be someone to vent to."

"Alright. But let me make you something to eat first. You have been pacing around all day, and I can't have you getting hungry."

He pulls me onto his lap with a warm smile on his lips. "Then you promise me you will tell me what is bothering you."

"Yes, I promise." I grin.

"Ok, then let's cook together. I am in the mood for pasta. Do we have cheese? I want to make a sauce."

"I saw some cheese in there, and mushrooms. There might even be bacon."

"Excellent." He stands up, lifting me in his arms, and carries me through to the kitchen.

It is such a relaxed atmosphere, as we both allow all our worries to drift away for the moment, and we just enjoy being near each other. I laugh as he throws grated cheese at me, trying to get it into my open mouth but getting it in my hair instead. When I try to throw a mushroom into his mouth, it just bounces off his chest. "You are too tall," I complain, having missed my target from a massive distance despite being only a meter away from him. I pick up another mushroom, and he steps forward, wrapping his mouth over my fingers and stealing it right from my hand.

"There, you have perfect aim." He chuckles.

"Oh, apparently, I don't need to aim for things. I can just stand here, and things will come to me."

"This thing is like a magnet to you." He grins, leaning down to kiss me.

I turn around to stir the cheese sauce and he glances over at me, taking the spoon from my hand, mixing it himself. "Hey, I thought I was in charge of this."

"Mm. But I am the expert with sauce."

"Is that so?"

"All sauces." He grins, running his hand over my stomach, across my pelvis, and between my legs.

"Hey, behave! They are hot here, and we don't want to get burned."

He steps away, laughing again. "The hottest thing in this kitchen is you, my love, and I handle you just fine."

When I turn back to look at him, his eyes are dark with mischief.

"One day, Antonio, I will be the one tying you up and doing whatever I want to your body."

He grins. "My beautiful baby girl. Hell will freeze over before that happens."

While we finish making the dinner, Antonio pours me a glass of white wine and reminds me again of how much he loves me.

I feel as though this is what my life would be like with him if I could only let go of this need for revenge against my father.

It is getting in the way and holding me back.

Antonio is so attuned to me he can tell that my thoughts have gone to other places.

"Come on, let's set the table and sit down to eat - and talk."

I nod, sliding off the kitchen counter where I was sitting. He sorts out the final bits while I collect plates and cutlery and place them on the dining table near the balcony.

Antonio dishes up food for both of us, and fills my wineglass, then comes to sit with me.

He eats, watching me but not pushing me. Just giving me the space to talk whenever I am ready.

After a few mouthfuls of food, which tastes amazing, I glance over at him and say. “It is my father, Antonio.”

“What about him? Has something happened?”

“No, nothing has happened. I just can’t stop thinking about what he did.”

“It is bothering you. That is natural. Why don’t you tell me what is on your mind?”

I sigh. “Well, I am kind of struggling with this internal battle. I want to let it go. I want to forget about him. I have you. I have found love. Nothing else should matter to me. But I can’t let go of the fact that I want answers from him. Why he did what he did? How he has lived with himself all these years. I want to confront him. I want to make him tell me. I want to know why he never contacted me. I can assume what he would say. I can assume things, but they are not satisfying my need to know the truth. I hate him. I am struggling so much to just let this go, like I know I need to.”

He places his fork on the plate and reaches out to take my hand from across the table.

“Seraphina, if you need answers, then you deserve those answers. Yes, you have found love, and your life is changing now, but closure is important.”

“But I don’t know how to get it. I don’t know what I should do.”

“You do whatever you need to do.”

I nod, staring down at his beautiful hands, his warm fingers stretched over mine.

“I want answers.” I nod, realizing that I need them.

“Whatever you need me to do, however, I can help you get those answers; just say it, and I will make sure it happens.”

"Let me think about it for a bit. Ok?"

"Of course. Talk to me when you know what you want to do."

Antonio moves his chair closer to mine and strokes his broad hand over my thigh. He smiles at me. "Do you like my cheese sauce?"

"*Our* cheese sauce," I correct him.

He laughs. "Fine. Ours."

"It is fantastic. And you were right; the paprika adds an excellent hint to it."

"Told you," he grins.

After dinner, Antonio runs a large bubble bath and pulls me toward the bathroom. He undressed me, stroking his hands over my body, then guides me into the warm water. He strips down and climbs in behind me, letting me rest my back against his chest. He runs his fingers through my hair, massaging my scalp, and while I lay against him with my eyes closed, savoring every moment I have with him, he whispers how much I mean to him.

I run my hands over his legs, where they are wrapped on either side of me.

"I have never felt this at home before, Antonio. With anyone, anywhere. And it's not the place; it's you. So wherever you go, I am going to follow you. Because you are my home."

"My beautiful girl, you are my world, and I will take you everywhere I go. These things that are bothering us now, that are stuck in our thoughts, we are going to sort them out together. And if anything else comes up, we sort that out together, too. The bottom line is that I am always going to be here for you, and I know I can always rely on you to be there for me. We are going to be an unstoppable force, you and I. And soon, we are going to be running New York."

I lean my head back and tilt it to the side so that I can kiss him. He wraps his hand underneath my chin and pulls my face toward his. Beneath the water, I feel his body respond to me, so I press my back harder against his groin, rubbing my body against his.

He runs his hands over my breasts and smiles against my mouth.

"It's you and me, forever," I whisper as he spins me over to face him and glides my body up onto his. We move against each other, letting the warm water rock back and forth over us.

Later, when we climb into bed, he pulls me right up against me and tells me I am the most beautiful thing in the world.

I fall asleep with a smile on my lips and warmth in my heart, feeling safe and loved.

He will help me get the answers I want. I don't have to worry about it; I just have to figure out what I need to do.

Wrapped in his arms, I fall asleep and sleep and, knowing that nothing in the world can touch me when he is with me.

Chapter 36

Antonio

At a coffee shop, sitting opposite Arton and one man who used to work on my father's security team, I explain to them what I want to do.

"Are you sure now is the right time to be worrying about this? Your friend is missing. Shouldn't that be your primary concern?" Arton asks, not challenging me but calling me to reassure him I have thought this through. I can respect that.

"She is the woman I love, and she is struggling without answers. I want to help her, and this is how I can do that."

"The man you are talking about kidnapping he has ties to the mafia. He has not been active for many years, but he is still a dangerous man with contacts."

"I am aware. That is why I will keep this private. I don't want the whole family knowing. Look, all we want to do is talk to him - away from his house, in an environment that I can control."

"I have a place you can use. And this is Diego. He is the muscle for things like this."

"Diego, can I trust you to keep this information a secret from the rest of the family?"

Diego sneers his lip, showing his distaste for what I want to do, but he nods. "Yes, boss. I will do as you ask."

"All you are doing is standing watch once the old man is secured. The girl will come in and talk to him. You are only to go in if she calls for your help. I don't know yet if she will want me there. It is a personal matter between her and the old man. I will be waiting in the car, though, nearby."

Diego nods again. "I understand. If I may share my opinion?"

"Go ahead."

"I don't think you should do this at all. The guy is a nobody. Honestly, I would prefer to not be involved in your plan, but you are the new boss, and I respect that."

"Thank you for your opinion. I appreciate you being honest with me, but this is happening."

He nods. "Understood, boss."

I eye Arton across the table. He nods as well. "Diego is a good man. I brought him along because we can trust him. He will do what we ask."

I sigh. I am fine with the guy sharing his opinion, but he better fucking do as he is told.

"Where can this happen? You said you have a location?"

"Yes, on the docks. We have a few containers there. I can have Diego bring the guy to one container, restrain him inside there, and your girl can have her talk with him. It is out of the way, in a quiet area, it won't raise any alarms. It is on our territory, sorry - your territory - and no one will bother you."

"Good. Set it up, plan it, tell me when it is happening."

"Also, your father had a personal driver and several cars. You can make use of him, obviously. I can give you his details. He will be happy to drive you around."

"I am fine for now. When I move into my father's property, I will make use of my driver. Right now, I am keeping it more low-key. Call me later; let me know."

"Will do." Arton stands up, Diego following his lead. "I'll get in touch later this evening and confirm everything."

"Thanks, Arton. It was good to see you."

I watch them walk away from the coffee shop. There is something about Diego that I don't like, but if Arton trusts him, I will take the risk of trusting him as well.

I check my phone.

I haven't heard from Rei in a while, but I know I don't need to follow up with her. She will contact me if she finds out anything at all. She has been tailing Lucas for the last few days, hoping he will lead her to wherever Kalo is being held. I have not had another call from his captors. My two days are already up, but nothing has come of it yet. I know time is getting tight for Kalo, and I need to find him soon.

Once I sort out this thing with Seraphina's father, I am going to confront Lucas, even if it means that he and I have to have a face-to-face talk in a private location.

He looks like a man who will bend under pressure and pain.

I have asked Rei to make a note of what his security team looks like so that we can plan around it.

I wave the waitress over so that I can get the check. I want to get back to the hotel and let Seraphina know what I am planning for her. I guess I should wait until I have a time and day before

I tell her. But that will still be today sometime, when Arton gets back to me.

The waitress eyes me up and down and grins as she slides the receipt over to me. I narrow my eyes at her; I know that look.

She winks and walks away. On the receipt is her phone number. I stand up, crumple it, and drop it on the table.

The waitress looks at me with her lip curled upwards, and her nose crinkled. She puts her hand on her hip and glares at me with heated eyes. She is not happy about this gesture at all.

Sorry honey, I only have eyes for one girl.

I walk out of the restaurant and climb into my car. Sure, a personal driver is a luxury I am used to, but until I know what is around here, I don't want anyone to know what hotel I am staying at, including a driver. So, for now, I am driving myself.

I head back to the hotel and park underground. Catching the elevator to the top floor, I feel excited to tell Seraphina what I have arranged for her.

She has been so lost in thought over this for a few days now, and she never came forward to tell me how I could help her, so I took matters into my own hands.

I don't know if it is some kind of guilt for still waiting to have the answers she needs, even though she should be happy now - with me - or what is holding her back, but the bottom line is that if she needs those answers, she will get them. Her needing that has nothing to do with our relationship. She can be happy with us and still want closure with her father.

I step out of the elevator and push the penthouse door open.

When I walk into the ~~hotel~~ room, Seraphina comes rushing over to me, jumps into my arms, and holds me.

"I missed you." She mumbles against my neck.

"I missed you too, beautiful girl. What have you been up to?"

She laughs, "Nothing, actually. Just watching cartoons. It's been a very chilled day here at the penthouse."

"Sounds perfect. Are you still watching?"

"Yep, I ordered some snacks for you as well and some sugary treats, and I am going to just lay on the couch all day."

"Am I invited?" I chuckle.

"I already made you a spot."

I walk into the room, kick off my shoes, toss my jacket and shirt over the chair, and climb out of my pants. I pull on a comfortable pair of sweatpants and a t-shirt and wander back through to the living room. Seraphina is at the door, letting in the room service attendant. The food smells amazing. I was getting hungry at the restaurant earlier, but I waited until I got back here - so that I could eat with Seraphina.

"Thanks so much," Seraphina says, letting the guy out again.

I browse over the selection of foods she has ordered for us. "Ribs, nice touch. Chicken wings. Prawns. Looks like you were in a carnivorous mood."

"I also got some veggies, but yes. Pretty much exactly right. Go sit down and relax. I will bring it throughout."

"Mm. My little hot in-house waitress." I slap her ass.

"You better leave me a good tip." She laughs.

"Just the tip?" I raise my eyebrow with a cheeky grin spread across my face. "I thought you preferred the whole thing?"

"Antonio," she says, with fake shock. Then runs her hand over my cock.

"Mm. Baby, be careful."

"Sorry, sometimes I can't help myself. Now go sit. Let me take care of you."

I sink into the sofa, lift my legs onto the coffee table, and take a deep breath. Damn, it is good to come home to such a beautiful woman with a smile, a laugh, and who wants to spend time with me? It is perfect; everything about this is perfect.

"What are you smiling about?" she asks, putting a big platter on the table, dishes up with a variety of the foods she ordered.

"Nothing," I say because words aren't enough to tell her how happy my heart feels about the idea of her.

"It doesn't look like nothing."

"Well, then everything. I am happy about everything." I lean forward, grab her around the waist, and pull her onto the couch, laying my boy over hers and kissing her.

When I stop to look into her eyes, her soft expression, I feel such peace in my heart that it almost takes my breath away.

"I really love you," I whisper, running my fingers over her cheek.

"I really love you," she replies, kissing me again.

"Now, get off me and let me get the cutlery," she laughs.

I roll off her, and she stands up. I grab one of the rib pieces. "Mm. These are damn good. Very good choice, my love."

"I am happy that you are happy."

She slides into the seat next to me, sitting sideways with one of her legs draped over my lap. She hands me a plate, a fork and a serviette.

"I chose cheesecake for dessert. Blueberry. It looks so good."

I grab the back of her head and kiss her again. She is too beautiful for me to keep my hands off.

"Mm. Those ribs are good," she says, licking her lips after our kiss.

She picks up her own rib and bites into it, grinning.

Halfway through our meal, with cartoons playing in the background, even though we are paying attention to the television, my phone rings.

I glance down at the screen, ready to decline the call. But then I see it is Arton.

"I am sorry, my love. This is an important call that I was waiting for."

"It's no problem. I will be here. The rest of the ribs might not be, though." She reaches over and takes my plate from me so that I can stand up. I shake my head, smiling as I answer the phone.

"Arton, what can you tell me?"

"Tomorrow, I recon around three o'clock. I will be in touch with you to let you know once we have him and we are on the way to the docks, but we can ballpark for three. Is that alright?"

"That is perfect, thanks. I will hear from you tomorrow, then."

"Yes, tomorrow. Have a good evening."

"You too."

I walk back into the living room.

"You have a meeting tomorrow?" she asks, wiping her hands on a serviette.

"Actually, my angel, you do."

She sits up straight and tilts her head to the side, curious. I have her full attention.

I sit down with her again and take her plate out of her hand, placing on next to mine on the table.

"My love, tomorrow, at three o'clock, you are going to talk to your father."

Her mouth drops open, and her eyes grow wide with shock.

"My father-"

"Yes, I have made all the arrangements."

"How? He won't want to talk to me. He will probably do everything in his power to avoid me like he has done my entire life."

"Trust me, he will be open to talking to you. I have made sure of it."

"Why did you do this for me? Don't you have other more important things to worry about right now?"

"Nothing is more important than you. I love you, and I will do anything for you."

Her eyes shine brightly with the threat of tears, but she blinks them away and leans forward to kiss me. "Thank you, Antonio. This means everything."

Chapter 37

Seraphina

"What do you mean, you don't want me to come with you at all? I was just going to wait in the car." Antonio says, looking upset.

"No, honestly, I appreciate everything you are doing for me - but this is something I *have* to do on my own." I shift from one foot to the other. I don't want him to think I'm ungrateful, but I need to have my strength. If he is there with me, I'll just lean into his strength.

He closes his eyes for a moment and then nods. When he opens them and looks at me, his features are softer. "I get it. I understand. But, Seraphina, you keep your phone on you at all times, and if I call, you answer. No exceptions."

"I will."

“I'll et Arton to drop you off at the location where you are meeting him. He is someone I trust. I don’t like this, though. I had planned to at least drive you there myself.”

“I was hoping I could just drive?” I pull my mouth tight, knowing that I'm pushing my luck a bit.

“You want to drive there alone?” He is shocked.

“Yes, Antonio. I can drive,” I laugh.

“Fuck me, you are really going to make me worry, aren’t you? Fine, here, take my keys. I'll message you the location so you can follow the maps. There will be a man waiting there for you; he is going to monitor you and will be if you need help.”

I take the keys from him, grateful that he is letting me do this.

“Fuck, I don’t like this.”

“I'll be alright.”

“I know. I know you will be fine. I just thought - anyway - it doesn’t matter. Go, they are ready for you.”

I stand on my tiptoes to kiss him, and he holds me for a moment. I can tell he is not happy about this at all. He is battling by allowing me independence and following me there.

“Antonio, I'll be fine. If anything at all happens, I'll call you right away.”

He nods. “Good.”

I leave the penthouse and rush down to the basement parking.

Punching the location onto the map, I see it's right on the docks. What a strange place to meet with my father. Anyway, it doesn’t matter where it happens. I just want to get there - and get this over with.

I'm nervous and excited, tense and eager. In fact, there are so many emotions rushing through me right now, I just feel overwhelmed.

I'm standing in front of a container right alongside the water. Behind this door, my father is waiting. My stomach knots and churns. I take a deep breath and push the metal door open.

My eyes take a moment to adjust to the light. It isn't dark; there is lighting overhead, but compared to the bright sunlight outside.

I stare at the man in the back of the container. He is tied to a chair, his head is hanging forward on his chest.

My heart hammers. He looks up at me with pain on his face.

He has been beaten, his lip is split and bleeding, his eye is swollen and blue, and he looks exhausted.

I was not expecting this.

For some reason, though, it doesn't bother me in the least.

"Marcus Moretti," I say his full name, and his eyes narrow toward me.

"Who are you?" his hoarse voice whispers. He clears his throat and asks again. "Who are you, girl? What am I doing here?"

I step toward him, picking up the chair that is against the side wall of the container and placing it in front of him. I sit down, staring at his face. My father's face.

I stare at him for a long time before I answer.

"My name is Seraphina."

His eyes grow wide in absolute shock. He gasps and leans back.

"Sera - Seraphina," he stammers, his eyes trying to take me all in.

"Yes, Seraphina. Your daughter."

"My daughter." My father's voice is churning with shame and guilt; his face falls, sullen and fearful of the fact that he has come face to face with the person he has avoided for almost twenty years.

He cries, heavy, chest-wrenching sobs that cause his body to shake.

I watch him with my head tilted to the side.

"Does it upset you? To meet me?"

"You do not know how long I have dreamed of seeing your face," He sobs.

"Is that so? Yet, you never reached out to me."

Despite my calm demeanor on the outside, I'm raging with anxiety on the inside. I have dreamed of coming face to face with the person who killed my mother for my entire life, never expecting it to be my father. Here I am, watching him sob. Seeing him in pain.

"Seraphina, my daughter. You are more beautiful than I could ever have imagined."

"Please, stop this bullshit. I don't want to see your tears. I have no pity for you. I know what you did."

He falls silent, puffing. "You know what I did?"

"And I hate you for it," I scream, unable to keep myself in control. I stand up and throw my chair across from the container. "I hate you! Do you hear me? Do you feel my words? I hate you with every piece of me."

His face pinched, silent, ashamed.

"Have you got nothing to say for yourself? Murderer. Killer. Don't you want to tell me you are innocent, beg me to believe you?" I'm shouting so loud my throat is hurting.

"Please," he murmurs.

"Please, what? What do you deserve, you sick, ugly, worthless human being? You deserve to live in pain, alone, hated by your own daughter. And I came here to tell you I hate you - to your face."

"Seraphina. I chose your name. An angel. That is what it means. Seraphim. My angel."

My angel. That is what Antonio calls me.

"Don't you dare call me that? I'm nothing to you. You made that clear in your actions and every day since you killed my mother. You have made it clear by not even bothering to know that I exist."

"I had to." He screams back at me, overcome with desperation. "I had to do it. You don't think it eats at my soul every single day. Every breath I take. You don't think I'm in agony just by existing. You don't think that every morning I wake up and cry because all I want is to die in my sleep, to end my existence? I had to do it. I loved her. She was everything to me. She was my world, my life, my person. The only person who ever existed to me."

I stare down at him. The intense emotion that has just flooded out of him has shocked me. I don't know what I expected, perhaps arrogance? Perhaps false remorse? But not this. Not this pain that is so clear in every word that he choked out now.

"You say you had to? But you say you love her. If someone told me I had to kill the person who I loved, I would never do it." I spit my words at him. Of course, I'm thinking about Antonio. I couldn't kill him. I would rather die myself.

"You don't understand, child."

"I'm not your child. And seeing as I don't understand, why don't you try to explain it to me, old man?"

I'm too agitated to sit down, but I can't pace anymore. I stand in front of him with my hands on my hips, my body so tense I feel like one sudden movement would tear me apart.

"Do it!" I scream. "Tell me how you can justify killing my mother. Your wife. Tell me how you can justify tearing her from my life like that and tossing me aside as though I was nothing to you."

He fights against himself for a moment, his eyes squeezed shut. I wait. I wait because I have waited my whole life for this, and now that I'm here, I don't know if I want the answer. No answer can ever bring her back. No answer can change what I went through. Nothing can justify what he did.

Tears are falling from my eyes, flooding over my cheeks. I don't even move to wipe them away. I can't. I can't move at all. All I can do is breathe and wait.

"I should never have brought her to New York. That is where I made my first mistake." He talks without looking at me, his gaze locked on the floor at my feet.

"We should have stayed with her family, but I wanted her to know me, to see my world. And she loved it here. She was so excited. You were born here, and we had a family. We were so happy. So happy." He swallows hard. I wait.

"My family, the mafia, they were angry. I was accused of marrying a spy. They hated her. They never accepted her. I tried so hard to get them to understand. Then I tried to make plans to leave, to take her back home, but I was too late. I realized how serious they were - too late."

"So you killed her," I say, with pain in my voice.

"They gave me a choice, Seraphina. And they meant it. I had seen them doing it to other people before. I just thought, seeing as I was in the organization, that it would not happen to me or to my family. They gave me a choice. Either - I had to kill my wife - or they would kill my wife *and my child.*" He is sobbing again.

"Seraphina, I did it because it was the only way to get you out of New York. They would have killed you both. How could I be so weak to watch them kill my child? I made the hardest choice I have and ever will have to make in my life. I took the life of my wife, the person who was my entire world, in order to save our child. And I know, believe me, I know - that if I had asked her, if I had had that chance to ask her - she would have told me to kill her."

I walk over to the container wall, where the chair is lying on its side. I pick it up and slump down onto it. My legs are shaking. I can no longer hold myself up.

"Seraphina, please, my daughter, please believe me."

I stare at him, silenced, shocked, processing, but unable to think.

"Say something, Seraphina. Tell me I'm a monster. I know I'm. I deserve it. But even now, I would make the same choice again. I would make that choice, and I would force myself to live in pain every day. Do you know why I have not killed myself?"

"Why?" I ask, my voice a mere whisper.

"Because I don't deserve that kind of relief. I deserve to feel this agonizing guilt."

I stare at his pain, the years of anguish that he has experienced etched in every wrinkle on his face.

"Why didn't you try to reach out to me?"

"I didn't deserve to."

A simple answer that tells me so much.

My father is dead inside. He hates himself more than I could ever hate him for what he did. And, honestly, I can't even hate him anymore. Did he even have a choice?

I sit for ages, staring at the wall opposite me, unable to look at him, my thoughts getting more and more distant.

After an unknown amount of time has passed, I stand up, picking up the knife from the table nearby, I walk over to him.

He lifts his head, revealing his neck as though asking me to kill him.

I step behind him and slice the ropes off his wrists.

I hand him the knife, and he stares at me in shock.

"Cut your feet free," I say, without emotion.

He does and then tosses the knife to the floor. He takes his time standing, his legs unsteady and shaking.

“Seraphina,” he says, but I'm already walking away. I need to get out of here.

I turn back, glancing over my shoulder at him. “You are free to go.”

“Seraphina.” He calls my name again, but I walk out of the container.

Outside, there is a man watching me. He stares at me with dark eyes, his arms folded across his chest, a look of hate across his face. I glare at him. I do not know who he is.

My father steps out of the container and stands next to me.

“Get in the car. I'll take you home.”

He follows me without a word.

He sits in the passenger seat in silence. The car is heavy with tension.

I pull up outside his house. The sky above us is dark and moody.

Before my father gets out, he turns to me and says, “Seraphina, you are my daughter; you have always been my daughter, and I have always loved you. I'm sorry. I'm so sorry.”

I nod, unable to speak, and my father gets out and limps toward his house.

Chapter 38

ANTONIO

When Seraphina walks into the penthouse, I knock her over, pulling her against me. Her body is tense, stiff, and unresponsive.

"My love?"

"I let him go."

"Alright."

I wait for her to tell me more, but she pushes away from me and walks toward the bathroom. She closes the door, and I hear the shower turn on. I pace up and down, needing to know if she is ok. She does not look ok.

I knock on the bathroom door. "My love, are you alright?"

"It's open," she says from inside.

I push against the door and step inside. She is drying herself off, and even though I know that now is not the time to appreciate how incredibly sexy she is, my eyes lock onto her curves, and I struggle to pull them away.

"You let him go, but you spoke first?"

"Yes, we spoke. He told me everything."

"He gave you the answers you needed?"

"He told me why he did it and why he never contacted me, so yes, I guess he did."

She takes a moment to explain to me what her father had told her, and I listen, taking in her facial expressions as she sits on the edge of the bath, her eyes on the ground.

When she has done talking, I wrap my arms around her and hold her. There is nothing I can say right now, nothing that will help her, but I can be here for her.

I hold her until she pulls away.

"There was a man outside the container. He looked angry, not very nice. An Italian man."

"Don't worry about him; he was there to look out for you."

"Can I make you some tea, my angel?"

"Seraphim," she murmurs.

"Yes, an angel," I smile.

"My father is the one who chose my name."

"He chose well. You *are* my angel. Can I make you some tea? Or perhaps something stronger? A whiskey?"

"Whiskey," she replies.

I kiss her forehead, then leave to organize a drink for her.

When I come back through, she is in the bedroom, lying in bed, with the covers pulled over her naked body. The towel is lying on the floor, and her wet hair is spread over the pillow. I pick up the towel, put her drink on the bedside table, and sit on the bed next to her.

I wrap the towel around the sections of her hair, squeezing some of the water out of it.

After some time, she sits up, taking the drink in her hand; she tilts the glass back and swallows all of it in one go.

“Would you like another one?” I ask, with no judgment.

She shakes her head and lays back down.

She closes her eyes, and I lay down behind her, wrapping my arm around her waist.

“I’m right here, my love.”

She doesn’t respond.

I lay with her until she falls asleep, then I get up to change into something more comfortable and climb back into bed, holding her again.

In the morning, she is still distant, and her eyes look lost and far away from me.

“Would you like to go out today? We can do something special, see something. I'll arrange it for us.”

She shakes her head. “No, thank you.”

She is sitting on the sofa with her legs curled against her chest, staring out of the balcony window at nothing in particular.

“Can I get you anything at all? You didn’t eat last night. Let me make you some food.”

“No, thank you.”

I clench my jaw. I don’t know what to do for her. All I want to do is see her smile.

But I also understand that the conversation she had with her father must have been very intense and emotional.

I pace around the hotel, feeling useless and lost.

When I see she has fallen asleep again, I decide I have to do something. I can’t just sit here and wait for her to feel ok again. I have to solve this for her.

I write a note, telling her I won't be gone long, and that I didn't want to wake her. I tell her to message me as soon as she wakes up.

Then I get into my car and drive toward her father's house. I need to know what happened. I need to know if he said anything else to her that might cause deeper issues than I can understand.

I knock on his front door, half expecting him to come outside with a shotgun and blow my head off.

He opens the door, his face swollen and blue.

"Yes?" he says, not looking at all bothered to see a stranger on his doorstep, even after the last strangers who arrived here kidnapped and beat him.

"Marcus, my name is Antonio."

"Antonio. You are the man who had me taken yesterday; they told me your name. They said you are the new boss."

"That is correct. And you don't look bothered to see me?"

"Why would I be bothered? I thought you were going to have me killed yesterday. I was hoping you would come back today to finish the job." He turns away from me and walks into his home.

I step inside, not waiting for an invitation.

"I came here to talk to you about Seraphina."

"What about her? Is she alright? Is she ok? She didn't look ok - when I told her." His face scrunches, emotions distortion his features.

"I'm here because I love your daughter, and I want to know how to help her work through this."

"So you are the man she loves. The way she spoke about love, I thought there might be someone. I hoped that there was. I want her to know what love feels like." He picks up a bottle of wine and sits down on the old sofa, sipping from the bottle.

I take a seat opposite him.

"Marcus, I need your help."

He scoffs. "I would do anything for her, you know. I would give my life if that is what she needed, apart from that, I have no use. I'm nothing. I'm a waste of air."

"Do better than that," I demand, tired of his self-pity.

"The only way to help my daughter is to end the war between Hong Kong and New York. You brought her here, into the heart of the city where her mother died, for being from Hong Kong. She will get over the pain that I have caused her; she will forget about me, but if you want to give her a good life - you need to end this war."

I sigh.

"What? You are the new boss. Don't you have that power?"

"The war between Hong Kong and New York has been improving. Things are not as bad as they used to be."

"Is that so? Isn't it your friend who went missing? Because of his nationality? Because of half of yours?"

I raise my brows, leaning toward him.

"What do you know about my friend?" I say.

"I can find out where he is if that is what you want to know. I stay out of the comings and goings of the organization, but I still have my contacts."

"Find out right now."

He nods.

"Will you help my daughter, then? Either get her out of New York, back home, or end the war before I lose her as well."

"I'll . I'll do anything for her."

"Good. Then give me a moment. And I am going to see what I can find out about your friend."

He stands up, leaving the room, and I hear him in the kitchen talking on the phone.

For all I know, he could phone someone to inform them that I'mhere, that I'malone, that I'man easy target. It would be a mistake if that was what he was trying.

I wait until he comes back into the living room.

He hands me a piece of paper with an address scribbled in pencil, in a messy handwriting that I can only just make out.

"What is this?"

"Someone has owed me a favor for a long time. I just called it in. That is the address where your friend is being held. He is still alive, but if I were you, I would get there now."

I stand up, pushing the paper into my jacket pocket.

"Thank you, Marcus. We are going to speak again."

"Any time." He replies. "And I believe you that you would do anything for her. I mean, you kidnapped her father so that she could confront him. Not very many people would go that far for the one they claim to love. So, I guess what I'mtrying to say is thank you."

"You are thanking me for kidnapping you?"

"Well yes. I'm thanking you for what you will do for my daughter."

I nod.

In the car I message the address to Rei and tell her that I'mon my way there right now. She confirms she will be there as well and that I should wait outside for her.

I drive toward the address, my hands gripped around the steering wheel. I don't know the location; I don't know what to expect. All I know is that I have to get there, and the only person I trust with Kalo's life is Rei.

While I'mdriving, Seraphina's father's words are in my thoughts.

End the war between Hong Kong and New York. You are the boss now, you have the power.

He is right. Seraphina will never be safe until I do that. And I'min think power to orchestrate it. I have connections on both sides. My business is on both sides of the war. I could have called for help, from my cousin especially, but I don't trust anyone with this. I don't even know who has him yet.

I pull the car to the side of the road and locate my gun and Kevlar. Getting ready for what I'msure will not be a simple mission. But at least they don't know we are coming, and with a smaller team, we can move fast.

I'll need to think about it and figure out a way to do that for her.

Right now, though, I need to focus.

Kalo needs me, and I know where he is.

Outside the building, Rei steps toward me, seeming to appear out of nowhere.

I nod at her, and she steps to my side, her sword in one hand and her handgun in the other.

"Ambidextrous?" I ask.

"And many other things," she replies with a grin.

Both of us know that this is not a quiet operation. We have to go hard and fast.

I kick the old wooden door with one solid strike of my boot.

It splinters and falls aside.

Rei rushes in, as silent as the wind. She is already up the stairs before I have set foot on the bottom one.

She peeks over the railing, a floor above me.

"Eight men." She whispers.

I take the stairs three at a time and stand beside her, our bodies against the wall.

With one slight nod of her head, I know we are going in.

We storm through the door, opening fire.

Someone screams as a bullet shatters their kneecap. Rei rolls across the floor and lands catlike on her feet, then shoots the screaming man through the skull.

I fire two shots, and two bodies fall to the floor.

Another man drops to my left. Rei moves along the back wall, ducking as some fires toward her. I shoot him in the throat, and blood fountains out of him.

A man turns toward me, lifting his gun. I freeze, knowing I won't be able to shoot him first, but then a blade pierces from behind him, pushing out between his ribs, right through his heart.

The blade slides out, and he falls to the floor, with Rei standing behind him.

I move, taking shots at the other two men who are still in the room. One falls, then the other dives through a window, disappearing from view.

"Must I chase him?" Rei runs to the window. "I don't know which direction he went."

"Let's get Kalo out of here." I run to where my friend is hanging, suspended by his wrists, semi-unconscious, his face swollen and distorted from the beatings he has received.

He looks up at me as I pull him down.

"Ant - you - took your - time," he chokes. With a twisted grin on his face, his lips were too swollen to smile.

"Better late than never?" I laugh, pulling this arm over my shoulder as he winces. His ribs making cracking sounds against my body.

"Go, I'll cover you," Rei says.

I head toward the stairs, eager to get out of here as quickly as possible.

Behind me, I hear gunfire again. Shit.

I move down the stairs as quickly as I can.

As I step out of the door, two more shots fire. This time, I feel the impact. I have no choice but to drop Kalo. I spin around and fire at the men standing behind me. Rei arrives at the top of the stairs and fires as well.

Everything falls silent. “There were so many,” Rei says, breathless and worried.

I turn to Kalo, blood coming from his mouth. “Kalo,” I shout, pulling him onto my lap as I sit on the stairs.

“Get - out of - here, Ant,” he says, gasping for air.

I push my hand against his chest, where the bullet punctured his lung.

He gasps, the gurgling sounds grow louder. He is drowning in his own blood.

Then his body goes limp, and his eyes glaze over.

Rei pulls at my shoulder. “We have to go. More are coming.” She pushes me hard.

I stand up, letting Kalo slip from my arms, my body in shock.

“Move,” she screams in my ear.

I run toward the car, diving in. She dives into the passenger side, and I slam my foot against the accelerator.

“Turn here.” She points, I turn. “My car is here.”

I park, understanding that my friend is gone.

“You did everything you could,” she whispers.

I nod.

“The bullet went through his back, into yours. You need to see a doctor.”

“I can’t even feel it,” I mumble.

“I’m sorry, Antonio,” she says, climbing out of the car and walking away.

When I walk into the penthouse, I'mstill in shock.

Seraphina leaps up and runs over to me.

“Antonio, what happened?”

I stare at her.

Chapter 39

SERAPHINA

Antonio stands in the hotel's doorway room, covered in blood. His expression is terrifying.

I rush over to him and grab his waist. "Antonio, what happened?" I say, anxiety pushing my body apart.

"Are you hurt?"

"I don't know."

"You don't know? Whose blood is this?"

He stares at me.

"Antonio," I shout.

"It's Kalo's blood. Kalo is dead."

"Oh no, Antonio, I'm so sorry."

I wrap my arms around him and him. I hold him and try to soak his pain into my body. I try to take it away from him. I try to make him feel alright.

He hardly moves at all. I step back, taking his hand.

“Come, let me take care of you.”

He follows me without thought or words.

I take him to the shower and undress him. I run my hands over his body and check to see if he is hurt. On his back, there is a small puncture, but it's not bleeding too much. The rest of his body is covered in blood, but it's not his.

I push him into the shower, beneath the warm water, and step in naked with him.

I carefully cleanse him, gently caressing the smooth, sudsy cloth over his form, cleansing the blood, acknowledging his emotional turmoil.

“Antonio?” I whisper as the water runs off his body clear, not tainted with Kalo’s blood.

“Do you want to stay in the water a little longer?”

He shakes his head.

I lean around him and switch it off. Then, take his hand and lead him out of the shower. I stand on my tiptoes to dry him, then wrap the surrounding towel.

“I need to find a medical kit. Your back is bleeding a little.”

“It’s a bullet wound. You need to get the bullet out.”

“Oh.” My stomach twists. I have never done that before, but I stay calm because that is what he needs right now.

I scratch around in the bathroom cabinet until I find the medical kit. I pull it out and find a pair of long tweezers. “Will these work?” I ask.

“Yes, you are going to dig around in there until you find it.”

I swallow hard, and Antonio sits on the edge of the bath with his back toward me.

He does not even wince when I stick the sharp ends into his back and move them around until I feel the bullet. I clamp the ends onto it and pull it out; blood flows behind it. I press a clean gauze against the wound and wait for a moment, then lift it, apply disinfecting cream, and cover it again, sticking a bandage over it.

"It isn't too bad; it didn't go in deep."

"Give me the bullet." He says, holding his hand out. I drop the misshapen pieces of metal into his hand.

"It didn't go in deep because it went through Kalo first." He says, staring at it.

I pull his face up toward mine. "What happened, Antonio?"

He tells me everything; about how he went to see my father to find out if he could somehow help me and how my father told him where Kalo was. He told me about what happened and how Kalo died. I listen, in awe of everything that happened.

"I have to keep you safe, my angel," he says, pulling me into his arms. I lean my entire body against him, relieved that he is coming back to me.

He picks me up and carries me to the bedroom, and we climb into bed, naked, holding each other.

"I'll keep you safe, and I'll get revenge for Kalo's death."

I stroke this face and tell him that I'll do anything for him. I'll help him with whatever he needs.

He falls asleep before me, and I stare at his face for a long time, thinking about what he told me.

He went to see my father, and my father helped him.

My father forgave him, even after he kidnapped him and had him beaten. My father did that for me. And Antonio did that for me. They both love me, even if sometimes I feel unlovable. They both love me.

I close my eyes.

Maybe I should call ah gung tomorrow. If I can resolve things with my father, then I can resolve things with him, too.

But for now, I'm so happy, even with everything that is going on. I have something so definite, so real, in my life. I have love.

I'm grateful beyond words.

Over the next few days, I'm very attentive to Antonio’s needs.

He is distant and struggling, but he does not push me away. He lets me help him, he lets me take care of him, he lets me love him.

This is what he does for me, and it's what I'll always do for him.

One evening, Antonio comes through to the living room and says, “Get dressed. Let’s go for dinner. I think we both need to get out of here for a bit.”

“I would love that.”

He drives us to a restaurant with the most beautiful views near the waterfront. We are sitting near the window, but Antonio is not relaxed. And because he is not relaxed, I'm unable to relax.

Our plates have been delivered, and our food is sitting in front of us. Antonio has eaten a small amount, and so have I.

“What is bothering you?” I ask, running my hand over his leg beneath the table.

“We are being watched, I think. Two black suits to the left of the bar.”

I lean close to him, kissing him on his neck, and when I do this, I glance toward the bar to see the men he is referring to.

“I see.”

“I don’t like it. With everything that has happened, I should not have risked bringing you out here until I knew more.”

“What do you want to do, Antonio?” I ask.

“I want to keep you safe. We have to leave.”

“I think we can make better food at home, anyway.” I grin.

He stands up, holding his hand out for me to take. I slip my hand into his, and he leads me out of the restaurant. I notice how he always keeps his body between me and the men at the bar. They watch us as we walk past.

We climb into the car, and Antonio reassures me it's armored.

"I think I have some work to do." He mutters as he drives back toward the hotel, making sure that no one is following us. "I have to weed out the rotten apples from inside the organization. My family needs some change."

"Was it your family watching us?"

"No, well, it wasn't anyone that I recognized. It could have been one of the rival families. But they knew where we were, and that means someone on the inside has let them know who I am. Also, someone in my family killed Kalo. I have to figure it all out before I lose anyone else."

He reaches out, and his hand grips my thigh. I intertwine my fingers between his.

Chapter 40

ANTONIO

I have not let Seraphina leave the penthouse for three days now; she has not complained once, understanding that all I want to do is keep her safe.

My phone rings, and I jump to answer it. I am waiting for this call.

"Arton, what can you tell me?"

"I am so sorry. It was my fault. I should have handled it myself, but I let Diego manage it."

"Just tell me what happened."

"Diego hired an extra man to help him with your girl's father. That man killed Diego, and he went to the container alone. He saw Seraphina. I need to find out who he was. But he was definitely one of our own."

"So we have a few rats on the inside."

"Yes, we definitely do."

"I need you to call a meeting for me. Only, and let me be very clear about this, only people we can trust. I'll send you a list of the ones I know and trust. You can add to it yourself. I want them there, and I want to sort this out. This ends now."

"The list of people I actually trust at this point is pretty small," He complains.

"Mine too, but I don't care if there are three guys there or ten. I just want to sit face to face with people who are on my side."

"Understood. I'll set it up for tomorrow tonight."

I sit down on the balcony, thinking about the pieces on a chessboard. Each one has a purpose, some of them. Their purpose is to sacrifice themselves, to protect the king. Others die as a lesson.

But every move matters.

I have to be so careful with how I conduct things from here forward. Every move has to have a purpose. Every piece I play has to be a step toward an end goal.

I look inside the hotel room toward the sofa where Seraphina is reading.

I dial room service and order us a very luxurious dinner. We did not get to have our date the other night, but that does not mean I can't recreate it here for her.

She is so lost in her book she does not see me moving around, pulling out the white tablecloth, laying it over the table outside, laying out plates and cutlery, and lighting candles.

The view from the hotel is more beautiful than the view from the restaurant. And all that matters is that we are together.

Thirty minutes later, there was a knock at the door. Seraphina has been told that she may not answer the door, so I have to be extra careful. She calls my name.

"I am coming, my love. It is our food."

"Food. Oh my goodness, I just realized how hungry I am." She sits up, dropping her book on the coffee table.

"Wait there," I tell her as I take the trays from the man and kick the door closed behind him.

" I can help you carry, though." She moves to stand up.

"Angel, what did I tell you?"

She grins and sits down again. "Wait here."

I carry the food out to the balcony and lay it out, then go back inside.

I hold out my hand toward her.

"My love, may I take you on a date?"

She places her hand in mine, and I pull her against my body. "Does it include dancing?" She grins.

"Of course it does."

I twirl her around and dip her backward, watching her face light up and savoring the beautiful sound of her laughter.

I guide her outside to the balcony where our candlelight dinner awaits. Above us, the stars are shining brightly.

"Antonio, what in the world? When did you do this?"

"I am just grateful you were so into your book." I laugh.

She jumps into my arms and kisses me, pressing her lips into mine. She slips her tongue into my mouth, and I pull her closer to me.

Then I hold her chair out for her and push it in behind her.

"I am surprised they let me into such a nice restaurant wearing this." She laughs at her pink tracksuit.

"I have never seen you look more elegant or more beautiful."

She rolls her eyes, brushing her hair away from her face, trying to tuck the loose strands into her messy bun.

"Funny," she says.

I grab the edge of her chair and pull her closer to me.

"I am serious, my angel. Every day, you get more beautiful to me."

She leans against me, grinning. Then, out of the blue, she picks up a spoonful of sauce and pressed it onto my shirt.

"Excuse me?" I say in shock.

She grins. "I can't have you looking so sexy while I am wearing a tracksuit."

I grab a handful of prawns soaked in lemon butter, and she screams, trying to dart away from me, but I grab her arm and rub the sticky mess into her hair.

She rolls off her chair, laughing so hard she can breathe.

I fall off my chair, trying to hold on to her, and land lying on top of her.

I wipe my butter-covered hand across her mouth, and she licks her lips.

"It's fantastic," she laughs again.

"Let me taste," I say, then press my mouth against hers, kissing her. Then I lick her face, and she laughs and screaming again. "Stop that." She tries to wiggle away, but I pin her down and run my tongue over her cheek.

When I lean back to look at her face, my heart shudders in my chest.

"How I love you."

She wraps her hands around my face and pulls me toward her to kiss me again.

I stand up, lifting her to her feet, and then hold her chair out for her again with a naughty smile.

"Why, thank you," she says, sitting down despite the prawn stuck in her hair.

I pull it out and show it to her. She laughs again.

"I feel even hungrier now."

"Good thing I ordered enough for an army."

I sit down next to her again, pulling her leg over mine, wanting to be as close to her as possible.

I use the cotton serviette to wipe her face and then dish up some dinner for her.

We eat, grinning at each other and, now and then, laughing at how messy we both look.

She takes away my worries and has proven that she will stick with me through anything.

After dinner, I carry her to the shower and take my time with her, running my hands over every inch of her body. We touch, taste and enjoy every part of each other. Then, I push her against the shower wall and satisfy her in other ways. Watching the water run over her arched back as I thrust into her beautiful body.

The next evening, I step into the meeting space that Arton has arranged.

I sit down at a table of five familiar faces.

"Thank you for coming," I say to everyone.

Arton speaks, "Antonio, we have all been sick and tired of the way things have been going. Our family is not as united as it should be, and we are ready for a change."

"Well, we are here to figure out the best way to do that. I need to know from each one of you. Who do you trust, why, and who do you think is a problem?"

We go around the table, each person taking a turn to share their opinion and any ideas they have toward resolution.

I listen to everyone and take mental notes. We talk for a few hours, working our way through a long list of names, everyone in the family and everyone who works for the family.

I'll have a solid idea of who's who by the end of the night.

"Men, I have one more request. I want to know who handles the death of my friend, Kalo. An attack on someone close to me is an attack on me, and I take it personally. I want to know who orchestrated that so that I can deal with it myself."

"We have an idea," Arton says.

"So do I."

"I don't have proof yet, but I'll get it. My father has never played by the rules, and he has never been very good at being anything but resentful."

"If your father is the one responsible, I won't expect you to take part in what has to be done."

"I hate him."

I nod, "that does not make it any easier when it comes time to take action."

"I know. I just want you to know that whatever needs to happen must happen."

We talk a little more about what each of the men is going to focus on gathering information. By the end of the meeting we are all tired, but I have a strong feeling that things are going to get better from here forward. These are the people who have my back and the people who want to change as much as I do. This is the new generation, and it is time for us to move in and set our plans into action.

I stand. "I appreciate every one of you. You all have my number. I ask that you stay in touch with either myself or Arton. Keep us up to date on whatever you find out, no matter how insignificant it may seem. It might be a key piece of information that someone else needs."

"Yes, Antonio."

"Will do."

"Of course."

The men stand with me, shaking my hand and commenting that they are looking forward to the changes I plan to make. I wait for all of them to leave, then turn to Arton.

"Arton, you are proving yourself to be precious. I just want to let you know I have noticed this, and your future in this family is going to be a good one."

He smiles, nodding. "Thank you, Antonio. I want the same things you do."

I drive back to the hotel feeling a hundred times better. Things are coming together.

My beautiful girl will soon be able to move into the mansion with me, and we will start our lives together. I can't wait to give her everything she deserves and so much more.

When I arrive, I find Seraphina asleep on the sofa. It is way past midnight, and the meeting having run late. I pick her up, hoping not to wake her. But she stirs in my arms and snuggles against me.

"Why didn't you go to bed, my angel?"

"Not without you," she mumbles.

"I am sorry I kept you up waiting. But the meeting went very well. Soon, everything is going to be sorted out, and we can leave this mess behind us and start our lives together."

She smiles against my chest. "As long as you are with me, the world can be burning, and I won't care."

I chuckle. "I'll bring the marshmallows."

"Pink ones. I only want pink ones."

"I will buy the entire factory and ban them from making any other color."

"Good. That sounds perfect." She leans against me and closes her eyes.

I step into the bedroom and lower her onto the bed, resting her head on the pillow.

"I am going to get changed, then I'll be right with you, my love."

"Mm. I am waiting for you." She smiles.

Chapter 41

SERAPHINA

Antonio and I are standing in the hotel's kitchen room; he has a grin on his face as he reaches around me to pick up the milk so that he can finish making the coffee. His arm wraps around my waist, and he nuzzles his face into my neck, trailing kisses across my skin and sending delightful shivers down my spine.

I tilt my head to the side, and a soft moan sounds from my lips.

"Last night was fun," he whispers in my ear.

"Every night is,"

His phone vibrates against the kitchen counter, and he groans, annoyed by the interruption.

"Antonio speaking," he says in his deep voice. The phone is on speaker, so I can hear everything.

This gesture on his part shows his trust in me and that he has nothing to hide from me anymore, and I'm grateful for it.

"Antonio, it's Arton. I have something I have to tell you. The men have been looking into everything to find out who was responsible for Kalo's death. It is difficult for me - I just - uh."

"It was my father. You already know that my father and I have not seen eye to eye for a long time now. He was fighting against Massimo, and now he is fighting against you. He does not act in the best interest of the family–only in his own interest. He is still my father, but it is not my prerogative to look out for him any longer. I have been dealing with his ego and cruelty for far too long."

Arton pauses, and I study his expression. There is a determination in his eyes, one of a man who is taking steps to stand up for himself, for what he wants, and for the family's overall progression and harmony.

"Lucas took Kalo? He planned the whole thing? You are sure of this?"

"Yeh. I hope you know I was in no way involved. I wanted to be the one to pass on the information to you, just to make sure that you understood that."

"I understand that. I appreciate you telling me. You understand I can't let this go?"

"I do. I wouldn't expect you to."

He hangs up the phone, the muscles of his jaw flexing as anger runs through his veins. I can see it in his eyes, the need for revenge, the deep-seated hatred and fury.

"I'm going to kill him."

"So, it was your uncle, as you had suspected?"

"Yes, it was."

I step behind him and wrap my arms around his waist; I lean my cheek against his back. "Let them know they can't get away with this. Show them you are not a man to be messed with."

"And that is what I'lldo."

He turns to face me. I still have my arms looped around him. He lifts my face toward his with his hand under my chin. "But for now, I'm going to have breakfast with the most beautiful woman in the world. Lucas is not going anywhere, and now that I know who is responsible, it is just a case of bringing my forces together into a plan of action."

"Antonio, if you need to skip breakfast, I understand. This is something that is very important to you." I stare into his eyes, knowing what the need for revenge feels like. I can't imagine how he could sit here and enjoy time with me when that is on his mind.

"My little bird, you are the most important thing to me, and yes, I'll have my revenge at the right time, with the right plan in place. But right now, I'm here with you, and I value that more than you might understand. You are my peace in this chaos. And I need that peace."

I stand up on my tiptoes to press my lips against his, letting my tongue slip inside his mouth so that I can taste him.

Outside on the balcony, Antonio and I sit close together, with our legs touching beneath the table. We eat together, but he is quiet and pensive. Thoughtful and focused. His hand is on my thigh, and he is rubbing his fingers over my skin as though it is soothing his thoughts and helping him think.

I love being near him like this. I love he needs me and that somehow, in even the smallest way, I can help him just by being there.

When we are finished eating, he stands up.

"I'm going to get going soon, little bird."

"Alright, will you stay in touch today, to let me know you are alright?"

"I will, whenever I can."

I stand up as well, gathering our plates and empty coffee mugs. "I think I'm going to see my father. I have been thinking about it, and I want to get to know him, you know - just build some kind of connection with him. I don't even know if it is possible; after everything, I'm still processing it all, but I want to try."

He turns to face me with narrowed eyes, tainted with a brooding darkness. "Little bird, what I have to do today is going to be dangerous. I don't know what is going to happen, but it is not something to be taken. I would prefer it if you did not leave the hotel until I get back. I just don't want to be worrying about you while I sort this out. Please, will you stay here? You can see your father tomorrow."

The look in his eyes tells me he is asking, but he won't take no for an answer, and I understand why.

"Yes, it can wait. I don't want to be a distraction for you."

"Thank you, little bird." He wraps his hand around the back of my neck and pulls me close to him, kissing me. "I'll be back later tonight."

Then he leaves, and only once he is gone do I realize the gravity of what he is about to do. He does not know his uncle very well, but family is family, and going after his uncle is going to cause a great disruption in the entire mafia family. His uncle made the first move, though, so he is justified; I just hope everything goes according to whatever plan he has pieced together.

The morning drags by, and I don't hear from him. I try to read, and I try to watch a movie. I sit out on the balcony, and I try to enjoy the beautiful views. But inside, I'm a knot of anxiety, worried and tense, waiting to hear from Antonio. I just want to know that he is ok. I become more and more fidgety, pacing around the hotel room, like a caged animal, trapped and agitated.

I can't take it anymore, and even though I don't want to interrupt him, I call him.

The phone rings for ages, and he does not answer.

This makes my stomach tighten, the knot inside me growing larger.

I bite my lower lip and dial again.

Again, he does not answer.

He is busy or not in a position to answer his phone. I can't overthink this.

But then I'm pacing again. If I could just go out and walk around, I might feel better, but I told him I wouldn't leave.

When it grows dark outside, after the sun has set, and the day is over, and I have dialed his number more times than I can count without getting through to him, I'm past the point of being able to placate myself. I can't just sit here anymore.

But who do I call? What can I do?

The only number I have is Kalo's, and that will not get me very far at all.

What if he needs my help? What if something has happened to him?

I do my best to wait it out, but around one in the morning, I'm in such a state of worry that waiting is no longer an option.

My father is the only person I know who has a connection to Antonio's family and the mafia, and that is where I'm going to go. Maybe he knows something. Maybe he heard something, or maybe he has someone he can call to find out for me.

I grab my handbag and rush out of the hotel to wave down a taxi. We drive through the city. The streets are still busy with the people who prefer the night.

In the back of the taxi, I'm plagued by dark thoughts about what has happened and where Antonio is. I don't know what I would do if I lost him. Somehow, he has become such a large part of my life that the thought of being without him terrifies me.

The taxi pulls to a stop outside my father's house. I pay the fee and climb out, rushing up to the front door.

The lights are still on inside despite it being so late. I knock and wait.

The door pulls open, and my father's surprised face greets me.

"Seraphina, is everything alright?" he asks, with worry in his voice.

"Actually, not really. Can I come in?"

He steps aside to let me into his home.

"Can I make you some tea?" he asks. I nod and follow him into the kitchen.

I wait while he works, unable to start a feeble conversation about the weather, but not wanting to dive straight into a heavy conversation about Antonio being unreachable.

My father carries the tea through to his living room, and we sit down on his old sofas.

"Why don't you tell me what is bothering you, Seraphina?" he asks.

"Antonio's gone. He figured out who took his friend and went after him. But something went wrong, and his friend was killed. This morning, Antonio found out who masterminded the whole thing that led to Kalo's death. He said he was going to deal with it and left the hotel. But he hasn't come back yet. He promised he'd stay in touch, but I haven't gotten a call or message since he left."

"Have you tried to call him?"

"Many times. He doesn't answer."

"I see."

My father sips his tea.

"I'm sorry for coming here with this, but I have nowhere else to go. I don't know who to call or any other way to reach him. I hoped maybe you know someone, or maybe you heard something?"

"Seraphina, I have not been part of that world for a very long time. The man who helped me when I told Antonio where his friend was is now dead. This is a very dangerous world that you are becoming a part of, and if I had my way, you would stay very far away from all of it."

"That will not happen. If you can't help me, I need to go back to the hotel and figure something else out."

"Don't do that. Don't go back. You don't know if anyone has figured out where he was staying; they might have him, and they might come for you to use you as leverage against him. Please, don't go back."

"I can't just sit around drinking tea." I huff, frustrated.

"Seraphina, if they find you - you know what they do. You know how this works. I can't lose you. I lost your mother, and I can't lose you, too. I'm was not begging you, don't go back to the hotel. Just stay here until you can reach Antonio on his phone. You have yours. He can call you, please, just don't go back."

Staring into my father's eyes, I can see the sincerity and concern in them. Deep, intense concern. Life and death. He is terrified because he knows what they are capable of. This makes me more worried about Antonio.

But, after a quiet moment of reflection, I have to accept that he is right. I'll be safer here, especially if something has happened to Antonio. And what would I achieve by going back to the hotel? I don't know how to contact anyone.

"Alright, I'll stay. At least for now."

I lean back against the sofa, feeling lost and helpless.

Where is Antonio?

Chapter 42

Antonio

"Lucas put a hit out on her," Arton confirms.

"Seraphina? They know who she is? How?"

"He has had his men trailing you for a while now, not in person, but through your phone. We just found out."

I pick up my phone off the office table. We are in the warehouse I have inherited from my father, trying to organize and plan our attack against Lucas. It has been a long day, and it is already past midnight. Looking at my phone, I realize I have not messaged her all day. It is probably for the best if they have been tracking me. We don't currently know where Lucas is, but the team is pulling together efficiently and ready for action.

I stare at the device in my hands, my mind rushing over everything that was on it. If they have accessed my phone, that means they have access to my messages, my call logs, and my locations.

They will know exactly where Seraphina is. They will know which hotel we are staying at.

Fuck.

I pull the SIM card from the device. I can't even risk warning her, as they get the message as well. I break the card and drop the phone to the floor, smashing it beneath my heavy boot.

"Get me a new phone," I demand, speaking to one man standing nearby.

"Yes, sir. There are burner phones in the safe. I'll get you one of those for now."

"Do you want me to send someone to the hotel?" Arton asks, seeing the tension on my face.

"I'll go there myself. I want to ensure that every man is armed and ready because as soon as I have her safely with me, I want to launch an attack. This man is going to feel the full wrath of what it feels like to fuck with me."

"I'll cover everything here and keep you in the loop. It won't take long now. We have sent out the request for a family meeting, and most of them have responded. Once my father responds, and we know he will be there, we will be ready."

I slip the new sim card into the new phone and switch it on, but even with this phone, I don't want to risk phoning her and warning her, as her phone or even the hotel lines might be traced. I need to go there. It is the best way to do this.

"I won't be long. I am just going to fetch her."

"Alright."

In my car, I speed through the city street toward the hotel and Seraphina. It is already past one in the morning, and I feel terrible for having left her for such a long time without calling her. She will be anxious. I got so caught up in the plans and having to deal with the teams that I lost track of everything else.

I pull into the underground parking beneath the hotel and climb out of the car. Pressing the elevator button, I wait, feeling ill with worry.

Finally, I reach the top floor of the building and the entrance to the penthouse. The door is locked, which is a good sign, I hope.

I push it open and walk inside, calling her name.

“Seraphina?” I rush through to the bedroom, where I hope to find her sleeping, but the bed is empty, still made, not a thing out of place.

“Seraphina?” I shout louder, with more urgency in my voice.

I run from room to room and find nothing at all.

She promised me she would not leave, and in asking that of her, I made her stay in the most dangerous place of all - right where they could find her. I should have taken her with me. I should have had her by my side.

“Fuck.” I shout angrily.

They have her.

They took her right from the hotel.

I pick up a glass vase and fling it across the room. It shatters against the wall, sending a rain of glittering shards into the air.

“What have I done?” I say with anguish.

I pull my new phone out, dialing Arton.

“They have her.” I snarl into the phone. “Get that family meeting set up right now. And find out exactly who set up the tracking on my old phone.”

“We know who it was.”

“I want them in the warehouse by the time I get back.”

With one last glance around the hotel room, a hopeful gesture of despair, wishing that I had done things differently, I storm out and back toward the parking garage.

While I drive, I am thinking, plotting and planning.

I am the mafia boss now, and that gives me a position of immense power. I have been very diplomatic so far in dealing with those who voice their opposition toward me, but that ends tonight. Tonight, everything changes. It is time for me to establish myself properly. I know the players; I know who is who, and I know that this needs to happen now in order for me to save the woman I love.

When I arrive back at the warehouse, Arton is waiting for me.

"Do you have them?"

"We paid them a late-night visit at their homes. We have the two men responsible for setting up the tracking."

"Who are they?"

"One is a cousin of ours, and the other married into the family. Both have been working for my father."

"Have they been talking?"

"Oh yes, they have been very forthcoming with their information. With a little persuasion, of course."

"Take me to them."

I follow Arton through the warehouse, past the teams of men, and down a flight of stairs leading to a bunker room.

Two men are chained to a wall, beaten and bleeding. One of them is crying. I snarl at them, disgusted by the weakness on display. "I hear you have been conspiring against me?"

"It won't happen again." The first man splutters, spitting blood.

"I know it won't happen again," I say, drawing my gun.

"No, wait, Antonio, we are family, please -"

The bullet penetrates his skull with such force that his head snaps backward. A loud cracking sound echoes against the cement walls.

The second man's eyes are so wide with fear that he looks frozen, almost comical.

"Antonio, I can help,"

"How do you suppose you can help?" I ask dryly.

"Lucas, he threatened my family. I had no choice. I had to do what he asked."

"You had a choice. You could speak to me. You definitely had a choice. Unfortunately, you chose the wrong side."

A second shot fires from my gun, hitting him in the throat, causing a fountain of blood to erupt from him. He begins to gargle and splutter, drowning in the thick red sludge of his own body.

I watch closely as the life drains from his eyes.

"Have the bodies put on display somewhere. I want every member of the family to know what happened." I say, turning my back on the carnage of blood and death. "It is time to let them all know who I am and what happens to traitors."

Over the next day, my actions cause a massive ripple effect through the family. My message was loud and clear, prompting people to respond and pledge their allegiance to me, assuring their commitment. It is a dark world where the best way to have people respect you is through death.

But it is the world I am running, and I'll do *anything* to get Seraphina back.

"The family meeting is set. Everyone has confirmed that they will be in attendance," Arton confirms.

"And your father?"

"He will be there. I don't believe he knows we know what he has done. When I spoke to him, I made it sound as though we believed those men were working independently of anyone else and that we believed the threat was now resolved."

"Good, but we still need to be very alert for anything he might have planned."

"Your numbers have increased considerably since your *message* reached the family. I don't think he has much of a force left on his side. But I agree, we should be ready for anything. The meeting is tonight at your property. We have given the impression that it is a sort of welcoming gesture regarding you moving in there."

At eight o'clock that evening, I was standing in what was once my father's dining room with my entire family around the table. The room is so packed with people that some of them are standing, and some are seated. "I wanted to thank all of you for being here tonight," I say to the room of people.

"Thank you for having us."

"We appreciate the invite."

"It is about time we all came together like this."

I nod. Running my hand across the head of the table, a sly smile on my face. Seraphina is in my thoughts as she has been almost constantly since she went missing. But I push it away. Right now, I have something to do that requires my full attention.

"I know things have been unstable since my father passed away. And I wanted to see each of you, face to face, to let you all know that from here on out - there will be no more of that. The instability of the family has been something I have been looking into and dealing with, and tonight, the final piece of that puzzle is about to be resolved."

I nod toward two of my security men. "Please, will you escort my uncle Lucas to stand by my side?"

I look toward Lucas, who shifts uncomfortably in his seat. "Antonio, that is unnecessary."

"Lucas, please,"I gesture politely, and he stands, pulling his arm away from one man who tries to grab it.

While he makes his way through the room, I continue to address everyone.

"Lucas and I did not see eye to eye in the beginning, and that was a disappointment to me. My father's own brother, he was someone I had hoped to look up to. However, we don't always get what we wish for, and I guess it is just one of those things."

Lucas reaches the head of the table. "Tonight, as I said, I want to put an end to all the instability in the family, and that means that all secrets should come to light."

The room is thick with tension as they stare at me. I turn to Lucas. "Lucas, my uncle, it would appear that you have been conspiring against me. I don't appreciate having my phone tracked, my position challenged, or the people close to me put in danger. I know it was you who took Kalo."

His eyebrows shoot up, and his eyes grow wide. "Antonio, it was a misunderstanding."

"A misunderstanding. I see. Where I am from, we don't call it a misunderstanding - we call it what it is. You are a rat."

I pick up my gun, and Lucas's eyes lock on my hand.

"I underestimated you. I am sorry about your friend. You are twice the man your father ever was. You and I can do such great things together," he stammers as I lift my hand and press the gun against his temple. "Antonio, you need me."

"So you admit your involvement in the murder of Kalo?"

"Yes, I admit it. I was acting impulsively. I thought I was doing what was best for the family."

I see the look of a man who will say anything to save his own ass. His confession is good, but the damage is already done.

"Where is Seraphina?"

"Who?" He looks confused.

"Don't play games with me, Lucas. Where is she?"

"I don't know who you are talking about." He replies without emotion. His eyes were steel gray and cold.

"Dad, just tell him what he wants to know." Arton stands up and glares at his father. I can't blame him for trying to get his father to confess, perhaps hoping that his life might be saved, but it is too late for Lucas.

He murdered Kalo. He went against me. He has overstepped every boundary since the day I arrived here. I can never trust him.

My finger hovers over the trigger of my gun. If I shoot him, he can't tell me where Seraphina is, but if I let him live after confessing to killing Kalo, I'll look weak in front of the family.

For a moment, my thoughts churn.

Lucas notices the hesitation and thinks he has a chance.

"Antonio, I know your friend meant a lot to you. It was a stupid,"

"Where is Seraphina, Lucas?"

"I don't know. I had nothing to do with that. I give you my word."

"Your word?" I snort an unamused laugh.

"Lucas, this is your last chance."

"Dad, just fucking tell him, stop being a fucking idiot."

"I am not the fucking idiot here. You two are. You think you are strong enough to run this family. What a fucking joke. You two are imbeciles. You are morons. You are weak, mean, who doesn't know what it takes to survive in this world?"

"You mean by betraying your family? Surviving by screwing over everyone around you?" Arton is getting angrier by the second.

"You need me, son, more than you realize. Both of you do. I did what was necessary—eliminating that spy from Hong Kong. You think he's one of us, but he's not. He's a wolf in sheep's clothing, ready to tear us apart. We've built this family's legacy with blood, sweat, and tears. I'm the one who knows how to protect it, to lead us forward. Who's with me? Who'll stand by me through thick and thin? I'm begging you; you need me. Without me, we're all going to lose our way. Please."

My finger presses harder against the trigger. His façade of regret and remorse has quickly slipped away under the smallest amount of pressure. He never plans to step down and stop seeking his own desires over and above the needs of everyone else.

“No, Lucas, I don’t need you.”

I pull the trigger, and his skull muffles the sound of the shot. I see the crowd of people flinch and turn their faces away as my uncle’s body slumps to the floor. I place my gun back on the table and turn to face my audience again.

Lucas is staring at his father’s body. His face is free of expression. Free of pain or guilt or anything that tells me he doesn't agree with my actions here tonight.

The muscles of my jaw feather for a moment, and then I address the room. “I don’t take lightly to betrayal, and every single one of you would do well to understand that.”

People nod and whisper confirmation, and not a single person in the room makes a move to protest.

“Seraphina is missing, and anyone who comes forward, anyone who worked with Lucas to take her — you have an amnesty for twenty-four hours. After that, I will go find her, and when I do, there will be no leniency for those involved.”

I look around the room. No one gives away a thing. Not one of them looks guilty. I'll give them the twenty-four hours to come forward while I continue my search. And I'll honor my word.

"Now, seeing as this is a night of resolution, does anyone have anything they would like to say?"

One of my second cousins stands, his hands pressed against the table as he leans his weight into them. "Antonio, on behalf of the family, I wanted to welcome you into your new position and assure you that you have our love and respect, as did your father."

"Thank you, Geraldo. Now, everyone should enjoy the rest of the evening. Appetizers are being served outside; help yourself to a drink, and please, enjoy my home."

I step away from the table and turn toward Arton.

"There is no need. You did what you had to do."

"Alright, then, is there any news on Seraphina? With Lucas gone, I assume anyone involved is skittish. They are bound to slip up or just let her go."

"Nothing yet."

I grit my teeth, looking across the sea of faces around me. One of them knows something. I just need to find out who.

Chapter 43

Seraphina

Marcus places a plate of food in front of me at his small dinner table. I push it away.

"Eat, Seraphina."

"I can't. I have been waiting here for two days, and not only is he not calling me, but now his phone has been turned off. The line just stays dead."

I push the plate further away from me and stand up.

It has been two days of hell, waiting to hear from Antonio. My heart is convinced that he is dead or in serious trouble. What other reason would he have for not getting in contact with me? This is too much to bear.

"I have to go back to the hotel. I have no other choice."

"No," Marcus says. "You can't. I can't lose you."

"And I can't live without Antonio, so I would rather risk going back there to find out what is going on than just waiting."

"They will kill you." Marcus's face is strained.

"Like I said, I'll risk that. I can't live without him."

"At least wait until the morning?"

"No, Marcus, I have waited long enough. It is time for me to face whatever it is I need to face."

I take out my phone and call the taxi company, telling them where to pick me up.

Marcus nods, sullen and withdrawn, knowing that this is not an argument he is going to win. My mind is made up, and he did well, keeping me safe here for two days, but I can't hide here forever.

"Thank you," I say, stepping toward him and wrapping my arms around him. He stiffens. This is the first time I have ever been affectionate to him, and I can feel he is not sure how to process it. "Thank you, Marcus, for letting me stay here."

He lifts his arms and wraps them around me, hugging me back.

"Please, take care of yourself, Seraphina. Please stay in touch and let me know what is happening. You have my number now. Use it."

"I will."

"Call me if you need something. I don't know if I can be of any help, but I'll try."

I step back, looking at Marcus. Marveling at how drastically things have changed in my life.

"I'll call soon."

Then I walk out of the house, pulling the door closed behind me, and climb into the taxi waiting outside on the street. It is time for me to find Antonio.

At the penthouse, standing in the center of the living room, I feel panic rise in my chest. There is a vase smashed on the floor, as though someone fought or struggled. Everything else seems in order, but that shattered glass has my mind reeling.

"Where are you?" I whisper into the space. "I need you."

I'm hit with a frenzy of nervous, angry energy. I search everywhere for anything. Any clue, any hint of who took him or where they went. Anything at all to give me a lead. I'm lifting things, tearing the blankets off the bed, pulling draws open. The longer I search, the more anxious I become. I don't find a trace of evidence.

After an hour, I slump onto the floor with my back against the sofa, staring at the broken glass.

Tears stream down my face as I try to figure out what to do.

I have to go back to Marcus. I have to make him give me a name - any name of any person inside the family. I'll start there and work my way through people until I find someone who can tell me where Antonio is.

I grab my handbag and rush out of the hotel room, into the elevator, and down into the foyer.

"Mrs. Aoi, I did not see you come in."

I turn toward the voice, and the receptionist is smiling at me. I eye her, wondering if this is a trap of some sort.

"I'm so sorry I missed you. I have a message for you."

I step toward the desk, every muscle in my body tight with nervous energy.

"What message?"

"I was told, under very strict instructions, to not deliver it to anyone but you. It is a message from your husband. Mr. Aoi."

My breath catches. My heart pulses at a dangerous speed.

I reach out, with a shaking hand, to take the white envelope from her hand.

“Thank you,” I whisper as I walk away from the desk, staring at the sealed envelope.

There is nothing written on the outside. It is a plain, white envelope.

I walk toward the waiting area and sit down on one of the golden yellow couches.

I flex my hand to get them to stop shaking, and then I pull the glued edges of the envelope open. The white papers tear, and my heart thunders.

I reach into the envelope and pull out a single, white, folded piece of paper.

I drop the envelope at my feet and unfold the page.

Inside, in immaculate handwriting, is a note.

I had to get a new phone. Call me as soon as you get this.

Then, written beneath that, is a cell phone number.

I pull out my phone and dial the number, holding my breath as it rings.

“Hello?” His deep voice answers the call, and every cell in my body screams with relief.

I can speak when I try to answer him.

“Antonio,” I stutter.

“Seraphina,” he says, excitedly. “You got my message? Where are you right now?”

“I'm at the hotel. I thought something happened to you. I thought you were dead. I came back to find out what was happening. I was so lost and scared without you.” The words rush out of my mouth between desperate sobs of relief. All the worry and fear from the past few days floods out of me, streaming down my face.

“Where have you been?” he asks.

"When you didn't come home that first night, I went to Marcus, hoping that he knew someone or something. I didn't know what else to do."

"You did the right thing. I had to get rid of my phone after I found out that they were tracing it, and I could not call you on your phone, as I assumed they were tracing yours as well. They had a hit out on your name. They wanted you dead, and when I went back to the hotel, and you weren't there, I thought,"

His words choke for a moment, and I hear him taking a deep breath. "I thought you were dead, or that they had taken you. I have been looking for you."

"If they have a hit out on my name, am I in danger? I'm at the hotel right now, sitting in the foyer."

"Go back up to the room. Wait for me there, alright? I'm coming right now. I'm already getting into the car. I'm on my way to you, little bird."

"Please, hurry. I need to see you."

For a moment, after hanging up the phone, I can't bring myself to stand. I have so much emotion rushing through me that my body is not in my control. My legs are shaking, and my hands are barely holding my phone.

I drop the phone into my lap and rest my face in my hands as more tears flow from my eyes. I sit for a long time, trying to catch my breath and get myself under control.

I thought he was dead, and I thought I had lost the person I love most in this entire world. But he is alive, and he is on his way to see me right now.

"Mrs. Aoi? Are you alright? Is there anything I can do to help?" the receptionist is standing near me, leaning over my seat. I look up at her with bloodshot eyes.

"No, thank you, no. Everything is fine."

"Are you sure?" she asks, unconvinced.

"I'm sure. I'm going back up to my room. Thank you for your help," I say, standing up, feeling embarrassed, and expose my feeling in the foyer, under the public eye.

I hurry into the elevator and up to the penthouse. Inside, I wash my face in the bathroom, splashing cool water over my eyes to soothe them and regain control of myself.

I'm staring at my reflection in the mirror and dabbing the clean white towel on my face when I hear the door opening.

At first, I freeze, remembering what he said about there being a hit out on my name, but then I hear his voice, and I drop everything and run toward it.

"Seraphina," he says as I leap into his arms. I am holding him tighter than I have ever held him before. I can't help it when I cry again, overcome with the emotion of seeing him, able to accept that he is alive and now with me.

"Antonio, I was so worried."

He lets me drop to my feet, my body sliding against his. I can smell him and feel the warmth of his skin. I can touch him and hear his voice.

He cups his hand beneath my chin, and with his thumb, he brushes my tears away. "Little bird, everything is fine now. Everything is perfect. I have you in my arms. My heart has never been happier than this moment."

Chapter 44

Antonio

I stand over her and stare down at her beautiful face, stained with tears and red from crying, but still beautiful.

"But Antonio, should we even be here, though, if they have a hit out on my name? Are you safe?"

"We are both safe here. The people who tried to organize the hit are dead. The person behind it all has been dealt with, and the threat is gone. We have nothing to worry about now."

"Who was it? Was it your uncle, as you suspected?" she asks, still looking anxious despite my reassurance. I guess I can't blame her. It has been a very strenuous few days. She has been through a lot.

"It was Lucas. Yes, he was unhappy that he was not the heir. He wanted my position and tried to take it with force. But he underestimated me, which was his own mistake, and for that, he paid the price."

"And the rest of the family. How do they feel about all of this?"

"The rest of the family has welcomed me, and I'm now established in my position as head of the family. There will be no more issues from here on out. I, of course, will not let my guard down. I still have reservations about certain people, but overall, I believe things have settled."

She leans into me, resting her head against my chest, and I run my fingers through her hair, letting her scent wash over me and the warmth of her body soak into me.

For the first time in days, I feel calm.

"I thought I lost you. I thought you were dead," I whisper against her hair, with my eyes closed, taking her in.

"I thought the same thing," she sighs, and I know she has been as worried as I have been.

"Can I order us some food? And we can just relax here, together, and forget any of this happened. I need to be with you. I just need to have you in my arms," I ask, wanting nothing more than to have her near me.

"Yes, that sounds perfect. Honestly, I couldn't eat for the last few days. My stomach was in such a knot of anxiety. I never want to experience that again, Antonio."

I dial downstairs to the hotel reception and place an order for room service. I don't like the fact that she has not eaten, or that she had to go through any of that. I don't like that I'm the one who brought her into all of this.

While we are waiting for the food, Seraphina climbs into the shower. I hear her humming from the bathroom, and it makes me smile. I can't believe the impact that this girl has had on me and how much my life has changed since I met her.

In all the world, I never thought I would meet someone who would make me feel this way, who would make me want nothing but just one person. Her.

I mean, obviously, my life has changed in a lot of ways, but somehow, everything else feels meaningless unless she is with me. Without her in my life, everything else feels empty and pointless.

She walks out of the bathroom wrapped in a towel, smiling at me as she comes toward me.

She adjusts the towel around her body, letting it fall open to reveal her gorgeous, naked skin. My eyes take her in, and my cock stirs, demanding to be inside her.

She presses herself against me, and I let my hands run over her hot skin.

I'm about to lean down and kiss her when there is a knock at the hotel door.

“Room service,” a voice calls from the other side.

I slap her on the ass. “Go to the room. No one else may see your body but me. Get dressed, we can eat, and then we have the entire night to play.”

She grins, her entire face lighting up in the most mischievous way. She steps away from me and lets the towel drop to the floor. For a moment, she stands revealed, looking me up and down. Then she walks toward the bedroom, and my eyes can't look away from her gorgeous figure.

When she is out of my sight, I go to answer the door and let them in to deliver our dinner.

All the while, I'm waiting for them to hurry and get out again because I don’t think I can wait until after we eat. I want her now. She has teased me in that brief yet very suggestive interaction that my entire body could not take another moment of waiting.

Once the room service is delivered and I have closed the door behind me, I turn and walk toward the bedroom to rip whatever clothing she has put on off her body.

But when I step into the room, she is lying on the bed, on her stomach, with her feet shining in the air. I pull my clothes off right away, staring at her as she tilts her head to watch me. She moves, spreading her long, slender, toned legs apart, teasing me even more.

She rests her chin on her hands, with the most innocent expression on her face, as though she was not the most sexy creature on this planet.

With my clothing tossed to the floor, I stand behind the bed, looking down at her. She is still lying on her stomach, so I grab her ankles and push her legs open even further. Then I kneel on the bed, my cock throbbing, and I push my knees between her legs, lowering myself over.

I trail kisses down her spine, and she arches her back. I grab a handful of her hair and pull, lifting her breasts off the bed and running my hands over them.

She lays still, letting me touch her and play with her body.

But I can't wait long, and I'm so desperate to thrust my swollen cock into her. I'm already lowering my body over hers. Her back is against my chest as I press my cock between her legs, letting it slide over her wet pussy.

She lifts her ass toward me, and I slip the tip of my cock into her. She moans.

I thrust my hips forward in one strong motion. My cock buries inside her, all the way in her pussy, and my body shudders with pleasure. I growl and pull out. She rocks her ass toward me, her fingers gripping the blankets beneath her.

"Fuck, you are so beautiful," I say as I thrust in again.

She cries out, not hiding her pleasure.

With my hand still knotted in her hair, I slam into her, feeling her body bounce every time I thrust. But I want more. I want to be deeper inside her, so I lift her hips and push her knees beneath her body so that her little pussy is pointing right at me. I press her face into the mattress as I fuck her again.

Her voice is muffled against the bed, but she is gasping and moaning with pleasure, crying out and calling my name.

I rest my hands on her hips, wrapping my fingers around her slender body and holding her as I fuck her harder and faster. The pleasure is building up so much, and I feel her pussy pulse over my cock. I know she is about to come on me.

"Come on to my cock. Let me feel you."

Her fingers are gripping the bedsheets that she is pulling them off the mattress. She rocks her hips upwards toward me and then screams as her pussy tightens, then convulses in wave after wave of pleasure.

I lean forward and wrap my hand around her throat, fucking her pussy deeper and feeling as though my cock is about to explode. Then my orgasm fires through me as I thrust into her and moan, satisfied.

She rolls onto her back, resting her feet against my chest, grinning up at me.

"I might be hungry now," she laughs.

"Me too, but don't get dressed. Stay here. I'll bring the food through."

I climb off the bed, my lip curled into a half grin, watching her.

I leave the room just long enough to pick up the tray of food that was delivered and then carry it back to the bed.

Lying next to her, I pull the tray next to us and lift the lid.

New York steak strips with mushroom sauce, thin-cut French fries and roasted vegetables.

"Oh my gosh, this looks like what I have been craving."

I pick up one of the streak strips, dip it into the mushroom sauce, and then hold it out for her. She opens her mouth, and I slip the meat into it. She smiles as I wipe the sauce off her lips with my finger. “Mm. It is delicious,” she says, closing her eyes and savoring the flavor.

I'm interested in the food at all. My eyes are on her face, her lips, her gorgeous features. As soon as she swallows her food, I lean forward and kiss her. “I can’t believe you are here with me now. I was so scared that I had lost you, Seraphina. You are everything to me. I never want to be without you.”

Her fingers slip across the back of my neck and up into my hair as she kisses me back. Our lips play across each other, tender and slow, seductive and intimate.

I lean back with a smile on my face. “Sorry, I should not be interrupting your dinner. "

She laughs and pulls me into another kiss.

“Stop this and eat.” I laugh with her.

After enjoying our New York-style steak strips, we lay on the bed, naked, wrapped in each other’s arms. My legs intertwine with hers, and I trace my fingers along the curve of her side, feeling the softness of her skin.

“I start negotiations with Hong Kong. I plan to put an end to this war from the perspective of entertaining a healthy business relationship. I have contacts in Hong Kong, but the person I'm going to be talking to is your grandfather.”

“Ah gung?”

“Yes, between him and me, we can build something solid, and once that is established, I want you to move in with me. I have inherited from my father’s estate.”

Her eyes shine for a moment, and a soft smile covers her lips. “You want me to live with you?”

“Of course I do. I don’t want to have ever not you by my side again. If I had my way, we would move in there tonight, but because of your heritage, it will cause a stir. I’ll not take a single risk with you, not like that. I came too close to losing you once. There is no chance I'm going to do it again. So, I'll do this. Business and money, that is the language I'll push for this. My family can't deny the benefits of a relationship with Hong Kong. And I know, underneath it all, it would be incredible to end this century-long war.”

“Whatever the future brings, Antonio, I just want to be with you.”

I pull her closer against me and kiss her, letting my hands slip lower to tease her all over again.

Chapter 45

Seraphina

I walk through the streets of New York toward the coffee shop where I'm meeting my father for lunch, and I think about the day I arrived here.

I felt so out of place, lost in the wonderful noise, color, and chaos of this city.

Now, just a short time later, I feel at home here.

I step into the coffee shop with a smile on my face, and I spot my father, who stands and waves as I walk in.

I go over to him and hug him, a gesture which he returns this time, feeling more comfortable with the intimacy of it compared to the last time I hugged him.

I sit down, and he sits opposite me.

“You look lovely today and are thrilled. I'm so glad that everything worked out and everyone is safe, Seraphina.”

“Thank you again, Dad, for letting me stay with you for those few days. I appreciate it, and so does Antonio. He told me you did the right thing by not letting me go back to the hotel.”

My father nods with a smile on his face.

“How are things between you and Antonio, sweetheart?”

I grin. “Dad, I have never been in love before, but I am. I'm in love with him, and it feels wonderful.”

“You look just like your mother when you get that look in your eyes.” He laughs.

“What was she like? I wish I could have known her, everything about her. Tell me about her.”

My father leans back in his chair as the waitress arrives to take our orders. I ask for a coffee and cheeseburger, and my father tells her he will have the same.

When she has left, he leans forward again, resting his elbows on the table.

“Your mother.” He sighs. “She was the most magnificent and beautiful person I have ever met, even to this day. I still love her so much. I don’t think it will ever go away. It hasn’t even faded. She is still my entire world.” He stares out of the window for a moment, lost in the memory of her.

“You still miss her?”

"Every day, every moment of every day, she was there, you know? She was this incredible force of strength, and her love for life was boundless. She adored cooking, exploring, she just had this immense love for everything."

“She loved you.”

“I have never felt love like that. I'm so grateful that I experienced it and so bitter that it was taken away from me. I try to tell myself that she had the choice, that she chose the outcome

- and she did. She knew what I had to do and why I had to do it. But. But I still can't stop blaming myself. If only I had never brought her here."

The waitress arrives with our coffees, and my father stops speaking for a while.

I sat down next to him and grabbed his hand, needing him to really get what I was about to say. "Dad, I've been so angry for so long, and it's been eating me up. But getting to know you and Antonio has helped me see things differently, understand our family better. It's like I've been carrying around this tremendous weight without even knowing it. I'm done blaming you for everything. I know now that you and Mom did what you had to do, and it made sense at the time. I just want to let all that go, start over. I want a life where there's love, you know? And I want you to be part of it, not just on the outside looking in. It's time to drop the guilt. Mom was okay with the choices you guys made. She wouldn't want you to spend all these years feeling bad about it."

He smiles, shaking his head at me. "You are just like her, you know. I can't believe the similarities. The small gestures, the way you smile, the way you raise your eyebrows when you speak. Your entire face lights up just like hers did. And you speak with so much strength, so much self-confidence and assurance. You are her daughter; she lives on in you, Seraphina."

"Will you ever be able to let go of everything? Do you think you will ever be able to find happiness again?" I ask, looking into his eyes with hope.

"I never imagined that I would sit across from you, my daughter, and having lunch and talking about the past. I never dreamed it was possible. So, I think I can accept that I don't know what is possible. Anything, so why not happiness? I never thought you would forgive me if you ever found out what I did.

And yet, here you are with me." He pauses for a long while, and I study his face, the lines of age and worry, the deepness of his wrinkles. His eyes are soft and kind. "Seraphina, I think, with you in my life, I might feel happy again."

"I hope so, Dad. I want that for you."

"I'm proud to be your father. I'm so proud of the woman that you have become, and I know your mother would be, too. You are an inspiration and a beautiful human being. Any father would be lucky to call you their daughter."

I tell him about moving in with Antonio and how well things are going with the family. I tell him a little about the negotiations that are going to take place between Antonio and Hong Kong over the next few days in positing peace and ending this war that has taken so many lives. My father says it is about time that it was resolved, and he hopes for the best outcome for everything.

After lunch we say goodbye, and I walk along the main street, taking in the sights and smells of New York again, as I make my way back to the hotel where Antonio is waiting for me.

I feel light and playful. My life feels like it has only just begun, with all the pieces falling into place in just the right way.

I'm happy and hopeful about what the future holds.

When I walk into the hotel room, Antonio is there to greet me.

"You are glowing. I take it that your lunch with your father went well."

"I was amazing. We get on well. He told me about my mother and how she was, and he said I'm just like her." I grin.

"Well, if you are just like her, then he was a lucky man to have met her."

"I think they were both lucky, in a way, because love like theirs is rare."

"It is, and I don't plan to let it slip away from me now that I have found that rare love for myself." He pulls me close to him and kisses me.

When I lean back to look into his face, his eyes are a little more serious.

"Seraphina, I'm meeting with your grandfather tomorrow afternoon. We are going to discuss everything in person. The negotiations are going to start. Over the phone, we spoke, and he was as keen as I was to find a resolution. We both know that money is at the heart of all of this and if we can show both sides that it will be beneficial to end all of this animosity, then we will do business together. And then, my little bird, you and I'll be free to be together with no issues or difficulties facing us."

"An gung is a powerful figure in our family, and I'm sure that between the two of you, two powerful forces, everything is going to work out just how you want it to." I smile at him, knowing that he is capable of anything.

"Kalo's death will be the last life lost to this war. He will not have died for nothing."

I nod, pulling myself against him, holding him close to my heart. I can't wait to experience a future with him. He is everything I never even dreamed was possible.

Chapter 46

Antonio

Before the afternoon meeting with Muchen Hanoi, Seraphina's grandfather, I first attend a meeting with the highest members of my family, to inform them of what is about to happen. I have been keeping them updated, and they know that a member of the Hong Kong family arrived in New York yesterday, but my goal is to keep them as well informed and involved in the process as I can to help them feel reassured that I'm doing this with the best intentions for the family.

When I arrive, the men and women are seated around a table, sipping coffee and water, waiting for me to begin.

I drop a folder on the table and sit down. "I'm sorry for making you wait." I touch my hand to the folder. "Thank you to each of you for providing me with your ideas and contributions toward how our family might work with Hong Kong. I have gone through each of them, and I'm very impressed with what has been presented. I'll add my own ideas to these, and by the end of today, I'm confident that we will have a new, very lucrative business deal in place."

I take a sip of coffee and use the scan the surrounding faces.

They all look relaxed and receptive, and to my relief, nobody looks sour about the fact that we are talking about working with Hong Kong.

"While he is here, know that he is in New York as my invited guest and that Muchen Hanoi and his men are off limits. No one may approach them for any reason, and no harm is to come to him. All communication will go through me, and from his side, all communication goes through him. Once a deal is in place, we will branch out from there. If negotiations are successful, we will have dinner with our family and his family, and everyone will be introduced."

"What if negotiations don't go as planned?" One of my cousins asks.

I knew this would be one question came up this morning, and I'm ready for it.

While I'm one hundred percent certain that this meeting with the Hong Kong representative is going to go as planned and we will end our differences, I also have to let my family know that my loyalty lies with them.

"If negotiations don't go as planned, then that is another story. But we can cross that bridge when we come to it, and nothing is to happen without my confirmation. Is everyone clear on that?"

"Agreed. Yes, we are all clear on it. Are you meeting with him today?"

“Yes, we are having our first meeting today. Then, we will each discuss the outcomes of that meeting with our respective people and meet again, if needed. I’ll keep all of you in the loop and call you in for another meeting to discuss the options. I value your opinions and input. And again, thank you for your contributions.”

“But Antonio, are you sure you want to meet him alone? Don’t you feel that It'srisky to do that?”

“No, not with my background and history. I have the upper hand. I know how they do business, and they have a high standard of respect for agreed terms. We have called a cease-fire from both sides. There is no danger for the time being. Also, the smaller the meeting, the more intimate, the less risk I believe there will be.”

The men nod.

I stand, ready to move on to the next thing. I have a lot to do today, and I don’t want to be roped into a long conversation about this.

“Thank you for coming in this morning.”

One by one they stand up and make their way out of the boardroom, and I wait, watching them, my body tense and my mind busy. I'm building my presentation piece by piece in my mind.

This is a huge burden I have taken on, and even though I'm sure It'sgoing to work out, there are always risks. No matter how many possibilities you try to prepare for, things can go wrong. I have faith in the fact my family is open to this, but I also have to accept that there might always be someone who wants to play a bad hand in the game.

I'm determined, though, and when I set my mind on something, no matter how big a task it is, I make it happen.

Besides, there is more at stake for me than business negotiations. This is about the girl that I love and my future with her. Our lives will be so much easier with this feud ends.

Not long after my morning meeting with my people ends, I'm headed toward the boardroom to meet with Seraphina's grandfather. It's a large, open space, hosting a massive mahogany table in the center, stainless steel and leather chairs around it, and massive windows that stretch across the entire room, filling the room with light - and, of course, the most magnificent views of New York City.

I arrive early so that I can get my bearings. I walk into the very impressive space and my two bodyguards follow me in, so I turn toward them, gesturing for them to wait outside.

They look a little puzzled, knowing that I'm meeting with a member of the Hong Kong mafia, but they do as they are told.

Muchen Hanoi arrives ten minutes later, and before he enters the room, I see him talking to his bodyguards, gesturing to them they should wait outside as well.

I watch for a moment as each of our security team's eyes each other, but it remains respectable. Good.

Muchen arrives wearing a black high collar suit, in traditional style. His gray hair is swept back, and his shoes are polished to perfection. He looks older than I remember, but I know that the one and only time I have ever met him face-to-face was many years ago.

The deep lines etched into his face give him a wizened appearance, a man of much experience in many aspects of life.

He walks with dignity and poise, entering the room with an aura that demands respect.

His voice is firm and confident.

"Good afternoon, Antonio. It's good to meet you." He nods his head in greeting.

"And you, Mr. Hanoi. I hope your flight here was a comfortable one?" I bow.

"Oh, yes, very comfortable."

"Is it your first time in New York?"

"I was here so long ago, and so much has changed that it may as well be my first time. The world moves, growing. New York is not the same city I remember it to be."

"Cities change, and people change, and I hope today we can change the way things have been between our families."

"As do I, Antonio."

I gesture for him to take a seat at the table.

He sits down and rests his hands on the table in front of himself. His back is up straight, and his old eyes are bright and alert.

I sit opposite him and pour us each a glass of water.

"I know you have traveled far to come to this meeting, and I want to start off by saying thank you for doing that. I also know that even with our agreement in place, there is always a risk involved in this kind of process, but I want to assure you I have been very clear with everyone here in New York that you are here as my guest, and should be treated as such."

"Of course, I will travel far because this is an important matter. You know, even *without* business and financial benefits involved in our discussion today, I believe that this meeting is long overdue between our two families. I applaud the fact that you have done this. A new generation of leaders, with a new vision for the future."

"We spoke about Kalo, my associate, on the phone,"

"My associates in Hong Kong will not be seeking retribution or revenge for the death of that young man. From what you have told me, you have already sorted out that issue, and Kalo's murderer came to face the consequences he deserved. There will be no further action from our side."

"Thank you, Mr. Hanoi. Then I guess the only thing left to do is to figure out how to present a good business deal to our families that ensures benefits for both sides to end this war."

We discuss different options and what each of us is able to offer. I go through the shipping routes, the products we have available, and how we can move production across to save costs, and not have to worry about transport risks. I go through each of the options my family has pieced together on my behalf and then add my own ideas to it. Muchen has come just as prepared as I am, and after an hour, we have a very secure, very attractive deal on the table, which we are both happy with.

And from what we have both shared today, in an open and diplomatic way, we can both see that this is only the beginning. There are so many more avenues of growth and symbiosis to explore in terms of business.

Though, one thing was obvious in all our conversations. And it had nothing to do with financial benefits or company growth. It was much more simple than that - we both love Seraphina very much and on a personal level, in our private thoughts, we are both here today because of her.

She is the driving force between the wager of peace between two families that have been fighting for over a century.

People go to war for love, but today, we want to end a war for love.

Muchen sighs, looking satisfied with our meeting.

He pushes himself up from his seat, standing and admiring the view from the window.

"It's a beautiful city. I can see why my granddaughter wants to stay here. You know, ever since she was a little girl, she has spoken of New York. Not always, but from what I understand now, things for her have changed." He eyes me, waiting to see how I'll reply.

"Seraphina has resolved and come to terms with a lot from her past. I understand she told you about her father still being alive?"

"She did, yes, and it broke my heart to tell her I knew about it. I didn't intend to hurt her by keeping the information from her. I do hope she understands that?"

"Mr. Hanoi, how long are you here for?" I ask.

"I didn't set a date for my return flight yet, I wasn't sure how long negotiations would take, but, there are so many positives to our families working together that It's already a sealed deal, but, apart from that, I was hoping to see Seraphina. Do you think she would be interested in joining me for dinner, perhaps tomorrow night?"

"Seraphina is an impressive young woman, and she has strength in her that even surprises me. I'm sure she would meet with you. I'll ask her tonight, and she can contact you with her response."

"Then perhaps you can also recommend a restaurant for me to take her to? I want to experience and try New York cuisine." he grins at me, his eyes lighting up.

"I know just the place. Let me make a reservation for you." I smile.

After saying goodbye and confirming that we will be in touch soon, I head back to the hotel.

I'm feeling very positive about how everything went. In fact, with the option on the table for us, the future profits of my business are looking to increase.

I walk into the penthouse, and Seraphina rushes to me, wrapping her arms around me.

"How did it go? I missed you," she gushes.

I lift her into my arms, kissing her and enjoying the warmth of her greeting.

"It was very good. Things are going well. Tomorrow morning, I'm meeting with my family to tell them everything, and I know there is no way that they can argue against what I have to show them. Your grandfather is a very dignified and impressive man, Seraphina."

"Ah gung has always been the source of strength and inspiration in my life. I admire him and love him."

"He would like to take you to dinner tomorrow night. Would you be willing to meet with him?"

She shifts in my arms for a moment, biting her bottom lip.

"I have been wanting to speak with him for quite a while already. I didn't think it would be in person. I have been so nervous just to phone him, but I know we need to speak. I want to have dinner with him. It's time."

"Well then, I'llmake the arrangements and book a table for the two of you at the Emerald Raven for tomorrow night. It will be on my account there, and I'll make sure I don't have any plans myself, just in case you need me for anything."

"Thank you, Antonio." Her eyes look distant, lost in thought.

"Do you want to call him to confirm? Or would you like me to pass on the reservation information?"

"Please pass on the information on my behalf. I'll speak to him in person tomorrow night."

Chapter 47

SERAPHINA

All day, I have been feeling wound with nerves for tonight's dinner with ah gung.

Antonio sent me out to buy a new dress, even though I didn't need one. I think he was trying to help me take my mind off everything. And I admit it was fun doing a bit of shopping.

Ah gung is used to seeing me dressed in jeans or slacks and with my hair pulled back. He is not familiar with the version of me I see standing in front of the tall hotel mirror.

I stare at my reflection, almost unable to recognize myself. The long pale pink dress makes my skin look more tanned than usual. My eyes are shimmering with a soft touch of gold makeup, and my long dark hair is falling over my shoulder in glossy curls.

The gold high heels complement the dress and make me look sophisticated and elegant.

"You look incredible, little bird," Antonio says, handing me my gold clutch purse.

His hand trails down my back, settling on the arch above my butt. My skin heats underneath his touch. "If you were wearing this out to meet anyone else, I might be feeling jealous." He smiles, the dimples in his cheeks catching my eyes in the mirror's reflection.

"You? Jealous? What a silly idea."

"Why would that be silly?"

"Because there is not a soul on this planet that can steal my attention from you." I grin.

He turns me away from the mirror toward him, and his hands drift over my waist.

"Perhaps I should stay here with you?" I whisper.

"There will be plenty of time for us to play after your dinner."

I sigh. "Well, I guess I'm ready," I say with a nervous knot in my stomach.

"Then let me drive you there."

He takes my hand and leads me out of the penthouse to the car, and with an anxious heartbeat, I prepare myself to see ah gung.

When I step into the restaurant alone, I spot ah gung right away. He is standing so poised, with such self-control, at the bar. His presence is hard to miss as he looks out of place in New York. But he looks confident and calm.

"Ah gung," I say, walking toward him.

He looks at me, confused for a second. "Seraphina?" he asks in shock.

I laugh as I wrap my arms around him and pull him into a hug.

"Seraphina, my girl, you look so different." His eyes are wide with shock. "For a moment, I could have sworn it was your mother walking toward me," he whispers.

"My dad also told me I look just like her."

"In every beautiful way possible."

The waiter arrives to lead us toward our table, and although my heart is beating fast, seeing him again feels good.

We sit and place our orders based on what Antonio has recommended that we try.

Then, sipping my martini, I watch ah gung with soft eyes and an open heart.

"Seraphina, I wanted to call you so many times, but it is not a simple conversation to have over the phone."

"I know Gung Gung, I felt the same."

"I always know that your father was still alive and living here in New York. I knew what happened and why it happened. I just couldn't tell you for fear that you would go looking for him and the same thing would happen to you. Your father also made me promise not to tell you. He thought it was best if he remained out of your life in every way possible."

"I understand why he felt that, but he was wrong. And, ah gung, you were wrong, too. Someone should have told me. I could have handled it then, as I have handled it now."

"You are much older now, much wiser, and the circumstances in which you find out these kinds of things shape the way you react. I know you think you would have handled it well, but how would it have changed your life?"

I sit for a moment, considering his words.

"I guess everything that happened the way it was supposed to happen at the right time."

"And that is why life is so beautiful."

"Can you tell me what else you know about what happened?" I ask.

"The people who threatened your father and made him do what he had to do to keep you safe - those people were old rivals of Antonio's family. They were against anyone from Hong Kong, as was all of New York, and the families that run the city. They would have killed both you and your mother. Your father acted, even though it destroyed him as a person. He acted with your mother's consent. She-"

He pauses for a moment, taking his time to pull his thoughts together. I wait.

"Your mother, she called me the day before it all happened. I didn't understand, but she was saying goodbye. She said the most beautiful things to me, and I to her, and I'm so grateful to have had that call with her. You know, I also went through years of anger. The rage and hatred inside me caused me to make some bad choices, wanting revenge as well, but then, because I had you in my life, I started focusing on you. You saved me from my anger, Seraphina."

We dive into deep conversations about my mother, my father, and all the events that unfolded. I lay all my questions on the table, and Ah Gung responds with honesty and openness. With nothing left to hide, our discussion helps us clear the air, bringing us closer than ever before.

"What do you have planned, Seraphina? What happens from here on out?"

"I'm going to stay in New York. Antonio has asked me to move in with him on the property he inherited from his father's estate. I have not been there yet, but I understand it is something quite spectacular. Either way, it could be a cottage in the forest, and I would want to live with him. He makes my heart happy. He makes me feel alive, loved, and whole. So, I'm going to make a life here in New York for myself."

"But you will visit me often?"

"Of course," I laugh.

"I must say, I have quite enjoyed my visit to New York, but I'm too old for this traveling now. I enjoy running my business from the comfort of home. I don't know if Antonio told you, but the future of business between our families is looking very impressive."

"He told me a little, and he sounds as excited as you do about it."

"That is good to know."

Chapter 48

Antonio

I drop a set of keys into Seraphina's hand and close her fingers around them. I grin down at her smiling face as we stand on the massive curved step that lead up to the front doors.

"Welcome home, little bird." I smile. I'm so excited to be bringing her here for the first time. It feels like the start of something big. A new season in my life and a new beginning.

"Are you ready to look around?"

She nods and wiggles her hips. I gesture toward the front door, and she steps up to it with her keys in hand and slips the key into the lock.

The door clicks, and she pushes it open, stepping inside with wide eyes, trying to take in everything at once.

The grand entrance hall doesn't disappoint, and I grin as I watch her spinning in the center.

"What do you think?"

"It's incredible. I can't believe how open and spacious it is."

I have had almost all of my father's belongings removed and put in storage. The walls have been painted, and all the lighting has been modernized. I point out the new features and the things that I have already changed as we walk deeper into the house.

"I want to redo the bathrooms and the kitchen as well, but of course, this is your home too, so you need to choose designs with me. Then, once you have looked around today, we have to go shopping and choose sofas, beds, carpets, standing lamps, statues, art - anything your heart desires."

I take her hand and pull her toward me.

"I want this to feel like home for you, Seraphina. I want this place to reflect *us*, the next generation, a new start and a new era."

Seraphina laughs as I pull her from room to room, showing her every part of her new home. My heart is so happy, watching her face, bright with excitement over all of it. Everything has worked out for us; I can't believe everything that we have been through to get to where we are now.

After a tour, we sit down on the living room floor to make a list of the things we think we need.

"Right over there. That is where I want it." She points to the space beneath the window.

"Blue?" I say, sounding horrified.

"Yes, a blue sofa, right over here?" She grins.

"Like, a gray-blue color?"

"No, like a bright primary blue color."

She flicks through her phone, looking for a photograph of this monstrous blue sofa she is trying to convince me to get. When she holds the phone out toward me to show me, I roll my eyes back with relief. He rolls his eyes back with relief. "That isn't even close to blue. That's stone gray."

She packs up, laughing. "I know. I just wanted to see if you would have agreed to a blue one."

"Unfortunately, I would have. Because I would do anything for you. Have you not worked that out by now?"

I push her over so that she is lying on her back on the floor, and I move onto her with my body pressed against hers, pinning her to the ground. She grins up at me, and I press my lips against her mouth, slipping my tongue inside her. We kiss, enjoying the moment, enjoying everything.

When I stop, I pull her back into a sitting position.

"Do you want to go shopping?"

"Yep," she replies. "I'm so excited to choose new things, our things, to make this space our own."

"Me too, my little bird. I'll have the driver bring the car around."

The entire day, we roam from designer boutiques to custom furniture shops, and we have so much more fun than I could have expected.

We argue over some items and laugh at others. We seem to have the same taste in things, though, which is very good. All the furniture and items we have chosen will be delivered over the next few days.

And those days are filled with joyful chaos.

Seraphina loves bossing the designers around, making them move things from one corner to another to see how it would look. She has a flair for interior decorating that impresses me, and but the space becomes more and more our home.

Last week, my grand piano arrived, and we had it placed in the music room, where I can now relax and meditate by playing. Seraphina sits on the high back sofa by the window, while she reads and listens to me playing.

After a few weeks of mayhem and laughter, our home is almost fully completed.

Seraphina arrives back after a brief shopping trip to find the perfect piece for the corner of our entrance foyer, and when she walks in, I take her hand and lead her out into the back garden.

I have set up a surprise picnic for her. We have been so busy with the move that we have had little time to just sit together and enjoy each other.

I lead her to a massive tree, its old branches stretched out over the lawn. Beneath it, I have set up a blanket and a very impressive spread of food. Biscuits, jams, cheese of every kind, figs, strawberries and cold cuts. Salads and sauces, champagne and, of course, chocolates and cakes for dessert.

"Antonio, this is so beautiful," she says, and I sit down next to her on the blanket, pulling her close against me and handing her an empty glass while I pop the champagne.

"Here is to us, my little bird, and our future together."

I pour us each a glass of bubbling liquid and tip the edge of my glass against hers.

"To us," she smiles and leans toward me, kissing me.

With her back leaning against my chest, we snack on the assorted foods and look out over our garden.

"I wonder if my parents ever had a picnic beneath this tree."

"I think your parents, and your grandparents, and even their parents - this tree looks like it has been here for centuries."

"I like the idea of sitting here, in the same place they sat, looking at the same views, and feeling at home as they would have."

"Do you think it was difficult for your mother? I mean, back then, things were very different. Even now, this resolution is so new still. I can't imagine that life for her was without challenges."

"She most certainly would have faced some very difficult situations, and it can't have all been easy for her or my father because I imagine all he wanted to do was keep her safe and make her happy." I wrap my arms around Seraphina's waist and turn her so that she is facing me.

"But, my little bird, things are very different now. This is a whole new world, and you will be safe here with me."

"I know. I know you would let nothing happen to me," she whispers as she kisses me again. I pull her onto my lap so that she can feel what her kiss has done to me.

Every time she touches me, my body lights with fire and need.

She giggles as I pull her sundress up over her hips and unbuttoning my pants.

"Someone will see us," she whispers, trailing kisses down my neck.

I free my cock, and she feels it pressing against her. I'm throbbing with need, staring into her eyes. I grab a handful of her hair and tilt her head to the side.

"Let them watch," I growl against her ear, lifting her hips and guiding my cock inside her.

She gasps and wraps her legs around my back.

I grip her hips in my hands and push her back and forth on my lap, at first grinding her against me while I'm buried deep inside her.

The small sounds she makes are driving me wild with lust and have me wanting to hear her scream with pleasure.

I rock her faster, pushing harder against her, and she cries out, then clamps her hand over her mouth.

I pull her hand off her face. "Be as loud as you want, my love. This is your garden. Don't hold back."

She stops trying to control herself and leans backward, resting her hands on my knees, letting me move her however I want to.

Her moans get louder and louder as I rock and thrust into her.

Then I lift her hips and fuck her hard.

She cries out. That is what I wanted to hear.

That is what I have been waiting for.

My cock grows harder, and her pussy clamps down on me. Then her legs shake, and soon, her entire body is shuddering with pleasure. With one loud scream, I feel her coming on my cock, and a deep, vibrating moan runs from my chest as I explode into her.

She sits on my lap, my cock still inside her, when we are both spent, and she smiles at me.

I run my hand up the back of her neck, into her hair, staring into her bright green eyes.

"You seem to get more beautiful every day, my little bird."

"I love you, Antonio. More than I have ever thought was possible," she whispers.

"I love you, Seraphina, more than I could ever have dreamed of."

For a moment, neither of us says anything as I stare at her, thinking about everything that we have been through.

I can't believe that when we first met, either of us could have imagined that this is where we would end up. And with her seeking revenge and my father dying, our lives have changed so much. Somehow, we both ended up here in New York, facing challenges together and apart - and somehow, through it all, we supported each other.

We belong together.

We are still together through everything that has happened, and that can only mean one thing.

This is true love, and I never, ever want to lose it.

Sitting here, in the garden, with Seraphina on my lap, our bodies still connected, I know in my heart what I want to do. And I smile, the widest, happiest smile I have ever felt play across my face.

"What are you grinning at?" She tilts her head, watching me. "You look like you just received the best news in the world."

"In a way, I did," I reply, still smiling. Because I'm going to make her mine. Forever.

Chapter 49

SERAPHINA

"Can I take the blindfold off yet?" I moan, feeling nervous, walking without being able to see.

"Do you trust me?" he says, with laughter in his voice.

"I do. Is it still daytime?" I chuckle.

"The sun will set soon, and that is why we have arrived at just the right time. There is a step in front of you. Good, there you go."

My sneakers pad against what feels like a metal grate, and the sound of water splashing against a wall fills my ears. Then I step onto flooring that is moving, drifting up and down.

"Are we on a boat?" I ask, feeling surprised.

"Yes, we are. We are on a boat. But not just any boat."

I feel his hands pulling the blindfold off my face, and when it falls from my eyes, I blink a few times, adjusting to the light. Then I look around.

We are on a yacht, a beautiful yacht, with crisp white decks and dark wood accents. We are standing on the deck, looking into the yacht through a gorgeous arched doorway. Above the doorway is the name of the yacht.

"Seraphim," I whisper.

"It is your yacht, my little bird."

"You bought me a yacht?" I spin to face him in surprise.

The smile on his face, seeing my reaction, fills my heart with joy and love.

"And now the captain is going to take us out to sea so that we can watch the sunset and enjoy dinner together."

He looks very pleased with himself as the yacht heads out into the open waters, and we stand against the railing, watching the ocean crash against the hull. The fresh, salty air fills my lungs, and I can't stop smiling.

One of the boat crew walks toward us with a tray of cocktails, and Antonio takes them, handing one to me.

"Too many adventures with the love of my life."

"Antonio, this is so magical."

"The night is only just beginning, beautiful girl. There is still so much more magic coming." He spins me and then pulls me against him, sipping his cocktail with a glint in his eyes.

When we are out on the open ocean, a man comes to tell us that dinner is ready to be served. He guides us toward a second, higher deck, where they have set up a gorgeous table with fairy lights around it and soft music playing.

Antonio holds the chair for me as I sit down and then pushes it in behind me.

He sits next to me, with his hand wrapped over my thigh and his eyes locked on me.

They serve our first course. Oysters in chili vodka sauce with a splash of lemon.

We have another drink, and then they bring out the main course, calamari and prawns, in lemon garlic butter, with crispy thin-cut potato chips, fried golden brown.

We laugh and talk and watch the sun sinking below the horizon across the ocean. The sky turns bright orange with fire tones, and then when it turns purple and pink, Antonio holds out his hand, inviting me to dance with him.

He pulls me onto the dance floor behind our dinner table, and the music grows louder. I lean my head against his chest as he sways my body back and forth.

"Little bird, when you came into my life, I did not know the things that you would do to me. The ways in which you would change me and how you would show me what love truly is."

I tilt my head back to look up at him.

"Seraphina, I love you. I will always love you. You are my entire world, and I never want that to change."

He steps back and downs onto one knee.

"Will you marry me, my little bird?"

My mouth drops open with surprise, my eyes grow wide, and the surge of emotion that explodes inside me has me laughing like a little girl. I leap into his arms where he is kneeling, shouting, "Yes. Yes, I will marry you."

He catches me, laughs, and kisses me. Pressing my lips hard against his and making my heart beat so fast with excitement and happiness that I feel as though I am made of nothing but love.

Then he stands up, pulling me with him, and slips the most beautiful ring I have ever seen in my life onto my finger.

It catches the light and glitters vibrantly.

I glance up at him. My heart is screaming with joy.

"You said yes," he grins.

"Did you expect me to say anything else?"

"I was nervous when I asked," he laughs.

"I will say yes a thousand times for the rest of my life."

He kisses me again, and the most beautiful stars glitter above us.

A few months after Antonio proposes, I am sitting at breakfast with my Gung Gung, who has flown to New York for our wedding in two days.

"How is business going, Gung Gung?" I ask as I pour him a mug of tea from the cast iron teapot.

"It is better than it has ever been. This resolution between our two families has revealed just how much we were all holding ourselves back, so focused on war instead of on growth. Our profit increase is through the roof, and everyone is thrilled about it."

"That is so good to hear. Antonio says that everyone on this side is also surprised and very pleased with the outcomes so far. They are looking to expand further from what I have heard."

"Yes, we are looking at each taking over a section of production for the other to allow us to reduce shipment costs."

He sips his tea, eyeing me. "But enough about business. How are you doing, my granddaughter? You are looking healthy and happy, which makes me thrilled to see."

"Gung Gung, I would struggle to express in words just how happy I am. You know, I was worried that his family would not accept me, but they have been wonderful to me. There is no tension or awkwardness. Everyone has welcomed me. They treat me like family. I could not ask for anything better."

I grin. "But the question I want to know is, did you bring it? Did everything go well?"

"Of course, I brought it. As part of my wedding gift to you, I also brought the most famous designer in Hong Kong, Khimmy Leniva, to have it tailored to fit you. They are coming to your home this afternoon to see you." He glances at his watch. "Soon, I suggest we finish up here. We can't have you missing such an important appointment."

After breakfast, I rush home, feeling so excited that I can hold it in.

I arrive there at the same time as the designer, who is carrying a black garment bag slung over his arm.

"Mr. Leniva, thank you for bringing it safely." I smile.

"Please, just call me Khimmy. Seraphina, oh, what a lovely surprise. I thought there were going to a be a lot of adjustments, but seeing you in person, I can tell you that you are almost exactly the same size as she was. This dress is going to need such minor adjustments."

He follows me inside and into one of the back rooms, where Antonio has no chance of accidentally walking in on us and spoiling his first sight of me in the wedding dress.

He hangs the garment bag on the closet door and unzips it, pulling it aside to reveal my mother's wedding dress.

My heart leaps in my chest. It is so much more beautiful than the pictures, and with some small changes, it will be modernized and taken in fitting me perfectly.

I stand on a small box as Khimmy works around me, pinning, clipping, and mumbling about what he plans to do. I just stand there, smiling at my reflection in the long mirror that has been placed in front of me. I think about my mother, and how she felt wearing this same dress, and the nervous excitement she would have experienced on her wedding day. I run my fingers over the soft lace and white silken fabric. The dress looks like a mix between elegant Japanese culture and lacy bohemian styles. It has a clean, close-fitting shape that flares out over my hips. The sleeves are long, white lace that hints at my skin beneath. The front of the dress will be adjusted for me to have a v-shaped neckline, and the back already dips low, to reveal a hint of my caramel skin.

Antonio is going to love it.

And I can't wait to see his face when I walk down the aisle.

Khimmy holds up a large white box. "I have brought the veil as well. Did you want a veil?"

"Oh, yes, definitely."

He lifts the lid and stands behind me to clip the sheer fabric of my hair. He drapes it over my face and, seeing myself in the mirror, I get a fright, as I could be looking at a photograph of my mother.

"You are right. The veil is perfect."

My Gung Gung loops my hand over his arm as we stand at the entrance to the church, about to walk down the aisle.

He has been my father figure, and while my father is here at the wedding, I had my Gung Gung walk me down the aisle and give me away. But the father-daughter dance will be with my real father. They both mean so much to me, and I wanted them both to play an important role on this special day.

"You look perfect, Seraphina." My Gung Gung smiles at me as we take our first step onto the carpet, leading toward where my future husband is waiting, just through those doors.

The music plays, and the veil floats around my face.

We walk into the church, and Antonio's face lights up with shock. I see his eyes grow wide, and his mouth drops open as I walk toward him, beaming with pride.

That beautiful man is going to be my husband.

My father stands at the end of the aisle opposite Antonio.

When I reach them, my Gung Gung nods his head in respect and steps away. My father turns toward me, grinning, and gently lifts the veil off my face. He kisses my cheeks and then nods, stepping away as well.

Then I turn to face Antonio, whose eyes are locked onto me as though nothing else in the world exists.

The preacher talks, and Antonio mouths the words' *my angel.*

In front of our families, we promise our love to each other. We promise our lives, our trust, and our honesty. We promise to be there for each other through everything, we exchange rings, symbolizing all our words.

"I now pronounce you husband and wife. You may kiss your bride." The crowd in the church cheers and laughs, clapping, as Antonio lifts me into his arms and kisses me passionately, holding me close, not letting me go until he has had his taste of my lips.

Then we walk out of the church, hand in hand, as rose petals fall around us, and everyone tells us how beautiful we look together.

At the reception, after the most beautiful speeches, and a lot of love is shared, Antonio leads me to the dance floor for our first dance as husband and wife.

I can barely hold back my tears of happiness when the music drifts through the air, and the lights turn low, with a soft spotlight on us.

Perfect, by Ed Sheeran. Antonio chose it, and the words make me smile. It will forever hold a special place in my heart.

When I look up at Antonio, his eyes are intense, dark with emotion, as he stares down at me.

"My wife," he whispers, and I feel as though we are alone in the room.

"My husband," I whisper back, then lean my head against his chest.

After we have danced, my father steps forward to steal me away for our dance, and I am lost in thought about how lucky I am to go from having almost no family to having two families. His and mine come together in circumstances we could not have predicted.

After a long, happy night, Antonio leads me into the honeymoon suite of our hotel room, his eyes drifting over my body as he pulls me toward the bedroom.

"Little bird, I have waited all night to make love to you."

I slip the sleeves of my dress off, one by one, as he pulls his back suit off, piece by piece.

My eyes drift over his muscular chest, the ridges and dips in his toned stomach, and the size of his rock-hard cock, pressing against his pants.

As I step out of the dress, letting it fall to the surrounding floor, he tosses his pants aside.

"Mm," he huffs, taking in the sight of me in white lingerie. "Fuck," he snarls. "I want to tear you apart."

I move to unclip the corset, and he stops me. "Leave it on."

He lifts me, carrying me to the bed and laying me down on it. He leans over me, grabbing my legs and pulling them apart as he grins, licking his lips. He pulls the thin lace fabric of my panties aside.

Then his tongue is on my pussy, and heat is rushing through me. He flicks his tongue over me and slides it down, dipping it inside me.

I squirm and moan, wanting more.

He holds my ass cheeks in his hands, lifting me toward his mouth, fucking me with his tongue as I grip the bedsheets.

Then he drops my hips onto the bed, grabbing my panties in his hands. He tears the fabric open.

He crawls over me, his arms flexing as they press into the bed above my head.

"If only I had my knife, I could paint that white lingerie red, as though it was our first time together," he grins and runs his tongue over my neck.

I rock my hips up toward his cock. It is throbbing and massive, and I want to feel it inside me.

"Are you ready for me, little bird?"

I nod, biting my lower lip.

He presses his cock against my pussy, and then slowly, he thrusts into me. Inch by inch, he fills me up and spreads my pussy wide open. A heavy, deep breath of pleasure escapes my mouth.

The air between us is charged with need and lust.

He thrusts, rocking hard against me, his cock slamming into me.

With each jolt of my body, I cry out, and my fingers dig into his shoulders.

His eyes are filled with whispers of darkness that touch a smile upon his lips and send shivers down my spine.

"Mm. That's my girl. Take all of me. Feel my cock inside you."

He entices me and teases me, the deep vibration of his voice running through me like electricity.

The deeper he pushes into me, the more pleasure I feel, the more connected I am to him, and the closer I get to an orgasm.

He fucks me faster and harder, and I moan and gasp.

"That's it, my angel. Come for me."

My body shudders with delight as my orgasm rushes through me. My pussy pulses over his cock, and he groans loudly and explodes into me.

It is the most perfect night, and it doesn't end there. Antonio continues to pleasure me until I practically have to beg him to stop because I can't take it anymore.

Then I fall asleep in his arms, with a soft smile spread across my lips.

I am his wife. He is my husband.

Chapter 50

Antonio

"I have a very busy day today, my little bird," I say into the phone, which is pressed against my ear.

"I know, but I want you home early for dinner. I have a surprise for you," she giggles.

"What surprise is that?"

"If I tell you now, it won't be a surprise now, will it?"

I chuckle. "I guess not, but how am I supposed to make it through the entire day with that kind of suspense? Is it a big surprise?"

"Yes. A big surprise."

"Alright, my love, I will be home at five and not a second later than that."

"Good, I can't wait." I can hear the smile in her voice. I wonder what she has for me.

These little things she does for me mean so much. Last time she told me to be home early for a surprise. She had booked us a weekend away, because I was looking a little stressed from work and she wanted to make me feel better. And she did all weekend.

The time after that, when she told me she had a surprise for me, she had booked me helicopter flying lessons. That was amusing and a lot more fun than I expected it to be.

I can't even imagine what surprise she has for me tonight, but when I glance at my watch, I see it is only eleven in the morning, and there is still a long day ahead of me, with a lot of things I need to get done.

I guess if I knuckle down and focus on the work, it might go quicker.

But even though I am very busy today and have several things that require my attention, I feel excited and curious to find out what she has for me. This is distracting me.

I shake my head as I walk out of a meeting, realizing that I listened to anything the team was saying about shipments coming in this week. I will need to ask my assistant to send me a spreadsheet for all of them, so I can go through it later.

After three more meetings and a long hour and a half at the docks, I am on my way home.

I would call her when I leave the office, but not tonight. Tonight, I am sneaking in, and maybe I can surprise her as much as she is going to surprise me. I grin, parking around the back of the property and walking to the front door on foot so that she doesn't spot my car.

I open the door quietly, nodding toward the security standing on either side of it.

When I am inside, I glance around, trying to figure out where she might be and where she might hide my surprise.

When I peek into the kitchen, I find her there, bending over the stove next to the chef.

“Little bird,” I say when I am right behind her, and she jumps and screams.

She spins around and punches me in the arm. “Antonio, you know you may not sneak up on me like that.”

I chuckle, and she grins up at me when I pull her into my arms and kiss her.

“Where is my surprise, then?”

She pushes me away, shaking her head. “You are terrible. You still have to wait. I was making us a roast, but I think I messed it up a bit and had to call Leonard back into the kitchen after I gave him the night off.”

“You were making a roast?” I peek over her at the dish the chef is pulling out of the oven.

“Mrs. Aoi, this looks perfect. I don’t know what you were worried about.” He smiles, placing the meat on a board to rest.

“The roast looks amazing, my love. Now, can I know what my surprise is?”

She rolls her eyes and throws her head back. “Out. You, out of the kitchen. Put your things down, freshen up, do whatever, just get out of the kitchen.”

“But-”

“Antonio,” she grins and tilts her head with her brows raised in warning.

I put my hands up, “Alright, alright, I am leaving. But, honestly, that smells amazing. And I am starving. Don’t make me wait for dinner as long as you are making me wait to find out what my surprise is.”

I back out of the kitchen, staring at her ass as she bends over to pull the roasted vegetables out of the oven as well. “Mm,” I mutter with a sly look on my face.

I head upstairs to change out of my work clothes into something more comfortable.

I slip on a pair of jeans and a black t-shirt, then freshen up and head back down to the dining room, where I can hear her humming.

When I walk in, I am greeted by a beautiful scene.

My gorgeous wife is leaning over the table to light the last candle. The plates are laid out with sparkling water, champagne, the *fancy cutlery* as Seraphina likes to call it, even though, for the life of me, I can’t tell the difference between that cutlery and our other cutlery.

“Sit, sit, my love,” she says, holding my chair out for me.

“Oh, well, this is different, isn’t it?” I remark, sitting down in front of plates. Then, on a whim, I check under the table.

“What are you doing?” she asks, confused. “Were you looking for your surprise?” She packs up, laughing.

I grab her around the waist and pull her onto my lap.

“That’s it. I am not letting you go until you tell me you have tortured me enough.”

She rolls her eyes at me again. “Ok. You can have your surprise now, then,” she grins.

She pushes off my lap and runs to the other side of the room to grab a box off the mantle place. Then she runs back to me and climbs back onto my lap. She sits with her legs sideways over me, so that she can watch my face. I wrap one arm around her back.

She hands me the small box.

I grin, wondering again what it might be this time.

She wraps her arm around my neck and watches me while I open it.

I stare down into the box. She doesn't say a word, and I don't say a word. My jaw drops open.

“Is it," I stammer.

“Yep,” she grins.

“Are you?" My breathing quickens.

“Yep,” she nods.

“I am going to be a dad?”

The two solid lines on the pregnancy test stare up at me, and everything clicks into place in my mind. “We are having a baby?” I shout, standing up with her in my arms, swinging her around, and laughing. “We are going to be parents?”

“We are going to be parents,” she laughs as I stop spinning her and hold her against me.

“My angel, my life, my little bird. This is the most incredible surprise you could ever have given me. This is my favorite one by far.”

I cup her face in my hands and kiss her deep and slow.

I can't stop smiling as we sit back down at the table, and she dishes up our dinner.

“How long have you known? How did you keep the secret? When did you find out?” I fire off a series of questions, too excited to calm down.

She giggles. “If you thought you had a long day waiting to find out what the surprise was, imagine how long my day has been waiting to tell you about it.”

“Oh, my word, yes.” The massive smile on my face grows wider.

She places our food in front of us, and I pull her chair closer to mine.

“So, when did you find out?”

"I went to the doctor this morning because the last two days I have been feeling nauseous, and then this morning, after you left, I felt very ill. I thought I just had a tummy bug starting, so I went to get medicine. But he insisted I take a test after asking me some questions and realizing that I am two weeks late."

"You didn't even suspect it?"

"Not even a bit. I guess I wasn't keeping track. But then, when he told me he wanted me to do a pregnancy test, everything made sense, and I wanted to call you right away - but I held back - and wait to tell you in person."

"I can't believe it. I am so happy, little bird. You know I have wanted this for a while now."

"I know, and I thought I wasn't ready yet, but now - I am just so excited. I can't wait to experience all of this with you. You are going to be the most amazing father. We are going to have a little family, Antonio."

Epilogue

Antonio

A lifetime later…

We are all sitting at home, out on the back patio, overlooking the pool. The afternoon sun is shining down on us. Seraphina is next to me, smiling and laughing. My beautiful wife. The mother of my children and a grandmother to theirs.

Her skin has become wrinkled over the years, and yet she is as beautiful as the day I met her. No matter how much she changes over time, her heart radiates through her body. She remains magnetic and enticing.

I look down at my hands, creased with age and years, and then I look back toward my wife. The love of my life, the person who has been by my side through everything.

Sitting here today, I feel very nostalgic, thinking about my father, how he lost my mother far too soon, and how he ended up very alone in his last years. I have been much luckier in time, and not only do I have my wife, but I have a big, exquisite family that has walked these years with me. I have never felt alone, not since I met Seraphina, and I know I'll never have to endure that kind of pain.

We had three amazing children together, Seraphina and I. Each of the kids is so different from the other. They are all confident, capable and smart, but their personalities each shine as individuals.

We had two boys and one girl. The boys are older and were very protective of their little sister growing up, and our entire family has always been very close. Even when they got older and moved out of our home into their own, they stayed in our lives as a big part of our daily experiences.

When Seraphina and I are no longer in this world, they will take over this house and call it their own; they will be the next generation. And the generation after. My oldest son, Diego, will be the heir to the empire that I have created, and he and his brother, Marcus, are already very involved in the business.

In the pool, playing and shouting and laughing, I watch my children and my grandchildren.

They are throwing a ball back and forth, diving to catch it and dunking each other to fight for it. The older grandchildren are enjoying the boisterous game with their fathers, and the younger two are holding onto the edge of the pool with their mothers, wrapped up in buoyant swimwear while they learn how to swim. My daughter is lying on the edge of the pool, soaking up the sunshine and sipping on an iced tea, watching the mayhem of the game.

Next to me, Seraphina laughs as one of the grandchildren climbs onto my older son's shoulders to wrestle with his sibling.

Both of my sons are married and look thrilled. They were married young and now have children of their own. My daughter is more free-spirited and wild at heart. She doesn't want to settle down yet and has spent the last two years traveling the world, sending us postcards from all the beautiful destinations that she has visited. She spent a lot of time in Hong Kong, learning about the culture there and visiting the places where her mother grew up.

She studied law and specialized in criminal law, where she graduated top of her class. But Isabella was not ready to work yet as she wanted to experience the world first.

She has never had a boyfriend, and in the beginning, it saved me a lot of worry, but now, as I grow older, I hope she will find love one day because as wonderful as it's to be so free; I want her to know what it feels like.

I want her to have what I have. I want her to meet someone who loves her as deeply as I love Seraphina. She deserves that.

I think about my father, sitting alone out here in his old age, staring at an empty pool with an empty home behind him, as he longs for my mother and searches for me.

I understand more and more, as the years go by, why he became so obsessed with finding me at the end. I was all he had left. I was his last connection to my mother, to the person who he loved so deeply and lost.

Those years must have been so hard on him. OF all the things I might be strong enough to endure in my lifetime, losing Seraphina is not one of them. My father was a stronger man than I'm to survive the loss of my mother.

I often watch Seraphina as she busies herself in the garden, planting her favorite flowers or playing games with the kids and the grandkids. I love to watch her. I love the way her face lights up with love and happiness, and the sound of her laugh still makes me smile.

I love everything about her, and it's because of her that my life has been the richest one possible on this beautiful earth.

I'm rich beyond gold and diamonds and bank accounts. I'm rich in a way that many people don't get to experience. I'm rich in the things that money can't buy. Although I would give up everything, I have to keep it, if it came to that.

I still can't believe that I went from having no family at all to having all of this. What gift the universe has given upon my life? Every day, I wake up, and I'm grateful for what I have. I have not once, not even for a moment, ever taken it for granted.

Every chance I have, I dote upon my wife and let her know how much she means to me. I have never stopped courting her, as she deserves to know, every moment, that she is the most precious thing in my life.

I reach my hand out toward my beautiful wife and lift her hand off her lap. I wrap my fingers through hers, and when she looks at me, I smile and say, "I love you, little bird."

The radiant smile she gives back to me lights me up inside, and I know that if I died tonight - my life has been full, happy and rich with love, I would be ok with it.

It has been better than I could ever have dreamed of, and I would not have changed a thing.

I have everything I could ever want right here with me.

The most beautiful woman in the world to call my own and the wonderful family that we made together.

THE END

THANK YOU for reading Heir of Corruption! Kindly leave a review. Your seal of approval means a world to me.

While I'm busy working on the next book in the series, you can start with "Grump's Unexpected Baby" an Age Gap Billionaire Boss Romance.

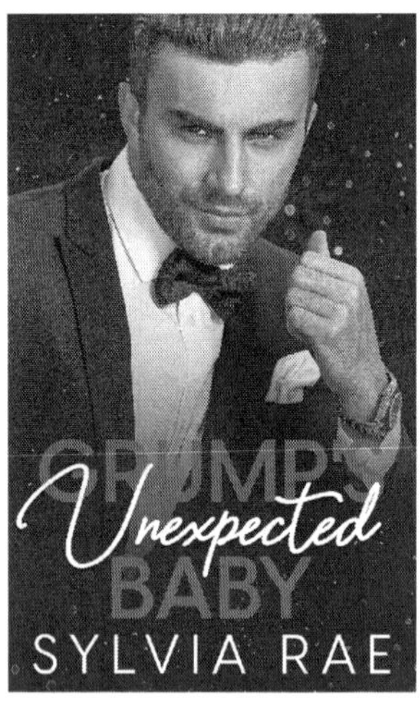

I broke the rules by getting pregnant by my grumpy boss.

I agreed to be his assistant for six months, for a guaranteed promotion.

His gorgeous face and piercing gaze had me wanting more.

But he was my boss.

I didn't want to submit to my wicked desires, yet his stare penetrated my soul.

Of course, nothing went as planned.

In a moment of weakness, I fell under his spell.

The intoxicating and inevitable pull was undeniable.

He whispered dirty things in my ear that makes me melt.

His touch magnified all my senses.

We were both betrayed by people we had trusted in the past.

So boundaries were set and agreed upon.

But two innocent lines changed everything.,

Will he accept the baby, or will I end up with a broken heart again?

About the Author

amazon.com/author/sylviaraebooks

facebook.com/profile.php?id=100089071685208

bookbub.com/authors/sylvia-rae

https://tiktok.com/@sylvia.rae.books

instagram.com/author_sylvia.rae/

Sylvia Rae, a #1 Amazon Best-Selling author, crafts angsty, fast-paced steamy contemporary romances with a twist of suspense that keeps you hooked. Her stories promise pulse-racing moments, tinged with enough thrill to make billionaires rethink their choices.

Living on California's Central Coast with her senior dog Treasure, and her husband, she's on a mission to convince him to star on her next book cover. When she's not writing, she's Googling her next travel destination or rewatching Friends, The Big Bang Theory, and Breaking Bad.

You can sign up for her newsletter to get exclusive content and be the first to know about upcoming releases and sales.

Newsletter Sign up

Don't miss the fun! Follow me now!

amazon.com/author/sylviaraebooks

facebook.com/profile.php?id=100089071685208

bookbub.com/authors/sylvia-rae

https://tiktok.com/@sylvia.rae.books

instagram.com/author_sylvia.rae/

For feedback, comments, or questions, please email:

SylviaRae@SylviaRaebooks.com

Also By Sylvia Rae

You can read ALL books for FREE on Kindle Unlimited, and you can read them as standalone.

Billionaire's Forbidden Fruits Series

- **Silver Fox professor**
- Billionaire's Accidental Baby
- **Secret Baby With The Boss**
- **Silver Fox Baby Daddy**

- Grumpy Boss's Secret
- **Bossy Grump's Secret**

How I Met Your Daddy Series

- **Grump's Unexpected Baby**
- **Bossy Enemy's Secret**
- **Faking With My Brother's Bestie**

The Gates Brothers Series

- **Bossy Billionaire's Secret**
- **Faking With The Frenemy**
- **Daring Enzo**

Billionaire Bad Boy Series

- **Contract With The Bad Boy**
- Shattered Echoes
- Silent Night Temptation

Silent Night With Alessio

Kings of Corruption Series

- **Cold Corruption**
- **Heir of Corruption**

FREEBIE

- Falling For The Grump

Printed in Great Britain
by Amazon

62329886R00229